by

A.J. Ó Coileáin

978-1-906018-93-1

A CIP catalogue for this book is available from the National Library.

Published by Original Writing Ltd., Dublin, 2009.

Printed in Great Britain by the MPG Books Group, Bodmin and King's Lynn

Foreword:

By Jack C. McGillicuddy, T.D.

Minister for Propaganda and Extramarital Affairs

It is my supreme privilege to introduce this new book dedicated to one of literature's most cherished icons, even if the author did let slip that I was only forty-seventh on his celebrity wish list. Belly-aching aside, Peig has left an indelible impression on generations of Irish schoolchildren. As a schoolboy myself, she was literally beaten into me and I may have suffered irreparable brain damage as a consequence - an unlikely deterrent from entering public office, as many of my colleagues will attest.

So how does one sum up Ireland's most revered matriarch? Thus far, I have only glanced at the front cover and I am truly sold on her unique androgynous charm. Moreover, my girlfriend was most impressed by the extracts posted to the constituency office. According to her - and I'm willing to go along with almost anything she suggests; "Peig is the embodiment of the spirit of Ireland, vibrant, strong and unvanquished by the forces of nature and man, especially man."

Perhaps it's best to judge her for yourself, but Peig - Cultural Heresy is the sort of book that I'd happily recommend to my wife and fourteen children.

Happy reading,

Jack C. McGillicuddy

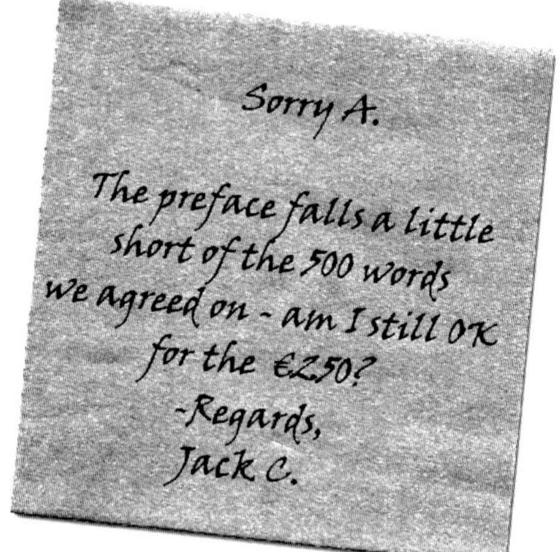

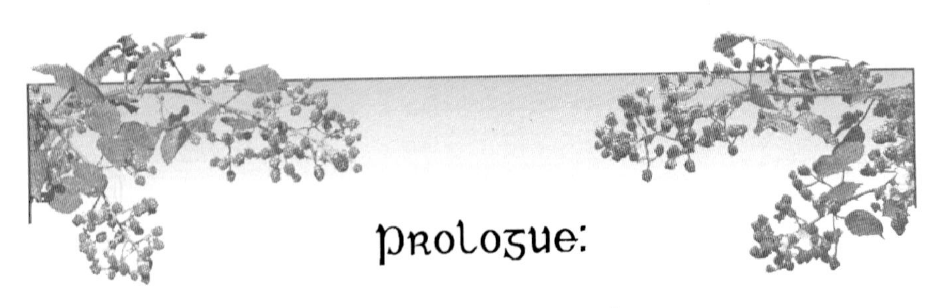

Prologue:

A chronology of dastardly deeds

In a land steeped in history and majestic landscapes, there is

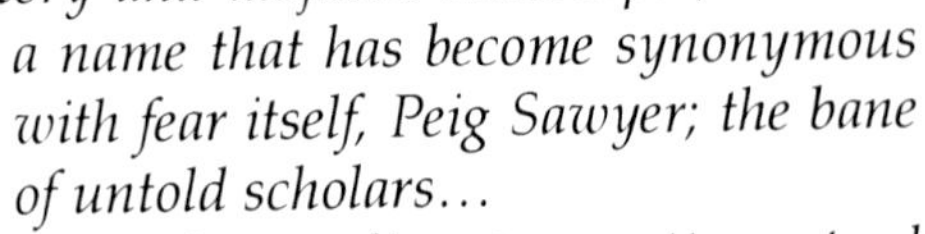

a name that has become synonymous with fear itself, Peig Sawyer; the bane of untold scholars...

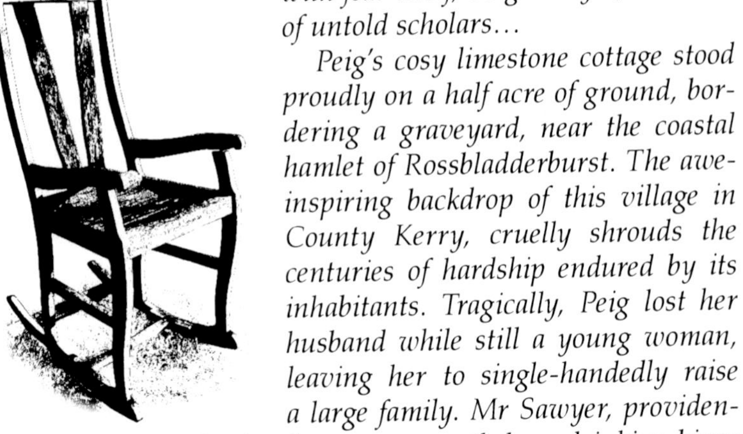

Peig's cosy limestone cottage stood proudly on a half acre of ground, bordering a graveyard, near the coastal hamlet of Rossbladderburst. The awe-inspiring backdrop of this village in County Kerry, cruelly shrouds the centuries of hardship endured by its inhabitants. Tragically, Peig lost her husband while still a young woman, leaving her to single-handedly raise a large family. Mr Sawyer, providentially, resurfaced having been on a month-long drinking binge in Tralee.

The Village

For years, the sea was the lifeblood of the community. The sea provided all; fish for food and seaweed to fertilise the soil, and Rossbladderburst was a mere stone's throw from the nearest shore; provided you were an Olympic hammer-thrower. The eleven kilometre trek was a regular pilgrimage for Peig, whose home was filled with furniture, fashioned from the flotsam and jetsam washed ashore. But it was the vibrant meals she prepared from the dead fish and half-masticated crabs found lying around the sandy beach, that were frequently the talk of the town.

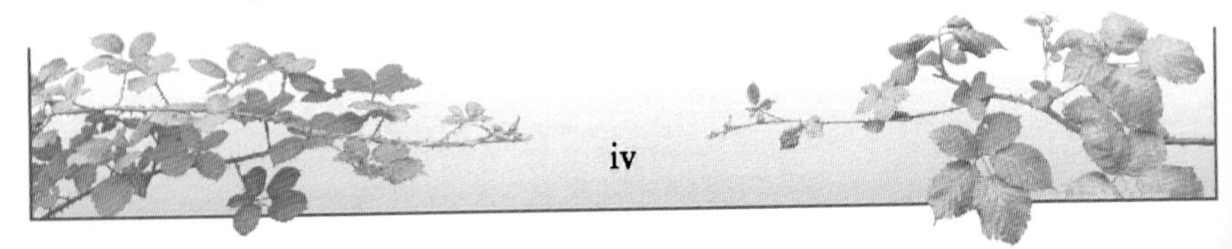

The name Rossbladderburst is derived from the old Irish name Rás Bríste Blagárd, which translates Race of the Blackguard's Trousers. During the eighteenth century, this was anglicised to Rossbladderburst, when its original churlish meaning was lost. With fifteen public houses to its name, Rossabladderburst once boasted more bar taps per person, than any other town in Ireland. Their claim to fame was quashed when nine pubs were gutted in the great fire of '66. By an odd coincidence, the six remaining were solely owned by the Buckley family. The Buckleys, however, lost their foothold when forced to sell on five of these, to cover legal expenses in a court case involving arson. While the villagers have never been short of a drink, the nearest convenience-store is inconveniently located in the neighbouring town of Knockyadown.

Paint Galore

In addition to the breathtaking vistas on its doorstep, there is another reason why this idyllic and leafy village is considered so 'green'. In 1957, several hundred barrels of luminous green paint were washed ashore on Bladder Beach.

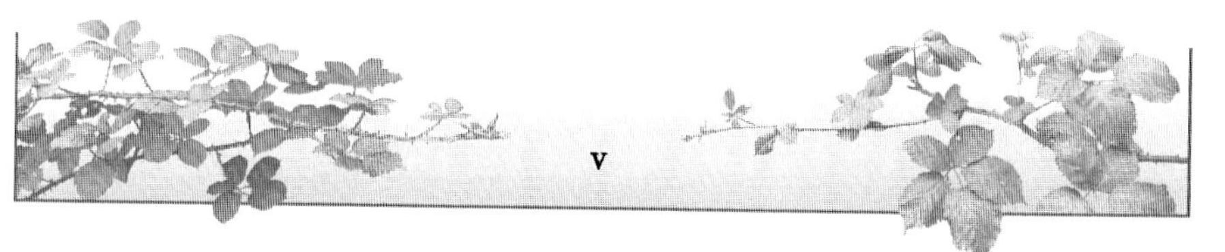

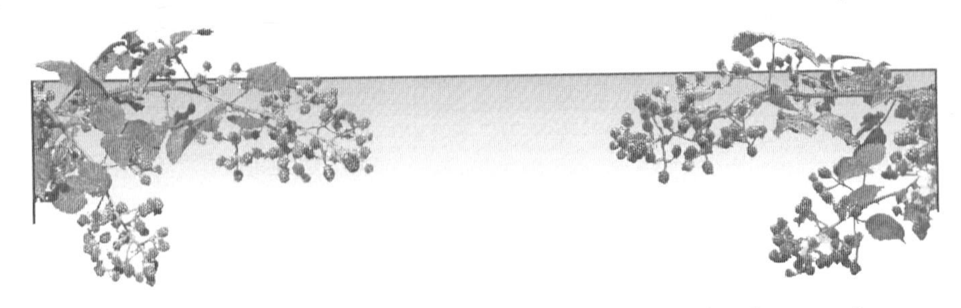

People gathered from miles around to share in this bounty, believed to be lost cargo from a passing ship.

All night parties ensued, as locals painted the town green. Adults and children alike, sauntered merrily about, painting faces, livestock and entire houses, with brushes fashioned from donkey-bristle. Some over-indulged just a shade and became seriously ill having used this peculiar glow-in-the-dark substance. Years later, a leaked British Government memo revealed that this was possibly radioactive waste, washed down from the north-west of England, following a nuclear mishap there. It was also disclosed that contact with this contaminated material could 'significantly shorten lives', but that given the quality of life in the area, 'recalling the barrels' was 'not a priority'.

The Wicker Wars

A hub of innovation, many cottage industries have emerged in Rossbladderburst, through the decades. Local man, Benny O'Sullivan (1897-1963), affectionately known as 'The Wicker Man', was considered to be the greatest basket weaver in Ireland. A man of extraordinary talent, O'Sullivan's dexterity amazed everyone. As legend has it, he lost all but one finger having contracted a virulent strain of 'potato blight', when he was five years old.

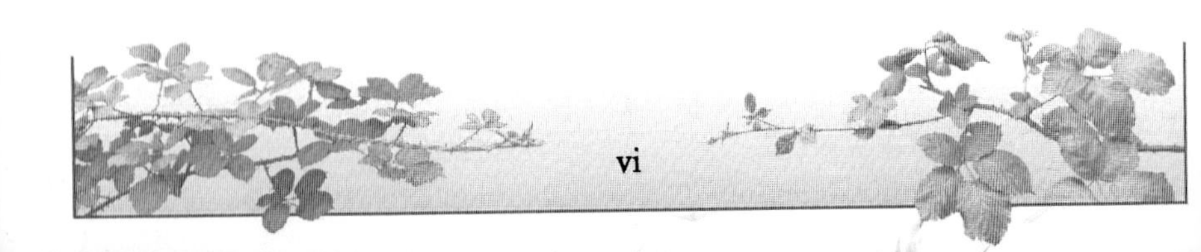

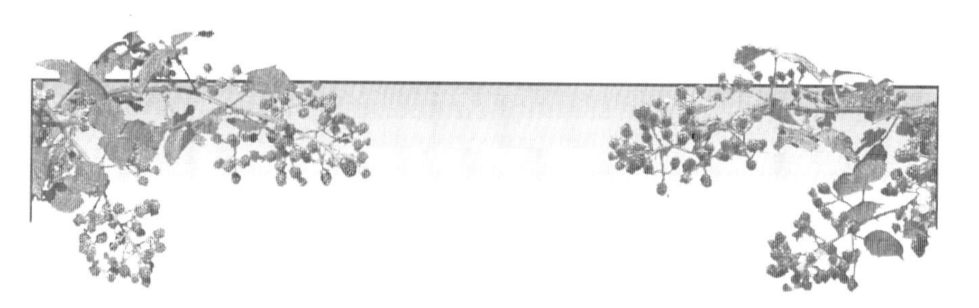

When O'Sullivan's baskets proved popular with the tourists, many more boarded the wicker wagon. All too soon, the village was brimming with shoddily crafted replicas. The competition for wicker became fierce, and its limited availability forced people to forage for alternative raw materials such as: straw, fibreglass and animal hide. Nothing was sacred.

Events took a turn for the worse, when a cartel (whose sole member was Peig Sawyer) attempted a hostile takeover of the industry. O'Sullivan refused to capitulate and three days later, was found in a ditch, with several metres of wicker wrapped around his neck. A verdict of 'death by mis-adventure' was recorded at the inquest; unsurprising, given that the acting coroner at this time was none other that Peig herself. The previous incumbent was exiled to Australia, twenty-four hours earlier, for stealing a pound of tripe; a charge he vehemently denied. The publicity, unfortunately, alerted the revenue commissioners to this profitable enterprise, and in 1964, the 'Wicker Licence' was introduced. The imposition of a levy saw a drastic decline in basket production.

Peig's tenure as coroner was short but fruitful. Ancillary undertakings, such as funeral director and grave digger, all turned a penny and helped Peig support her sixteen children.

Wicker Man: Benny O'Sullivan, shortly before meeting his maker.

When prominent local Dan Buckley succumbed to the hereafter, his will decreed that his coveted collection of gold sovereigns should be buried with him. After a lifetime of hard drinking and debauchery, old Dan anticipated having to bribe his way through St. Peter's gates. Peig was so touched by his plight, that she magnanimously replaced all the cash in the coffin, with a cheque for twice the amount. When slow-witted, grieving relatives, finally came to their senses, there was no refund; as Peig claimed to have squandered the entire hoard at a casino in Killarney. The incident triggered an on-going feud between Curly Buckley (Dan's eldest son) and Peig Sawyer, which has lasted to this day. Peig was finally ejected from her post, when rings and jewellery that were supposedly interred with their deceased owners, began to surface in nearby pawnbrokers and auction houses. Her attempt to blame the Leprechauns misfired, as everyone knew they had been wiped out during the famine.

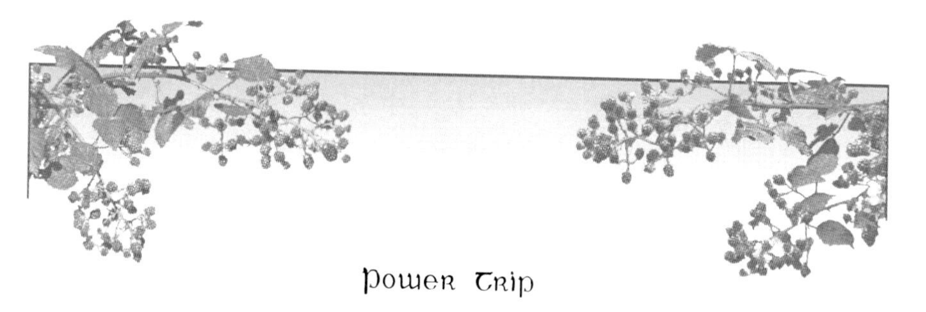

Power Trip

When electricity eventually reached this tiny backwater, Peig Sawyer was one of its most vocal detractors; "That auld electric is the devil's invention," she would say. Electrical appliances like radio and television sparked even more distrust; "I don't want little people in a box spying on me, in my own home. It's an invasion of privacy," she declared.

Sceptical neighbours suspected that such primitive scare-mongering was only a ploy to veil her frugality. But Peig, like everyone else, gave way to the supernatural and was soon basking in the delights it had to offer.

Her first (and last) purchase was a fifteen-watt light bulb, which not only illuminated, but heated the kitchen, as never before imagined. Mr Sawyer, meanwhile, splurged on a washing machine, as an anniversary gift for his wife. Initially, Peig almost clubbed him to death for eating into their bank account, but mellowed when she discovered the machine's miraculous properties. With such a large family to look after, the old twin tub was a cost-effective and labour saving device. The only drawback was that with more time on her hands, the size of Peig's family doubled, which in itself, created an even heavier workload.

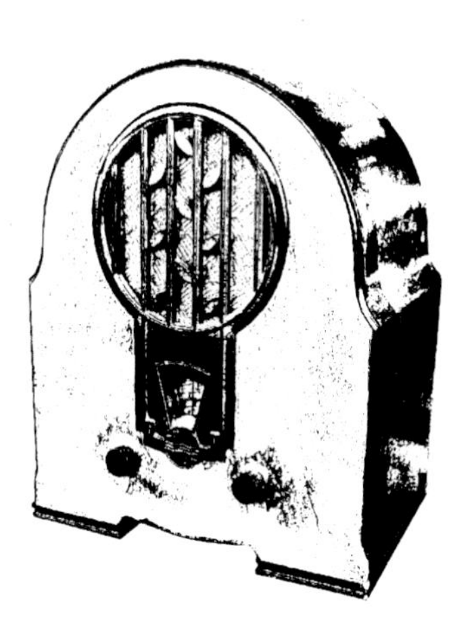

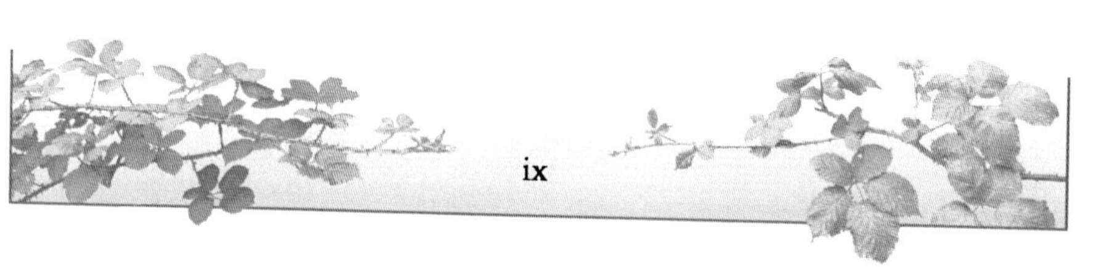

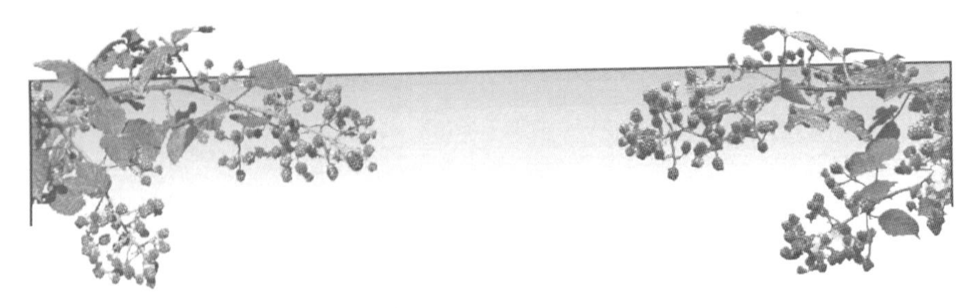

The Butter Mountains

Like others across Ireland at this time, Peig hit upon the idea of using the washing machine to make butter. Some complained that this practice was unhygienic, but to Peig it was a welcome relief from the strain of using a traditional churn. Since much of the butter she produced was sold at market, the washing machine paid for itself several times over.

As time marched on, a progressively health-conscious nation began demanding so-called healthier or convenient alternatives to butter. Margarine was in vogue and in a desperate bid to compete, Peig carried out a series of experiments in the hope of perfecting a substitute. Various chemicals were added to the process; the most dangerous of which, was Peig's revolutionary concept of dissolving butter by cyanide solution. It was an unmitigated disaster. Most of the black slime residue ended up in the nearby river Sualach, leaving death and decay in its wake. The cleanup operation is said to have cost the Irish taxpayer in excess of three million pounds. Peig, for her crimes, received a ten-year suspended sentence and her margarine factory was ordered to be put beyond use, though she still whips up the occasional batch, on the sly.

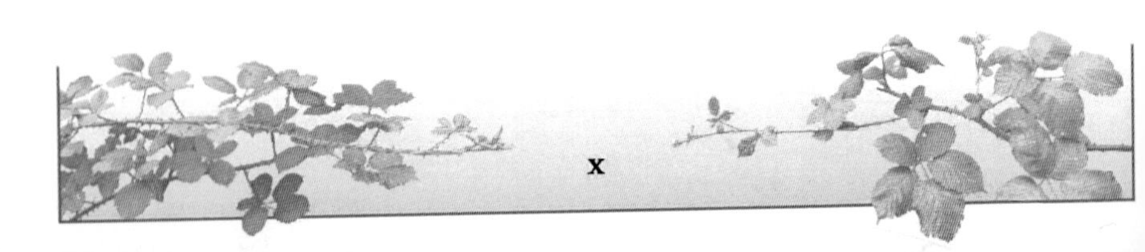

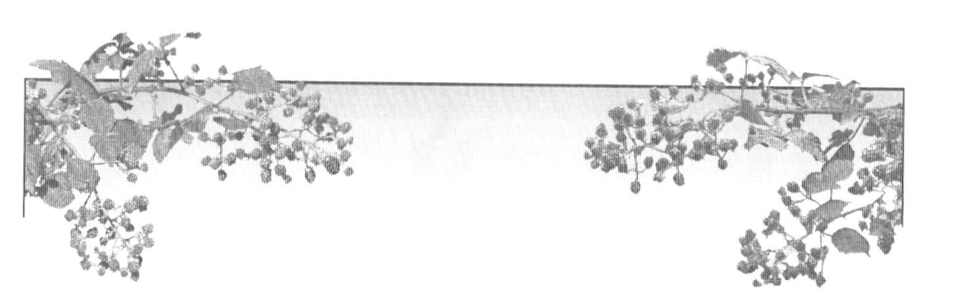

Instead, Peig focused on trading her home grown rhubarb and free-range farm eggs. Ever conscious of escalating overheads, however, palming off supermarket-eggs as free-range, became common practice from the late 1970s. "Animals ate profits," she claimed, and her livestock therefore, was phased out over several dinners.

'Phased out over several dinners'

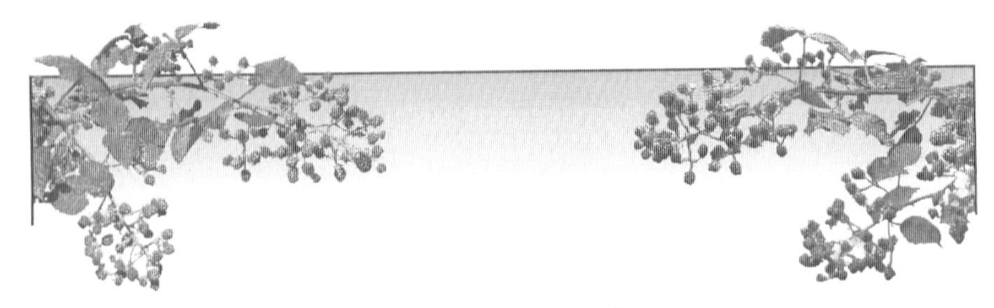

Summer Schools

Ireland's economic slump during the 1980s cut a swathe through the landscape and indeed, through the Sawyer family. Unemployment was rife and the only option open to seventeen-year-old Tommy, (the youngest of Peig's children) was to emigrate. The real clincher, it must be said, was finding a new lock on the front door, courtesy of his mother. With this gentle nudge, Tom Sawyer was bound for the land of opportunity and like Peig's fifteen other children was never seen or heard of again. Peig's husband had long since been tidied into the grave, which according to some, was 'his only decent bit of rest in years'. In later life, Mr Sawyer had been obligated to accompany his wife on her daily jaunts; primarily as a drudge, but also so that she could keep an eye on him.

He was always 'such a worry', 'for fear he'd wear out the furniture', 'answer the door to strangers' or 'eat something' in her absence. As his arms grew longer, Mr Sawyer's feet grew shorter, causing a neighbour to remark at his funeral; "She wore that poor man's last legs down to stumps."

Meanwhile, the great farmers' market crash of '87 saw Rossbladderburst hit a crisis point. With the sales of baskets and butter as stagnant as the merchandise, the villagers were dredging other channels to fill their coffers.

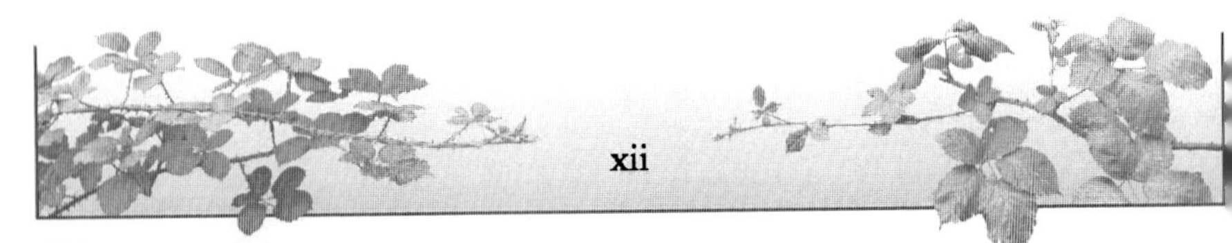

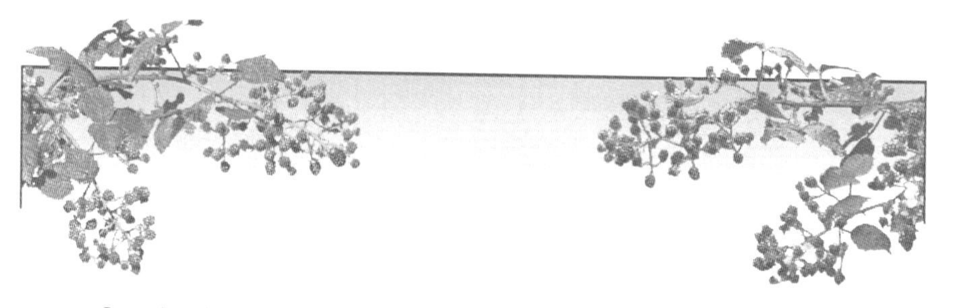

Inspiration struck when someone caught wind of events arising in a neighbouring town, where students from all over Ireland were arriving in their droves. The lure was a newly established summer school, specialising in the cream of Irish culture; music, dance, literature, arts and crafts, and Gaelic, the traditional Irish language. With reports of similar frenzied migrations to the likes of Connemara, Mayo and Donegal, it seemed that a Gaelic revival was sweeping the nation. Parents were especially keen, judging by how gamely they shelled out on dispatching their loved-ones to these thinly veiled brat camps. With the sweet music of cash tills ringing in the air, Rossbladderburst was not about to be sidelined. Although not officially recognised as a Gaeltacht♣ area, fat city was soon within their grasp. In true entrepreneurial spirit, villagers seized a crash course in Gaelic and, one greased public servant later, Gaeltacht status was extended to the area. As guardians of their cultural heritage, the good people of Rossbladderburst were soon reaping the benefits of Government subsidies and a bumper crop of students every summer.

Over the next two decades, it was pioneers like Matthew Begley, the principal of Coláiste Nathair Naofa, who rescued the village from the fringes of obscurity. Begley's pious devotion and the tireless efforts of his wife Catherine (vice-principal and teacher), firmly established Rossbladderburst (and its new Cultural Academy), as the fourth finest Gaeltacht in south-west Munster. Peig Sawyer was first in line when this gravy train came to town, raking in as many students as possible. That first year was also something of a learning curve, as she discovered that six students per bed, including Peig herself, was regarded as 'unhealthy'.

♣ Gaelic hotspot

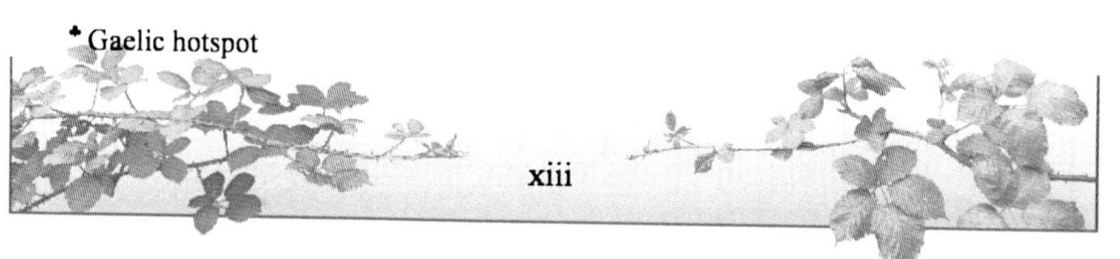

Few students survive from this era, but thanks to those who didn't, a code of conduct was introduced, which was widely ignored.

Shaped by years of poverty and deprivation, albeit self-inflicted, Peig Sawyer knew the true meaning of adversity and fervently believed that others should too. It was amazing the sacrifices this woman was prepared to make for the love of her country, her heritage, but mostly for money.

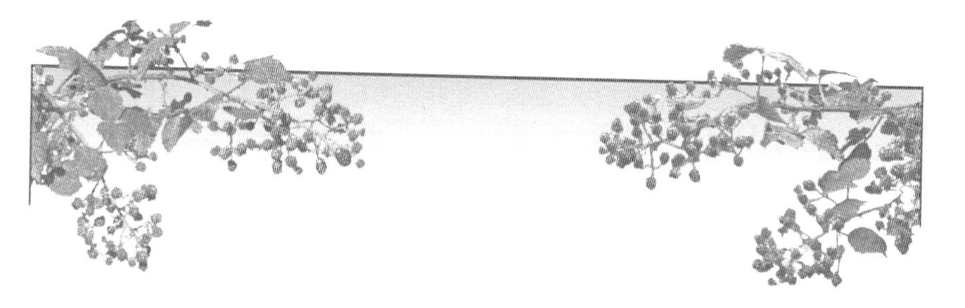

The River Sualach - An ecological disaster

1. The Trauma Unfolds

Catherine Begley lowered her reading glasses to cast a scornful eye over her husband. He was sprawled across an armchair, stroking his greying sideburns while cooling himself with a handheld battery-operated fan. An eleventh-hour paperwork bomb had detonated on the lounge coffee table, leaving spreadsheets, letters, files, photographs and cheque books scattered everywhere. Catherine nonetheless, struggled to maintain a veneer of professionalism as she sifted through the muddle. Her orderly manner was reflected in the style in which she thrust her jet-black hair into a tight bun and in her choice of apparel, a formal grey suit.

"What time did he say he was coming?" she said tersely.

Fraught by the recent heat-wave and the beastly humidity, Matthew Begley approached their assignment with apathy and fatigue; "Eight o' clock," he sighed.

"Well it's twenty to nine now. I hate leaving everything 'til the last minute. We've had months to do this! Months! We've three coach-loads arriving from Dublin tomorrow and everything is in a heap! We've no itinerary set out! Nothing! I haven't half the cheques written and I don't know who's doing what or where half the children are staying!"

Matthew suddenly jerked to attention. "Did you send that letter to Peig Sawyer?"

"Good God! Yes! I delivered it by hand too, to guarantee its safe arrival. Now look, we've so much to get through this evening and there'll be hell to pay if people don't get their money at the assembly tomorrow. I don't know what's keeping that man, but if he's going to be holding us up this long, somebody had better be dead or dying." On cue, Catherine and her husband were alerted by a gentle tap on the window. Low and behold, a grinning figure, dressed in black, was peering through.

"There's the grim reaper now!" Matthew quipped.

"Whisht up, he'll hear you," his wife hissed through clenched teeth, "And tidy yourself up for goodness sake!"

As the door swung open, Catherine assumed an entirely new persona. "Well hello there Father Buttimer, come on in, you're very welcome," she said with a radiant smile.

The large framed cleric returned the compliment with a flash of pearly whites through his untamed bushy beard. "Good evening Mrs Begley, how are you all?"

"Grand, grand-"

"Ahoy there!" he signalled across the room to Matthew Begley, now in an upright position. "Another sweltering evening, isn't it?"

"You're telling me," Matthew acknowledged. "Come on in and take a load off!"

Father Tom Buttimer gladly took a seat at one end of the large sofa and was joined by Catherine at the other. "Thanks very much, oh, but listen folks, my apologies for keeping you so long. A bit of commotion over at Mrs Schalplatten's, as you may have heard?"

"No, what?"

"She's dead."

Mrs Begley chewed her lip in contrition.

"Yes indeed and apparently for some time too." Their visitor pushed himself to the edge of the sofa as he prepared to recount the grisly details. "They found her at the bottom of the stairs earlier this evening. Nothing suspicious they say, but given all the hot weather we've been having lately, well, to put it mildly, it played havoc with the decomposition."

Catherine began to squirm in her seat.

"There was evidence of vermin and the flies had begun to lay their-"

"Ex-traordinary!" Catherine suddenly cried. "Now, where's Jennifer with that tea? Jennifer?!!"

"Sorry, I wasn't being too graphic, was I?" Fr. Tom offered.

"Nonsense, you're fine! Jennifer?!!!"

As they settled down again, an attractive but dour looking teenager came stomping down the wooden stairs. "What?!" she demanded.

"Tea and scones for Father Buttimer, please!" her mother declared.

"Hello?" the teen huffed petulantly. "Like my *Leaving Cert* starts tomorrow?!"

But the matriarch exposed her clenched teeth again, a sign that surely meant business and without dallying about for a second warning, the young lady barged through the louvre doors leading into the kitchen.

"Actually, I won't bother with tea, if that's okay?" Fr. Tom said apologetically.

"Oh sorry, I forgot you don't drink tea, Father!"

Catherine cast her head towards the kitchen, "Just two teas and a glass of milk for Father Buttimer, while you're in there, Jennifer!"

"All right, I'm getting it!" an acid tipped voice spouted from within.

Mildly embarrassed, Fr. Tom smiled humourlessly and straightened some imaginary creases in his blazer. "So I was wondering then, do either of you remember the last time you saw Mrs Schalplatten?"

"No, we rarely spoke," Matthew grunted. To the chagrin of his wife, he had violated the armchair again, by draping his leg over the armrest.

"Wasn't she German or something?" Catherine glowered.

"Eh no, but she was married to a German officer," Fr. Tom elucidated. "A fighter pilot too, apparently. The story goes that he crash landed into her back garden during the war and she hid him from the authorities. And indeed, there he stayed, until his death in 1979-"

The Begleys did their best to appear interested. "Is that right?" Matthew nodded.

"I only asked since you were her closest neighbours-" the cleric sustained.

"Actually you'll find that the O'Shea's are a bit closer, I think," Catherine hastily added.

"Oh. It didn't strike either of you as odd that twenty-eight litres of milk had accumulated on her doorstep?"

"That's incredible!" Matthew declared.

"Yes, it's sad to think that not one person in the entire village would take just a few moments to check on an elderly dear living on her own-"

"I didn't know they delivered around here," Matthew continued.

"Oh that's right, Buckley's have been doing it for years!" Catherine asserted.

Fr. Tom caught the whiff of sabotage, but nonetheless made one final stab. "So, it was James Buckley who spotted the body through the window after he turned up to settle the unpaid account-"

"Ah no! Jim Buckley? Not exactly the brightest spark! Still, you'd think that he'd have noticed something a bit sooner. Ah well, life goes on, I suppose."

Jennifer's fortuitous reappearance with a tray of light refreshments terminated the barbed exchange. "Ah, here we are now!" Catherine cleared an area on the cluttered coffee table.

"How's the study going, Jennifer?" Fr. Tom enquired.

"Ah fine, not too bad," Jennifer replied amiably, setting the tray down. But the vexed teen gave her mother a cold look before stealing away again.

"And tell me, Mrs Begley, where are the other two scallywags this evening?"

"Eh? Oh, Daniel's in bed and eh, Derbhla's staying over at a friend's," Catherine replied, as she distributed the beverages. "Now, why don't you help yourself to a scone, Father?"

"Ooo! Thanks very much!"

Fr. Tom duly selected a buttered fruit scone and sampled it.

"Mmm, they're lovely! Did you make these yourself?"

"Eh no, they're shop ones actually."

"If those were hers, *you'd* be the one pushing up the daisies!" Matthew jibed, before a dark scowl from his wife buttoned his lip.

"Ah sur' they're grand anyway! Now I suppose we'd better get cracking on the old itinerary then?" Fr. Tom suggested.

"Yes of course. And thank you again for helping out and, as always, for the use of the hall!" Catherine declared.

"Yes, I'm sorry you got roped into this again, Father," Matthew added.

"Ah, don't mention it. So now, where do we start?"

Catherine handed him a clipboard and tetchily flung another at Matthew who barely bothered to acknowledge it. Unfortunately, her husband had now truly breached the boundaries of etiquette by further sprawling across his armchair in a most indecorous manner.

"Now this is the timetable for extra curricular activities," Catherine began somewhat edgily.

Fr. Tom concentrated on the blank spreadsheet before him. "Right, Monday the sixth," he began, "Any thoughts?"

Catherine toyed with her spectacles for a moment;

"I suposeit might be nice to start off the first night with a *céilí*♣?" she said ponderously.

"Yes a *céilí* would be nice. I'll mark that down. Now Tuesday evening, how about a little bingo?" Fr. Tom enthused.

"Oh no-no-no-no! Bingo is nothing short of gambling, the disease of barbarians, and definitely a bad example for the youngsters."

"Uhm, okay, well, maybe another *céilí* so?"

"Yes, another *céilí*, that would be fine."

"Grand, and I was thinking we could organise a little talent contest on Wednesday night, once they've all settled in a bit?"

"To single out one individual for glory while others, trying their utmost, are stamped as inadequate? What would that do

♣ Early form of disco

for their self-esteem, when the majority of them are hopeless anyway? No, it's best for morale if we just stick with a *céilí* for that night too."

A dejected frown began to take hold, as Fr. Tom pencilled down details. "Okay, if you say so, and Thursday?"

Catherine looked to her husband. "Matt, have you any suggestions for Thursday?"

"I dunno," he shrugged.

"Come on now, you haven't made any input all evening!"

"Stock-car racing?"

"Look, if you're not going to make the effort, it'll just have to be another *céilí*!"

By now, disenchantment was setting in and Fr. Tom's lips began to curl downward in defeat. "Perhaps we ought to have something special on Friday evening?" he chuckled, with strained optimism. "Like a play or a concert?"

Catherine's eyes bulged at the mere concept. "Too expensive! No-no-no! Let's make it a double *céilí* on Friday, instead."

"And Saturday-?"

"Double *céilí*."

"Sunday-?"

"Double *céilí*."

"And the following week?"

"*Céilí*."

"And the week after that?"

"*Céilí*."

"They're spoilt for choice, aren't they?" Matthew rolled his eyes.

Fr. Tom wisely averted his gaze and downed his milk, leaving Catherine to once more, shoot down her husband with the iciest of glares. "It's *too* good they have it!"

♣ ♣ ♣ ♣ ♣

It was bedlam outside the community hall the following morning. Double and triple parked cars created a horrific cacophony of horns, heated arguments and tailbacks a mile long. Inside, however, things were a little more regimented, with Fr. Tom, Catherine and Matthew seated at respective tables at the top of the hall. Below them, three orderly queues had formed in eager anticipation of their 'special packs'.

"There you go Mrs O'Shea and thanks again," Matthew said cheerfully, as he handed the over a beige folder.

Mrs O'Shea carefully placed the item into her wicker shopping bag and arose from her chair. "I can still keep more, you know!" she declared.

"I know, but the numbers are down from last year and competition is up!"

"Ah well, but wasn't it awful about poor Evelyn?"

Matthew's face drew a bemused blank. "Who?"

"Evelyn Schalplatten over the road, they say she was half eaten by-"

"Oh yes-yes-yes-yes, an awful-awful-awful business. But tell me, you haven't heard when they're having the eh, you know what?" he said, with an expressive wink.

The woman's eyes widened with mischievous glee. "Not yet, but I'll keep you posted. Listen Matty, thanks a lot and I'll see you later!"

"Okay, good luck so!" And as Mrs O'Shea departed, the principal checked her off on his list. "Next please."

His smirk quickly vanished as he looked up to discover who was now seated opposite. It was an elderly, if rather shabbily clad, woman of short stature. Her dark beady eyes gazed intently upon him.

"Mrs Sawyer! I, eh, hello, I wasn't ex-expecting you!"

The unwelcome guest parked her wind-burned jowls a little closer.

"Failed to make the grade this year, is that right?" she said, plucking a fibre of cabbage from her homemade yellowed dentures.

Matthew hastily shut his organiser. "D-did didn't you get that letter we sent out?"

"The letter? Oho! Go 'way! Since the dawn of time I have been nurturing your children as if they were my own kin. I've worked my fingers to the bone. And now, after all the years of blood, sweat and toil, you'd bury me like a festering sack of potato peelings."

Matthew massaged his brow in a state of semi-anguish, as he reflected on Peig's 'kin' and how quickly they had fled the nest. Further adding to his frustration was the jingling of change in pockets and heavy sighs of those still waiting in line.

"Nuturing? Rumour has it, you're no stranger to the strap" he whispered, with all the restraint he could muster.

"Children need to be disciplined," she warranted, "And what's wrong with that? When I was growing up we were beaten black and blue and it never did us a bit of harm!"

"Evidently not."

Pulling a small diary from the inner pocket of his blazer, Matthew flicked through its pages. "Now listen. Last year we had a barrage of complaints, resulting in two very nasty out of court settlements, which practically bankrupt the Academy!"

"What's that got to do with me?" Peig raucously defied his efforts to remain inconspicuous.

"Shhh! For goodness sake woman, these were students in your care!"

Mathew unfolded a sheet of paper he had been using as a bookmark "Look here!" he pointed feverishly, "A solicitor's letter stipulated that several of the girls in your care, were left, and I quote, 'emaciated and traumatised'."

"Pity about them," she countered, "Most of those girls looked half-anorexic to begin with."

"So how do you explain that one girl was left so disturbed that she had to be institutionalised? And I'm told by her father that she still hasn't been able to speak a word of her ordeal!"

Peig folded her arms and looked towards the window. "Culture shock?"

"Besides," Matthew continued, "I did say you were welcome to take that Superintendent's job, over in the school. Wouldn't that be a nice little number for you?"

"If you pay peanuts you get monkeys," she quivered haughtily.

Concealing his notebook again, Matthew adapted a solemn approach. "I'm sorry Mrs Sawyer, but the fact remains that I can't give you any students and it's more than my job's worth to do so."

"Oh all right so, yera, if that's the way you want it."

As Peig edged away, a wave of relief swept over the principal.

"Oh but listen," she swooped back down again, "I almost forgot to show you my holiday snaps from last year."

"Look Mrs Sawyer! There are scores of people waiting in line. This is hardly the time or place for reminiscing over old photographs!"

Blatantly ignoring his plea, the old woman whipped out a large brown envelope from her bag and dropped it on the table. "Ah but these should be of particular interest to you!"

Matthew looked on in bewilderment. There was something about the tone of her voice that fuelled feelings of anxiety. Deciding to indulge her for a moment, he watched as she leisurely slid the photos from the envelope and placed them in his hands. "Oh right, it's the end of season party we held here last August," he unenthusiastically acknowledged.

"Keep going, there's plenty more," she oozed.

Leafing through the pictures, Matthew soon discovered an unflattering testimony of his alcohol intake. "Yes, well, we all like the occasional jar, don't we?" he said, defensively.

The next image, unfortunately, packed such a wallop that his jaw practically hit the floor.

"Yes, I liked that one too!" the old woman hissed with glee. "It's that nice au-pair who stayed with you last year, isn't it? But now, what's your tongue doing in her ear? Tell me, is that what they call *aural* hygiene? And what happened to her anyway?"

His ghastly pallor more than hinted his discomfiture with the subject.

"She- she went back to France."

But his shock soon turned to anger. "Now look here! Nothing happened and these photographs don't prove anything. They're- they're taken out of context! It's not what you think!"

"It never is," Peig sympathised mockingly.

"Is this some sort of threat?

"No, it's blackmail."

"Right! What is it you want?" he seethed.

"You know damn well!" Peig slammed her mitts down on the stack of photographs.

"Shh! Keep it down! I told you I can't-"

Matthew glanced nervously across the hall and was horrified to discover his wife staring inquisitively at him. With a shame-faced shrug, he turned his back on her again.

"Maybe we should consult your wife on the matter?" Peig threatened. "Or perhaps Father Buttimer would be interested in a copy for his parish newsletter? Oh yes, what a lovely story that would make! I can see the headline now; *Principal spends time lechering instead of lecturing.* Wouldn't be too good for business, would it now? Bad news for the whole town, I suspect. So tell me, is it still more than your job's worth, or even more than your life's worth to give me students?"

Matthew imagined his nemesis keeling over and writhing in agony from the effect of having a large boulder dropped on her head. Sadly, it was only wishful thinking and snapping out of his reverie, he opened his ring-binder.

"Mrs Schalplatten was to have taken three lads from Dublin." he handed her a beige paper folder. "But as you may know she exceeded her expiry date a bit sooner than expected. This file includes all you need to know, plus an introductory letter from each student."

"Only three?" she groused. "I kept eleven girls last year!"

"Only nine of which went home!" Matthew hastily referred to his notebook.

Peig averted her eyes.

"Anyway," he said, shaking his head in despair. "I can't help it, if several schools have bailed out on us, this year. Word must be getting 'round."

"Where's the lining in this thing?" Peig insolently flashed the file in front of his face.

"Don't worry, you'll get your blood money!" he growled contemptuously. "But first, I need some insurance."

Grabbing Peig's fist, Matthew released the photographs beneath and furtively slid the incriminating article into his organiser.

"You may as well have your money's worth," she endorsed. "I can always produce more copies from the negatives."

The prospect of a lasting threat enraged the principal. "Where did you get them?!" he snarled.

"Ah sur' didn't one of the girls leave them behind last year-"

"More like you rifled their luggage, I suspect!"

From the myriad of paperwork on the table, Matthew picked up a white envelope and extended it. "These kids need proper food- *not* the weeds and horse testicles you've reportedly been serving year after year!" he warned.

"You can eat all that stuff," Peig tugged at the envelope. "It's the best of food!"

"Children today have more refined tastes than you'd think!" he maintained his grasp.

One final tug liberated the envelope. "Isn't it tender their bag is?" she hissed.

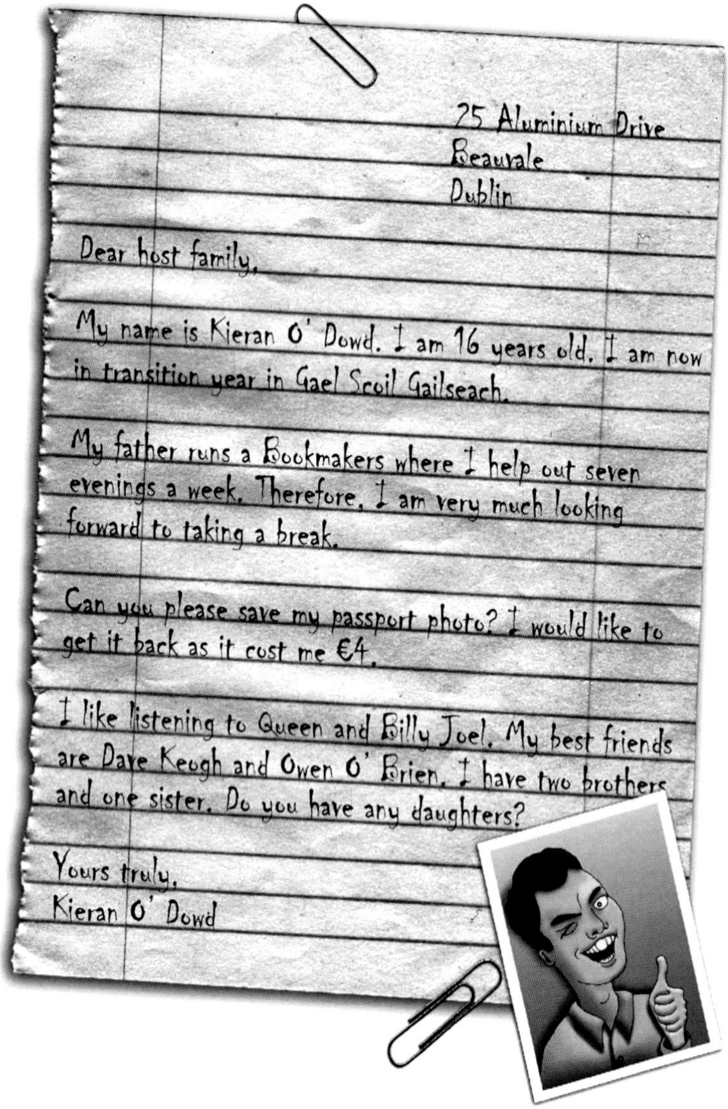

25 Aluminium Drive
Beauvale
Dublin

Dear host family,

My name is Kieran O' Dowd. I am 16 years old. I am now in transition year in Gael Scoil Gailseach.

My father runs a Bookmakers where I help out seven evenings a week. Therefore, I am very much looking forward to taking a break.

Can you please save my passport photo? I would like to get it back as it cost me €4.

I like listening to Queen and Billy Joel. My best friends are Dave Keogh and Owen O' Brien. I have two brothers and one sister. Do you have any daughters?

Yours truly,
Kieran O' Dowd

Unit 4008 D, Joyride Industrial Estate, Co. Dublin

Tel: +353 1 555-70250 Fax: + 353 1 555-70251 E - mail: sales@bbb.com

'Tír Na nÓg' Villa
Pastry Crescent
Portbrook
Dublin

To whom it may concern:

Hi! My name is Owen, I am 15 (but nearly 16!).

I am looking forward to spending three weeks in the country as I love animals; especially Pork and Beef.

My hobbies include soccer, rugby and Gaelic games, all of which I prefer to watch on television.

I am an only child. Dave Keogh and Kieran O' Dowd are my best mates.

C.U. soon!
Best Wishes.

Owen O' Brien

'You can't lick Bottoms, Brown & O' Brien for better hygiene'

Directors: Jack Bottoms, Latrine Brown and Brian O' Brien

167 Bauhaus Terrace
Taladale
Dublin

Dear Bean An Tí

I have never been away from home before, but mother insists that it is a wonderful opportunity, so I am trying to look forward to it.

Mother is a part time counsellor in my school - Gael Scoil Gailseach. I have three sisters, but they live in America, so I just live with mother.

While I am in the Gaeltacht I shall miss mother, but she has promised to visit.

Mother has written an 8-page booklet for you to read on my required medication.
My best friend is probably mother.

Yours sincerely,

Rory Waters.

P.S. I can't eat meat.

If Kieran O'Dowd had an inkling of the cruel blows fate was about to bestow, he might never have left the wholesome confines of his father's betting shop. But for now, the well-groomed, handsome teenager's greatest challenge was mastering a portable computer game, belonging to his friend, Owen O'Brien. Enthralled by the rolling scenery, Owen was seated by the window, to Kieran's left. Equally, this ginger-haired and faintly heavy-set adolescent remained blissfully unaware of their impending calamity. In fact, there was a general sense of optimism on this glorious June morning, as their coach glided through the scenic countryside.

"So what else do you know about this Ross-thingy place?" Kieran said, without averting his eyes from the game.

"Not much," Owen replied. "As I said, the brochure looked promising, but I really don't care, so long as the food's good."

"It'd better be. We paid enough for it!"

Directly behind the pair, their especially blithe friend, Dave Keogh, was sprawled across two seats, using his kaki jacket as a blanket and not unlike the twenty-eight other boys of *Gael Scoil♣ Gailseach,* was still subdued after their appallingly early start that morning.

At the front of the bus, the group's liaison teacher, Miss Colic, confirmed the time before standing up to address the passengers. A bespectacled spinster in her mid-thirties, Miss Colic was basically a good natured, but staid woman, whose most noteworthy 'quality' was her affinity for flowery frocks.

"All right simmer down everybody!" she decreed, while probing her clipboard. "It's time to announce your host families and housemates. And please, I don't wish to hear any objections. If you don't like it, it's not my fault! Everything has been prearranged by the course coordinators. Right, first up; Damien Nolan, Sean Higgins and Jason McLochlann, you three will be staying with Candy O'Shea."

A rapturous cheer erupted from the rear. "Candy? Ooooh Yeah! Sweet babe!"

♣ Gaelic language school

Glimpsing down the aisle, Kieran O'Dowd spotted a dubious object in a brown paper bag being passed from mouth to mouth.

"Daimo, Higgo and Locko, all the wasters under one roof," he murmured discreetly to Owen.

"Okay, quiet down there," their liaison teacher continued. "Next we have Kieran O'Dowd, Owen O'Brien and uh, Rory Waters, you'll be staying with eh, Evelyn Sk-Skalplatten-"

Kieran leapt from his seat. "What? That's a mistake, surely! What about Dave, isn't he with us?"

Miss Colic ran her finger down her clipboard; "You mean David Keogh? No, I don't think so, according to my list he's staying in Mags Buckley's house along with David Morrissey and Ambrose Cleary."

"But that's ridiculous! You can't have two Daves staying in the one house, they'll get mixed up!"

"I'm sure they'll manage!" Miss Colic pledged.

Owen O'Brien interrupted the proceedings. "Yeah, it doesn't matter because there's good Dave," he pointed to Dave Keogh, "And there's bad Dave!" he pointed across the aisle to David Morrissey.

Morrissey who, with a Stanley Knife, had been carving his initials into the seat opposite, soared into the air. "Who's the bad Dave? I'm not the bad Dave! *He's* the bad Dave!" he flashed his blade at Dave Keogh.

"That r-reminds me," Miss Colic quivered nervously, "Your Mum asked me to give you these before we left." She proffered a small jar of tablets to Morrissey, who snatched them from her trembling hands and on returning to his seat, proceeded to embellish his artwork with a heavy duty green marker.

"It's not fair!" Kieran groused. "Dave Keogh should've been staying with me and Owen."

His trifling quibble prompted heckles from the rear.

"Aw poo' wittle Keewaan," they sniggered.

Kieran's face turned crimson. "Shuddup! I was only worried that poor Rory might miss his Mammy!"

Now in the limelight, the bespectacled and studious looking Rory Waters, lowered his novel and tackled Kieran in his customary aloof manner. "If you must know she's coming down at the weekend."

"Ooooooh!" the entire bus mocked in unison.

"That's enough!" Miss Colic raised her arm. "And sit down Mr O'Dowd! I don't want any more lip from you, either!"

The teenager abandoned his protest and slumped back into his seat.

Dave Keogh cropped his head from behind. "Hey, it doesn't matter, they're all done arsebetically anyway."

"That's for sure," Kieran sulked. "I just hope I'm not expected to tuck him in at night."

Dave raised his hand to summon the teacher. "Miss Colic, Miss Colic!"

"Yes what is it, Mr Keogh?"

"Is your husband's name *Al*?"

"No, I'm not married. Why do ask?"

"Oh nothing, I was just wondering if you had an *Al Colic* in the family?"

Gales of laughter filled the air.

"Stop-it now! That's enough horsing about!" she ruled.

But as the liaison teacher tried to focus on her objective, someone began repeatedly stomping his feet on the floor. The notion caught on and the thumping spread rapidly, until the entire complement on board were galloping and whinnying. The unfortunate Miss Colic was now at her wit's end. "Stop-it! Stop-it! Stop-it! Stop-it!" she shrieked.

When a bump in the road caused her to swagger, the predictable onslaught of heckles, jeers and accusations of drunkenness followed.

"Sorry about that folks!" the bus driver announced over the intercom. "But the last time this patch of road saw a fresh coat of tarmac, St. Patrick himself was doing the rounds."

The apparent attempt at humour swiftly restored a sense of sobriety.

The route to Rossbladderburst was in every sense a precarious one. Firstly, it was plagued with potholes; a common problem with Irish roads not frequented by politicians and dignitaries. Secondly, a junction at the foot of the village was so treacherous that even the 'Accident: Black Spot' sign was removed after 'it' collided with several vehicles. It was hoped that the Rossbladderburst bypass would alleviate this problem; unfortunately its development went askew, when a wealthy (and allegedly well-connected) land-owner managed to overturn the compulsory purchase order on his property. Hence, the Rossbladderburst bypass was re-routed through the centre of Knockyadown, a town four times its size. However, these inconveniences paled compared to the hazards within the village itself and while being burdened with Rory Waters may have seemed torturous for Kieran O'Dowd, his worst affliction was yet to come; Evelyn Schalplatten had been superseded by Peig Sawyer, Rossbladderburst's most dubious hostess. Rest assured, these students were about to embark on the trip of a lifetime, a trip that would leave a mark on them for the rest of their lives.

Accident: Black Spot:
The perilous intersection just outside the village

2. Celestial Greetings

It was late morning and outside St. Millipede's hall, the villagers were patiently awaiting the new arrivals. The smell of freshly written cheques had formed a smile on their rosy cheeks and as they chatted gregariously, many could be seen caressing their pecuniary glands (a.k.a. pockets). By the roadside, members of a uniformed brass band were warming up for a recital, while on hand was Catherine Begley, discussing their programme with the conductor.

Peig Sawyer, meanwhile, appeared unimpressed with the contents of her special envelope, but nonetheless pocketed her 'meagre' remittance. The file on her imminent visitors was briefly skimmed over, before being contemptuously discarded into a nearby hedge. What did rouse the elder, however, was the presence of a tall burly figure dressed from head to toe in tweed. This, she warranted, was a man who simply did not belong here. In the midst of an animated discussion with other local bigwigs, including Garda Superintendent Leo O'Meara and publican Bernard O'Shea, Curly Buckley very much appeared to be the life and soul of the conversation. But most sickening of all, was the beige folder under his arm. Of course, given their chequered history together, the flamboyant Mr Buckley and the arcane Mrs Sawyer were never likely to see eye to eye.

Inches away, Fr. Tom Buttimer was pouring himself a cup of milk from the hospitality stand, which consisted only of milk, when from the corner of his eye he spotted Matthew Begley emerging from the hall, squinting in the daylight, looking pale and despondent. Intuitively pouring a second cup, Fr. Tom strolled over and handed the principal a complimentary beverage.

"Well, here we go again," the cleric said cheerfully, "And you couldn't hope for better weather to start the season off. Warm sunshine and good company, what more could you ask for?"

Matthew gazed glumly into his polystyrene cup. "I wish I was on a beach in the Bahamas sipping Piña Coladas, away from this cesspit of vultures. But no, every year June arrives that bit earlier and I'm locked into the same charade. Twenty years of relentless bile. And where does it get you at the end of the day? Your kids despise you. No one respects you. Everyone wants a slice of the cake and not only that, they *all* want the lion's share. So called friends and neighbours would sooner stab you in the back than look at you. And now, look at them salivate, as they prepare to draw fresh blood, their unquenched thirst mightier than ever. How many more lives must they destroy before they've had their fill? I'd offer myself as a sacrificial lamb, but still, they'd crave for more and more, until they drowned in a pool of their own avarice and iniquity."

Fr. Tom stared at Matthew for a moment, "Still, it's a nice day for it?"

The principal rubbed his weary eyes, only to find Peig Sawyer charging towards him as he opened them again. "Oh *no*," he groaned.

"You! That man is a criminal!" Peig bellowed, pointing to Curly Buckley. "What are you doing giving him students? How many is he getting?"

"Shhh, calm down," Matthew implored. "He's getting exactly the same as you and everyone else, only three per household!"

"I am calm!" Peig retorted. "You can't give students to a man who deliberately tried to infect his cattle with B.S.E! He's a crook! A menace to society! Anyone who would do what he did, in an attempt to defraud the state, is a monster! You can't trust him!"

Matthew folded his arms as he tried to reason with her. "You can't hold a grudge forever, Mrs Sawyer, and while I won't condone his actions, Curly Buckley served his time and ultimately deserves a second chance."

Ditching the mulish principal, Peig tried to evoke the sympathies of the parish priest. "Curly Buckley's great-grandfather put a cross on our family's barrel of barley during the famine. Now what does that tell you about the Buckleys? They're lepers! That's what they are! Lepers! Not to be trusted. And you know what they say? A leper never changes its spots."

"Ah come on now, that's all in the past," Fr. Tom chuckled. "Mr Buckley has repented, so I think we ought to let bygones be bygones."

Rossbladderburst: during tea-time rush hour

"I have to agree with Father Buttimer," Matthew concurred, "Curly Buckley has been very eager to show us how much he's reformed. Look! This year he's even splashed out on that brass band to welcome our visitors."

"Oh is that right?" Fr. Tom looked on.

Peig's expression, however, was one of disdain, which increased exponentially when she spotted Curly Buckley's gaze locked on her. Doubtless, his ears had been burning and the scorn was evident in his frosty glare.

"Not only that," Matthew continued, "But James and Jeremiah Buckley arrived this morning and surprised us all with half-a-dozen crates of complimentary milk!"

Fr. Tom Buttimer recoiled in horror. Having just taken a large sip himself, he anxiously churned the stuff around in his mouth, while over by the hospitality stand, six-year-old Daniel Begley sampled and at once rejected the same white lumpy substance. Fr. Tom was in trouble. With his cheeks bulging, he hardly knew which way to turn. Worse still, Curly Buckley himself was approaching, which, unsurprisingly sent Peig scurrying away.

"Hello there Father!" Curly boomed, with a hearty slap on the back, forcing the hapless cleric to swallow. "You like your milk, I see!" he declared, while still maintaining a keen eye on Peig, who was now slinking into the crowd.

Nauseated, Fr. Tom stared into his cup and chided his own negligence. "Oh, yes indeedy," he responded diplomatically, while wiping his tongue on a handkerchief.

Curly suddenly held the priest aside as if to engage him privately, but yet, spoke in a manner that was rather ostentatious. "Listen Father, there's plenty more where that came from, and it's all fine for drinking or baking or whatever, and we've plenty of extra stock in at the moment. So you just say the word and I'll send a stack of crates over to you!"

"Ah well, I'd love to but ah-"

"Grand that's settled!" Curly decreed. "Hello Matt, grand day for it!"

Exasperatingly, Buckley had already deviated before Fr. Tom could properly decline. Further discussion was ruled out when the band broke into a thunderous rendition of The Irish Emigrant.

"Two coaches spotted at the crossroads!" Catherine Begley exclaimed, as she negotiated her way through the jubilant horde. "So I've just asked the band to start up!"

As Matthew looked on in anticipation, he raised the paper cup to his lips.

Aboard the first bus were the boys of *Scoil Gailseach,* while in hot pursuit, were the girls of St. Grizelda's, albeit several hours of agony for Christy, their driver. There was nothing extraordinary about the task of delivering thirty-two young ladies from Dublin to Kerry, but, chauffeuring thirty-two compulsive chain smokers on a 310 kilometre journey, was strictly martyr territory. The torture began at 6.00am, when Christy first found himself immersed in second-hand cigarette smoke. Amazingly, old Mrs Breslin, liaison teacher to the girls, appeared to be sleeping through it all in her front row seat. Was she really unmindful to the fact that every one of her students was flouting the rules? Or was she merely turning a blind eye? Once again, Christy attempted to rouse her.

"Mrs Breslin?" he pleaded, with one dehydrated eye still on the road. "Mrs Breslin?"

With no reply still, the driver picked up his microphone. "I would like to remind passengers that there is a strict no smoking policy on board this bus," he croaked. "There is, in fact, a heavy fine for anybody caught smoking, so perhaps you might all like to consider extinguishing your cigarettes-"

Suddenly, there was a hiss and a crackle and his voice no longer resonated through the speakers. "Hello? Hello? Testing-testing?"

Puzzled as to the reason he had been cut short, Christy inspected the microphone. The cable was unexpectedly limp and with one sharp tug, he discovered why. His P.A. system had been sabotaged. Several rows behind, a set of pliers was surreptitiously making its way down the bus, before being stored in a

Gucci Bag. Given their reputation, it was unsurprising that St. Grizelda's had earned the nickname, St. Rizzla's.

As the band regaled the locals, Fr. Tom glanced casually across the road to *Coláiste Nathair.* He wasn't certain, but it appeared as if somebody was thumping angrily on a window over there. Concerned that something was awry, the cleric alerted Matthew with a tap on the shoulder. "Don't the state exams start today?" he cried.

"Yes, that's right," the principal acknowledged, with a cursory squint in the same direction.

"Won't the noise bother them?"

"Ah no, I'm sure they're fine," he said, with a dismissive wave.

But despite Matthew's heedless assurance, something was horribly wrong within those school walls. The exams had been well underway when the clamour from outside reached seemingly untold decibels. Jennifer Begley wrapped her arm around her head in an attempt to stifle the din, while an ineffectual invigilator jigged nervously about, hammering at the window.

"How can we concentrate with all that racket?" Jennifer eventually snapped.

"Shhh! No talking! I'm doing my best to alert them. Just finish your paper or we'll all be in trouble," the invigilator said feebly.

Others too were becoming extremely irate. "My whole future is tied up with this exam and now I'm doomed to fail, because of the circus outside my window!" one student exclaimed.

Sadly, the stress was overwhelming for the so-called invigilator who, moments later, fled the ruckus speaking in tongues, leaving a group of forty-odd Junior and Leaving certificate students in a state of anarchy.

Outside, with all eyes on the band, Peig produced from beneath her shawl two litres of milk, lifted from the hospitality stand, earlier on. Having discovered their origin, however, her taste for them had curdled. Rather than return this tainted milk, both cartons were tossed into a ditch. It was a rare and exceptional incident, in which pride was placed above pragmatism. The ritual was completed with Peig fanatically wiping her hands on some leaves. Carefully observing the crowd as she discarded the leaves, Peig found something else that riled her. Among the familiar faces was Domingo Murphy, who was delighting himself and others by pretending to conduct the band. The real conductor clearly saw the funny side and yielded to Domingo's expertise. Peig wasn't amused, she didn't care much for his style or his baton, a rolled up beige folder.

Despite his troubles, Matthew Begley couldn't help but warm to these shenanigans and was even tapping his foot in rhythm with the music. Regrettably, his relief was abruptly terminated, when a malicious entity grabbed his shirt collar from behind. As he struggled for air, Matthew's ring binder fell on the ground. Viciously wrenched from the crowd, it was no surprise to find that this was the calling card of a certain pain in the neck. "What is it now?" he gasped, while straightening his shirt and tie.

Peig pointed to the moustachioed gentlemen, who was larking merrily about. "What's he doing here?"

"Who? Domingo? Ah come on, everybody loves Domingo!"

"Well I don't!"

"Well he's great with the kids, so what's the problem?"

"That man doesn't speak a word of English let alone Irish!" she huffed.

"What difference does it make? These city kids haven't the foggiest notion what we're on about at the best of times! Besides, it was Catherine's idea, I suggest you take it up with her!"

"Oho! You can be sure I will! And tell me, how many is he getting?"

Matthew hesitated for moment. "Ehm, f-five-"

"What? Five?!" Peig roared.

But before she could voice any further objections, two coaches rolled towards St. Millipede's community hall, spurring an ecstatic ovation from the crowd.

Kieran O'Dowd sprung from his seat. Seemingly, this miniscule hamlet and its haphazard layout had crept up on them without warning. "Hey, we're here already!"

"Oo-er! They've even brought their duelling banjos!" Dave irreverently remarked.

"Please stay seated until we've come to a complete stop!" their liaison teacher frowned disapprovingly. "And that means you, Mr O'Dowd and you, Mr Keogh!"

With that, Dave plunged into his seat, clutching his abdomen in agony.

"Miss Colic! Miss Colic!" Kieran cried.

"What is it now O'Dowd?"

"It's Dave, Miss, I think he's sick!"

"This had better not be one your tricks!" she warned.

But when Dave yielded a harrowing cry, Miss Colic came rushing down the aisle.

"A-a-are you a-all right?"

Dave vented another heart rending howl.

"It's not appendicitis, is it?"

"No!" he clutched his stomach. "I think it's- ooh! I think it's- aah! It's the *colic*!"

An explosion of laughter suddenly hit Miss Colic.

"Go on, get off the lot of you!" she fumed. "Straight into the hall for the assembly!"

As the door to St. Grizelda's coach hissed open, a steady stream of blasé faces emerged from the haze. The indiscriminate dropping of ash everywhere suggested that none were overly impressed with their new surroundings. Their driver didn't waste any time in administering, to himself, a substantial dose of oxygen from the medical kit. As the thick layer of smoke began to dissipate, it emerged that Mrs Breslin was still in her seat. Unable to fathom how she had slept through the whole affair, Christy lumbered towards her and nudged her arm. "Mrs Breslin?" he wheezed, "Mrs Breslin?" To his horror, she keeled sideways, banging her head on the window.

♣ ♣ ♣ ♣ ♣

By midday, all factions had assembled within St. Millipede's hall for the obligatory Rossbladderburst welcome. Seated on a platform facing the auditorium, the staff wearily awaited the principal's customary opening address. But as Matthew took to the podium, he realised that his ring-binder was missing. Even more distressing, was its rediscovery on his wife's lap. Spotting his hesitant onset, Catherine 'pre-empted' his requirement and opened the organiser. "Get a move on!" she urged, handing him an A4 sheet, fortunately resting on top.

Clearly uneasy with the arrangement, the principal had no choice but to proceed. "Good afternoon *Gael Scoil Gailseach*," he declared. "And of course, St. Grizelda's. Rossbladderburst welcomes you with open palms, eh, arms. But before things get underway; we've just learned that *Coláiste Cruimhín* will not be arriving today as scheduled." Murmurs of disenchantment arose from the floor. "In fact, we have just received a call from their liaison teacher, who claims they've been held up in Limerick- literally. Apparently, they were bus-jacked at knife-point earlier this morning and it may be a while before alternative transport can be arranged. Some have been treated for shock, but the good news is that there were no fatalities."

Noting Catherine eyeballing the heavens, Matthew regretted this elaboration.

"Erm yes, moving on," he continued, "In a few short moments you will become acquainted with your delegated host families who, no doubt, will extend to you the warmest of hospitality. But first, let me give you just a hint of what promises to be an experience to die for. At *Coláiste Nathair Naofa* Cultural Academy, we pride ourselves on our unique seal of excellence. Our exclusive and progressive master classes will undoubtedly leave you clamouring, uhm, for more. And among the extra curricular activities to enjoy, we have *céilís* and-" He glimpsed down at the lean agenda. "*Céilís*, and much-much more! Your schedule is simply bursting with life-"

An embodiment of death inharmoniously burst through the side entrance, as James and Jeremiah Buckley casually wheeled a coffin into the auditorium. Horrified at first, the throng whispered excitedly as Fr. Tom Buttimer sprung into action.

"Lads-lads-lads, what's going on? Can't you see we're in the middle of an assembly here?" he glanced anxiously over his shoulder.

Curly Buckley's simple minded offspring seemed equally perplexed by the large crowd gaping at their pine box. "Sorry Father, b-but you said to d-deliver the coffin this afternoon," James stuttered.

"What? Oh right, Mrs Schalplatten, but not here, I told you to take her into the chapel, next door!"

"We tried, but the door was locked!"

"No, it isn't. It can't be! Wait a minute, did you actually try pushing the door *in*?"

"Isn't that exactly what I told you?" James looked sternly at his brother.

Jeremiah ruefully eyed the floor. "Sorry Father, I'm always getting mixed up with the old *pull* and *push* thing."

Rather than loose his temper, Fr. Tom simply bit his tongue. "All right just take it back out of sight and once we're finished here I'll deal with it!"

Hence, James, who was at one end of the coffin, endeavoured to heave the trolley back towards the exit, but with the castors at an oblique angle, it remained stationary.

"Pull!" he ordered his brother at the opposite end.

"I am!" Jeremiah replied.

But as James looked up, he saw evidence to the contrary. "No you're not, you're *pushing* it!"

"What? No! I'm *pulling* as hard as I can!" Jeremiah thrust his entire weight upon the trolley.

Just as the parish priest was just about to intercede, James decided to release his grip. Naturally, the laws of physics prevailed and Jeremiah and the trolley were sent hurtling towards the centre of the auditorium. As the pine box plunged into the crowd, its half-decimated contents unfurled on the laps of a dozen hysterical girls. The sight of a mangled corpse strewn in the aisles sent many fleeing in horror. Principal Matthew Begley felt only his knees weaken, as yet another travesty notched itself onto what was becoming an awfully long day.

3. Straight From The Frying Pan...

Following the premature suspension of the assembly, the students were soon being ferried away to their designated corners of the village. Outside St. Millipede's hall, Catherine Begley, having assumed command, was shepherding the flock with some degree of efficiency. Matthew hovered anxiously in the background, almost ill with worry, concerning the organiser now in his wife's custody.

"Only a few more before we break for lunch," Catherine turned the page. "Right, can we have David Morrissey, David Keogh and Ambrose Cleary, please?"

Three heavily burdened students presented themselves. "Yes, eh, ye lads will be going with Mr Buckley- *Mr Buckley*?"

Larger than life, Curly Buckley bounced towards the hesitant looking youths with an outstretched arm. "How do lads? Welcome-welcome-welcome!"

Grabbing each of their hands respectively, he wrung them with such vigour that Ambrose Cleary fell to his knees. "What's wrong with you, at all? Is your bag too heavy?" Curly asked him, in all innocence as he grabbed the holdall. "Let me take it over to the car!"

In passing, he turned towards the principal. "We'll have to put a bit of strength into these city lads, won't we?"

"Oh that's right Curly," Matthew chuckled synthetically.

"And maybe we can find them a good barber too!" Buckley hinted at Dave Keogh's unkempt greasy mop.

The three boys followed their new patron and were visibly over the moon to find a vintage golden Rolls Royce awaiting them. Kieran O'Dowd couldn't help but feel a little envious, noting the other group had fallen on their feet. Even so, he and Owen might yet be blessed with an equally affluent host.

As Catherine turned another page of his wretched ring-binder, Matthew swabbed the beads of anxiety from his brow.

"Finally we have Kieran O'Dowd, Owen O'Brien and Rory Waters-"

Equally laden with heavy bags, the trio plodded into the foreground.

"And you lads are with- Matt! What's this skull and crossbones doing here?!"

"Ahem, eh, Mrs S-Sawyer," he mumbled uncomfortably.

"What? But she's been expunged from the roster!"

"Ahem, no, change of plan. I erm, just," he trailed off with a shrug.

"Right, well, where is she?" Catherine enquired suspiciously, as she scanned the yard.

Curly Buckley, meanwhile, didn't have the grace to depart on a quiet note. Upon igniting the engine, he hammered the car horn and waved regally to his minions. As the sleek vehicle glided away, there stood Peig in all her glory. Though she may not have been short of a bob, unfortunately for Kieran, she was more closely associated with effluence than affluence. Alas, formal introductions were inauspiciously scotched by an almighty clap of thunder, followed by a precipitous cloudburst. The old woman didn't so much as flinch, as the rain streamed down her face.

"Hello lads, ye're with me!"

Kieran O'Dowd regarded her cruel thin-lipped smile. Surely this repugnant fossil was mistaken? He turned to ask the principal only to discover that he and the other teacher had suddenly vanished.

"Where are you parked?" Owen naively enquired.

"Right here," she said.

He looked around, but there was no sign of a vehicle in the immediate vicinity. "No, I mean, where's your car?"

"Car? What car?" she retorted.

Kieran, Owen and Rory looked at each another with a united sense of foreboding. Kieran, in particular, looked decidedly green around the gills, his matinee idol features already drowning in a torrent of fear and anxiety. It was now sheeting down and he and his comrades were soaked to the bone. More thunder and lightening followed, almost certainly a portent of impending doom.

Metres away, both Begleys were fleeing towards their own car when a parched voice summoned them by surprise. "Mr Begley-?"

It was St. Grizelda's driver sitting on the steps of his own coach, holding an oxygen mask over his mouth.

"Christy!" Matthew cried. "What's going on? Are you all right?"

"I will be, but that's more than can be said for poor Mrs Breslin," he wheezed, thumbing in the direction of the front row seat.

As the pair looked up, they beheld the chilling apparition of Mrs Breslin's face pressed up against the window. Her eyes were glazed over and with the rain trickling down on the glass outside, it appeared as if she was weeping, posthumously. Horror-struck, Catherine instantly turned away.

"There-there," Matthew comforted his wife. "And here, let me take *that*," he added, finally reclaiming his folder.

♣ ♣ ♣ ♣ ♣

Having bolted the main doors shut, Fr. Tom marched towards the opposite end of the hall, where the cowering Buckley boys were awaiting his instruction. "Now lads," he said gravely. "Has Mrs Schalplatten been taken care of?"

"She has indeed, Father," James said, meekly. "She's out of sight and out of mind, until the funeral this evening, so you needn't worry about a thing."

'Out of sight', unfortunately, meant that poor Mrs Schalplatten's coffin had been left outside the back door in the pouring rain, surrounded by stray dogs who had congregated to investigate the pungent odour. It was a shame too, that they neglected to leave the brake on the trolley. But the priest, for whom it had been a trying morning, was simply looking forward to his lunch. "All right so," he said, allowing a little latitude, "And perhaps the pair of ye might move aside those chairs, for the dance this evening?"

Nodding in agreement, James produced a docket and extended it. "Daddy said you needed to sign this."

"What's it for?" the cleric asked warily.

"The milk."

"What milk?"

As the young man pointed to a six-foot high stack of crates by the back door, poor Fr. Tom almost fell out of his standing. "Ah no!" he cried, shaking his head in despair.

♣ ♣ ♣ ♣ ♣

Any residual delusions of grandeur were quickly dispersed as Kieran O'Dowd set eyes upon Peig's modest bungalow. Still, he and the others would be glad to take refuge after trudging to the most outer reaches of the village in torrential rain.

"Come on lads, ye're dragging your heels!" the old woman said, as she opened the front door. "A drop of rain will do ye no harm."

Kieran, Owen and Rory bravely stepped into her lair, where at least, burning embers in an open hearth took the chill out of the air. The kitchen-cum-living area encompassed a sophisticated amalgamation of neo-classical, post-apocalyptic décor. Its unique and subjective elegance was clearly governed by a non-existent budget, a style only the most cynical detractor would classify as tacky.

"Well lads, make yourselves at home. There's no need to stand on ceremony here." she said, hanging her dripping shawl behind the door.

Owen, who was quite breathless after his jaunt, dropped his bag and happily took the first available seat. It was the only armchair in a room of mismatched furniture.

"That's *my* chair!" Peig bellowed.

Owen jumped up. "S-sorry, I-I didn't know!"

"Ah sur' take it easy. Relax. You can sit there if you like," she immediately changed tactics. Observing an almost leathery veneer of dirt on the textile armrests, Owen opted to sit at the table instead. Rory cautiously joined him, as did Kieran, who angled his chair towards the fire. A white marble table top was one of the more impressive features in the kitchen; though curiously covered just half the table. Similarly, the hearth rug beneath Kieran's feet appeared to be stitched together from miscellaneous carpet samples.

"I suppose, ye'll be wanting to get out of those wet clothes?" Peig offered half-heartedly, as she began stoking the fire.

"Ah, there's no hurry," Kieran instinctively replied.

In actual fact, it was pure agony basking in saturated garments and as fresh turf was added to the hearth, Owen pinched the clinging fabric on his thighs, in an attempt to aerate his trousers.

"What about food? Ye're not hungry, or anything, are ye lads?"

"Ah no, we're fine," Kieran said.

Despite the tepid nature of her proposals, Kieran's impulse to decline caused Owen to frown. He, on the other hand, would have gladly welcomed a decent square meal. Alas, it was an empty gesture anyway. "Good, because I haven't been to the shops yet," she added.

That's rich, Kieran thought, *she had rakes of time to prepare for our arrival.*

"But ye'll have a cup of tea anyway, lads, won't ye?"

"Ehm yes, that might be nice," Kieran said, biting the bullet for fear she wouldn't ask a second time.

"Yes please, I'd love a cup, Mrs Skalplatten!" Owen clasped his hands.

Peig wrenched a red hot poker from the fire and brandished it at the portly teenager. "*Schalplatten*?" she hissed, "Sur' she's dead! *I'm* Peig Sawyer!"

"I- I'm s-s-sorry, but th-that's what they told us e-earlier on!" Owen recoiled.

Though she undoubtedly instilled fear in their hearts, the fact that their assumed hostess had been suddenly written off, was particularly unsettling.

"What about you, the boy with the goggles there?" she pointed the poker in Rory's direction. "Do you want tea?"

Clearly stunned by the entire induction, Rory mustered a squeak. "O-okay."

"Grand so, tea for three!" she affirmed, tossing the poker into a copper coal scuttle.

Sliding open the door of her green dresser, Peig produced a tea caddy, which she unlocked with a key from the pocket of her filthy apron. Owen also observed that as the only storage unit in the kitchen, the dresser seemed alarmingly bare. A pinch of tea was sprinkled into an old aluminium teapot, and as the old black kettle adorning the hearth came to the boil, Peig unhooked it and poured its boiling contents into the pot.

"Now gentlemen, I'm out of milk, I'm afraid, so you'll have to do without!"

Three mugs were taken from the dresser and placed on the table. Or at least they used to be mugs, Kieran mused. The rim of his was chipped at 360 degrees. He could just about decipher the faded lettering 'Italia 90' emblazoned on the exterior, while the revolting coat of tannin on its interior, suggested that the marvels of dishwasher technology had evaded this part of the country. Still, he couldn't grumble; at least his mug had a handle.

"And I hope ye don't take sugar," Peig continued, "As I never use it myself. But sur' aren't we better off without it anyway?"

There was hardly a chorus of approval as she poured, and it wasn't exactly the strongest brew they had ever seen, but it was adequate and warming.

Inspired by the war-zone like surroundings, Kieran couldn't help but ridicule their situation by simulating shell-shock, when Peig's back was turned. The jape lost its appeal when he and Owen noticed that Rory had the same party trick, offering a precision performance that was bordering on genius.

"So lads, ye're from Dublin, are ye?" Peig casually enquired, as she joined them at the table.

"Uhm, yeah," Kieran replied.

"Dear-dear-dear, what an awful-awful-*awful* place," she bleated.

"Have you *been* there?" he frowned.

"Oh God no! What business have I going to those places? No, I've never been outside Kerry in my entire life. Sur' nowadays when you turn on the wireless, all you hear about is gang warfare, murders and armed robberies."

Owen was reeling. It wasn't so much the affront to their beloved capital, but another startling realisation. His eyes explored every nook and cranny, before ascertaining that there was, in fact, *no* television set. The concept was demoralising; goodbye premiership matches and European championship football. Already, his nauseating desperation for a fix left him feeling as if he had been force-fed a box of *Brillo Pads*.

Kieran, meanwhile, found his landlady's fixation with their bags extremely disquieting. A long, awkward silence followed, after which Peig arose to add more fuel to the fire. "Do ye see much turf in Dublin, lads?" she idly asked.

"Yeah quite a bit," Kieran replied, without really paying much heed. "My father is a turf accountant."

"Well-well, and does he have his own bog?"

Her line of questioning was mystifying, to say the least.

"Erm, yeah, there's two in the back of the shop."

"Begod, that's a fair stretch."

"Perhaps you don't understand, what I mean is, my father's a bookmaker."

"Oh he's a writer?"

"No, he's not!"

"He prints them, then?"

"Uh, sure, why not?" he wearily suggested.

"And what about the rest of ye, do ye have yer own bogs as well?"

"Owen's auld fellah works in a toilet paper factory!" Kieran divulged with relish.

"He doesn't *work* there!" Owen grimaced disapprovingly. "He's a senior partner in *Bottoms, Brown and O'Brien*, an international manufacturing firm who just happen to have toilet tissue on their assembly line!"

"Oh really? What else do they make?" Kieran contested.

"They produce soap, man-size tissues-"

"Snot rags! Snot rags and toilet paper!"

"All right, fine, maybe you *do* have a point," Owen conceded. "But at least *my* parents aren't so cheap that they keep a tray of used betting slips in the bathroom!"

Kieran clamped up and just glowered quietly for a moment.

"What about the boy with the goggles? He's very quiet," Peig observed.

"M-my n-name is Rory!" he blurted.

"Oh now, he has a tongue, after all!"

But when Rory failed to elaborate, Kieran happily obliged. "Rory's auld one is the school shrink!" he scoffed. "Unfortunately, she hasn't been able to do much to help him!"

"Is that right?" she said vacantly, "Well-well-well."

While off the cuff references like these left Peig in the dark, her spin on the vernacular was mutually perplexing to her guests. "Right then, let's get ye fixed up," she announced, just as they were beginning to unwind. Hoisting herself from the table with a gratuitous grunt, she viciously wrenched the mug from Owen's jaws. And as the rest of the cups were gathered, the old curmudgeon dropped a bombshell. "Once ye're settled then, it'll give ye a chance to sort me presents out."

Kieran's eyes bulged from their sockets. "What?" he mimed at the others.

Equally surprised, Owen shrugged incredulously and reached for his holdall.

Apart from the front door, there were three other doors leading from the kitchen, two to the left and one to the right. Trundling over to the one on the right, Peig ran her fingers over the architrave. A key dropped onto the frayed linoleum and Kieran went to pick it up.

"You'll be glad to know that I only have one rule in this house!" she plucked the key from his fingers.

Well that shouldn't be too difficult, he figured.

"And that is, that you do everything I say."

Somehow, this revelation wasn't altogether surprising. As she turned the key to unlock the door, Peig regarded Rory, who was still seated at the table. "What's wrong with that boy, at all? Is he a bit delicate?"

Unsure of her precise meaning, Kieran pledged that such behaviour was normal where Rory was concerned. "Ah no, he's always like that."

Aware that he had become the subject of conversation, Rory eventually arose. What he failed to observe, however, was that a thread of his woollen sweater had snagged a nail jutting from his chair, causing it to unravel as he crossed the room.

"Check out Rory's jumper!" Kieran howled. "That's flea market gear for you!"

But the loud and imperious guffaws ceased, as Peig opened the door to their sumptuous new accommodation. It was a small and musty dormitory with three primeval and decrepit bunk beds. The linen was strewn everywhere, ostensibly left un-cleaned from the previous occupants. Otherwise this veritable dive was bare, apart from the most revolting donkey head; stuffed and mounted on the opposite wall. Kieran, Owen and Rory simultaneously dropped their bags on the floor, overwhelmed, no doubt, with their colourful new environment. Owen winced at the sight of the partial animal and mistaking his revulsion for curiosity, Peig engaged him. "That's Old Healy as we used to call him. The late Mr Sawyer fancied himself as a bit of a taxi-farmist, I'm afraid."

Kieran shivered as he edged away from the draughty window. "What about you, Rory?" he enquired, "You haven't splashed out on some Waterford Crystal for our charming hostess?"

Seated on one of the lower bunks, their reticent comrade was too busy sending a text message to reply.

"Rorrrry!" Kieran heckled.

"Yes! I'm giving her a tea-cosy, if you must know!" he pointed agitatedly, to an object nestled in his open holdall.

"A wha-?" Aghast to discover that he was the only one without a strategy, Kieran tottered over to investigate. It was a distinct, if slightly garish, hand-knitted cosy, festooned with fluffy kittens frolicking around its circumference.

"We could say this is from all of us?" Kieran wistfully proposed.

Rory rolled his eyes in censure. "Mother spent a fortnight knitting that!"

Owen too, was unimpressed. "Come off it Kieran. One measly tea-cosy between the lot of us? You're so cheap!"

"Listen, I paid nearly three thousand Euro for this trip and I don't see why I should have to shell out for presents on top of that!"

It was a sturdy argument, but Owen deemed it best not to antagonise the natives. "I've brought a couple of Swiss Rolls with me," he said, reaching into his own holdall, "You can give her one of these, if you like."

"Thanks!" his thrifty roommate accepted, moistening his lips in anticipation.

Gathering the remainder of his wet clothes, Owen entered the kitchen again, where he found Peig in her armchair, darning her nylons. "Eh, I was wondering if I might give these a spin in your dryer for a couple of minutes?" he ventured softly.

Peig paused in mid-stitch. "Machines are only for the idle and foolhardy! But if it's airing your clothes need, you can throw them on the line over the fire!"

The student meekly obeyed and hastened back towards the dormitory, avoiding further eye contact with his belligerent landlady.

"A streak of misery! That's what she is!" Owen exclaimed, as he slammed the door behind him. "And why on earth does she keep picking on me?"

"Sounds like Owen's got a secret admirer!" Kieran offered unconstructively.

"Seriously! I'm being victimised here!" Owen cried. "In the car park, for example, she nearly bit my face off, and *again* when I sat in that disgusting armchair. Next, she practically bludgeoned me with a hot poker and then almost knocked my eye-teeth out when she grabbed that mug. Now, I've had yet another earful!"

"Perhaps her rage is a manifestation of the latent desire she harbours for you, and one day you shall both overcome adversity and be united in your eternal love," Kieran deduced.

"What's *that* supposed to mean?"

"Sorry, I was just paraphrasing the blurb on the back cover of one of Rory's trashy romance novels," Kieran said, flaunting a paperback.

Rory instinctively jerked and hit his head on the wooden frame above. "Ow! Give me that!" he seized the book. "And keep your paws out of my stuff!"

"Ooo! Begging your pardon, sir! One didn't realise your bag was a sacred temple!"

At this point, Kieran's wet clothes had been ditched in favour of a smart navy blue flannel robe and just as Owen had done, his sodden garments were bunched into a ball. "Now, if you'll excuse me, I must ask Owen's new girlfriend if I can bung these into her dryer."

"For your information she doesn't have a dryer!" Owen added bluntly.

"Ah, so you admit she's your girlfriend?"

"No! I'm just saying she doesn't have a dryer; only a length of cord stretching from one end of the fireplace to the other."

As Kieran O'Dowd entered the living area, he discovered that Peig had slipped out of sight. Interestingly, one of doors opposite was left slightly ajar, though not enough to reveal anything as he sneaked a passing glance. Nevertheless, he could hear shuffling inside, leading to the supposition that this was *her* room. As he approached the fire, Kieran noted with contempt how Owen's baggy jeans had commandeered the prime spot. Pushing them aside, he gave preferential treatment to his own garments. Unfortunately, before reaching the dormitory again, the hapless teenager was ambushed. "Oh now! That's a lovely coat you've got there!"

Peig soared across the room to inspect his elegant bathrobe. "Oh it's lovely," she purred, gently stroking the fabric on his shoulder.

Her body language (and odour) left him feeling distinctly chilled. It was imperative to evade this creepy troll without delay.

"Did you buy that in Dublin?" she grilled, despite the 'Florida Keys Hotel' badge emblazoned on the front.

Recalling how he had misappropriated this merchandise during a holiday trip to the sunshine state the previous year, Kieran fudged a little.

"Uhm, yeah," he replied somewhat guiltily.

"Listen, come here to me, do you know how much a Singer sewing machine cost in 1953-?"

Kieran failed to see the relevance and feared that any answer could open the floodgates to an epic account of her life's story. "Uhm, two hundred quid?" he hazarded.

"Thirty pounds!" she sighed, with a reminiscent squint.

"Oh really?" Kieran feigned interest. "Eh, well I have to go now-"

But Peig wasn't done yet and thwarted his escape with a firm clasp of his arm. "In those days, we all had to make our own clothes from whatever materials we could find. Sack cloth was all the rage you know. We always had our Sunday best, of course, but the rest of the time we had to make do with an old bag."

"Yes, I know the feeling," Kieran twittered, while endeavouring to disengage himself from her clutches.

"Tell me, what time are ye heading out?" she said, clinging tighter still.

"I think there's a *céilí* around seven? Down at- what's the name of the place?"

"And what's your name again, by the way-?"

"Kieran," he peeped nervously.

"Cian?"

"Kieran!"

"That's what I said!" she hissed.

Kieran didn't dally about splitting hairs, but wiped her venomous spittle from his face and retreated to the dormitory.

Back in relative safety, Kieran closed his eyes for a moment and breathed a quivering sigh of relief. That wretched beast, he decided, didn't so much need a Swiss Roll, as an industrial sized bottle of antiseptic mouthwash. "Uh! She's horrible! Horrible-horrible-horrible!"

The others appeared unconcerned by his feat of endurance. Rory was curled up on his bunk, looking more angst ridden than usual, while Owen was seated opposite, clutching a pair of mobile phones. "Here, you'll never believe this," he declared.

Kieran braced himself for the next potential kick in the teeth. "What?"

"Our phones don't work! We can't ring anyone! We can't even send a text message! Zip! Nothing! No signal, whatsoever!"

"So?"

"Oh yes," Owen suddenly recalled, "Mr O'Dowd doesn't own a mobile, Mr O'Dowd's too mean!"

"I'm not mean! I just heard that those things can fry your brain, by transmitting microwave oven signals - though I suspect that won't affect either of you."

Leaving Owen to caper about with the mobiles, Kieran decided to appraise the bed situation. It was grim to say the least. His roommates had predictably requisitioned the two lower bunks, unsurprising given Rory's fear of heights and Owen, well, he was just plain lazy. As for the remaining unit, it wasn't fit for garden mulch. Ascending to inspect the upper bunk of Owen's unit, Kieran threw himself upon it, to test it for size. "Pure junk, but better than nothing I suppose," he sighed.

Lying there for a breather, he counted the cracks in the ceiling and reflected on how his horrendous day had unfurled. *Stranded in the arse end of nowhere with virtually three grand down the tube*, he brooded. *Still, I'm here now, and I guess once you know the score, it's not too bad knowing the worst is behind me.*

Suddenly there was a tingle on the back of his neck. Kieran scratched repeatedly, but instead of finding relief, the itch intensified. Scouring incessantly for several moments, he paused to glance at his hand when *it* too began to itch. Alarmingly, he discovered that the worst was not only behind him, but all around him; the young man's entire upper body was crawling with weevils.

"What the? Aaaah! Get them off! Get them off! They're all over me!" he yelled feverishly. Within seconds, his face was suffused in tiny black dots. Kieran was paroxysmal. Thrashing about in his bunk, he bumped his head on the ceiling before toppling onto the hard floor. Immediately fearing an outbreak of Bubonic Plague, Owen and Rory recoiled in horror, hardly astonishing given these less than salubrious conditions, while Kieran continued to jig about in a fanatical display of terror.

Several exhausting hours had elapsed by the time Owen and Rory had managed to pluck all the lice from Kieran's mane.

"That's the last one, I'm sure!" Owen declared.

"But my scalp still feels itchy," Kieran whined.

"It would, so I suggest you take a shower."

"Eh, no, let's not bother Mrs Sawyer about that."

In truth, Kieran didn't care to draw trouble on himself, since their landlady didn't seem entirely amenable.

"Here's the source of you problem," Rory brandished a filthy canvas-like sack, at the end of a *Bic* biro. "Your pillowcase appears to be stitched together from an old flour sack. Clearly it's never been washed and the weevils were probably thriving on residual grain particles inside."

"Just keep it away from me, please!"

Though he didn't milk the situation, Rory undoubtedly drew some satisfaction from seeing his haughty classmate taken down a peg or two. Raising the window's lower sash, he hurled the pillowcase into the yard.

As time for the *céilí* drew near, the students prepared to set off again. Stepping back into the kitchen, however, the trio were immediately struck by a rancid smell of burning. Peig was kneeling by the hearth, stoking a hearty fire, while a gaping hole just above, gave Kieran cause for concern. "Here, where' my clothes?" he demanded.

Peig raised her poker. "In there," she replied.

Gob smacked, Kieran stared helplessly into the flames, just as one of his designer labels turned to cinders. "Wh-wh-what wh-wh-*why*?" he burbled, shaking his head in sheer disbelief.

"It must have been a spark, when my back was turned," she shrugged. "But sur' they caught fire and had to be destroyed, for fear they'd set the place alight."

"They're hot pants now," Owen quipped.

Scowling unappreciatively, Kieran slumped into the nearest chair and watched his cherished threads go straight up the chimney. A moment's silence was observed, as a mark of respect, before Owen nudged Kieran again.

"Psst!" he whispered, "Where's the bathroom?"

Stirring from his trance, Kieran looked to the two doors on his left and pondered for a moment. Since one had been accounted for, the other, he logically concluded, led to the bathroom. "The second on the left, I think," he gestured.

"Cheers," Owen acknowledged, casually wandering over.

But as he reached for the door handle, a flying turf sod thrashed Owen's hand.

"And where in the blazes do think you're going?" their hostess exclaimed.

The stunned teenager glanced down at his hand where specks of blood were already beginning to surface. "I- I was just-"

"You were just what?! That door is out of bounds! Do you hear me? Forbidden! And that goes for the rest of you too!" she hissed, exerting yet another sod.

The late Mr Sawyer's hobby frequently bewildered animals

Dreading what this fanatic might do next, the students scrambled towards the front door where Rory floundered with the latch. "Come on, come on!" Kieran urged.

Peig beat them to the punch, grabbed the handle and swung the door wide open. Outside, horrendously, it was still lashing rain. "Get out, the lot of you!" she roared.

Dithering in the doorway for a moment, they looked forlornly at their hostess, as if seeking clemency, but there was no hint of mercy in her cruel glare.

"You are never-ever-ever to go near that door again! Do you hear me?" she warned.

"Yes of course, I'm so sorry," Owen pleaded. "I was only looking for the bathroom!"

Pausing to wipe away the foam from the side of her mouth, Peig's demeanour surprisingly mellowed. "The bathroom? Oh! Well, it's over there," she pointed to a dilapidated wooden shack at the side of the garden.

On cue, the cubicle door creaked open, revealing all the wonderful amenities inside; one bog-standard bog. "I realise that this may be an inopportune time to ask," Kieran hazarded, "But what are the chances of a shower this evening?"

Looking up at the sky, Peig's forecast was curt, but succinct. "One hundred per cent!"

Following her line of vision, he swiftly grasped the sarcasm. "Or a bath perhaps?" he ventured.

Peig gestured to an upside-down tin tub leaning against the outer wall. "There it is!" she decreed. "Saturday night is usually bath night 'round here! And bath water must be shared!"

Oh marvellous, Kieran pondered. "Well in that case I'm going first!" he stipulated.

"I always go first!" she asserted, "Now clear off! I'm tired of looking at ye!"

Shunted into the pouring rain, the door was shut and bolted behind them. Although appalled at the very idea of sharing bath water, the notion that she actually bathed, proved to be the most startling concept of all.

♣ ♣ ♣ ♣ ♣

With so many visitors gracing their village, chests swelled with pride, and more importantly, with hefty returns. In the Begley household, this auspicious occasion was celebrated with Catherine baking one of her special coffee layered sponges for tea. She was attentively hacking off the burnt crusts when young Daniel charged into the kitchen, waving his toy aeroplane. "Mind!" his mother warned.

Typically, the tearaway threw caution to the wind and collided against the radiator where his father had recklessly abandoned that ring binder. The whole organiser was swept clean onto floor and its contents scattered far and wide.

"Pick it up!" Catherine ordered.

Daniel grudgingly obeyed and from the heap arose the inevitable 5 x 7 glossy, instantly captivating the youngster's imagination. "Ish dat Daddy?" he tugged innocently at his mother's grey skirt.

Catherine submitted a superficial glance before proceeding to skim butter-icing over her sponge. "M-hmmm, that's right," she hummed vacuously.

Daniel gave the photograph further consideration. "And ish dat you?"

"Yes, that's righ-" Suddenly, all the colour drained from Catherine Begley's face and just as it was slipping away in the hands of a six-year-old, the lewd snapshot was intercepted. "You!" she shrieked. "Come back with that!"

Following a chaotic morning at St. Millipedes, Matthew Begley took time out to catch up on some light reading. Seated in his favourite armchair, his feet adorned one end of the pine coffee table, while at the other end, eleven-year-old Derbhla ploughed assiduously through a colouring book. This picture of tranquillity was disrupted by Jennifer who, judging by her murky appearance, had brought much of the storm indoors. Lowering his Beano Summer Special, Matthew looked up to greet his elder daughter. "Hello, Oh! You're like a drowned rat! Why didn't you take an umbrella?"

Jennifer wrung her hair, deluging the carpet. "Well I didn't know it was going to rain, did I? Earlier this morning, the sun was splitting the stones!"

"So tell me, how did you get on?"

"What clever clogs came up with the idea of having a band outside the school today?"

"Yes, they were brilliant, weren't they?"

His daughter groaned resignedly and headed towards the stairs. "Never mind, I'm going up to study."

"Listen, you wouldn't do us a little favour?" he hollered. "We need somebody to work the cassette player down at the hall, for this evening's *céilí*?!"

Jennifer stopped in her tracks, quite unable to fathom *why* she was being continually put upon, at this crucial juncture. "Ask Derbhla! She's old enough now!"

"She's got homework!"

"What?!" Jennifer squinted in the direction of the coffee table. "It looks to me like she's only filling in a colouring book!"

"That is her homework, and besides I don't want to keep her out late."

"Can't you grasp the situation?" Jennifer roared, making a ball of her fist for emphasis. "I'm in the middle of my final exams here!"

"But sur' can't you take your books with you?" her father suggested.

The argument ended as Catherine emerged from the kitchen with a tray of coffee slices. Daniel followed on, plunging himself into the large leather sofa, as he awaited the pending goodies.

"Oh there you are Jennifer," her mother hailed. "How were the exams?"

"Fine!"

"Grand. Are you for coffee cake?"

"No!" The irate teen clumped up the stairs and slammed the bedroom door behind her.

"Goodness! She seems to have lost her appetite altogether. Maybe she needs a good tonic? Now, would anyone else like some?"

The younger children squealed with delight as Catherine set the tray down on the table. Daniel grabbed the first available piece and surmising that Derbhla was deliberating on whether or not to pick the sole outsized slice, her mother shrewdly intervened. "Eh, shall we'll leave the big piece for Daddy?" she suggested.

"Okay," Derbhla replied, happily settling for another.

With that, Catherine sent the children on their way. "The pair of ye can go and play outside for half an hour."

With their cake in hand, the pair cavorted merrily towards the front door, but an almighty clap of thunder as they opened it forced a hasty retreat.

"All right, into the kitchen so," their mother ordered.

Once she and Matthew were alone, her warm affection receded into an icy politeness. "Cake?" Catherine extended the tray to her husband.

"Don't mind if I do," he replied, helping himself to the nearest and largest slice.

As Matthew bore into the crispy sponge, he observed a most peculiar expression on his wife's face. She was seated directly in front of him, with her chin resting on her palm, scrutinising his every move.

"Mmm! Ith delithith!" he assured her.

Unfortunately, the second bite proved somewhat less appetising. It tasted of either metal or plastic. Matthew froze. For one horrible moment he feared that his wife had slipped razor blades into his food. But as he separated the sponge into two halves, he discovered something equally distasteful. There he was in full glorious colour, grinning devilishly while brushing up on his French. As Matthew swallowed, the cake descended like shards of glass. Unable to look his wife straight in the eye, his excellent peripheral vision presaged a figure closing in for the kill.

5. Debasement In The Ballroom

It was one of the cruellest storms Rossbladderburst had seen in many years and our friends, Kieran, Owen and Rory, were in the thick of it. Their swift and harried departure saw them ill-prepared to brave the elements. Without hats, coats or sweaters, they braved gale-force winds that ravaged them to the core.

"What time is it now?" Kieran roared.

Owen swallowed before answering; even exercising his vocal chords was a challenge. "Qua-quarter to!" he gasped, rubbing the face on his wristwatch.

Despite the fact that they were, yet again, soaked to the bone, more misery followed when a passing vehicle completely swamped them.

"Ah for Godsssssake!" Kieran howled, as the muddied-brown water streamed down his face. "This just beggars belief!" When it emerged that the offender was the same golden Rolls Royce they had seen earlier that afternoon, all were positively livid.

Salvation arrived, moments later, when a red Mini Cooper Classic pulled up alongside. Rolling down a window, the driver summoned the three hikers. "Hey lads! Ye wouldn't be heading down to St. Millipede's?"

They nodded affirmatively at the ursine creature, comically crammed into his twee automobile. "Well I'm heading there myself, so ye can hop in, if ye like?"

"No thank you, we're fine!" Rory said, coldly.

"Forget you!" Owen roared, wading through the deluge and pushing him aside. Opening the passenger door, he thrust the front seat forward and leapt into the back. Kieran promptly followed his initiative, deserting Rory by the roadside.

"Get into the car!" Kieran ordered.

Thankfully, fear of abandonment prevailed over fear of abduction and Rory took refuge in the front. The driver vigilantly checked his rear view mirror, before setting off again. "You lads are *Scoil Gailseach*?" he asked.

"That's right!" Owen said, catching his breath.

"Yes I thought as much. I'm Father Tom Buttimer, by the way. Shocking weather, isn't it?"

The pair in the rear mumbled in agreement.

"Ah yes, It's horriblus, just horriblus!" the gregarious cleric rambled on. "It's such a shame, as it was so nice until this afternoon. But given its sheer doggedness, it'll let up soon, I expect. But sur' apart for auld rain, what do ye make of the place, so far?"

Kieran and Owen exchanged uncertain glances. "Uhm, yes," Owen scratched his head in search of the right words. "What's the story with mobile phone coverage around here? I can't seem to pick up a signal!"

"Oh jeepers! Well, to cut a long story short; a mast was on the cards this long time, 'til some local blackguards kyboshed the deal by holding out for a ridiculous amount of compensation. So what with all the hills around here, you'll have to go as far as Knockyadown before finding a signal, I'm afraid."

"Wha-wh-where?"

"Knockyadown, it's the next town over. It's about six or seven miles from here."

"Oh brilliant. Well, there must be a phone box in the village?"

"Yes, we had one, but it burned down more than twenty years ago."

"*Damn* it," Kieran fumed.

"But there's two in Knockyadown, or was the last time I checked," Fr. Tom said optimistically.

Owen and Kieran bowed their heads in gloom. Now they were truly marooned in this forsaken wilderness. Rory, too, was in mourning, having accepted a lift from a stranger; to defy Mother's prime directive brought shame and possibly a good throttling, provided he made it home alive. Sensing, perhaps, their brewing despair, the cleric offered some reassurance. "Ah sur' not to worry lads, ye'll soon settle in; they're a good decent bunch around here. We have the occasional oddball, of course, but sur' isn't it always the way? And tell me, who is it ye're staying with?"

"Peig Sawyer," Kieran grunted sourly.

Stupefied by the revelation, Fr. Tom swung to the opposite side of the road, narrowly avoiding a collision with an oncoming van, before recouping the steering-wheel and swerving back again.

"Goodness me, s-sorry about that, gentlemen!" he quivered.

Kieran's temples were fit to burst. For the briefest moment he almost wished they had crashed. To be killed or maimed, would rule out his return to the cottage and the definitive oddball within. Intriguingly, Fr. Tom clamped up for the remainder of their journey, rousing Kieran's curiosity. Why did the mere mention of her name derail him? Could he be withholding vital information? Whatever the case, it certainly warranted further investigation.

Before long, the red Mini veered into the grounds of St. Millipede's. "Here we are lads," Fr. Tom announced. "I've a funeral in the chapel next door, but I'll be in to see the *craic* later on."

The car had no sooner braked, when Rory made a dash for the hall. Owen followed suit, while Kieran, resolving to forage whatever titbits the cleric might throw his way, lingered behind. "Eh, you were going to say something about Mrs Sawyer?" he probed, while slowly stepping out of the vehicle.

"Not at all, I was just surprised to hear she was back on the roster!"

An economical answer, Kieran mused. But then came a parting shot that raised the alarm. "Especially after what happened to those two girls last year," the priest murmured, with a haunted glaze over his eyes.

"What?!"

The young man expected clarification, but Fr. Tom distractedly hit the accelerator and screeched across the car park with the passenger door still ajar.

With his informant out of reach, Kieran intercepted the others in the foyer.

"Here! Did you hear what he just said?"

"Yes! Unlike prison we don't even get a single phone call!" Owen snapped.

Inside the auditorium, all the chairs had been pushed aside, to make room for the *céilí*. To the left, were the girls of St. Grizelda's, and to the right, the boys of *Scoil Gailseach*. The self-imposed segregation signified that neither party had yet found their feet. As the trio slogged wearily through the hall, Dave Keogh, full of vitality, waved cheerfully in their direction; unaware that his smug grin was beginning to incite feelings of resentment. Having been through hell and high water, Kieran, Owen and Rory each collapsed into a hard plastic chair, failing to acknowledge their bosom buddy. Undeterred, Dave invited himself into their circle. "Hey! How's it going?" he greeted.

When Kieran waved his hand in a 'so-so' gesture, there was one logical conclusion. "Teething problems with Mummy's Boy, I suppose?" Dave whispered, excluding Rory from the loop.

"What?" Kieran puckered his brow. "Oh! Strangely enough that's the least of our problems at the moment."

Dave appeared taken aback; but the opportunity didn't arise to query their grievances.

"I'm starving!" Owen interjected. "Does anyone have any food?!"

"Did you try the vending machine in the foyer?" Dave asked.

"Yes, but I won't go far on just shillelaghs and cigarettes, thank you!"

"Well St. Rizzla's appear to be thriving on them anyway."

Across the room, a row of divas were puffing away with mechanical precision.

"If synchronised smoking were an Olympic event, they'd be gold medallists!" Kieran quipped.

"Either that, or they all form part of a hive mind," Owen added whimsically.

"So listen," Dave eagerly clasped his hands, "There are thirty-two of them and twenty eight of us. So, according to my calculations, that makes about one-point-five each!"

"Your calculations are seriously flawed!" Rory sneered.

"Nobody asked you, foetus-brain! Mummy isn't here now to rock your pram, so you'll just have to toe the line like the rest of us!"

Ignoring these obtuse remarks Rory busied himself, wiping his glasses dry with a miniature chamois. It was at this point, that Miss Colic entered the auditorium, her face warped as if a bad kipper had drifted beneath her nose. "What's going on here ladies?" she squealed, while shaking the droplets from her frilly pink umbrella. "You know that smoking isn't allowed indoors! Where's Mrs Breslin?" (Mrs Breslin, sadly, had taken her last puff earlier that afternoon). "Come on now, put out those cigarettes!" she ordered.

A law unto themselves, the young ladies passively blew smoke in Miss Colic's face.

Kieran, meanwhile, detected another missing person. "Hey, where's Morrissey?"

Maintaining a keen eye on the bevy of dance partners across the hall, Dave Keogh explained. "He fell down the stairs, having spent the afternoon sniffing a king-sized permanent green marker. Our landlady thought he had the flu and put him to bed."

Kieran rolled his eyes in apathy.

"I think I recognise some of those girls," Dave deviated, "Should I go and say hello?"

"Do!" Kieran enthused.

Once their bold friend was out of earshot, Kieran closed the gap. "Okay, where was I? Oh yes, according to Fr. Butterscotch, two of the-"

"It's Buttimer you imbecile!" Rory corrected.

"Whatever! Anyhow, from what I could gather, something diabolical occurred with two young ones who stayed with the old bat, last year."

Owen took a profound interest. "What happened?"

"I've no idea! But he mentioned something about her being 'back on the roster?' So maybe she's got a history, maybe she's even on probation. I honestly haven't a clue. But we've all seen what she's like, and you need only look at Dave's plum deal, to know we've been given the sewage treatment!"

"Too bloody true!"

"Whatever it was, Fr. Butt-face looked totally rattled! So I think we ought to knock this thing on the head and report her antics to Miss Colic, before we end up reading our own obituaries in tomorrow's newspapers?"

"Reading our own obituaries?" Rory carped.

"Shuddup Goggles Boy! You know what I mean!"

"Yes, but Miss Colic?" Owen frowned sceptically. "She couldn't run a bath!"

They turned to look at their liaison teacher, who was fanning herself from the smoke.

"We're only asking her to do her job," Kieran warranted.

Nodding in agreement, Owen prised himself from his chair. "Right, so what do we say?"

"Look at my clothes. Look at your hand. Look at *Rory*!"

Rory, conversely, baulked at the prospect of an altercation. "Maybe I should stay here?" he whined. "There's no need for me to get involved."

"Involved?!!" Kieran roared, "Listen here you cabbage, you're already in this up to your neck! So buck up!" Having rapidly swayed their reluctant comrade, all three meandered over to address their teacher.

"Miss Colic?" Kieran ventured softly.

"Yes Mr O'Dowd, what is it?"

"We'd like a word about our, uh, accommodation?"

"Oh look!" she snorted, "As I've already explained, it's too late to go chopping and changing, now!"

"Eh no, it's our *Bean an Tí*[*] actually. She burned my clothes and molested Owen with a piece of turf, and keeps shouting at us for no reason! Oh! And my bed was teeming with tiny black bugs!"

"Lads-lads-lads, you're in the countryside now, and the place is loaded with all sorts of creepy crawlies! It's only natural. Furthermore, what you might consider shouting often passes for normal speech around here, especially among the older generation. Some of their customs may seem strange and even startling at first, but after a couple of days, I promise, you won't take a blind bit of notice. Anyway, you're with Mrs Skalplatten, aren't you? From what I hear, she comes well recommended."

"No, eh, it's Mrs *Sawyer* actually," Owen amended.

"Who? What? *Peig* Sawyer?"

"Yes?"

Their liaison teacher suddenly grew fidgety. "Ooh! Yes, Mrs Sawyer is the pick of the litter all right, a warmer and more placid soul you'll never meet."

"Pure rubbish is more like it!" Kieran refined, "And the woman is as cold as a dead fish on a slab in the morgue!"

"Look it's out of my hands." Miss Colic said, gradually stealing away. "I suggest you speak to the Headmaster. He made all the arrangements; it's his department, not mine."

"Look, there he is now!" Owen gestured to the top of the hall.

Kieran noted a figure kneeling on the stage floor, unravelling some extension cable. "Yeah come on," he beckoned, "It couldn't hurt to ask."

"Ah, excuse me sir?" Kieran began.

Mr Begley looked up to reveal a massive contusion on the right side of his face. "Yes, what is it young man?" he slurred.

The trio cringed at the angry-red face that greeted them. "I-eye-eye-eye! I- I was just wondering wh-wh-what time the *céilí* starts?"

[*] Lady of the house

Matthew's tongue probed his gums, before spewing a fragment of broken tooth into his palm. "In a couple of minutes, just after I make a few announcements," he whistled.

Unfortunately, Kieran's dithering resulted in a missed opportunity. A hot and bothered parish priest, flanked by James and Jeremiah Buckley entered from the rear and immediately commandeered the principal. "Matt, we've a problem- oh dear lord, what happened to you?"

"I uhm, walked into a door," Matthew murmured hesitantly, as he arose to power up the P.A. system.

"I get that a lot too!" Jeremiah confessed.

"Whisht! This is deadly serious!" Fr. Tom scolded. "These two blackguards have only gone and lost poor Mrs Schalplatten on me! You haven't seen her lying about, have you?"

"Good God! No! Not since she dropped in on us this afternoon!"

"Right, we'll just have to keep our eyes p-peeled," the cleric winced. "No doubt, she'll crop up somewhere, eventually. God rest her soul."

Irrespective of her soul, Mrs Schalplatten's corpse was certainly on the move, as her coffin had, by now, rolled halfway to Shannon airport, while being trailed by a pack of deluded beagles.

As Fr. Tom and his task force took their leave, Matthew rifled feverishly through a tray of pain-killers. Observing this, Kieran couldn't help but shrink away. Somehow, a confrontation seemed ill-timed and ill-advised. Besides, he couldn't stand to look at that bruised face for a moment longer. Dismissing the other pair with a wave, Kieran turned to make his way back down the hall. Perhaps Miss Colic was right and they would grow acclimatised within a few days. *Perhaps the old bag might even be dead, by the time we reach the cottage*, he pondered hopefully.

At a point when his estimation of the locals was reaching its lowest ebb, from the corner of his eye, Kieran beheld a figure of divine creation. In a room where one was almost blinded by peroxide, her long, silky, dark hair was a delightful antidote, as it fell so casually over a pure-white-and-oh-so-huggable Aran sweater. Of course, Kieran wasn't to know that Jennifer Begley didn't form part of the Grizelda mob. Maybe it was the textbook at her fingertips, instead of a smouldering appendage, but this young lady was a cut above the rest. As he drifted towards her, thoughts of proposing marriage flashed through his mind. Alas, instead of dropping on one knee, he tripped over some extension cable and belly-landed at her feet.

The echo of raucous laughter filled the air, but Kieran's immediate concern was that his bumbling may have created an inauspicious first impression, and as he looked up, a withering stare from above confirmed precisely that.

"Sorry, eh, I was just inspecting the floor for, uh, termites," he ventured.

"Take a hike, jackass," she said coolly.

Stripped of his dignity, Kieran picked himself up and rejoined his friends.

The P.A. system was activated amid a burst of shuffling and scratching. "Ladies and gentlemen, I know you're all waiting for the *céilí* to get underway, but first I need to make a few announcements." Matthew began, with his tenor noticeably diluted, since earlier that day. "First and foremost, after umpteen cases of alcohol poisoning last year, the Department Of Education has ordered a crack down on the sale of alcoholic beverages to underage drinkers. Rossbladderburst's six public houses are now under the strictest orders not to serve minors."

While groans of resentment filled the auditorium Kieran caught a snippet of conversation among the nearby 'intelligentsia'. "Miners? What have bleedin' miners got to do with us?" Locko cried.

"Put away de hip flask, before someone sees it!" Daimo growled.

"Moving on," the principal proceeded, "At nine o' clock tomorrow morning, you will report to room 4C, in the school across the road, where your Academy Master Classes will begin. As you will be sharing the building with students sitting their state examinations, you are expected to conduct yourselves with the decorum befitting visiting dignitaries."

Jennifer sighed at the hypocrisy.

"As for St. Grizelda's, your teacher Mrs Breslin, is dead and hence will not be rejoining you, for the remainder of your stay."

Miss Colic blinked in disbelief. How utterly callous, that the death of her friend and colleague had been abridged to a mere footnote. But as she scanned the auditorium, it became clear that the lack of sympathy was universal. The girls, in particular, appeared more concerned with checking themselves in their three-tier vanity cases, or fussing over their inoperative mobile phones.

"Finally, in an unrelated matter, if anyone sees a coffin knocking about, please report to either myself or Father Tom Buttimer in the presbytery, next door!"

Had this been an ice-breaker, it would have worked a treat, as the only response it evoked was laughter.

"Stop it now, just stop it!" Miss Colic shrieked, stamping her heels into the floor, "A teacher is dead, for goodness sake! And a missing body is a grave matter!"

As Mathew prepared to sign off, his wife emerged from the wings. "Now as the *céilí* gets underway, I leave you in the capable hands of Mrs Begley, who will-"

Catherine brazenly grabbed the microphone. "Yes, let's start with a simple Barn dance, shall we?" she sidestepped her husband. "And later, maybe something a little more ambitious. Now, first of all, I want everyone to grab a partner. Come on now, there's no need to be shy!"

The entire hall was cast into turmoil. Luckily for our friends, Dave returned, escorting a trio of Grizelda's finest. "This here is Natasha," he announced, "And *her* two friends, Ashley and Sharon. Ladies, these are my best pals, Kieran and Owen."

"How are ya' puddin'?" the sturdy Ashley croaked, between drags of her cigarette, with her eyes fixed keenly on Owen.

"Eh, hello?" he whimpered nervously.

"You'll do!" she grabbed his arm and hauled him out of his chair.

"Uh, sorry *Rory*," Dave conceded, "I didn't bring one for everybody in the audience."

"You'd be wasting you time there anyway," Kieran grinned, "Rory prefers the mature woman. Isn't that right Rory? About forty years, more mature?"

"Shut your trap!" Rory snapped.

Sharon unexpectedly took pity on their bookish classmate. "Ah, poor lad!" she cried. "Come on, you can dance with me!"

The conceited smirk was wiped clean off Kieran's face.

"Ah, eh, *no*, it's all right," Rory whimpered.

"Come on, I promise I won't bite," she said, extending her arm, to seal the deal.

And so, as the three couples took to the dance floor, it was Kieran O'Dowd who was left high and dry. "Hey, what about me?" he groused.

Dave glanced over his shoulder. "Not the way I planned it, but what can you do?" he shrugged.

Catherine Begley liberated the microphone from its stand and mingled amongst the crowd. "Is everyone fixed-up now? Yes? Good! Okay, let's have some music so," she said, with a nod to Jennifer.

For the benefit of her mother, Jennifer dramatically raised her index finger and hit 'play' on the tape deck. When her theatrics went unnoticed, the teenager valiantly resumed her studies, despite the blare of traditional Irish music spewing from the speakers.

"We're going to begin now with a lovely dance, called *Staicín Eorna*," Catherine continued, "Which means 'Stack of Barley'."

Kieran, still out on a limb, quickly discovered a shortfall in the number of dance partners. *So much for Dave's calculations*, he thought. In any event, he only had eyes for one, but she appeared to be out of commission.

"You! O'Dowd! Get up here!"

Kieran looked up to find Miss Colic beckoning. "You're with me!" she summoned. "Some of the girls have taken sick and I've nobody to dance with."

A handsome woman, by and large, Miss Colic was a pariah in the eyes of her students. "Ah no, y-you're all right," he said, praying this horrid new dilemma would crawl away and die.

"Yes!" she snapped. "Now come on!"

Kieran's heart sank and he grudgingly arose. She extended her hand and he proffered his, albeit covered with the hem of his sleeve, for fear her skin might come in direct contact.

"Stop that nonsense!" she ordered. "I wouldn't expect that sort of folly from fourth class, let alone fourth year!"

In no time at all, and thanks to Catherine's competent choreography, the students were keenly kicking up their heels. Most forgot their inhibitions, including conscripts Owen and Rory, who gambolled admirably with their respective dance partners.

"So, is this your first time here, Ashley?" Owen attempted to make light conversation.

"Call me Ash!" she said, dropping some cigarette residue on his shoulder. "Oh sorry, love!" she croaked, inadvertently filtering more smoke into his eyes.

During the final waltz of the evening, Dave Keogh spotted an irresistible opportunity for mischief. Noting how Kieran's right arm was haplessly placed on the lower half of Miss Colic's back, Dave deftly goosed their teacher as he glided by. Mortified and incensed, Miss Colic raised her hand to strike her partner, but restrained herself, at the last moment. "Keep your hands where I can see them!" she barked.

Mystified by her behaviour, Kieran assumed the nagging to be part and parcel of having to dance with his cantankerous teacher.

As Dave capered by a second time, Kieran petitioned his help. "Please help me!" he mimed in jest. Fascinatingly, Kieran caught a glimpse of Jennifer looking his way, *and* with a smile on her face. But realising, almost at once, she had been detected, plunged behind her books again.

Shortly after nine, Catherine called in full time and the crowd began to disperse. Briskly discarding his shackle, Kieran scanned the room for his mystery girl, who to his dismay, had vanished.

"Well that was a good laugh, wasn't it?" Dave grinned, as Kieran rejoined him by the seats.

"Riotous," Kieran huffed resentfully.

Seconds later, Owen and Rory limped into their midst.

"Good man yourself, O'Brien!" Dave cheered.

As Owen was conferred a hearty slap on the back, he coughed up a puff of smoke.

"It was like dancing with Poolbeg Power Station," he wheezed.

"Toodle-ooo!" a hoarse voice hailed from nearby. It was Ashley and four others, including Natasha and Sharon, giggling and waving as they departed. "See you tomorrow!" she hollered, blowing Owen a kiss.

"Hey, you're well in there!" Dave joshed.

"Oh no! Do you think so?" Owen cried in despair.

"So any idea what's happening tomorrow evening?" Kieran asked.

"Same again," Dave replied.

6. Culinary Curiosities

A stunning sunset bathed the entire village in gold. Glistening droplets adorned every stem, while sweet songbirds serenaded a renaissance that was thoroughly astounding. Unfortunately, the storm clouds were still looming in the minds of three students as they began their return journey to Peig's cottage. A short jaunt through the sparkling countryside infused a faint sense of optimism, but as Kieran, Owen and Rory reached a quaint stone bridge on the river Sualach, the sight beyond, reinstated the grisly reality. "No luck," Kieran lamented, observing the black smoke billowing from her chimney. "It didn't get struck by lightening and burn to a crisp, which means she's still slithering about inside."

Each took a deep breath and subconsciously primed themselves for battle. The old woman must have had a sixth sense, because they had no sooner raised the gate lever when the green timber door swung wide open. "Ah lads! Welcome back! How was the *céilí*?"

In light of their earlier spat, her conviviality was genuinely surprising. Perhaps there was an element of truth in Miss Colic's hypothesis. "Yes, it was fine," Kieran frowned suspiciously.

"And ye're just in time too," she hobbled excitedly back inside.

The trio followed on and Kieran shut the door. A stack of dinner plates on the sideboard indicated that she had been in the throes of setting the table. The kitchen itself looked a touch cosier too, though poor lighting rarely failed to flatter filth.

"Ye'll be wanting to wash up, before ye sit down, I expect?" Peig suggested.

"Yes please, Mrs Sawyer," Owen replied, looking around for a sink, only to find there was none.

"Over here, lad!" she directed him to a dish of water on a chair.

A neatly folded white towel and a bar of soap were wondrously provided. Owen was pleased to find the water warm, and positively thrilled to discover that she favoured a familiar brand name. "This soap is manufactured by my father's company!" he said proudly. "Note the triple 'B' indentation in the centre; that's what they call a trademark!"

"Go way! Well-well-well!" Peig acknowledged, as she distributed the knives and forks.

Kieran, in turn, took the soap and analysed it. "How many horses did he massacre to make this?"

"None!" Owen glowered.

"I bet lower life forms, like squirrels and monkeys were fair game, though?"

"Look! Our soap is neither *tested* on animals nor does it *contain* animals! So give over!"

Despite his own comments, Kieran didn't stint on the lather. Comfort craving Rory, meanwhile, was captivated by the fluffy white flannel and rubbed it against his cheek. Remarkably, her choice of fabric softener was a true reminder of home.

"Psst! What about her presents?" Kieran whispered, while insensitively grabbing the towel from Rory's hands.

"Yes, God help us should we forget," Owen murmured.

As he moseyed into the dormitory an odd feeling struck Owen. He couldn't be sure, but it looked as if their personal effects had been tampered with. Specifically, Rory's tea-cosy had relocated to the floor and was now bejewelled with a dusty footprint. Ascribing the irregularity as a product of their fetid surrounds, Owen disregarded his instincts and picked up her obligatory gifts. He was still in a pickle regarding his forfeit. Soap was an earlier consideration, but had been irredeemably cheapened by Kieran's flimflam. Thus, delving into his holdall, Owen settled for something else.

Back in the kitchen, Kieran and Rory reprised their former positions at the table. Owen joined them and discreetly distributed the gateau and tea-cosy, accordingly. Once they had all settled, Peig trundled over. "Well lads, are ye ready to eat, now?"

"Ehm yes, I suppose," Kieran said sheepishly, "Uh, but first we have a few presents for you, to show our, erm, appreciation."

"Oh now! You shouldn't have!" she said, eagerly wiping her grubby hands on her even grubbier apron.

Slightly puzzled, Kieran glanced briefly at the others to gauge their reaction. "Well if you don't really want anything?"

But before he knew what hit him, Peig had snatched the Swiss Roll from his hand.

"Ooh, what's this?" she crowed, holding the box at arm's length and squinting at the label. "Oh now! Look at that! *Luxury Log, with raspberry flavour filling*. That's very nice, very-very nice, indeed."

Rory produced the tea-cosy from beneath the table, though noting its condition, scowled at Owen, before dusting it off. "This is from Mother and me," he said, handing her the item. "It's hand-knitted."

"Ooo! A woolly hat! Now you really have me spoilt!"

"And here's something I thought might be useful around the kitchen," Owen tendered.

Once again, Peig held the packaging at arms length as she tried to decipher the text.

"*Bottoms, Brown and O'Brien's Deluxe Quilted Kitchen Paper*! Deluxe *Quilted* Kitchen Paper? *Deluxe* Quilted Kitchen Paper?" she emphasised its multiple facets.

Owen blushed. Had he chosen poorly?

"*Ten times more absorbent than other kitchen towels,*" she continued. "Ten times? Well-well-well, what'll they think of next? Quilted Kitchen Paper indeed. Oh yera, we'll have to put that in a special place."

Owen mopped his brow with more Deluxe Quilted Kitchen Paper and breathed a sigh of relief. Placing the packet on top of the green dresser, the old woman basked in its magnificence. Finally, and with a faint smile still on her face, she fetched a large saucepan from the hearth and placed it before her baffled brood.

"So lads, do ye like pizza?"

"Yes, I love it!" Owen affirmed

"It's the best!" Kieran confirmed.

"Well ye can forget about that sickly dirt, now!" she huffed.

As the lid was raised, the dissipating steam activated a trio of twitching noses. Kieran knew he had caught a whiff of something peculiar earlier on, but suspected it was their hostess. It was an odd smell, a putrid smell, a fishy smell. Three heads triangulated as Kieran, Owen and Rory peered into the pan. Likewise, staring back at them was the most aesthetically disadvantaged sea bass nature had ever disgorged. Peig's gastronomic delicacy was beyond the pale, though she was too awestruck to notice. "Quilted Kitchen Paper," she blathered.

"Eh, Mrs Sawyer?" Rory ventured timidly. "You may recall a mention in my letter, of me, uh, not being able to eat meat?"

A long blank stare preceded a twinge of recollection. "Oh that's right, you're a vegetable, aren't you?"

Kieran and Owen snorted.

"A vegetarian," he amended.

"Oh yes, isn't that what I mean! Not to worry, I have just the thing for you here."

Sliding open the dresser door, she produced a small brown paper bag and emptied the contents onto Rory's plate. It was a slice of processed corned beef.

"But this is just more meat!" he cried.

"What? But it's *corned*!" she stressed. "Most of it is jelly, for goodness sake!"

The elder towered menacingly over this fickle youth, one hand on the table for support, the other on her hip, signifying her escalating impatience.

"Look, if it's too much I can take some of it away!" she exclaimed.

Grabbing a pair of rusty scissors from the mantel, she cut the slice in half and thrust the remainder back into the bag.

"But it's still meat!" he quivered, now on the verge on tears.

"I paid good money for that!" she pointed angrily to the bag. "Eighty nine cents from the supermarket's delicatessen counter. But sur' if you can't manage it, I suggest you make do with the salad side-dish instead."

Kieran gestured to the great void. "What salad?"

To his astonishment, a battered enamel dish, filled with dandelions and assorted leaves crash-landed on the table.

"Ah Mrs Sawyer," Owen gasped, "Th-these are just-weeds!"

"You can eat all that stuff!"

Ignoring the groans that followed, Peig busied herself, squirreling away her new hat and Swiss Roll. Kieran, sadly, was never to see an iota of the Luxury Log, with raspberry flavour filling.

Given the observably lightweight menu, Kieran picked up his scalpel to carry out an autopsy on the fish. A closer examination revealed it to be grossly rubbery and at best, boiling water had been poured over it, to give the illusion of being steaming hot. Even more worrying were the random segments that appeared, not so much tenderised, as chewed and spat out, while claw marks on the flipside suggested that its previous owner had raised a valiant fight before being robbed of its dinner.

"Excuse me," Kieran broached, "Are you sure this fish is safe? It doesn't appear to be fully cooked!"

"Safe?!!" she hissed. "Of course it's safe! It's been on, ages! If you were in a restaurant now, you'd be glad of that. You'd scarcely even know the difference. They'd have it all dressed up in these fancy sauces, full of chemicals! No, that fish is the best of food. It's good and it's wholesome. There's nothing wrong with it! It's fine!"

"It does smell a bit iffy?" Owen speculated.

Peig reached for the poker. "That's enough of yer auld slish, now!" she cried, finally drawing the line. "Just get on and eat and when ye're finished, ye can clear off the table. Under my roof, ye'll earn ye're keep, I guarantee you that!"

"Our parents paid three thousand Euro for this trip!" Kieran groused.

"*Three thousand*?" she sputtered. "I'm barely getting half of that! Who's creaming off the rest?"

"There are tuition and administration fees to take into consideration, I expect," Rory added. "Though I still can't understand why it's so expensive. Aren't you subsidised?"

"We get nothing of the sort!" Peig all too brusquely dismissed.

She scuttled over to the hearth to add more fuel to the fire. "I'll have to go to town on that principal of yours!" she wittered. "Anyone will tell you that the profit margin in keeping students is non-existent. I can't run on empty, you know."

"Neither can we," Owen whispered.

"That man's penny pinching is getting ridiculous! Twenty years I've been spoon feeding his strays. Has he no concept that inflammation is going out of all proportions? I mean like I ask you; eighty nine cents for a slice of corned beef? I remember a time when you could buy a small farm for that much and still have enough left over for a bag of potatoes. But those were hard times. Ye don't know how lucky ye are, with yer hot and cold running water and the like. I expect ye all have the electric and indoor plumbing now?" She looked towards the table again only to find that the trio had vanished. "Well now, they can't be too hungry, can they?"

♣ ♣ ♣ ♣ ♣

"I'm *ravenous*!" Owen exclaimed, as he slashed the foil wrapping from a large chocolate Swiss Roll. Once his jaws embraced the gateau, he liquefied with contentment into his bunk. The more disciplined Rory sat at the edge of his berth and opened a small Tupperware lunchbox on his lap. Inside, were the remainder of some neatly-cut salad sandwiches his mother had prepared for the journey.

"Look, Rory's on solids!" Kieran scoffed. "What happened? Didn't Mammy make you any Milupa?"

Rory said nothing. Now that food was in short supply, every bite was precious and he simply wanted to relish the moment.

"That reminds me though," Kieran digressed, "I've some leftover sandwiches too."

Rummaging through an exterior compartment in his burlap holdall, he produced a skewed bundle, wrapped in bread paper. Its crude presentation lacked the finesse of Mrs Waters' dainty creations. Unveiling his rations, however, Kieran beheld another startling oddity. "What the hell is this?" he cried.

"What's what?" Owen chewed nonchalantly.

"There's an obscene message printed on my sandwiches!"

Owen ceased ploughing. "Somebody wrote on your grub? Who-why-what does it say?"

"See for yourself, Sherlock!" Kieran said, flinging the graffitied snack onto his lap.

Owen leaned forward to investigate. "*Die you bleeding scab!*" he decoded from the blotchy inscription. "Not exactly Pulitzer material, is it? But whoever wrote it, certainly has you pegged, if you'll pardon the expression!"

"Who are you calling a scab?" Kieran roared.

"Face facts, O'Dowd, you're so tight that you have a P.O. Box as your address!"

"She did this! First she burns my clothes and fills my bed with bugs and now she's sending me hate mail!"

"Hold on," the budding graphologist said, as he inspected the indelible green ink, "Didn't Dave mention that Morrissey nose-dived, after going on a green marker bender?"

"Yes, I saw him vandalising a bus seat with one, earlier today," Rory recalled.

"Oh," Kieran suddenly winced.

"Yes?"

"During our picnic stop, this morning, Morrissey told me he'd forgotten his lunch-"

"And?"

"And I offered to sell him mine for five quid."

"Motive, means and opportunity," Owen unsympathetically returned the tainted article. "Enjoy!"

The unravelling of a minor enigma did nothing to quell Kieran's growling stomach. "Morrissey is dead!" he roared, hurling the bundle into the darkest recess available.

"At the rate he's going, I'd say his days are numbered, anyway," Rory estimated.

With his quota now spent, Kieran latched onto the lip-smacking chocolate log being devoured by his friend. "Mr O'Brien," he warbled, starting anew. "Are you sure you can manage all that by yourself?"

Owen extended the Swiss Roll and smiled. "Oh you'd like some, would you?" But the cake was immediately retracted and doused in saliva, rendering it undesirable to anyone but Owen himself.

"You filthy pig!" Kieran barked.

"I'll be damned if I give you any more today!" Owen warranted.

Overwrought by the everlasting torment, Kieran slumped to the floor and buried his face in anguish. "That sandwich was all I had left to eat in the whole wide world," he sniffled. "How could anyone deface good food?"

Struck by pangs of guilt, Owen and Rory quickly reassessed their stock.

"Uhm, listen, this cake isn't the bee's knees anyway," Owen said, setting it aside on his pillow. "How about a nice packet of cheese and onion crisps, instead?"

"You probably need them more than I do," Kieran meekly replied.

"Or a sandwich?" Rory offered, "I've still two left!"

"No, no, I won't deprive you."

Owen suspected a ruse, but observing that his friend was indeed, in need, arose and placed the crisps in his hand.

"And here," Rory extended the lunch box, "Have a sandwich anyway."

Kieran humbly accepted and gradually began to nibble. "Damn! These are tasty!" he swiftly regained his zest. "Who made them?"

"Mother," Rory blinked.

Once he had polished off the sandwich, Kieran attacked the crisps. Such was his haste, that a glut of them grazed his gullet, igniting an aggravated fit of coughing.

"Do you need a drink?" Owen enquired.

"Or a throat lozenge?" Rory suggested. "I've a tray of them in my bag."

When Kieran extended his hand in anticipation, Rory unzipped his holdall and produced a chic attaché-case from within. Inside was a plethora of every over-the-counter drug imaginable.

"It's a junkie's paradise!" Owen gawped.

"Mother says you always need to make contingencies," Rory stated grimly.

He handed the tray of green lozenges to Kieran, who opportunistically began knocking them back, one by one.

"They're medicated, you glutton!!" Rory snatched back the tray. "One is sufficient!"

As the dispensary doctor closed up his portable pharmacy for the night, an alien object nestled among his personal belongings, caught his eye. "Who left this mouldy threadbare tea towel in my bag?" he cried, extricating a vile cloth and flinging it onto the floor.

"That's one of Owen's snotrags." Kieran proposed.

Owen submitted a passing glance. "Heck no, I've never seen it before," he said, massaging his stomach.

"And what seems to be your trouble?" Rory observed.

"Nothing!" Owen said, returning to his bunk. "Just- ooh! Too much cake, that's all!"

Kieran arose to his feet. "I'd better turn on the light, I suppose, before we go blind on top of everything else."

Hobbling over to the door, Kieran expected to find a switch, but combing the walls, ceiling and floor, he merely hit yet another hurdle.

"Oh brilliant!" he cried, "We've no flaming electricity in here!"

♣ ♣ ♣ ♣ ♣

Kieran awoke with a start. Finding himself face to face with a crudely severed donkey head, provided a braying reminder of his bearings. Yet, to have survived one night under these insufferable conditions was no mean achievement. One down and only twenty more to go. For reasons that were revoltingly obvious, the upper bunk of Owen's unit had been deserted in favour of Rory's. This structure was anything but stable and creaked riotously with the slightest stir. Sliding his hand beneath his pillow, he produced a miniature digital alarm clock. 07:03 he noted from the Liquid Crystal Display. A myriad of brilliant beams penetrated Peig's tattered curtains, illuminating a rising tide of dust, as Kieran kicked back his disintegrating horse-hair blanket. The dust reactivated his irritating tickle and his eyes watered copiously as he tried to stifle it. Within seconds, an unavoidable fit of coughing erupted.

Owen rolled over and groaned witheringly on discovering a half-eaten Swiss Roll plastered to his cheek. Stripping away the flattened cake, he dropped it on the floor and wrapped the pillow around his face, in order to muffle the brouhaha.

"Rory?" Kieran croaked.

"Oooh," a voice beneath, moaned.

"I need another cough sweet!"

"Oooooh?"

"Please! I'm ready to drop a lung here!"

As the coughing intensified, the bed continued to creak. Suddenly, something, somewhere gave way and with an almighty crack, two bunks became one, leaving the hapless Rory sandwiched in the middle.

♣ ♣ ♣ ♣ ♣

An extremely dishevelled Matthew Begley drooped into the kitchen that morning to find his pouting wife crashing drawers and slamming cupboard doors.

"Oh 'tis yourself," he murmured, "I thought we'd burglars knocking over the place."

"Sit down!" she snapped.

Delighted to see a marked improvement since yesterday (at least now, they were on speaking terms), Matthew occupied his usual place at the breakfast table. As he poured himself a coffee, however, Catherine came perilously close, wielding a large frying pan. Matthew flinched, but rather than belt him, she merely emptied a fry onto his plate. His bacon and sausages were charred beyond recognition; still, nothing out of the ordinary there. Matthew, nevertheless, was unable to shake off an escalating sense of foreboding. "I'll need to set up the overhead projector in 4C," he said, hacking into his breakfast. "So I thought we might leave a few minutes earlier this morning?"

"I'm not going!" Catherine declared.

"What? What do you mean? What are you talking about?"

"I said I'm not going in today!"

"But you have to! What about the students? Who'll conduct the master class?"

"You look after it. I'm sick."

"You don't look sick?"

"Well that's what I am! Sick, sick of the whole bloody lot of you!"

"But I've a tonne of paperwork!" Matthew implored. "Plus we're short an invigilator, after Marcus McGinty's nervous breakdown yesterday afternoon! What'll I do?"

"I'm sure you'll find someone to lend a sympathetic ear, seeing as you're so good at licking up to people!" Catherine manhandled the crockery for punctuation.

"Now come on! As I've explained, I've no recollection of that incident! Besides, it was just a bit of innocent fun. It's that woman. I wouldn't be surprised if she touched-up the photo, just to implicate me!"

"No doubt the poor soul was mortified and did the only decent thing, by handing it in, for fear it fell into the wrong hands!"

Matthew almost choked. "It *did* fall into the wrong hands! She's evil incarnate and clearly her influence is spreading! In fact, it was only the other evening that you referred to her as a vampire, sucking the lifeblood from the community!"

Catherine drew a long, contemplative breath. "Well now I owe her a debt of gratitude, for opening my eyes to the tomfoolery going on, right on my very own doorstep!"

Realising he'd been whipped, Matthew wilted over his black fry.

♣ ♣ ♣ ♣ ♣

The tumultuous uproar that arose in the wake of the 'Great Bunk Bed Disaster' roused the great beast from her slumber. Peig Sawyer looked on as Rory Waters was dragged from the debris and propped up against the devastated ruins of his own cot. It was Owen O'Brien who posed the dreaded question. "Is he dead?"

"Don't be daft!" the old woman scoffed, drenching the comatose youth with the contents from an old basin.

"What was that?" Kieran twitched his nose at the dubious odour.

"What does it matter?" she said defensively. "See, he's coming 'round now!"

Rory's eyelids began to flicker; though any dosage of her pungent smelling salts was enough to raise the dead. Kieran, himself, had not emerged unscathed, suffering another knock on his forehead, but atypically gave priority to Rory's welfare.

"He looks pretty bad. Maybe we should send for a doctor?" he suggested.

Peig wouldn't buy it. "Ara, doctors are for people with more money than sense! Sur' he's fine!"

"Ooh, what happened?" Rory groaned. "What's that smell?"

"There's nothing wrong with you lad, that a nice cup of tea wouldn't fix!"

Satisfied that he wasn't a Darwin Award candidate, Peig made for the exit, pausing in the doorway to cast a scornful eye over the fallout. "Oh lads, look at me beds! Ye have me bankrupt!" she sighed, before waddling back into the kitchen.

"Oh *lads*?" Kieran gasped. "Look at that bed-post! That crack is donkey's years old! It's only support, was a piece of old fishnet, for crying out loud!"

As Owen assisted Rory to his feet, he spotted the remains of his half-gnawed Swiss Roll nuzzled among the rubble. Buoyed by its rediscovery he retrieved his encrusted confectionary and nursed it back into shape.

"You're not planning on eating that?" Kieran said warily. "There could be pockets of smallpox lying dormant in these parts, for all we know?"

"If I die, I die happy!" Owen said, digging in.

Soon, all three were seated around the kitchen table again, awaiting their first meal of the day.

"There ye are lads," Peig placed a dish before them. "I thought ye're appetite might have improved a bit this morning." The students couldn't believe their eyes. It was the same hideous abomination they had been served up the night before. "And here's a cut of bread for the boy with the goggles, since he's so delicate," she taunted, tossing a dry heel into Rory's bowl.

Retiring to her armchair, Peig removed her shoes and began picking her corns with the rusty scissors, previously used to cut Rory's corned beef.

"Go on Owen," Kieran urged. "I nominate you to eat it; otherwise we'll never see the end of it."

"Why me?"

"You've the constitution of a horse!"

"I'd need a tracheotomy to swallow *that*!"

"If not for me, then do it for Ireland."

"Oooh, all right." Rising to the challenge, Owen picked up his plastic knife and aluminium fork and severed a minuscule slither.

"Is it nice?" Kieran sprung, once the morsel had passed his lips.

"Not bad."

"No?"

"No, it's horrendous!" he whinnied.

But when his food tester didn't bite the dust, Kieran took a gamble. His assessment, regrettably, was even less favourable. "Damn!" he retched. "We should've told her we were vegetarians too, at least then we might have got bread and jam, like Rory."

"Jam? What jam?" Owen cast a curious eye over Rory's dish. "That's not jam! Look, it's blood!" he said, pointing to the steady trickle from Rory's nose.

Owen produced a clean tissue from his pocket, tore it in half and offered both pieces to his ailing comrade. "Take this, you're bleeding!"

Still visibly shaken, Rory sluggishly accepted and plugged his nostrils.

"I think he's half concussed!" Owen said, pushing him upright for the umpteenth time. "Maybe he ought to stay here for the day? What he really needs is bed rest, but let's face it, that could end in more carnage!"

On hearing this loathsome prospect, Rory suddenly salvaged his wits. "No! You're not leaving me here!"

Deep in thought, Kieran idly pulverised his fish into a paste. Twenty four hours ago, he had been tucking heartily into a plate of pancakes; now, he would have willingly donated a kidney for one bowl of cereal. But as he mucked about his breakfast, inspiration struck; could this tripe stick to the underside of the table? Daubing on a sample, the scheme, to his delight, actually worked.

"What are you playing at?" Owen enquired.

"I'm making it disappear," Kieran whispered.

"Good idea," Owen grinned, swiftly doing the same.

The boys were dead chuffed. Within minutes, they had banished the fish to the nether regions of the table. What they didn't bargain for, unfortunately, was the all-pervading shadowing capabilities of Peig Sawyer.

"What in the name of all that is holy do you think you're doing?!!!"

Seized by the scruff of the neck, Owen was arrested in his tracks. He had been so busy plastering, that neither he nor Kieran had smelled her advance.

"Just, uhm, t-tenderising it a bit," he quaked.

"It looks to me, you're just smearing it under my table!"

"No, no, I was going to eat it, honestly!" he unwisely pledged.

"Well, what are you waiting for? If it gets any more tender, you'll be able to drink it!"

Since she clearly wasn't going to let it slide, Owen began the compulsory mining and ingesting this putrefying puree.

Kieran thanked his lucky stars, she hadn't shopped *him*. But rather than bear witness to Owen's degradation, he simply crept away from the table.

"Oh, you're off, are you?" she peered.

"Ah yes. Mmm! That was a delicious, but if you'll excuse me, I must be getting ready for, uh, school."

Rory also made for the dormitory, proving that he was nobody's fool either, albeit, looking the part, with a pair of vibrant tassels protruding from his nose.

Moments later, Owen thundered through the dormitory with a pair of swollen cheeks. Hurtling straight towards the window, he raised the sash and fertilised Peig's front lawn. "You swine!" he spluttered.

"Don't blame me," Kieran retorted. "You were the one she nabbed!"

"It was your lousy plan!"

Moving away from the window, Owen grew wary as he spotted Kieran polishing off a titbit of uncertain origin. "Hey, what are you eating?"

"My sandwiches," Kieran said, wiping the green dye from the tips of his fingers.

"But that ink could be toxic!"

"Look, I was hungry! Okay?" Kieran snapped. "Besides you're grand after eating that Swiss Roll, aren't you?"

"Don't bank on it!" Owen kneaded his stomach.

In the interim, Rory had regained sufficient lucidity to appreciate the need to freshen up before rearing his head in public. "Has anyone seen a pair of white towels?" he enquired, while probing his kitbag. No one heeded the call. "Hello, white towels, anyone?"

"White towels?" Kieran listlessly scratched the bump on his forehead. "What colour were they?"

"White!!!"

"No, I don't recall seeing them."

"That's odd, Mother packed them herself and I'm sure I had them before the *céilí*? Listen, you were rummaging through my stuff, yesterday afternoon-"

"Oh yes and I took your saintly towels, did I? And I suppose you'd like to search my bag too?"

"As a matter of fact, I would, if you don't mind," Rory said suspiciously.

Kieran took exception to the inference. "Of all the cheek! Yes, I do mind actually!"

"O'Dowd, is this your carbolic soap in my bag?" Owen interjected.

Kieran glimpsed over his shoulder. "Carbolic?! I wouldn't touch that with a barge pole!"

"Is that so?" Owen distrustfully acknowledged.

"Right, just empty your bag and prove you don't have my towels," Rory persevered.

"Now look here, Goggles Boy, you'll need a warrant to come within a five mile radius of my gear!"

"Excuse me!" Owen, once again, interrupted. "Before anyone is hung, drawn and quartered, just answer me this: were your towels anything like the one Mrs Sawyer had last night?"

Rory pondered for a moment. "Yes, they were identical."

"Identical!" Owen juggled his bar of carbolic. "And something else just occurred to me; her soap, the triple 'B' Luxury Lather Special?"

Kieran grunted sardonically.

"Yes, Kieran! I'm getting to the point! That soap is manufactured for export only. There is no way she could have picked it up locally. And guess what? I'm missing two bars from my bag!"

"What? You mean she-?"

"Precisely! Now Rory, you found an old tea-towel in your bag, last night? Correct?"

"Matted microbes, I'd call it."

"And by some miracle, I've just gained half a bar of carbolic soap. So assuming we're not dealing with leprechauns here, someone," Owen expressively eyeballed the door, "Has been replacing our stuff with cheap knockoffs!"

"Bloody hell!" Kieran bellowed. "What is going on?"

Minutes later, three riled and circumspect students re-entered the kitchen.

"Yer away, so?" their landlady grunted from her armchair bastion.

"Eh, yes," Kieran replied, with a suspicious frown.

"Right-oh, I'll see ye back here, for dinner at six," she stipulated.

"Six?!" Owen cried. "The brochure said we were to get lunch here every day, at one!?"

"Did it? Oh that was an old brochure, maybe. Yes, they did away with that, long 'go. Sur' how badly-off are ye? Isn't there's plenty of wild berries out there, ripe for the picking?"

"Right, six o' clock it is. We'll look forward to it." Kieran fumbled with the latch.

"That auld thing has a mind of its own!" Peig struggled from her chair. "Let me get it for you."

As she opened the front door, a peculiar noise drew everyone's attention towards the table, where Kieran's fish pancake was disastrously peeling from its marble plane. It hit the floor with a cringe-inducing slap. The offender scrambled to escape, but the old woman swiftly collared him. "You!" she roared, "Get back here!!"

7. Blight On The Landscape

"I've never felt so violated in my entire life!" Kieran shuddered.

"Do you want to rest up for a bit?" Owen wheezed, evidently in the need of a breather himself. The unholy union of fish and Swiss Roll was threatening to seek an annulment. "After all, it was a bit harsh forcing you down on your hands and knees to lick that revolting slime clean off the floor!"

"It was downright criminal!" Kieran asserted. "And no! I don't want to stop! The greater the distance I put between her and me, the safer I'll feel!"

Something else, however, put a crimp in his stride. "No, no, *no*!"

"What is it?" Owen cried.

"Look!" Kieran pointed to a silhouette trotting along in the distance. "How can anyone in her early hundreds move so damn fast?"

Owen paused and squinted. "What? No! It can't be. You're right, it is!"

"More to the point, how did she get so far ahead of us?"

Owen scanned the surrounding landscape. "She cut across the graveyard, I expect. It figures she'd know all the short cuts."

"Nothing but mindless repetition!" Kieran carped. "Everything is fine! There nothing wrong with anything! And that kitchen paper! God! I thought we'd never hear the end of it! What are the odds, that right now, she's on her way to scrounge from wheelie-bins for our supper, this evening? But don't worry, it's all fine!"

Owen, similarly, had his bone of contention. "That brochure wasn't out of date! It was only issued about a month ago! And it clearly outlined that we were to receive a full meal at midday."

"*Oh, isn't there's plenty of wild berries out there, ripe for the picking?*" Kieran mimicked.

"The only thing ripe for picking was our gear!" Owen added. "I mean, how did she reckon we wouldn't tumble to that one?"

"I honestly don't know, but I'll bet she's so thrifty that she's calculated her entire day down to the last calorie." Kieran decreed. "And the state of her gaff! No light and not so much as a chest of drawers in our room!"

"A home without a television is a home without a heart," Owen added morosely.

"And what was all that shiteology about a forbidden door? Anyone would think she had a stack of dead bodies hidden inside!"

Owen contemplated the possibility. "You know, those girls you mentioned? Well supposing, just supposing now, she butchered them, harvested their organs and that's where she keeps her stash!"

"For snacks?"

"Maybe," Owen shrugged, "And every once in a while she needs to regenerate, so she keeps a fresh supply of spare parts, you know, just to keep her ticking over. She's probably even keeping their shrunken heads, on a stake, as trophies!"

"But you'd think that if we were on this week's menu, she'd at least fatten us up a bit first?"

"Speaking of food, I'm running dangerously low on goodies. So keep an eye out for a supermarket."

Kieran musingly stroked his chin. "Yes, I believe I saw a Dunnes Stores or SuperValu just beyond the next brow."

"Good! We'll drop in on the way. Wait a minute, I don't recall seeing either of those, yesterday?!"

"No? Well, you can't miss them. You take the second left, just after Liberty Hall and they're directly opposite the Eiffel Tower," he offered glibly.

"Ah come on, has anyone here seen any shops? What about you Rory?"

"Is he still with us?" Kieran peered over his shoulder.

Trailing behind, their forlorn comrade was still with them in body, if not in spirit.

"Shops?" he replied listlessly. "No, not in the village anyway, you may have to go as far as Knockyadown, I suspect."

"That place is like ten miles away, which is what, twenty kilometres? Well, there's no fear I'm making a forty kilometre round trip, on foot, just for a lousy doughnut."

"Ah, I think forty is a bit of an exaggera-"

"Here!" Owen blurted, as another shocking realisation hit home. "My birthday is next Saturday! And any prospect of a half decent scoff is looking bleaker by the minute!"

"Well, there *is* one consolation there," Kieran said wistfully.

"What's that?"

"The way things are looking, we may all be dead by then."

"Thank you very much! That's a real comfort all right!" Owen cried scathingly.

If nothing else, the students certainly had food for thought, as they as they plodded languidly along this quiet country road. Each formulated their own theories surrounding the odious developments since their arrival. The faltering testimonies, the forbidden door, the dormitory atrocities and the humiliation at the breakfast table; deeds which, even in hindsight, seemed quite incredible. It was no wonder then, they were fostering the notion that their landlady could be criminally insane.

"So will you be speaking to Miss Colic again?" Owen queried.

"That feckless mule?" Kieran sneered, "She's a dead loss! No, they're bound to have either a phone or internet access in the school. At least then, we can get 'word to our parents. Otherwise, we'll have to try the principal again or Mrs. Begley, yes, she seems quite approachable."

♣ ♣ ♣ ♣ ♣

Matthew Begley stole into the lounge, sporting a pair of sunglasses that concealed a multitude of sins. The queen bee was sprawled across the length of the couch with a box of Milk Tray on her lap, staring inertly at the television set. Anxiously chewing his lower lip, Matthew made a last ditch effort to enlist her help. "Uh, are you sure you won't change your mind?"

Catherine reached for the remote and amplified the volume. "*Today on the Olivia Plunkett Show: The woman who sold her idle good-for-nothing husband into slavery for a sandwich maker and a Dublin taxi driver who has been reincarnated as eight-year old boy's pet hamster*," a high-pitched melodramatic voice blared into the living room.

The message was loud and clear, Matthew was out on his ear.

"Jennifer? Are you ready yet?" he cried towards the ceiling.

Contrary to expectations, the teenager made a grandiose entrance from the kitchen. "Yes, I'm here."

"Have you had your breakfast?" her mother enquired, without straying from the television.

"Yes, I'm eating it!" she huffed, while exerting a miniscule triangle of toast.

"Right come on, we're late enough as it is!" Matthew tapped his wristwatch.

As her husband and daughter made their departure, Mrs Begley dropped a strawberry fondant into her mouth "Betht of wuck with the egtham, Thennifer!" she gurgled; parting words that went down like a lead balloon.

As the silver Renault Laguna Estate backed slowly down the drive, its occupants were accosted by their meddlesome next-door-neighbour, Candy O'Shea. Without warning, Mrs O'Shea poked her head through the driver's side window.

"Hello Matty, grand morning, isn't it?" she grinned.

In no mood for exchanging pleasantries, Matthew nonetheless grunted affirmatively, whilst pondering on her unsightly collection of facial moles.

"And how are the exams going, Jennifer?" she probed.

"Fine."

"What's on today?"

"Irish, paper one."

"Oh yes? And how many subjects are you doing?"

"Nine."

"Oh nine? My niece Audrey, in Dublin, has eleven! Is it honours or pass you're doing?"

"Honours, of course!" Jennifer specified. "What about Audrey? What's she doing?"

"Eh, you must be very proud of your daughter, Matty!" Mrs O'Shea digressed. "I expect she's a bit of a genius?"

Matthew, on the other hand, was still rapt by something else. "Wart?" he bungled, "I mean wh-what?"

A slight grimace fell over Mrs O'Shea, but as usual she persevered. "I was just saying you must be very proud of your daughter?"

"Oh, yes-yes, very proud."

"Tell me, though," she continued, "What's happening with Mrs Schalplatten, at all? I was down at the chapel yesterday evening and the next thing I hear, the funeral has been postponed indefinitely?! And come here, wasn't the *you know what* scheduled to take place later today? Is there any word on that now at all?"

"No, but I'm sure you'll be the first to know. Now if you'll excuse me, I must go and open the school!"

Matthew hit the accelerator, forcing the woman to disengage from the vehicle. Remaining on the footpath, Candy O'Shea observed briefly, as the car rolled several metres down the road and veered into the school yard.

♣ ♣ ♣ ♣ ♣

Kieran, Owen and Rory were among the final few stragglers filing into 4C, at ten past the hour; relieved, ironically, that they had arrived before their instructor. With a complement of sixty, the airless classroom was already jam-packed. Scanning the perimeter for an ideal bolt hole, a shrill whistle focused their attention on Dave, on the far side of the room. But as the trio navigated their way through the crowd to join him, an unidentified hand groped Owen's posterior.

"Mornin' sugar!" croaked a voice from behind.

Owen shot a glance over his shoulder and was met by the nicotine-stained smiles of Ashley and her vacuous cohorts. Understandably, she had been relegated to the back of his mind, given that he had enough on his plate, or too little, to be precise. Yet, since enemies were in no short supply, Owen discounted the incident with his customary good grace.

Kieran O'Dowd threw down his jotter and pencil and quietly assumed residence in a window seat opposite Dave Keogh. At this point, even the course curriculum offered a welcome diversion from the miseries of Peig's draconian regime. Unfortunately, with Mrs Begley now out of the frame, that too was pure fantasy. Indeed, a further fifteen minutes had elapsed before the principal breezed into the large classroom.

"Good morning all, and apologies for the delay," he announced. "Firstly, I'll need you all to sign your names on this sheet of paper, for the register," *And that should fritter away a good half hour while I think up a few more menial tasks.*

Leaving behind a blank A4 sheet, and somewhat recklessly an expensive ball-point pen, Mr Begley breezed out again. The customary reprimand for smoking was also overlooked, as he feared that antagonising these yobs might be hazardous to his own health.

On entering his poky little office, the winded principal was piqued by another faintly objectionable odour. The source promptly identified itself, when his swivel chair rotated by 180 degrees. Matthew had an intruder.

"What on earth are you doing in my office?" he cried.

"Aren't I here about the job, of course?" Peig Sawyer nonchalantly replied, setting in motion his Newton's Cradle desktop ornament.

"What job?"

"That superintendent's job you offered me."

"Ah no, that was before you muscled your way back onto the roster! And I hope those students of yours are being well treated, too!" he warned.

"I'm spoiling them something rotten."

"Yes that's what I'm afraid of."

Matthew halted the balance balls in mid swing. "You're busting my balls here! And look!" he removed his sunglasses. "Look at what you've done to me!"

"Ah ladeen, you're under a lot of stress. Sit down there now and take it easy. Besides, I already know that a vacancy arose yesterday afternoon."

Matthew eyed the ceiling. "Someone blabbed, I suppose?"

"No, I just read your report to the Department of Education," she pointed to a file on his desk.

His pigmentation turned an unhealthy shade of purple. "That's it! Get out!" he roared, "Those files are confidential! Go on! Out!"

As she was elbowed towards the exit, Peig decided to play her trump card again.

"How about a few visual aids to slip in with your auld letter to the department? A photograph or two, maybe?"

"Oho! That ship has well and truly sailed!" he quivered indignantly.

Matthew picked up a roller deck from the bureau and brandished it at his tormenter.

"See here! I've plenty of old colleagues to call upon for a favour," he flicked through its pages, "Friends, retired teachers, plenty! All these people would have to be dead and buried before I'd even consider you!"

The old woman expelled a disparaging growl and slammed the door behind her. With a sigh of relief, Matthew reclaimed his province and began weighing up his options.

"Right now, let me see," he plucked forth the first card, "Orla Casey. Yes, I'm sure she would be delighted to sit in on- oh wait no, they cremated her last year, didn't they? Ah, here's one, Seamus Devane, oh blow! He's dead too. A massive heart attack, if memory serves. Ah jeepers, Cyril Donovan; he died of cirrhosis over five years ago! And Leonora O'Sullivan, she was jailed for fraud last October!"

Thumbing his way through his list of contacts proved to be a real eye opener. "Dead, dead, emigrated, dead!" One by one, each card was dropped into the waste paper basket, until there were none left. All of his professed connections, it emerged, were either out of circulation, or deceased. "What a shambles!" he exclaimed, hurling the entire roller deck into the basket.

Suddenly it hit him. Slowly but surely, he had allowed himself to cruise on his wife's directive, detaching himself from school's mundane operations. Realising that he had been taking her for granted, Matthew resolved to make amends. He would have to, if things were to return to normal, i.e. nice and cushy. Moreover, if he hurried, he might just apprehend that other wretched beast. Clearly, she was a degenerate, but what did it matter, so long as the Department was footing the bill. Scrambling to his feet, Matthew swung open the door and was aghast to discover that Peig Sawyer had never actually left.

"Neglecting our housekeeping, have we?" she crowed, while massaging the kink from her lower back.

♣ ♣ ♣ ♣ ♣

A tirade of vitriol engulfed Matthew Begley as he entered the examination hall, accompanied by an invigilator of dubious eminence. Desperation had formed an uneasy coalition.

"What's going on Mr Begley?" one Leaving Certificate student raged.

"Yes, we were meant to have started over half an hour ago!" another ranted.

The principal raised his arms in an effort to placate the angry mob. "Please, calm down! Mrs Sawyer here will see to all your needs!"

Entrusting her with a stack of sealed exam papers, Matthew relinquished command.

"And don't worry, you'll all be given time in lieu, at the end," he assured the students, on his departure.

Peig began sluggishly distributing the papers. "Ye can pretty much start whenever ye want," she announced.

This flagrant breach of protocol met with opposition from those still awaiting their papers. "Hey that's not fair!"

Rossbladderburst's Cultural Academy: Coláiste Nathair Naofa (Proudly declared an 'Asbestos Free Zone' in 1994)

"Ah please yourselves, sur' isn't it all much of a muchness at the end of the day?" she replied, before contemptuously lobbing the remainder in front of Jennifer. "Ara, here, you do the rest! I'm getting tired."

As the principal's daughter reluctantly complied, another candidate raised his hand. "Excuse me, Miss? May I use the bathroom, before we begin?"

"Didn't you hear what the principal just said?" Peig hissed. "You'll be given time for the loo at the end!!!"

It wasn't without a smattering of guilt, that Matthew had unleashed this monster upon the masses. Yet, if anything did go awry and if questions were asked; *he* had performed his perfunctory duty and *they* could always repeat, the following year. Back in the office and brooding over his next course of action, a knight in floral armour suddenly graced his doorway.

"Eh hello Mr Begley, I was just-"

"Oh Miss Colic! Am I glad to see you!"

"You are?" she grinned, while fixing her hair.

"Yes, Mrs Begley has taken ill and I need somebody to fill in for her."

Though the smile was diffused, Miss Colic remained eager to please. "Oh yes of course, but as you know, I'm only here in a supervisory capacity and I've nothing really prepared-"

"I have complete faith in your abilities," he ushered her down the corridor. "Just stick on a tape and ask them to write a report. You'll do just fine."

♣ ♣ ♣ ♣ ♣

Back in 4C, a completed roll sheet abounded with the names of cartoon characters and miscellaneous celebrities. In order to alleviate boredom, one faction had resorted to pitching a rotting orange about the room. Rory's head, notwithstanding its many problems, attracted the fruit on numerous occasions. The game culminated with the orange narrowly missing Miss Colic as she wheeled in the audio-visual unit; rupturing as it hit the wall, directly behind.

"That's enough of that!" she warned, examining her frock for possible fallout. "Remember now, you are all privileged visitors here!"

Observing from the corridor, Matthew formed a circle with his thumb and index finger, before gently closing the door.

"Okay everyone, we're going to watch a video!" their substitute teacher announced. "But first I need a volunteer to show me how this contraption works."

"Go on, O'Dowd, tell her how contraception works!"

With his verve in decline, an encouraging shove, courtesy of Dave Keogh, sent Kieran crashing to the floor.

"O'Dowd! Get up here, seeing as you have so much energy!" Miss Colic demanded.

"Thanks a bunch!" he growled.

The conscript lumbered towards the A-V unit, to lend his expertise. The television itself was something of a marvel, indisputably the cutting edge of technology, back in 1980, judging by its wooden casing and archaic tuning dials.

"Now, where do I insert the tape?" she said helplessly.

"Oh God, it's one of those ancient top-loaders," Kieran said, as he plugged the unit into a nearby power outlet. "You'll need to press eject first."

Miss Colic complied, though Kieran's heart sank as he spotted the video label; *Make Your Own Lobster Pots in 40 Easy Steps.*

"This tape doesn't fit!" she squealed.

"It should! Oh wait a minute, that player says Betamax!!!"

"So what do I need to do?" she persisted.

"Hire a skip!" he retorted.

"You mean it won't work?"

"No! You need a *VHS* player to operate a *VHS cassette*! But good luck to you, because that too is a contender for the National Museum!"

Miss Colic's orifice skewed as she chewed over other potential avenues. "Right well, maybe there's something on television instead!" she said optimistically.

♣ ♣ ♣ ♣ ♣

With the candidates in the examination hall already on tenterhooks, more high jinks followed, as their invigilator paraded up and down, pilfering sweets from desks. One incensed student made the mistake of protesting, as he was being robbed of almost half a packet of Milky Moos. "Here! They're mine!"

"Ah, don't be so mean! You've a rake of them there!" she growled.

With her pockets bulging, the old woman rustled towards her own desk, to tally her pickings. "What time do they serve the tea and biscuits around here?" she demanded.

The unfortunate cluster in closest proximity shrugged diffidently, as they attempted to compensate for lost time.

"Right!" she barked, noting the time on the wall clock behind her, "I'm heading out for a spell, so don't any of you so much as even *think* about looking at a text book, while I'm gone!"

While Peig's announcement was met with wide-eyed astonishment, the fact that she favoured the window as an egress, left them simply stunned.

♣ ♣ ♣ ♣ ♣

With his elbow on the desk and his chin in hand, Kieran pondered on the lush grassy fields beyond the schoolyard. What a cruel irony it was to be stranded indoors one of the finest days of the year, straining his eyes on a small screen, no less than twenty feet away. To top it all off, the inadequacy of the wire-coat-hanger antenna limited their selection to only one channel and with severely compromised picture quality, at that.

"Three thousand bleedin' Euro I paid just to sit here and watch reruns of *Murder She Wrote*," he groused. "I could be doing this in the luxury of my own front room for free and at least then, I wouldn't have to watch the damn thing through a snowstorm!"

Owen, who welcomed television in any size or form, didn't share his sentiments. The final straw for Kieran came when a hunchback in familiar garb drifted by the window. Rubbing his eyes in disbelief, he nudged Owen again, to alert him to this monstrous development.

"Shhh! What is it?" Owen whispered petulantly.

"I've just seen Quasimodo again! I think she's stalking us!"

"Nah, you're seeing things, now!" he dismissed.

Although Kieran's toxic breakfast had left him feeling a little queasy, he was certain the sighting was no figment of his imagination.

♣ ♣ ♣ ♣ ♣

Breakfast at the Buckley homestead, was seldom a lean ritual. It was late morning and the aroma of sizzling bacon brought the great man walloping down the stairs. In contrast to the grand apparel he had worn the day before, Curly Buckley was dressed in a filthy vest, with braces hanging by his sides. The kitchen, however, was a good century ahead of that of his arch-nemesis, Mrs Sawyer. This was in part due to Mags Buckley's adroit housekeeping, but also in accordance with Curly's dogma of having to part with a pound in order to earn two. And thanks to his proclivity for the fullest of Irish Breakfasts, Curly was certainly piling them on. The self styled entrepreneur was seated at the table, stirring his tea, when his sister served up the customary mountain of cholesterol.

"There's something missing, is there?" he eyeballed the platter.

"Like what?" she frowned.

"Well I don't know yet. Three eggs, four hash browns, five rashers, six sausages, half a tomato, eight pieces of black pudding and wait, there's no white! Where's the white?"

"We're out,"

"But I'll starve!"

"Ah, would you go 'way! Isn't it high time you started pulling back from the trough? You'll have a heart attack one of these days!"

That was a moot point, as far as Curly was concerned, but unworthy of further discussion, for fear of jeopardising his late morning fries.

The breakfast table itself presided over much of the Buckley ancestral empire and Curly frequently enjoyed absorbing the scenery whilst absorbing his saturated fats. Yet, it was Mags who spotted an incongruous entity lurking in plain sight, as she paused to take a swig of her own tea.

"Have you someone working in the field below today?" she squinted.

"No, why?"

"Well there's somebody out there now, digging!"

Launched into a state of heightened awareness, Curly swiftly pinpointed the trespasser. "Begod, there is all right!" he galloped around to the front door.

But as Curly stepped outside, the only hint of an incursion was a patch of disturbed soil in a deserted field. “Blast! It was that lighting cow, Peig Sawyer, I’ll stake! I’m sure she’s the one who’s been thieving my spuds!”

“Hasn’t this feud between the pair of you gone on long enough?” Mags scolded. “Why not bury the hatchet for once and for all?”

“I’ll bury her one of these days!” he quivered.

“Oh, may God forgive you!” she said in condemnation, while opening the oven door and producing a second fry.

“Where are you going with that?” Curly said, marching over to the table again. “Sur’ haven’t I enough, as it is?”

“It’s not for you! You big pup! I’m taking it upstairs to that poor lad who collapsed from exhaustion, yesterday!”

“Oho! Wait just a minute!” he cried, stampeding towards her armed with a fork.

Curly Buckley excitedly sunk the utensil into three pieces of white pudding, stuffed one into his mouth and dropped the other two on his own plate.

“No white, my foot!” he growled.

♣ ♣ ♣ ♣ ♣

A free rein in the examination hall ended with a loud thud. On looking up, the startled students found their invigilator scaling back through the window with a heavy sack in tow. Alerted by a click of the door handle, Peig slinked behind her desk again, not a moment too soon. As the large oak panel door creaked open halfway, Matthew Begley’s head cropped through. “Everything okay?” he whispered.

“Without a doubt!” she winked reassuringly.

Satisfied that everything was in perfect order, the principal quietly withdrew. At liberty to pursue her own stratagems again, the old woman dipped her hand in the bag and threw a potato on the table. Curly Buckley, of course, was on the money and though his dairy produce may not have been up to her exacting standards, clearly his crops were. Unfortunately, the morning sprint had drained the old adventurer and it wasn’t long before she drifted off in her chair. Soon, Peig’s guttural snores resonated throughout the entire hall, leaving the furious students in yet another quandary.

As Matthew heaved a box of videotapes from the stores, he contemplated a liquid lunch. His morning had shaped up far better than expected that surely he deserved a treat. But events took another shady turn, as the principal encountered a trickle of students exiting prematurely from the exam hall. Among them was his own daughter.

"What's going on?" he demanded. "You're not finished already?"

Jennifer angrily flung a bag over her shoulder. "I'm finished all right!" she stormed down the corridor.

"Why? What's wrong?" he tailgated.

"Listen, I thought the eejit you hired yesterday was bad enough, but that's an absolute barrel scraper!" she thumbed in the direction of the hall.

Matthew abruptly changed the subject. "Uhm, while you're here, you wouldn't do me a small favour?"

"What is it now? I've revision to do for this afternoon!"

"Well it's a bit late for that, isn't it? Anyway, it's only a small job. Just take these tapes and leave them outside 4C for Miss Colic and when you're done, nip down to the stores and bring up the overhead projector too."

Unburdening the lumber into his daughter's arms, Matthew skived off for his, severely needed, midday tipple.

Nearby, the privileged dignitaries in 4C were enjoying countless reruns, leaving many with a sensation of being stuck in a 1980s time warp. Worse still, the lack of ventilation was slowly suffocating Kieran O'Dowd, while an unsavoury breakfast wreaked turmoil in his digestive tract. An earlier request to open a window was rejected, on the grounds that the noise might interfere with the proceedings in the exam hall. Resolving that he had been tortured enough, Kieran arose and approached the teacher. "May I be excused please? I'm as sick as a dog!"

Miss Colic checked her watch. "Can't you wait another half hour?"

"Sure, if you'd prefer me blowing chunks in your face?" he beseeched.

"Oh, all right go on!" she yielded.

Replenishing his lungs with wonderful fresh air, the light-headed student stumbled over a box of videotapes, abandoned in the corridor. Fortunately, his swift reflexes prevailed and he tottered along briefly, before regaining his balance. Unfortunately, real disaster was looming just around the corner, when a chance encounter with the arm of an overhead projector, sent Kieran hurtling into oblivion.

8. Up In Arms

"Oh my God! Hello? Are you all right?" a voice surfaced from the volley of dazzling stars.

Struggling to his feet, Kieran instinctively fingered his forehead. "Ow! Yes, I think so." Though the blow hadn't been particularly severe, their rapid succession was enough to render anyone a quivering wreck.

"Shall I get help?" the voice enquired.

"Ah no, I- I'm fine," he affirmed.

But as the stars subsided, Kieran was doubly stupefied by the attractive brunette hovering in his presence.

"Are you sure?" Jennifer Begley persisted, noting his disorientated gaze.

"Hah? Oh! Yes of course. No-no, I was walking all over the shop, as usual!" he said, attempting to absolve her of the blame.

"Don't be daft! I was the one charging along at ninety miles an hour wielding a blunt instrument. And look at that bruise! We really should- oh, wait a minute! You were at the *céilí*, last night, weren't you?"

Suddenly, she too grew flustered. "What am I saying? Of course you were there! Why wouldn't you be?!" she hesitated, before striving to make light of the situation. "You were investigating the, ah, woodlouse, isn't that right?!"

"Termite inspector! Eh, yes, guilty as charged. Sorry, I was a bit stumped for words at the time!" he shrugged.

Jennifer cringed as she replayed the incident in her own head. "I was a bit of a creep myself, and now I've nearly brained you!"

"No fear, I'm working up a nice callus there now," Kieran gently tapped his forehead.

Jennifer glanced over her shoulder. "Ordinarily I'd recommend the school nurse to examine it, but she's been on sick leave for the past eighteen months."

"Nah, it's fine, really, honestly!"

"Listen I'm awfully sorry and if there's anything- oh look, I'm Jennifer, by the way!"

Kieran arched his swollen brow. "*Jennifer*? Oh! Hi, I'm eh, Kieran O'Dowd of the- clan O'Dowd!"

"Okay then, Kieran O'Dowd of the clan O'Dowd, maybe you'd like a cup of tea, instead?"

Kieran pondered for a moment. "Is that the universal medicine in these quarters?"

"Yes, I suppose it is," she grinned, "Or coffee, if you'd prefer!"

"Great! Or if there's any food going, that would be tickety-boo too!"

Thirty seconds later, Jennifer Begley boldly descended on the teachers' lounge.

"Good! We have the place to ourselves," she declared.

But Kieran, being on foreign turf, had reservations. "Uhm, are you sure about this? It says teachers only on the door!"

"Yes, and if you stuck that sign on the door of a funeral parlour, it would still read the same!" she quipped.

Vacillating between amusement and bemusement, Kieran accepted her warped logic and stepped inside. Though the décor was hideously dated, it was a damn sight more comfortable than the chamber of sensory deprivation from which he had just escaped. He also observed how at home Jennifer seemed, as she pottered about the kitchenette, filling the electric kettle and plugging it in. Something else twigged too, her rural brogue.

"So you're local, then, I gather?" he said, naively.

"Actually, a coach load of tourists left me behind a few years ago, but I decided to stay on for a laugh," she replied.

"Oh, ah, you just know your way around the staff room, th-that's all," he stuttered.

Jennifer smiled as she placed two mugs on the counter top. "You can relax, they're all on holidays at this time of the year! Now I'll make the tea, while you fetch the biscuits from the press behind you."

Kieran's eyes bulged as he opened the cupboard. It was crammed with countless scrumptious varieties. So full, in fact, that as he made his selection, several packets tumbled out, knocking him on the head.

"Oops! Are you okay?" she grimaced.

"Sorry, eh, butter fingers! Although I'm not usually this accident prone, you know."

Gathering an assortment in his arms, the hungry teenager withdrew to a chaise longue where he immediately began tearing into a packet of Fig Rolls.

"So at first, I thought you might be with St. Rizzla's," he elaborated. "But let's face it; you're hardly in league with that reeking bunch of old scags!"

His comments ignited a horror laden gasp. "I beg your pardon?!!"

Terrified he had jeopardised a promising new alliance, Kieran quickly backtracked. "Sorry-sorry! That was tasteless, wasn't it?"

To his astonishment, her stern expression morphed into a crooked smile. "Yes, they're rancid aren't they? Each one of them billowing more smoke than a crematorium functioning at full capacity!"

Kieran was taken aback. Her cynicism was most refreshing, though it did seem strange to be its recipient for a change. Soon, the kettle came to the boil and Jennifer poured.

"Milk?

"Yes please."

"Hmm," she twitched her nose at the carton, "Buckleys' milk is always a bit rank. Sugar?"

"Yes please!"

"One or two?"

"Five."

"*Five*?!!!"

"Yes, my blood sugar levels are a bit low at the moment."

As the hot drinks were stirred, Kieran hastily stuffed an already empty Fig Roll packet under a cushion. Placing the mugs on the coffee table, Jennifer sat down beside him.

"Ah terrific!" he accepted. "Say, they must really love their biscuits around here!"

Jennifer eyed the two remaining packets. "Yes, they buy them wholesale, so don't hold back!"

"Well, if you insist," he bleated timidly, before ripping into a packet of Chocolate Hob Nobs.

"So you must be in the throes of your Junior Cert?" he offered her the open packet.

"The *Leaving* Cert," she ticked a little depreciatively, declining his offer.

"What?! How old *are* you?"

"Oh now, gentlemen shouldn't ask, but seventeen if you must know-"

"And when's your birthday?"

"March."

Kieran took two biscuits and dunked both in his tea at the same time. "Oh brilliant, so you're only a few months older than me, and yet, you're two years ahead, in school!"

"Well, I did skip transition year. My parents said I'd be wasting my time. Though I suspect, they were more concerned about a different kind of waste and fast-tracking me into gainful employment!"

"No, that was a smart move!" he sloshed. "I'm beginning to wish I'd done the same, myself!"

"What? And miss out on all the *craic*, here?"

"Oho! We've had to wear plenty of old crack, all right!" he quivered.

"Yet, you danced so beautifully with your teacher, last night," Jennifer added with another hint of glib whimsy.

"Yeah, that was a trip all right. Miss Colic is a real *classy* chick."

"But not quite so gracious, when your friend pinched her rear end!"

"Who? What friend? Was it the guy with the long hair and army jacket?"

"Yes, that was him."

"That swine! I got a right bollicking over that! Oh well, never mind. Here, I'm hoping to send a couple of e-mails, today. Is there a computer room with internet access around here?"

"Computer room?! Internet?!!" she gasped. "Come here and I'll show you our internet!"

Jennifer led Kieran back through the corridor and around the corner to the storage closet. "There's our *internet*!" she opened the door and pointed to an enormous mound of yellow plastic.

"Uh, what exactly am I looking at?" he frowned.

"Well, a few years ago, the school received a government improvement grant, right? But rather than risk it all on a 'passing fad' called the information superhighway, they opted for something a little more tangible; something equally *fun*, but with the potential to reap real returns. A bouncy castle!"

"A wha-?"

"And it wasn't long after a spate of injuries and one teacher's broken spine, that it was decommissioned."

"No internet?"

"No internet! No computers! No computer room! Just one deflated castle, one massive lawsuit and a string of small claims!"

With so many options being slashed, Kieran too, felt deflated.

"What kind of ass could dream up such a mess?" he whined.

"My father, actually," she replied.

Kieran laughed at her apparent wit, though noting her sober expression, nervously trailed off. "Y-you mean y-you're r-related?"

"I'm afraid so," Jennifer sighed, glancing at her watch. "Anyhow, I think I've just enough time for a last minute cram, before this afternoon."

"Sure, and there's another *céilí* tonight, I take it?"

"Oh yes! You'll find no shortage of those. Well, wish me luck!"

"Hah? Oh, eh, good luck then!" he cried, as she scampered down the corridor.

Kieran returned to the lounge to quaff the last of his tea. Once there, the remaining biscuits on the coffee table enticingly beckoned. *Nobody seems to be eating those*, he pondered. *And there is nothing worse than allowing good food to go to waste.*

♣ ♣ ♣ ♣ ♣

As the lunchtime bell sounded, Kieran was seated on the outer school wall, milling through his chocolate biscuits. Two bedraggled heads surfaced from the outbound cascade and drifted over to quiz their housemate. "Where did you disappear to?"

"Biscuits!" Kieran said, sharing his windfall.

Owen perked up significantly. "Oh hey, my favourite, where did you get those?"

"Teachers' lounge! And there you go Rory, a packet of Lemon Puffs for you!"

"I don't like Lemon Puffs!" the strait-laced one retorted.

"Okay, well, have a Hob Nob instead," Kieran bartered.

"I'm not eating any stolen biscuits!"

"You nicked them?" Owen temporarily resisted the temptation.

"No, I didn't! Well, not exactly, they were just lying there and, let's just say, I'm recouping my losses! Okay?"

Owen tucked in regardless. "So, did you see a telephone?"

"I'm afraid not, and e-mail is definitely a lost cause! Plus, as you know, Mrs Begley has pulled a sickie, so that scuppers her for a day or two!"

"Should we try the principal again?"

"He's not such a keen strategist, I gather. So let's play it by ear-"

An intruder interrupted the debriefing. "What's this? A hen party?!! Dave Keogh scoffed.

Already flagging badly in the opinion polls, their devalued pal was doing nothing to earn extra brownie points. His new boon companion, Ambrose Cleary, was loitering nearby and presumably being tolerated as they were tethered for the duration.

"Ambrose and I are heading back for our lunch now- eh, you lot are going in the same direction, aren't you?" Dave indicated.

Kieran glanced briefly at the commune before answering. "I think we'll just, uhm, hang around here for while," he said, throwing a casual spin on their predicament.

"Biscuit?" Owen offered.

"No peasant food, thank you," Dave demurred, "Ambrose and I are saving our appetites for some quality nosh."

With the entire swarm, apart from themselves, making a beeline for their midday repast, Dave's parting jibe felt like a stiletto in the gut.

"Ooo! Ambrose and I are on our way to the Gresham for a four course lunch!" Kieran seethed. "Afterwards presumably, Ambrose and I will be on our way to the town hall, for a marriage license. Oh Kieran, will you be our bridesmaid? Why yes, of course, I'd love to!"

A rambling tirade triggered nervous stares. "Oh, but I've simply nothing to wear for the ball, apart from these old rags! You see my landlady burned all my clothes! No, you go on without me, while I stay here and eat this disgusting crap from the floor!" Kieran petered out, while staring into the cosmos.

"Biscuit?" Owen gestured towards Rory.

With starvation slowly grinding down his principles, one Chocolate Hob Nob was grudgingly accepted.

♣ ♣ ♣ ♣ ♣

The afternoon sitting in the examination hall was largely uneventful, providing you were impervious to the spectacle of an old woman using her fingernails to peel a dozen potatoes. For the visiting delegates however, the ignominy continued, with four hours of mind-numbing, pre-pubescent television. Kieran, at least, no longer cared, now that he had something else, or someone rather, to engage his thoughts.

But when will I see her again? he mused. *She didn't mention if she'd be at the céilí. Come to think of it, she dashed off pretty fast*! The more he analysed the situation, the more his own insecurities began to plague him. *Oh God! It was that stupid remark about her father being an ass! Big mistake Kieran! I know, I'll write her a note of thanks. Yeah, women really lap up that sort of malarkey.*

Plucking a newly acquired ball-point from his pocket, Kieran opened his copy book.

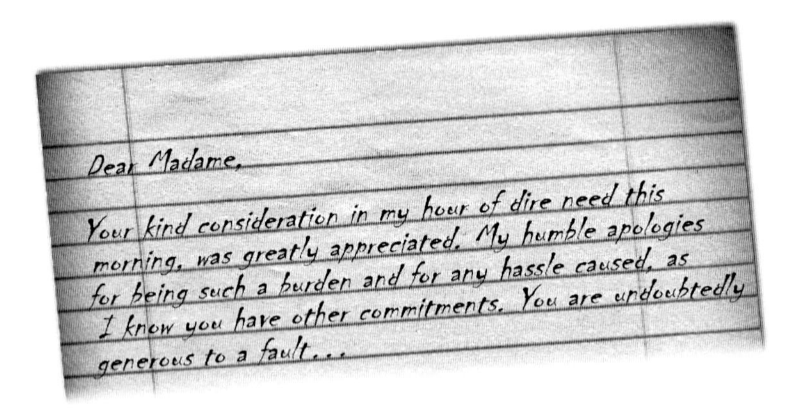

Dear Madame,

Your kind consideration in my hour of dire need this
morning, was greatly appreciated. My humble apologies
for being such a burden and for any hassle caused, as
I know you have other commitments. You are undoubtedly
generous to a fault...

Kieran paused to read the few sentences he'd written. Stagnant wasn't the word. Clearly Jennifer had a sense of humour and might appreciate something a little more tongue in cheek. Bearing that in mind, he proceeded to put pen to paper.

Let's face it, ever since the céilí, I've been falling head
over heals for you! Wink wink! And given that we're both
drop dead gorgeous, why not make the most of the next
three weeks and have some fun? In fact, just say the
word and we can elope! Discretion is my middle name.
And hey, who cares about the slight age gap? Mind you,
don't expect a lavish honeymoon... this place has me
bankrupt!

With my undying love.
A 'secret' admirer!
X

Delighted with his witty epistle, Kieran closed the jotter and draped himself over his desk. He would figure out how to deliver it later, but for now, with the afternoon sun beating on his face, it was inescapably siesta time.

♣ ♣ ♣ ♣ ♣

Their homecoming that evening was marred by a shocking new attachment at the front of the cottage. Her three foils had no sooner been spotted on the horizon, through the lens of a telescope, when the old buccaneer zipped into the cubicle of her newly installed tollgate. The students could only gawp in disbelief as she lowered the iron bar, impeding their access through the front door.

"What's the meaning of this?" Kieran cried.

"It's my new system!" Peig cackled. "Admission is one Euro each!"

"Ah no way!" he reversed down the garden path. "No-no-no, this is just going too far! I'm heading back to the school to report this!"

As Kieran approached the gate, it automatically slammed shut.

"There's no going back!" she hissed.

Undaunted, Kieran reached for the lever, but an electrified jolt as he touched it stimulated a quick change of heart. Fear for his very survival soon eclipsed his financial anxieties.

"All right, I'll pay!" he whipped out his wallet. "Damn it! I've no change left! Hey Owen, have you any change?" Kieran looked around only to discover that his wily friend had apparently fled. "Where'd he go?"

"Dunno," Rory shrugged.

Spotting a banknote in Kieran's hand, Peig snatched it. "This'll do," she said, pocketing the money.

"But that was a fiver!" he roared.

"That's fine. I'll open an account for you!"

Though the iron bar was raised, an unexpected cloudburst deferred their entry.

"Oh dear! Time to bring in the tea!" the old woman sighed, scurrying from her cubicle to the clothes line.

Kieran observed in amazement as Peig gathered a dozen tea-bags which had been left out to dry. Unfortunately, as he prepared to step indoors, the bar descended again.

"Ah-aaah!" she scolded, "Your time has expired! You'll need to feed the meter!"

"What? That's a swindle! What about my account?"

"Yes, isn't that inflation a fright," she pouted with false sincerity.

The besieged teenager thrashed out his wallet again. This time, it was bare.

"That's it Rory, I'm skint! You'll have to cover us!"

Rory, bizarrely, appeared unfazed by the infringement of their civil liberties.

"Hah?" he grunted impassively.

"What's the matter with you? Snap out of it and get your cash out, before she brings on the water cannons!"

Perceptibly lacking any sense of urgency, Rory leisurely reached for his money belt. The tension proved too much for Kieran, who plucked it from his hands. To his astonishment, it was packed with banknotes. Another hand, inundated with liver spots, swooped down and seized the lot. The coup, however, was brief. "Ara what's this!?" Peig let the currency to slip through her fingers. "This is only monopoly money!"

Kieran couldn't believe his eyes. "Why, Rory? Why?"

"Mother won't allow me to play with real money!"

"You brainless plebe! How will we get any supper at this rate?"

Peig advanced menacingly towards the hostages. "Ye wouldn't have any other form of legal tender, would ye?" She grabbed Kieran's jaw and thrust his mouth open. "Like gold fillings, maybe? No? Oh, too bad!"

Hurling him aside, she seized Rory's throat. "Bah! Nothing there either."

A Celtic cross hanging from Kieran's neck grabbed the attention of her beady eye.

"Oh now, that is nice!" she clawed at the pendant.

"No! Please! That was my grandfather's. He died last year!"

"Well he won't miss it, will he?" she wrenched it clear. "Right, on ye go!"

Suffice to say, when the bar was raised a second time, the students didn't dally.

A spruced up kitchen was a turn up for the books, though undoubtedly the fruit of ill-gotten gains. Nevertheless, the velvet table cloth and golden candelabras gave the dilapidated domicile a faint air of refinement.

"Sit down gentlemen!" their hostess ushered.

"Well this doesn't look too bad, I suppose," Kieran noted the upgrade.

"And here are your menus!" she handed them each a gilded leather folder.

"Menus?!" Kieran gasped. "Now, this is more like it! Pity Owen did a legger, he missed a treat!" Inside the folder, bafflingly, was nothing more than a white sheet, with Owen's name printed in bold lettering. "Owen?" Kieran frowned.

Jotting something into her notebook, Peig turned towards Rory. "And what about you, Goggles Boy?"

"Hah?" he listlessly replied.

"Never mind, I'll put you down for the special too," she said, concealing the notebook in her apron pocket.

"What's she prattling on about, now?" Kieran whispered to his increasingly gormless housemate.

When it transpired that she was making for the forbidden door, a ghostly silence enveloped. Slowly, the door creaked open and the old woman drifted beyond. What finally emerged defied all expectations. It was gross, vile and downright despicable. Out she came, heaving a giant cauldron, brimming with his old chum, Owen O'Brien, though still alive and whistling without a care in the world.

Kieran leapt from the table. "What the hell is *he* doing in there?!" he exclaimed.

"What does it look like? I'm taking a bath!" Owen replied, unaccountably using a ladle to douse himself in his own gravy.

"What?! Are you blind? That's not a bath! Look! It's a cooking pot!"

Owen grew mildly vexed by the badgering. "Can't I have a minute's peace to bathe? Now leave me alone!"

The crone inserted her index finger into the water to sample the stew. "Mmm, it's lacking," she said wistfully, before adding salt, pepper and diced carrot to the mix.

"Can't you see what's happening? Kieran implored. "She's planning to eat you!"

"I most certainly am not!" Peig protested.

"Then how do you explain this?"

"We're *all* going to eat him!" she screeched.

"I can't!" Rory avowed. "I'm a vegetarian!"

"Don't worry, there's no shortage of vegetables. You can just eat 'round the meat!"

Belatedly growing anxious, Owen peered over the side of the cauldron and noting the fire beneath, bawled in terror. "Aieeee! This *is* a cooking pot! You *are* planning to eat me! Help me Kieran! Please help me!"

Kieran scrambled to assist, but Peig dished him a hard smack with the ladle.

"Ah-aaah!" she warned, pulling a meat cleaver from her seemingly bottomless apron pocket. "I was planning on saving you 'til last, seeing as you're my favourite, but try that once more and you'll be the next one inside that pot!"

As Peig circumnavigated the cauldron, jealously guarding her prey, Kieran began to perspire, though a mere drop in the ocean, measured up to Owen, who was now literally stewing in his own fat.

"For goodness sake Rory, do something to help!" Kieran pleaded.

Rory remained barely responsive. "Hah?" he hummed.

"Forget him!" Owen urged, "Get proper help! Get the principal! Get Miss Colic! Get anyone! If I don't make it, tell my parents I love-"

"Ah give over your bloody nonsense!" Peig roared, slamming a lid over the cauldron.

Wielding her blade at the dissenter, she closed in, with malice and with intent. "So, this is how you betray me! There are starving children in the world today, who would gladly give, not only their right arm, but their *left* one too, for a meal like this! It's the best of food! There's nothing wrong with it!"

Terror-stricken, Kieran backed up towards the table. "Come on, wake up you dummy! Let's get out of here!" he grabbed Rory's arm, which to his sheer horror broke away in his hand. "Stone me Rory!!!" he roared. "Your arm's just come off!!!"

But as he tipped his housemate's shoulder, Rory's head fell off and landed directly at his feet. A quick examination revealed it was made from hollow plastic.

"What the hell-? I always knew you were an airhead, but *this* takes the biscuit!"

At this point, it was every man for himself and to buy some extra time, Kieran lashed Rory's head into her chest, before tearing towards the door. It was to no avail.

"Ye don't know how lucky ye are! In my day, we had to do penance by chewing live wasps and crawling through broken glass!" she harped on.

Conquering the latch, in the nick of time, Kieran bolted. What he failed to consider was the iron girder located directly outside, causing him to stumble and land head first on the other side. Kieran blacked out for a moment, but could still hear voices.

"Wake up you dummy, it's time to go!"

"What?" he groaned.

Opening his eyes again, Kieran was agape to find himself back in 4C. Above him was Owen O'Brien, whose rotund proportions were clearly intact and nearby; Rory Waters, no longer shaped from plastic, though still reassuringly wooden. Kieran sprung to his feet and looked around the room. Everyone else had vacated, apart from Miss Colic who was plugging out the television set.

"Right, let's go and see what concoction the old witch has brewed up for our dinner!" Owen proposed.

"Yeah, I can't imagine," Kieran murmured.

As the trio exited the classroom, they crossed paths with a distillery in the form of Principal Begley. "Hello Miss Colic!"

He adjusted the dark glasses on the bridge of his nose. "Did everything work out all right today?"

"Ah Mr Begley! Not too bad! Although this video player won't accept these tapes of yours, so we ended up watching a bit of the old telly instead."

"Oh, why didn't you come down and see me? I might've been able to sort something out?" he suggested.

"I did come looking for you around lunchtime, but you weren't in your office?"

"Uh yes, an urgent appointment in the village," he muttered, while knocking back a mint Tic-Tac. "Tell you what, write down anything you might need and I'll see what I can do."

"Mrs Begley is expected to make a full recovery fairly soon?" she frowned.

"Yes, of course!" Matthew affirmed, despite his suspicions to the contrary.

"Okay, well, one the lads mentioned a V-H-S player?" Miss Colic said, as she regarded the A.V. unit.

"Hang on, we'd better make a note of this," he said, probing his pockets. "That's odd, I'm sure I had a pen- oh *there* it is." The glistening object was spotted on a desk, halfway down the classroom. Jostling through a maze of tables and chairs, Matthew retrieved his ballpoint and in addition, the copy book beneath it.

"Mmm, no harm in borrowing a page or two, I reckon," he murmured. "Now anything at all you desire, your wish is my command!" he proclaimed, yielding both items, with a friendly wink.

Miss Colic inattentively accepted the jotter and opened it. "What's this?" she whirred, with a look of wonderment sweeping across her face. "*Your kind consideration in my hour of dire need this morning, was greatly appreciated*?"

"What?"

"*My humble apologies for being such a burden and for any hassle caused, as I know you have other commitments. You are undoubtedly generous to a fault.* Oh Mr Begley! There was no need for this! But all the same, it's very nice!"

Matthew grew very uneasy. "What? No- I didn't."

"And wait! There's more! *Let's face it, ever since the céilí, I've been falling head of over heals for* you!!! Oh, Mr Begley! I had no idea!" she cried, passionately buying into the satirical prose. "*Why not make the most of the next three weeks and have some fun? In fact, just say the word and we can elope*! Oh my! Oh Mr Begley! *Discretion is my middle name. And hey, who cares about the slight age gap? Mind you, don't expect a lavish honeymoon, this place has me bankrupt! With my undying love*!"

By now, Matthew was truly flummoxed. "I- who- what- that's not- no- I- I- I- I didn't write that!"

"Oh course you didn't write it. It was my *secret admirer*!" Miss Colic squealed, throwing her arms around him and smothering him with kisses. "Oh Matthew! Eight years I've coming been here now and I knew we had this unspoken bond! Forget discretion! Who cares what others think, so long as we're happy! And what's ten or fifteen years between us? Love knows no boundaries! You've still plenty of time! We both do! We can travel. See the world! Live simply; backpacking, staying in hostels and surviving off the land! Oh Matthew, it's a dream come true, at long last we can be together!"

Though Miss Colic was too blinkered to notice, Matthew was unable to warm to her affections. Furthermore, he wasn't ready to renounce the relatively comfortable lifestyle he had grown accustomed to, for a reckless outdoor adventure.

"Please, Miss Colic! This is just an awful mistake! I'm a happily married man!" he implored.

"A sham!" she wrenched the sunglasses from his face and gently stroked his tarnished skin. "That's what it is! I understand you've been bankrupt, *physically* and *emotionally*. But wounds heal and soon your life will be a rich tapestry of marital bliss with me!"

As he struggled to extricate himself from her fanatical embrace, the voice of an intruder caught them unawares. "Just letting you know, I'll be off now?"

Like dazzled bunnies, caught in the headlamps of an oncoming vehicle, the pair gawped in horror towards the open door. Skulking in the corridor was Peig Sawyer, her eyes so conveniently filled with disgust and disdain.

"Mrs Sawyer!" Matthew gasped.

Before either party could fabricate a defence strategy, their judge, jury and executioner began to trudge away. Prising himself away from his amorous devotee, Matthew careered after the witness, before she tore his career and as well as everything else asunder.

"Hurry back, my love!" Miss Colic urged.

♣ ♣ ♣ ♣ ♣

"Oh damn, I forgot a couple of things!"

"Like what?"

"My copybook, for starters," Kieran patted his empty pockets.

"Can't you pick it up tomorrow?" Owen sighed.

"No, I want it for this evening, and besides, I suspect we could use a few extra biscuits for tea!"

With an inspired volte-face, Owen O'Brien led the assault team back into the building.

♣ ♣ ♣ ♣ ♣

As Kieran O'Dowd re-entered the classroom, he found Miss Colic vegetating by the window, with his rolled up jotter clutched tightly against her chest.

"Oh good! You found my copybook!" he scuttled towards her.

"Oh, Mr O'Dowd, what is it? Have you forgotten something?" she said, stirring from her besotted reverie.

"Just my copybook, that's all!" he replied, with a gentle tug.

To his bewilderment, her grip abruptly fortified. "What?!!" she blinked, suddenly developing an eerie tic.

"Uh, my copybook?" he frowned.

Panic stricken, she looked to and fro, from Kieran to the jotter and back again.

"This is *yours*? *Your* copybook?"

Kieran's suspicions were aroused. "Uh, yes, may I have it back, please?"

With an icy hint of psychosis creeping into her eyes, Miss Colic begrudgingly relinquished the article.

"Thanks, eh, you haven't opened this, have you?" he grimaced.

"Certainly not! What are you accusing me of?"

"Nothing! Nothing at all!" he whimpered, edging cautiously towards the door.

It had crossed his mind to ask about the pen, but given her peculiar behaviour, he ruled against it. Unsettled by her intense gaze, Kieran ripped the first page from the jotter, concealed it in his pocket and tore down the corridor to rejoin his friends.

Miss Colic lurched towards her chair in a state of hyperventilation. Moments ago her heart had been set aflutter, now she was suffering palpitations. Not only had she needlessly humiliated herself in front of the principal, but it transpired that one of her pupils was disturbingly obsessed with her.

I wasn't meant to read that letter, or at least, not yet!! she cogitated. *But that said it all! What did he say? 'Your kind consideration in my hour of dire need this morning, was greatly appreciated?' Against my better judgement, I let him out before time and now he believes it was favouritism! 'Ever since the céilí, I've been falling head of over heals for you' Oh dear God! It's my own, fault! I encouraged him! I led him on! 'And who cares about the slight age gap?' he said. Slight?!! I' m old enough to be his moth- older sister! Oh my goodness! I never knew the powerful extent of my allure!*"

♣ ♣ ♣ ♣ ♣

At the other end of the school, Matthew had intercepted Peig and was mid-way through pleading his case. "You see, Miss Colic appears to be going through a rather bad patch at the moment."

"You mean the bad patch on your face?" she cynically cross examined.

"What?! No!"

"Ah sur' what does it matter? Now, will you be needing me tomorrow, or not?"

Once again, she had him over a barrel and this was her sly demand for a back hander.

"Well, I suppose we could use-"

"Good lad!" she bestowed him with a patronising pat on the arm. "You're all right. Your secret is safe with me!"

As Peig pushed open the emergency exit door and stepped outside, Matthew followed on. "No honestly, there's nothing between Miss- just a minute, why are you leaving this way?" he frowned.

"It's quicker," she said, hoisting the first of two heavy sacks lying outside the door.

"And what have you got inside those?" he cried.

"Shopping!" she replied, setting off across the football pitch with both sacks in tow.

Shopping? The principal racked his brain for a moment, before rushing back to his office for an inventory of school property.

♣ ♣ ♣ ♣ ♣

The door to the teacher's lounge creaked open and Kieran's head cropped through.

"Okay, the coast is clear. Owen you're with me, Rory you stay by the door and keep sketch."

"Look, I don't really want any part in this," he objected.

"Listen here, you hypocrite! You've already sampled from the poisoned chalice! There's no going back now! Besides, it's hardly stealing now, is it? It's about survival!"

With a disapproving groan, Rory submitted to Kieran's interpretation.

"Right, just enough to fill our pockets and we're out of here! Kieran enthused. "No need to create too big a dent!"

Stealthily, they made for the cupboard and opened it. Pitifully, the only thing in store was disenchantment, as the entire compartment had been completely ransacked.

"What's this? The weight watcher's pantry?" Owen frowned sceptically.

"I don't understand it!" Kieran pined. "What kind of a sick, twisted individual- earlier this afternoon this place was chock-a-block of every type of biscuit imaginable! We're dealing here with a dark malevolent force, hell-bent on ensuring our perpetual misery! It's just been one cruel hoax after another."

"And there, possibly, is your perpetrator now!" Owen gasped with wide-eyed revulsion, pointing towards the window.

"Eh? What are you on about?" Kieran looked over his shoulder.

It was then, that he spotted the ageing marauder marching across the playing fields with a full consignment saddled on her back.

9. The Bloodsucker Proxy

Morale was low. Exceptionally low. The merciless wrenching of their only life-support sent our friends spiralling into a chasm of despair, while the prospect of a viper, lying in wait back at the cottage, significantly curbed their drive. The torpid trio were the very last to emerge from the gates of *Coláiste Nathair.* Across the road, however, there was a flurry of excitement in the grounds of St. Millipede's.

"What's the hullabaloo over there?" Kieran raised his chin from the shadows.

"An accident?" Owen squinted at the flashing blue lights.

With little else in the way of entertainment, morbid curiosity compelled them to investigate. Poking his head through a cluster of bystanders, Kieran bore witness to the chilling spectacle of a body bag being thrust into the back of an ambulance. At the heart of it all was Fr. Tom Buttimer, whose bearing suggested that he was orchestrating the affair. Once the vehicle doors closed, the surrounding onlookers began to disperse.

"What happened?" Kieran queried. "Was there an accident?"

Apparitions of the old wretch being dragged out into the moors and sacrificed to a pack of hungry wolves immediately sprung to mind.

"Oh lads!" Fr. Tom cried. "I thought everybody from the school had already left! I'm sorry you had to see this!"

"See what?" Owen probed, as the ambulance driver extended the priest a clipboard.

"It's Mrs Breslin, I'm afraid," he signed the release form, "They're uhm- sending her back to Dublin, this evening."

"Lucky stiff!" Kieran cried.

His unique spin on the tragedy baffled Fr. Tom and as they watched the ambulance pull away, Kieran began to wonder if they would all be going home in a body bag.

"Hey! I've just realised something! The three of us could have hitched a lift with Mrs Breslin! I'm sure she wouldn't have objected?"

"Ah now lads, things can't be all that bad?" the cleric contested.

"Well it isn't a complete loss," Kieran acknowledged, recalling just one agreeable incident.

"Our *Bean An Tí*," Owen interjected, "Were there problems with some of her students, last year?"

A troubled gaze, once more, shrouded the burly man's hirsute face, making Kieran even more determined to persevere. "Yes, Owen was wondering if she hacked them into little pieces?!"

The indictment caught Owen by surprise. "What? I never said *that*!"

"Someone had to ask!" Kieran warranted.

"Ah, come on lads, don't be silly!" Fr. Tom emerged from his wool-gathering. "Here, go and buy yourselves an ice cream," he said, drawing a twenty Euro note from his pocket and extending it to Owen.

"Oh thanks very much!" Kieran quickly usurped it.

"And don't bother your heads about it, at all! I'm sure everything will work out for the best," the cleric affirmed.

Nearby, more chaos erupted, as the Buckley boys engaged in a fencing tournament via two large batons. "Ah look at these blackguards! They're meant to be doing a job for me," Fr. Tom sighed wearily.

"All right!" he said, breaking up the duel, "Enough fooling! I want this whole mess wrapped up by tea time, if at all possible. That missing uhm, *package* isn't going to locate itself, you know!"

"Oh yes, sorry about that, Father!" James Buckley cowered, as he progressed to flog a nearby ditch with his stick.

"What missing package?" Jeremiah cried raucously. "I thought we were looking for a coffin!"

"Sh-shuddup! We are," James whispered, glancing awkwardly at the three unknowns.

"Oh right, yes, the missing package!" Jeremiah construed, long after the cat had been left out of the bag. Unfortunately, with Mrs Schalplatten currently wheeling through Piccadilly Circus in central London, the Buckley boys were on a fool's errand.

An unexpected bonus restored a slight spring in Kieran's step, as he and the others proceeded on their journey. "Fr. Butterly isn't a bad sort, really."

Owen on the other hand, remained a little more focused. "Mmm, maybe, though I notice he didn't actually answer our questions."

"What questions?!" Kieran leered over his prize.

"Now, you *are* going share that money? That ice cream was intended for *all* of us!"

"Don't worry, I'll look after you, as always!"

"Eh, need I remind you of the obvious lack of shops in the area?" Rory stated bluntly.

"Need I remind *you* to shut your face?" Kieran snapped.

"Fine, kill the messenger!" Rory scowled.

"He's right though," Owen mediated. "Maybe we should've asked Fr. Buttimer where we might find the nearest shopping mall?"

Kieran glanced over his shoulder just as the cleric was stepping inside the presbytery. "Mmm, yes, he's hardly shy of a good meal, by the looks of things."

♣ ♣ ♣ ♣ ♣

The prospect of Peig's white-washed cottage unleashed a bellyful of rabid butterflies. The absence of a toll-gate was a favourable sign, though recalling another electrifying experience, Kieran graciously allowed Owen to open the gate. A twitching curtain signified that not only was she already home, but was still violating boundaries. "Look!" Kieran cried. "That sow is in our room!"

Within a flash the green door swung open and there to greet them, was their charismatic hostess. "Ah ye're back! Come on in! The tea's wet!"

Despite their readiness to be on the defensive, Peig's pious greetings were continually disarming. A definite pattern was emerging, however, and that despite their best behaviour; something would inevitably ire her royal highness. They followed her through to the kitchen, where the table, reassuringly devoid of expensive table-cloths and candelabras, had been set.

"The dish and what-not is on the chair," she pointed to the usual sundries.

Owen immediately dashed towards the basin, in the hope of a second look at her soap, while Rory grabbed her white flannel. But as the former pored over the triple 'B' Luxury Lather Special, it appeared that any trace of its characteristic logo had been cunningly chiselled away. Similarly, Rory found only a stub where a tag had once been. This shrewd minx was one step ahead of them, every inch of the way. And so, after briefly dipping their hands in the water, the pair sat at the table, in silent disgust.

"Eh, you weren't in our room today, by any chance, Mrs Sawyer?" Kieran perilously probed, while taking his turn at the basin.

"Why?" she peered in askance, making for the hearth.

"Well, I, eh, *we* saw the curtain moving, just this minute-"

Peig focused on the small black pot suspended over the fire. "Sur' 'twas probably the wind," she huffed. "Or no, yes, just this minute? Yes, I was doing a bit of cleaning up in there, that's all!"

Kieran raised a sceptical brow in Owen's direction and continued to lather his hands. Pondering on the mystery of the forbidden door again, his imagination ran riot with the cries of tormented souls, who conceivably met their grisly demise beyond.

"All right, enough is enough!" Peig grabbed the soap from his hands. "You've squandered enough of that bar to scour an elephant!"

Kieran promptly dried his hands and sat at the table.

"Ye're all very quiet this evening, lads!" she observed. "Did ye learn much on yer course, today?"

Darting glances abounded. "Yeah, plenty," Kieran stated rancorously.

His current concern was regarding the possible bio-hazard soon to afflict their dinner plates. Unhooking the vessel from the hearth, Peig placed it on a wooden coaster before them. This time, something far more palatable emerged.

"Right, who's for mash?" she extended the first heaped wooden spoon.

Owen's chipped platter was first in line. "Me please! I love potatoes!"

On receipt of one serving, his plate remained elevated in anticipation of more.

"Next!" she barked.

Realising that this was the sum total of his meal, Owen glumly retracted his dish.

"Ooh! It's hot," he said, blowing gently over his meagre ration.

"It's what?!" she snapped.

"I was just s-saying it's g-grand and h-hot," he stuttered.

"Oh right, well, there's butter on the table, if ye want it!"

Butter?! Egad! Surely not? But raising the lid on the terracotta dish, one gleaming pound was unveiled.

"It's homemade and the best of stuff too!" she added pompously.

Owen swiftly capitalised on this momentous upturn, while their hostess doled out servings to Kieran and Rory, respectively.

"Yes, good simple food! That's all ye'll be getting from now on. Sur' what's the point in preparing extravagant dishes if ye're only going to be plastering it all over my kitchen! What's more, I'm getting too old to be doing separate meals for those with delicate palates!" she meaningfully hit Rory's plate with her wooden spoon.

There was ample potato leftover as the saucepan was returned to the hearth, though nobody had the gumption to ask for more. Instead, the students opted to season their meal with liberal quantities of Peig's homemade spread. Strangely though, Kieran's attempt to thrust a knife into the yellow mass met with an obstruction.

"What's wrong?" Owen enquired.

"It's still hard," he replied.

"It can't be hard!" the old woman yelled from the other side of the kitchen.

"Well either that, or its gone bad in the middle."

Peig closed in on the table. "Ara, go 'way! Butter doesn't go bad!"

"Well look! There's definitely something in it!"

"Try using your fork," Owen suggested.

Kieran complied and with a sudden jerk unscrambled a foreign entity from within.

"Euch! What's this?" he pitched the vile object at the end of his utensil.

Peering in for a closer examination, Peig snatched the deviant article. "Ah, isn't it one of my old stockings?" she cried, smoothing it down. "Well now, I've been looking for that this long-time! Ah sur' it'll do ye no harm."

The news came a little late for Owen who was in the throes of swallowing the last of his heavily buttered potato. And despite her firm warranty, this latest bout of bad taste only poisoned their appetites for Mrs Sawyer's special home blend.

"Right now, who's for afters?!" she rapidly moved on.

Fear of yet another nameless horror resulted in a stone cold silence. Peig, nonetheless, stepped into her private quarters, with her curdled stocking in hand and returned with a packet of Ginger Nut biscuits. "Right, and are ye all for tea?" she enquired.

With dehydration setting in, there were no objections.

"Yes please," Owen croaked, checking his glands for signs of swelling.

Peig scuttled over to fetch the teapot, which had been warming at the edge of the hearth. On this occasion, the brew appeared encouragingly strong, thanks, no doubt, to ample time allowed for the solitary tea leaf to draw.

"And there's yer afters," she placed the biscuits on the table.

"Oh right, thanks very much!" Owen said, reaching for the Ginger Nut.

In doing so, the ginger-headed youth received a sharp slap on the back of the hand.

"I'll distribute, if you don't mind!" she snapped.

"Oh, eh, s-sorry, I-I didn't realise-"

As Peig tussled with the packaging, Kieran noticed enough dirt under her fingernails for a sizeable cotton plantation. But even that couldn't repel the hungry teenager from eating the solitary biscuit thrown onto his plate. Budding agitator, Owen, was the last to receive his pudding, which landed on his plate in three broken pieces.

"That's enough now, for fear ye might be sick!" she conveniently presumed, while concealing the packet in her apron pocket.

The only thing more scant than the meal was the dearth of conversation that followed. And when the trio were enlisted to wash the dishes, even more unspeakable was the diktat that they use the same basin and water in which they had bathed, only moments before.

♣ ♣ ♣ ♣ ♣

Back in the dormitory it was apparent that she hadn't created much of a dent in her cleaning up either. A patch of wall, newly exposed following the bunk bed collapse, highlighted a rudimentary calendar left by one of their predecessors, but offered no clue of the fate that befell them.

"Where am I going to sleep tonight?" Rory pointed helplessly to his mattress now deluged in rubble.

Kieran surveyed the hashed bunk-bed and considered if anything was worth salvaging. Though the top bunk was a write off, the bottom bunk remained intact. Hence, with one violent lunge, he swept the surplus clean onto the floor.

"There now, are you happy? At least you still have a bed!"

Rory stood gawping for a moment, before sitting on his mattress to test its viability.

"Look at this rubbish!" Kieran lashed through the debris.

Owen observed from the window sill, while supplementing his dinner with another packet of his increasingly precious cheese and onion crisps. Mollified with monosodium glutamate, it didn't take long for the facetious banter to resurface. "Maybe you can use those bits to build a new bed?" he suggested.

"Some hope! It's a coffin I'll be needing next!"

Kieran flipped the upper mattress onto the floor. "There, that's *my* new bed!"

"I don't suppose *she* sleeps in a coffin?" Owen sighed, gazing wistfully outside.

"She fits the bill, all right! And next, she'll be demanding a pound of our flesh! *Oh lads-lads-lads, what have ye done to me beds? Ya have me bankrupt*!"

Lumbering about with his shoulders hunched and his face knotted, Kieran created a reasonable facsimile of their hostess. "*Oh well-well-well! Oh yera! Oh you there! Get down on your hands and knees and lick that floor clean*!" he bellowed in falsetto, unmistakably capturing her effervescent spirit.

"Oh I'd love to Mrs Sawyer, but I'm afraid I've just eaten!" Owen maintained the pretence. "Besides, it's littered with wood-chippings and rusty bed-springs!"

Kieran collared his quarry and compelled him to the lino. "*You'll Eat It! And you'll like it! It's the best of food! If you were in a restaurant now you'd be glad of that! In my day all we got was donkey-snouts and bum-fluff and it never did us any harm! There's nothing wrong with it! It's fine!*"

"Yes ma'am, but are you sure you got enough fibre in your diet?"

"*Silence! You impudent scamp! In my dominion and you shall abide by my decree, or suffer the consequences like those infidels who perished last year*!"

"Gee whizz Mrs Sawyer! I don't want to die! I'm too young!"

Grabbing a tattered sheet from the floor, Kieran draped it over his shoulder in order to simulate a royal robe. "*Bring forth a human sacrifice and I may show you lenience*!"

"How about this fine young specimen?" Owen munificently gestured towards Rory.

"*Ahh*! *Master Goggles Boy, I presume*!" Kieran said musingly.

Rory, who was busy dusting down his mattress, shunned their miniature farce. "Go away! And stop calling me Goggles Boy!"

"Hark! We have a traitor in our midst, oh noble one!" Owen cried, clearly relishing his role as the obsequious varlet.

"*Treason, eh? Clasp him in irons and banish him forthwith to the forbidden chamber! There he shall dwell until the end of his days*!"

"Oh you are delectably cruel, oh mighty one! Shall I sharpen the machete?"

Their tour de force abruptly terminated, when Owen's eyes met with an eerie shadow skulking at the base of the door. By rapidly drawing a finger across his own throat, he signalled for Kieran to desist. Assuming this to be part of the charade, the faux-Peig responded in character. "*What is it, knave? Off with his head?*"

But observing his roommate flailing frantically, Kieran followed his line of vision and immediately sobered up. It was mortifying. An intruder had been hanging on every last searing detail of their masquerade. For several moments, the pair remained in suspended animation until the shadow apparently grew weary and shuffled away.

"Oh God!" Owen gasped. "How much of that do you suppose she heard?"

"I couldn't give a rat's ass, at this stage," Kieran bundled his ceremonial dress into a ball. "I'm sure we're already knee deep in it, as far as she's concerned. Come on, we may as well get this stuff cleared before the *céilí*, otherwise we'll be left facing it again this evening."

Owen rolled up his shirt sleeves. "We'll need a colossal mat to sweep this under!"

"Just chuck it down at the other end! This kip was already a walk-in tomb for bunk-beds before we arrived." But as Kieran himself seized a pile of rubble, a pointed object calamitously sliced through the palm of his right hand. "Geeaaarrrggh!!!"

The excruciating cry triggered all around coronaries. "W-w-wha-what happened? What is it?" Rory whimpered.

Kieran's haemorrhaging palm rose from the wreckage. "I've gashed my flaming hand on one of those bloody bed springs!"

"Is it bad?" Owen cringed.

"What does it look like? As if I'm planning a finger-painting master class?!"

The makeshift emergency services dived into action. "Right, first we need to stop the flow!" Owen asserted. "Rory, have you any bandages?"

"Rakes of them!" their well-resourced comrade said, whipping out his portable pharmacy. Two clicks, the clasps were up and the attaché case sprung open. But disaster dealt Rory a sudden clout. "You thieving maggots!!!" he hurled the open case onto the floor.

"What? What is it?" Owen cried. "I don't see anything!"

"Exactly! It's empty!"

"Hello, I'm still dying here!" Kieran prompted.

Owen rushed over to his holdall where he retrieved a depleted roll of Bottoms, Brown and O'Brien's Deluxe Quilted Kitchen Paper. "Take this! It's all I have left! But it should help for the time being!"

"Thanks," Kieran said, pressing the two remaining pieces against his hand.

"Now Rory, w-what's this all about?" Owen pointed to the attaché case.

"It's obvious, isn't it?" he huffed. "I've been robbed!"

"Are you sure the stuff didn't just spill out somewhere in your bag?"

"Positive! Look! Everything is gone! All my inhalers, antihistamines, bandages, painkillers and those lozenges I gave Kieran yesterday. So either you or he-"

"It couldn't have been us!" Owen exclaimed. "Remember, you were with either one of us at all times and that only leaves-oh God!"

Suddenly the truth reared it beastly head; more petty larceny at the hands of their custodian, and since no shoddy substitutions were made, it was a safe bet that the pandemic had mutated.

"That kitchen paper you gave me has reached saturation point!" Kieran snivelled.

"Sorry pal," Owen said solemnly, "I'm all out of supplies. You'll have to ask *her*!"

"No way!" he retorted. "We're not asking that demented despot for any favours!"

"Mother says that a bad cut can lead to gangrene," Rory warned.

"G-gang-what?!"

"Gangrene! First it turns black and then surgeons have to saw it off!"

"Stuff that!" Kieran resolved. "This trip has already cost me an arm and a leg and I'll be dammed if I'm going risk loosing a hand too!"

Peig was in her armchair sipping tea as Kieran clomped into the kitchen to confront her.

"Yes, what is it Cian?" she said, shiftily wedging something down the side of her armchair.

"Excuse me Mrs Sawyer, but I've cut my hand on one of your rusty bed springs!"

"Save us and guard us!" she prised herself from her chair. "Bring it over into the light and show it to me!"

As they met by the window, Peig grabbed his wrist. "Sur' that's nothing!"

"You don't think I'll need stitches?

"Stitches?! What would you have me do? Get out the old Singer there? Sur' it's only an auld scratch! But just to play it safe, we should cleanse it of any auld toxins."

Without warning, the old hack sunk her jaws into his palm and drew blood with incredible zeal. Horrified, Kieran wrenched his hand free, but her eyes flared and she hissed back with feline fury. Kieran wringed his eyes shut, as he tried to recoup what was left of his sanity. Surely this was a mirage caused by his own light-headedness or the flickering sunlight from a passing tractor? It *had* to be. Thankfully, as he opened his eyes again, the mere awfulness of normality was restored.

"Need any help?" Owen enquired, as he and Rory stepped into the kitchen.

"Yera no, we're fine," Peig re-evaluated the laceration. "Now all we need is a dressing of some sort."

"You *do* have bandages?" Kieran presumed.

"Goodness no! Those luxury outfits are only props for malingerers!" she replied.

The endless string of absurd lies left Kieran speechless.

"Here, leaves are good, aren't they?" Owen intervened with a handful of green vegetation.

"Where did you get those?" she peered derisively.

"Over there by the front door."

"What?! They're rhubarb leaves!" she belted them out of his hand. "They're poisonous! Deadly-deadly poisonous!"

Despite being berated at every hand's turn, Owen still wanted to help. "How about some more kitchen paper?" he suggested, with a nod to her display above the dresser.

"Don't you dare!" she spat.

When it became clear he could do no right, Owen faded quietly into the background.

"This'll do," Peig grabbed a sickly looking dishcloth from the clothes line.

"Are you sure it's hygienic?" Kieran said anxiously.

"Of course it's hygienic! I washed it only yesterday!"

"In what? A septic tank?"

"Whisht your auld jabbering while I concentrate on this!" she scowled, while folding the fishy article around his hand. "You! Orange-ball!" she pointed at Owen, who was noting a partially hidden carton jammed down the side of her armchair, "Don't just stand there! Fetch me a safety pin from the drawer of that dresser!"

Owen obliged, but found himself in a bind, as he opened the drawer. "Which one? They all look rusty!"

"Just bring one over!"

Selecting a pin with the least corrosion, he extended it to Peig. Although quite agile for a woman of her age, Kieran quickly discovered that she wasn't so nimble with small sharp objects. "Oh-ow-ow!" he howled.

"Pipe down lad!" she roared, fastening the dish cloth. "I'll fix you up with a drop of medicine to counteract that. Sur' I've often had a lot worse myself, over the time."

As promised, Peig plummeted to the depths of her green dresser, resurfacing with a large bottle, almost gothic in its distinction. Pouring a measure of silvery liquid into a teaspoon, she lumbered towards the patient.

"Open up!" she commanded.

Casting a wary eye over her 'drop of medicine', Kieran baulked as he spotted the label. "That's mercury!" he exclaimed. "No way! I'm not taking that!"

"But it's good for what ails ye!"

"Actually, mercury is said to cause harmful side-effects," Rory interjected, with a smattering of his encyclopaedic knowledge.

"Ah go 'way with your auld science fiction! Isn't it the same stuff they're using in all these flu injections, today!"

But Kieran was adamant. "Look! I'm not taking any and that's final! Besides, the label reads: *Use by September 1958*?!"

"Those auld expiry dates are just a scam! Now do you want any or not?"

"No, I said. No, thank you!"

"Well, no point in letting it go to waste," she sighed resignedly, before swallowing it herself. "See? Nothing wrong with it. Sur' we practically grew up on the stuff!"

"Well that explains everything," Kieran murmured.

"What's that?"

"Eh yes, thanks for everything!" he cautiously backed away.

But Peig grabbed the wrist again for a parting look at her handiwork. "I suggest you look after it for a few days. After that I'm sure it'll be fine."

"Eh it's quarter to," Owen advised. "Time to go?"

"Oh wait, we can't have you going out like that!" she cried, viciously wrenching the shirt-sleeve clean off Kieran's arm.

"What the hell was that for?" he wailed.

"Here!" she draped the flaccid rag over his hand. "I thought y'might be needing a sling?"

♣ ♣ ♣ ♣ ♣

On route back towards St. Millipede's hall, the students trawled through their landlady's latest anthology of transgressions. "It just goes from bad to worse!" Kieran raged. "And she wasn't just cleaning up in there, she was cleaning us out!"

"My games console has been nicked." Owen pouted.

"Ouch! They're like, what, a hundred quid?"

"Two hundred and forty nine, ninety five."

"Damn! And is that all?"

"No, my toothbrush has gone walkies too."

"Gross! What does she want that for? Still, by the looks of things, our teeth won't be getting much of a workout for a while. And do you know what the old hungah was munching on, before we left?"

"Yes, I saw them buried down the side of her armchair-"

"Jaffa Cakes! So, no prizes for guessing who strip-mined the teachers' pantry this afternoon! We get one Ginger biscuit while she keeps the tastiest treats for herself. All her endless poor-mouthing, it's absolute hypocrisy!"

Owen plucked a biro from his breast pocket. "Has anyone got a piece of paper?"

"Are you ready to draw up your last will and testament?"

"Not yet, but I do feel we ought to keep a record of all the missing items so far. We need as much ammunition as possible, for our report!"

"What report?"

"For Mrs Begley I guess, when she comes back!"

Kieran plucked a folded piece of ruled paper from his pocket. "Here's some-"

"That'll do. Now, what items have you lost so far?"

"Apart from what went up the chimney, yesterday?"

"I mean valuables!" Owen specified.

"Hey! Clothes *are* valuable! Especially when they're in limited supply! And now that she's tasted blood, I expect our time is limited too!"

"No, I don't think we're on any death list just yet," Owen reflected. "Otherwise she might have been stuffing us to the gills with those poisonous rhubarb leaves. That's some consolation, anyway."

"See here!" Kieran created a tiny aperture between his thumb and index finger. "I was that close to having a hole drilled in my head! It'll be leeches, next! If we live to see the middle of next week, that'll be of some consolation!"

♣ ♣ ♣ ♣ ♣

The trio encountered James and Jeremiah Buckley still beating the same patch of hedge as they approached the community hall. Fr. Tom Buttimer peered anxiously from the presbytery window next door, with a serviette stuffed into his collar and a glass of milk in his hand. As Kieran had pointed out, the affable cleric was no stranger to food. Pausing meditatively for a moment, Owen placed the pen and paper in his shirt pocket. "You two go on ahead," he veered towards presbytery, "I'll catch up with you later."

Kieran and Rory proceeded into the hall where the air was slightly more garrulous than the night before. Again, visibility was hampered by cigarette smoke, but there was no mistaking one angelic contour, arched over a text book at the other end. Sensing a tremendous weight being lifted, Kieran strutted straight over.

"Well-well-well, fancy meeting you here!" he piped frivolously.

Jennifer Begley lowered her book. "Yes, I thought all the noise and distraction would be a good study aid!" she replied. "And who, pray tell, is *this* charming young stud?"

"Eh?"

Her reference, to Kieran's disgust, was to the fifth wheel that had been glued to his heel for the past two days. "Oh you mean Goggle- uh, Rory?"

"Gogglarory? That's unusual!" she extended him a friendly hand.

"No, just Rory!" the po-faced teen amended.

"Oh, sorry."

"What a day!" Kieran sunk wearily into the nearest chair.

Resigning herself to the notion that her swotting had reached an impasse, Jennifer abandoned her study materials. "You're telling me! It was one caper after another in the exam hall today! This invigilator we've got is a right auld fraud- oh, what's that?" she pointed to the greyish cloth swathed around his hand.

Kieran bashfully concealed the embarrassing lump. "Uhm nothing, just a slight accident earlier."

"You're all misfortune, aren't you?"

"Yes and there's no let up!" he gawped fearfully, "Colic alert, at twelve o' clock! She's probably got me lined up as her dance partner again!"

"Tell her you're dancing with me, instead!" Jennifer gently squeezed his arm.

Kieran's throat went dry. "Really?"

Before the conversation could go any further, the liaison teacher cast her shadow.

"Ah Mr O'Dowd! Just a quick word before the *céilí* begins. Now, you may have anticipated dancing with me again this evening. But I firmly believe it's best for, eh, everyone, if we both mingle. Is that fair?"

"What? Oh, ehm, sure!"

"I understand your disappointment, but what you must appreciate is that I can't afford to give special treatment to *any* one of my students. Am I clear on that, Kieran?"

"Crystal!"

While her argument was cryptic, Kieran was simply relieved when she drifted away.

"What was that all about?" Jennifer said, with a bemused frown.

"Beats me! But what a stroke of luck! Oh, and I suppose that leaves you off the hook, if you want?"

"Fair enough, I'll ask Rory for a dance instead!"

"Ooh very dangerous! Rumour has it, his Mammy is a bunny boiler!"

"Shut your lying face, O'Dowd!" Rory retorted.

Miss Colic's inner angst was a ticking time bomb, which unfortunately exploded as she ploughed into Matthew Begley in the foyer.

"Ah there you are Miss Colic!" he said, softly catching her elbow, "I've been looking everywhere for you. Listen, I thought it best if we just cleared the air about what happened, earlier this afternoon?"

Scowling at the depraved breach of her personal space, the liaison teacher violently extricated herself. "How dare you take advantage of me!" she fumed. "And you a married man! How dare you!"

"What? I don't understand. I just wanted to-"

"I know exactly what you wanted, you filthy animal!"

"No- wait- you've got it all wrong!"

But Miss Colic was already edging towards the exit. "I don't know why I bothered coming here this evening. I don't feel at all well. I must go and lie down for a while-"

With his latest deputy now gone, so too was his plan to unload the *céilí* in her previously eager hands.

"It's an epidemic," Matthew whined, as he clipped to the top of the hall, while signalling to Jennifer with a circular motion of his index finger.

"Time to crank up the juke box!" she acknowledged. "Now don't go away!"

As Jennifer made for the stage, Owen returned from his brief excursion.

"What have you been up to?" Kieran enquired.

"I've just been chatting with Fr. Buttimer," he said smugly.

"Oh right, and did you manage to shake him down for another score?"

"No! But he did say that the nearest shops are in Knockyadown!"

"Well that's flipping useless for a start!"

"Not if he's promised to give us a lift in!"

A flicker at the end of the tunnel renewed Kieran's sparkle. "When? This evening? Tomorrow morning?"

"Saturday morning."

"Saturday?!! Are you willing to lay bets we'll still be alive by then?!"

"That's his next trip into town, which I reckon is better than nothing! At least we might pick up some half-decent nibbles for my birthday and there should be ample opportunity to call home!"

"Mmm, or jump on the next bus home."

"Anyway, he said he'll collect us around eleven, which is fine, as we've no classes at the weekend."

"Yes, that is good news I'll admit, *if* we can survive the next few days. Although, if we're desperate, we can always eat Rory."

Rory on the other hand cast a cloud over the favourable forecast. "I don't know if I'll be able to go," he bleated. "Mother is scheduled to visit on Saturday, but as we haven't been able to get in touch, I've no idea what time to expect her, and If I go, I'm afraid I'll miss her, entirely."

"Listen num-nuts, you can go kayaking down Niagara Falls, for all I care, so long as you don't scupper what could be our only lifeline from a slow and painful hunger strike!" Kieran tactlessly replied.

"Good evening ladies and gentlemen!" the principal announced from the podium. "Please grab your partners, as the *céilí* is about to begin!"

Kieran winced as an amateurish jolt suddenly deluged the auditorium with some tediously familiar music. "Is that thing stuck on the same number the whole time?" he asked Jennifer, as she stepped down from the stage.

"No! There are sixteen different tracks on that tape!"

"Sixteen? But they all sound the same!"

"No, we played them yesterday! Thrice over! Don't you remember?"

"Oh right, s-sure," he fudged, before quickly changing the subject. "Eh, and this is Owen, in case you haven't met?"

"Hello, I'm Jennifer!" she extended her hand.

On the point of returning the gesture, a large masculine hand seized Owen from behind and whisked him onto the dance floor. "You're with me honey-bun!"

It was the death rattle of his entire evening. "You've haven't been trying to avoid me, have you?" his abductor grilled.

Owen smeared *Vicks* around his nostrils to neutralise the stench of cigarette smoke. "No-no, of course not Ash-Ashley, I just was on my way to look for you."

"Oh good. Here, what's *that* stuff?"

"It's uhm, for my allergies," he replied.

"Oh yes, I'm full of ah-ah-allergies too!"

Unluckily for Owen, this was the moment Ashley chose to parade one of these oddities. Forcefully gripping his shoulders for support, she let rip a series of Richter-scale-registering sneezes. "Ah- ah- ahhhsssskkk! Ah- ah- ahhhsssskkk!" she roared.

Owen looked to his friends, in a silent plea for an intervention.

"Don't look so *ash*-en!" Kieran quipped, as he and Jennifer took to the dance floor.

"You wouldn't ha- ah- ah- hab a tissue, on you?!" Ashley beseeched.

"I, I'm just out of them, actually!" Owen peeped nervously.

"Anytig wid do, I'b desperate!" A square of paper jutting from his shirt pocket caught her eye. "I'll jus' borrow dis, if you dote mide!"

"What? No! That's my-" But his catalogue was already soiled.

"Oh sorry, was this your shopping list?" she paused to inspect her creation. "Here, do you want it back?"

"No!" Owen recoiled. "You keep it!"

♣ ♣ ♣ ♣ ♣

Grace, synchronisation and harmony were all the qualities absent during Matthew Begley's solo bash as *céilí* ringmaster, a truly dire effort that exposed his need to lure Catherine back into the fold. Nevertheless, a few hours in good company raised spirits, particularly Owen's, after Ashley unfolded a love letter, she assumed had been written expressly for her. But the warm bubbly feeling subsided, as our three friends prepared to settle down for the night in their dank and dreary dormitory. Tilting a magazine towards the window, Owen attempted to wring out the last of the fading sunlight.

"This is outrageous!" he groaned. "My eyes are shot to pieces!"

"I could go and ask if there's a candle available," Kieran volunteered.

"Be careful now, you might break the bank!" Owen cautioned.

"Yes, but I hear it's government policy to bale out worthless spongers."

As Kieran re-entered the kitchen, Peig was stacking the dinner plates in her dresser.

"Sorry, to disturb you again Mrs Sawyer," he ventured, "But there's no light in our room and I was wondering if I might borrow a candle or something?"

"Demands-demands-demands!" she sighed wearily. "Yes, there ought to be one knocking about here somewhere." A quick rummage through the dresser drawer yielded one long white candle. "Bring me the sconce, there!" she ordered.

"The what?"

"The sconce! Look! It's behind you!"

"Hah?"

Impatiently rolling her eyes, Peig swaggered over to fetch a candle-holder from the mantel. "That's a sconce!" she slammed it on the table.

Kieran watched in wonder as she hacked the top off the candle with a bread knife.

"How's your hand?" she enquired.

"It's fine!" he replied, keeping it well out of harm's way.

Surprisingly, it was the smaller portion that was inserted into the sconce.

"There you go lad," she said, "You needn't want for anything!"

Kieran stared pessimistically at the paltry night light. "Uhm, have you got a light?"

"Well, if you look hard enough, you might just find just the ticket over there!" she huffed tartly, pointing in the direction of the fire.

A trail of singed eyebrows followed Kieran as he returned to the dormitory, ten minutes later. Goody two-shoes had already gone to bed, though Owen was still by the window straining his eyes. "Is that it?" he threw down his magazine. "I shed more ear wax in a day than that!"

"Good!" Kieran slammed the door. "It needs an extension!"

Setting down the candle, Kieran was slightly miffed when one of his remaining sweaters turned up behind the door, and particularly so on finding a pair of his jeans hanging from the curtain rail. But when he found an entire heap of his clothes strewn among the bunk bed wreckage, Kieran's rabid butterflies returned for an encore.

"Uh, Owen? Have you done a spot check on your stuff, since the *céilí*?"

"Straight after that dollop of potato she called supper," he replied. "Nothing else taken. Why? She hasn't been dipping into *your* bag, has she?"

"Mmm, all my gear seems to be here."

"So what's the problem?"

"It's my *bag* that's gone," Kieran stated grimly.

10. Sticky Fingers

It was soul destroying to say the least, as more and more items began to disappear from the dormitory. Clothes, medicine and toiletries all slipped into the ether, while 'the big raid' of Wednesday afternoon, waved goodbye to the last of Owen's treasured tuck. Even more perplexing, was the reappearance of Kieran's bag, only to see it vanish again *and* eventually resurface once more, on Friday morning.

A picture of poverty in his pathetic bed, Kieran rolled over and slid his hand beneath his pillow. A pebble emerged where his miniature alarm clock should have been. The ghostly pilferer knew no bounds. Hurling the stone against the door in disgust, the crack roused Owen from his slumber. "Eh whassat?" he grunted.

It was at this point that Kieran noted the elusive holdall abandoned just inside the dormitory door. Battered, bruised and browbeaten, he limped over to investigate. This was a pale imitation of the clean cut teenager who left Dublin only days ago. Large black circles had formed beneath eyes, while his right hand had swelled to the size of a turnip. "What is this?" he peered inside. "It's full of earth! What does she expect? For me to clean it out before she borrows it again?"

"Don't tell me she's been doing the rounds again?" Owen groaned.

"Yes!"

"Didn't I tell you to put a chair up against the door?"

"Yes!!"

"And did you?"

"Yes!!!"

"Ah no! What's the damage this time?"

And as Owen dragged his feet to the floor, he focused on a pair of decrepit black shoes beneath his bed. "Who owns these?"

"Not mine anyway!" Kieran shrugged. "They're at least three or four sizes too big!"

Panic gripped Owen. "Wait a minute, wh-where are my runners? No-no-no! Please! Not my Reeboks!" But a quick search confirmed his suspicions; Owen's footwear had been substituted. "That's it Kieran! This can't go on any longer!"

"Well hopefully Mrs Begley will be back today," Kieran yawned, with dog-eared optimism.

"There's no guarantee of that!" Owen exclaimed. "What about this friend of yours, Jennifer? Maybe she can put a word in with the principal?"

"Oh, did I not mention she's his daughter?"

"What?! Now he tells us! So what are you waiting for?"

"Hassle her during her final exams? She'd love that, I'm sure!"

"All right, scrub that. Now I know you said he isn't up to much, but surely the principal himself can't ignore all three of us marching down to his office and spelling out every last sordid detail of the past five days?"

"Worth a shot, maybe."

"Right that's settled and let's do it today before we become a statistic!"

Owen's nostrils suddenly flared. "Here, do you smell something?"

"I think it's those rotten shoes!" Kieran twitched his nose.

Hastily discarding his newly allotted footwear, Owen set about getting dressed. "Look at my pyjamas! I'm practically swimming in them now!"

No longer concerned by his milieu, Kieran tipped the dirt and rubble from his holdall into the middle of the floor. "Maybe she's been coming in and trying them on during the day?" he suggested.

"Please! I'm already feeling queasy enough as it is! And, if she thinks I'm going to wear what could very well be the late Mr Sawyer's shoes, she's very much mistaken! No way. No way in hell!"

But since Owen was halfway there, minutes later, he was tottering into the kitchen with the outsized pair flapping from his heels. Kieran, meanwhile, was literally staggered by another scurrilous development. While attending to a simmering pot, the old troll was shamelessly parading his very own navy blue robe, one of the many casualties of Wednesday's big raid. "That's my robe you're wearing!" he cried.

The landlady turned and shot him an icy glare. "How could it be yours if I'm wearing it?" she hissed.

"Of course it's mine! Look! It even has a Florida Keys Hotel badge right on-"

Peering closer again, Kieran merely encountered a gnarly hole where the trademark insignia had once been.

"You listen to me, Motormouth," she quivered, wielding her authority with a wooden spoon. "I've had this same robe for nigh on forty years! It was a present from my eldest son after he first moved to America! See here, it even has my name written on the lapel!"

Some coarse white lettering was submitted as proof of ownership; though plausibly shed more light on what happened to Owen's missing bottle of Tip-Ex.

"Just because you write your name on something doesn't automatically make it yours!" he retorted. "Your son didn't give you that, you just swiped it from my room!"

"How dare you!" she seethed. "Oh! You must have bad parents that they didn't teach you some proper manners! Very bad parents! Have you lost sight of the fact that you are a guest in my house?"

From the corner of his eye, Kieran spotted Owen making a facial gesture that seemed to hint at the futility of their quarrel. Grasping his friend's subtle message, Kieran suddenly abandoned his protest. "Sorry, my mistake. My robe is nothing like yours."

The u-turn momentarily surprised her. "What?"

"Come to think of it, mine didn't have Peig Sawyer written on it either."

"Of course it didn't!" she said, returning to the hearth. "Now sit down there and eat your breakfast!"

With the conviction that they were simply biding their time in custody of this duplicitous wretch, the pair shrunk quietly into their chairs. Rolling up with her customary dusky cauldron, she proceeded to mete out her usual meagre portions.

"There are only two of you this morning!" she eyeballed the empty chair. "Where's that other gangly looking geek with the goggles?"

Despite having had ample time to familiarise herself with her students, Peig stubbornly snubbed their rightful names.

"I dunno," Owen said, with a cursory glance towards the dormitory. "Shall I take his breakfast down to him?" But as his hand reached for the third bowl, it fell foul of her wooden spoon.

"No!" she snapped. "If he's too lazy to join us, then he can't be badly off!"

With the hoi polloi catered for, the aristocrat stole away to the privacy of her own quarters, to gorge herself on biscuits, no doubt.

Owen massaged his hand and frowned at the bland meal presented before him. "Mmm, yummy!"

"Yes, mashed potato three mornings in a row is stretching it a bit," Kieran moped. "She wasn't joking when she said, that's all we'd be getting from now on. And by having it in a bowl places it in the breakfast category, I presume?"

Kieran scooped up large dollops of potato and crammed them into his mouth. "Pothaaaathoooo!" he groaned, in a zombie-like fashion, allowing the purée to ooze back onto his plate.

"Oh God!" Owen wearily kneaded his eyes.

"Am I making you sick?" Kieran burbled.

"No! I just can't shake off the image of *her* rolling around in my pyjamas!"

After forcing down some much needed sustenance, Kieran and Owen swung by the dormitory again, to investigate Rory's absence from the breakfast table. They were somewhat surprised to find him still in bed, with a sheet drawn over his face.

"What's going on?" Owen cried. "If you don't get a move on, we'll be late!"

"I'm not going!" grunted the spectral mound.

"Eh? Why not?"

"I want to go home!"

Kieran threw his arms in the air. "Oh yes, I knew this was coming! From day one, I knew this was coming!"

Owen, on the other hand, was a little more sympathetic. "What's brought this on, all of a sudden?"

"All of a sudden?! I haven't thought about anything else since I arrived in this flea pit!"

"We're *all* in the same boat! But you don't see *me* complaining!" Kieran argued.

Rory furiously cast aside the blankets. The skin surrounding his eyes was an angry red, signifying either severe distress or advanced scabies. "You haven't done anything *but*, for the past week!" he bellowed.

Flabbergasted by this unfounded backlash, Kieran looked to Owen for backup. "I've been a *rock*, haven't I, Owen?"

"Actually O'Dowd, you do go overboard at times," Owen ventured cautiously. "And your three thousand Euro speech is getting so old."

"But it's true, isn't it? Anyway if he remains here, she'll have his head on a platter by teatime!"

"Exactly!" Rory glowered. "I just can't hack spending another fortnight in what I can only describe as a penal colony! Plus, still no news from home! No phone call, no text message, not even a postcard!"

"That is strange," Owen said musingly. "It's been several days now and there hasn't been so much as a birthday card from my folks. You don't suppose she's been snaffling the mail too?"

"I dunno, but it's worth a mention to old Begley later on," Kieran said, while dealing a hard blow to Owen's upper arm.

"Ow! What was that in aid of?"

"Your birthday beating, just in case I forget!"

"Thanks a lot! As if I haven't been mauled enough over the past few days!"

Owen's nostrils flared again. "That sour stench is back! And this time it's lethal!"

"I can't smell anything," Kieran said, with a quick sweep of the dormitory.

"All right Rory," Owen refocused, as the smell drifted away again. "We're just as anxious as you to ditch this joint. But if your Mum doesn't arrive tomorrow morning, worst case scenario, you should at least be able to call her from a public phone box in Knockyadown. Besides, we'll only be there an hour or two!"

"Mmm, seems logical," he conceded.

"In the meantime we need all your support in confronting the principal today."

With a submissive sigh, Rory reached for his glasses.

"Good man!" Owen said, anxiously checking the time. "And listen, I hate to rush you, but today's *Murder She Wrote* marathon starts in twenty-five minutes!"

♣ ♣ ♣ ♣ ♣

Slinking through the kitchen, the trio were accidental bystanders to another nauseating exhibition. This time, the old woman was licking the breakfast bowls clean. It was only when Kieran hit the awkward door latch that she glanced up like a startled field mouse. "Oh lads, I thought ye'd already gone," she wiped her face on a tea-towel.

"Eh, yes we're just leaving now."

"Well hurry up and get out! I'll be locking up, shortly!" she spat, as embarrassment turned to anger for having let her guard down.

"What a filthy dirt bag!" Kieran scowled, as they bustled into the garden.

"Shhh!" Owen cautioned, looking over his shoulder.

Clear of the Peig's front gate, the trio spotted a pair of familiar silhouettes loafing on the nearby stone bridge. "Don't tell me that's Dave Keogh?" Kieran squinted.

"And Ambrose Cleary by the looks of it," Owen confirmed.

"God, what do they want?" Kieran muttered, while in the same breath hailing the duo with a tepid smile. "Hey, top of the morning! What are you up to in this neck of the woods?"

"Just back from a fishing trip with old man Buckley," Dave said, as he and Ambrose met them halfway. "Up at the crack of dawn, we were!"

With Peig Sawyer as their only benchmark for local hospitality, Kieran couldn't imagine the benefits of such an outing. "Hate that," he commiserated.

"Ah no! It was deadly!"

"See here!" Ambrose motioned. "All this is Buckley's land, apart from the graveyard and that gammy looking bungalow."

The inadequacy of Peig's cottage being spouted from the mouths of peers was like bucketing vinegar over an open wound.

"Yeah, I think yer man was more interested in showing off his spread than catching any actual fish!" Dave grinned. "He's a real character, if a bit too needy, at times."

"So what's the scoff like?" Owen queried.

"Criminally good! Colossal Irish breakfasts every morning! Prime roast beef for lunch and massive steaks for supper in the evening! It's like having three dinners in one day! And every type of potato imaginable; jacket, roast, baked, boiled, mashed and chips. We've potato coming out the wazoo!"

"I know that feeling," Owen added numbly.

"Who does all the cooking?" Kieran asked, while wiping away the white scum that was beginning to encircle his lips.

"The wife, and she's a dab hand at it too."

"Actually Dave, I think she's his sister?" Ambrose noted.

"Yeah? Well maybe she's both?!" Dave smirked. "But the grub is fantastic!"

Dispirited, Kieran forged ahead. "But apart from that, it's nothing to write home about?"

"You must be joking! The auld lad is a real Jack of all trades! For starters he's got a pub in the village, not to mention a huge collection of vintage cars-"

"He's got a dozen racehorses!" Ambrose added with wide-eyed admiration. "Come to think of it, he's promised to take us to the track tomorrow morning and I'm sure he wouldn't mind if you lot wanted to tag along?"

"No thanks, we've got plans!" Owen pouted.

"Where's Morrissey?" Kieran enquired. "Is he still sick?"

"I haven't seen him since Monday." Dave shrugged. "He just stays in his room all day."

Rory stepped into the fore. "Wait, you've each got your own rooms?"

"Well sure, don't you?"

"Of course we do!" Kieran snapped, with a brooding glare intended to lure his housemates into a collaborative deception.

Dave cast a sceptical eye over the nearby premises. "Didn't we see you coming out of that house below?"

Kieran couldn't deny the blatantly obvious. "Well yes, but-"

"It doesn't look all that big to me!"

"Well *scale* isn't really the issue-"

"There's a big extension out back!" Owen blurted.

And with the support of at least one of his comrades, Kieran accelerated into spoof hyperdrive. "Yeah, that's right! It's a listed building and that's why the front looks so old. But it's dead cosy inside and we have our own lounge and kitchenette! And you know, after a long hard day, we just like to chill with a couple of beers in front of our sixty-inch LCD wide-screen television with surround sound and one thousand channels."

"You've got satellite?" Ambrose gawped.

"S-sure, why not?"

"I can't see any dish," Dave squinted.

"It's down in the basement!" Owen declared. "It's a whopping expensive one and must be kept out of sight, in case it gets nicked!"

"The basement?!"

"Yes, there's a massive cellar!" Kieran embroidered. "With a big rumpus room to boot! We've everything down there, a snooker table, kitchenette, the works!"

"Ooo! *Two* kitchenettes?" Dave observed, with mounting cynicism.

"Eh? Yeah. Our landlady always keeps the fridge fully stocked with cider, giving us the full run of the place!"

Hot on his heels was Owen with a further omnibus of ludicrous embellishments. "The best part of it is that she has two- no *three* drop-dead gorgeous daughters who happen to be lap-dancers in Knockyadown! And most evenings they like to practice their latest routines on us, you know, like a test audience. So it's basically like having our own private nightclub!"

While Ambrose Cleary lapped up every last detail, Dave Keogh was reluctant to swallow this outlandish yarn. "I suppose you wouldn't mind if we dropped in ourselves for a sneak preview, this evening?" he probed.

"Of course not- Oh wait, today's Friday. No, they'll be working tonight, I'm afraid!"

"That's convenient."

"Yes, sorry about that. We'll probably just settle down to watch a flick instead."

Dave's major nitpick was that he couldn't visualise the sanctimonious and strait-laced Rory participating in such debauched revelry. Suspecting that he might be unwilling to perjure himself, Dave decided to put the human polygraph to the test. "So Rory, is there any truth regarding the decadent nightlife in that cottage below?"

"Yes! Our *Bean An Tí* is a sinful, sinful woman!" Rory stated with conviction.

Suddenly, Dave no longer knew what to believe.

"Buckley's only got a lousy four TV channels!" Ambrose whined. "Do you think your landlady would mind if we dropped by some evening to watch some movies?"

Kieran scratched his temples, endeavouring to appear wistful. "Well she's in Sligo at the moment, for a potato picking conference, but I'll ask her when she gets back."

"Here! All this talk of television and we're going to be late for *Murder She Wrote*!" Owen fretted over his watch.

"Not necessarily!" Dave gestured reassuringly. Just then, Curly Buckley's golden chariot loomed into the foreground, heralding its arrival with several galling blasts of the horn. As the vehicle halted alongside, Ambrose wasted no time in commandeering the front seat. Dave, meanwhile, opened the back door and extended an open palm. "What are you waiting for? A written invitation?"

"You're offering us a lift?" Kieran gawped.

Dave poked his head through the window. "That's okay, isn't it Mr Buckley?"

"Work away lads!" replied the bristled beetroot, behind the steering wheel.

The trio seized the opportunity and leapt into the back. "Nice shoes O'Brien! Are they your Grandad's?" Dave noted the downgraded footwear.

"Mind your own business!" Owen retorted.

As the car began to glide along, Dave hoisted a large plastic container from the floor. "There's some drinks here in the cooler if you'd like one?"

Kieran could barely mask his glee. "Yes please!" he smacked his lips.

"Now it's just soft-drinks, I'm afraid. Nothing like the quality you've grown accustomed to, I expect?"

"Wh-whatever's going!" Owen drooled. As Dave opened the treasure chest, the eyes of the three destitute urchins instantly lit up.

"So whereabouts are ye lads staying?" their driver enquired, as the drinks were distributed.

"With Mrs Sawyer down the road," Kieran replied.

Curly Buckley spewed a lump of tobacco which hit the wing mirror. "That lighting cow?!"

"They've got satellite television, Mr Buckley!" Ambrose declared.

"They have, I'm sure!" Curly quivered sceptically.

Placing the cool contours of the bottle against his roasting cheeks, Kieran basked momentarily in its arctic radiance. It was a luxury he might have taken for granted a mere five days ago, back in civilisation. Owen and Rory, meanwhile, toyed with the idea of rationing, but fearing someone else might get their grubby paws on it, swiftly plunged into their beverages.

"So Owen, what are the names of these three drop-dead gorgeous girls of yours?" Dave asked, raising a curious and mischievous brow.

"Eh?"

Immersed in the invigorating effervescence of his drink, Owen O'Brien had almost forgotten his subterfuge. "Oh the girls! Yes-yes! Well now let me see, there's ah, eh, ehm, Ime- Imelda! And, an- a- Anne! Yes, *Anne* and ah, ghe- hghe- feh- ss- ch- je- ja- ehm-" Glancing briefly at Kieran's flushed face, inspiration struck. "Je-*Jennifer*!"

Kieran clenched his teeth in condemnation, but alas, the damage had already been done. Wavering between belief and disbelief, Dave Keogh shook his head as he reached for a bottle of orange. "Your own games room? Booze? A home cinema with one-thousand TV channels *and* lap-dancing? Looks like me and Ambrose drew the shortest straw!"

"Yeah, dead jammy!" Kieran murmured despondently, once more looking at his soft drink and at the surrounding opulence.

♣ ♣ ♣ ♣ ♣

The cold war in the Begley household had reached a stalemate. No amount of charm or cajoling could coax Catherine Begley from her industrial action. With her snow white pallor and tangled black hair, she was gradually developing the form of a banshee, signs of self-abandonment partly attributable to a steady staple of lurid daytime television chat shows.

Alone in the lounge, Catherine was curling up with a box of Black Magic to watch the latest Olivia Plunkett extravaganza when she was discommoded by a tap on the window. Cropping her head above the sofa, her eyes rolled as she saw a young man bedecked in a maroon baseball cap and matching polyester blazer. He was grinning foolishly and pointing eagerly to a bouquet of flowers cradled in his arm.

"Can somebody get that?!" she wailed. "Jennifer? Derbhla? Daniel? Anybody?"

Resentfully setting aside her chocolates, Catherine made a tardy attempt to make herself presentable, as she shuffled towards the door. "Yes?" she sighed wearily, swinging it wide open.

The young man extended the bouquet. "Hi, I have a delivery from Peter's Pansies for Catty Bagslady?"

Matthew belatedly came thumping down the stairs, while fumbling with his necktie. "Did somebody call? Oh good! It's the florist!" But his enthusiasm waned as he spotted this particular bouquet. "Just a minute! I ordered Roses, not Lilies! And isn't that a funeral wreath?"

"Very appropriate! Don't you think?" Catherine remarked.

Matthew's face drew a bemused blank. "Where's Peter? He usually delivers in person!"

"Away in Mauritius," the envoy replied. "I'm filling in and that's the last of our current stock, I'm afraid."

"I'm not surprised!" Catherine said, eyeballing the vast floral shrine, adorning the opposite end of the lounge. "He can easily afford a holiday, after the mint he's made on you, Matthew!"

You blithering idiot!" Matthew raged. "Does my wife look dead to you?!"

The harangued messenger tilted his cap back. "You want my *honest* opinion?"

"You cheeky little browel!" Matthew seethed, slamming the door shut, just as the young man was extending his palm for a gratuity. The courier responded, in turn, by disgorging his own dividend on the Begleys' front room window, though it would be sometime later before anyone discovered that little mess.

The past week had been a rollercoaster ride of scant thrills and many spills for the principal. The hectic schedules, the extra curricular activities and, since Miss Colic had gone to ground, an increased reliance on one objectionable invigilator, were all trying his patience to the last. But Matthew knew he must endure, in order to reinstate his standing as, not so much as a 'walking' principal, but a 'feet-up' one.

"Would you like me to put those in some water, my sweet?" he fawned.

Catherine dropped the bouquet on the coffee table. "You can dip them in Champagne with your French tart, for all I care, boyo!"

Matthew forcibly bit his tongue, "Certainly my dear, uhm, and are we feeling any better today?"

Returning to the security of her sofa, his malingering wife emitted a listless cough as her only answer.

"You do realise, I'm practically on my own, since Miss Colic baled out on us?" he broached.

"I hope it isn't because you made a pass at *her* too?!" Catherine glowered.

Ill-equipped with the poker face to deal with such jibes, the worry fissures around Matthew's eyes expanded. Would she ever have believed that quite the opposite was actually true? Unlikely. Furthermore, the possibility of her being prejudiced by a certain agitator remained a constant threat. "Right, well, time to go and open the school!" he hurriedly gathered his effects. "Now, where's Jennifer? Jennifer! Are you ready to-?"

The teenager made a deviously punctual entrance from the kitchen. "I'm here!" she declared.

"Right, let's get go," her father reached for the door handle.

"Have you had your breakfast?" her mother enquired.

"Yes, I'm eating it," Jennifer ventured, despite evidence to the contrary.

"My thoughts will be with you all day," Catherine said, amplifying the volume with the remote.

The pair had no sooner climbed into the silver Laguna when Candy O'Shea, heaving with excitement, cavorted up their driveway. "Matty! Matty! Have you heard the news?" she cried.

"What?" he replied jadedly.

"Half past seven this evening! Half past seven!!! That's when it's all happening over at Evelyn Schalplatten's!"

Matthew pondered for a moment before catching her train of thought. "Oh yes, the wife's brother mentioned it, last night," he slurred.

"And how *is* poor Cathy? I heard she's been a bit down in the dumps lately."

"She's taken up permanent residence there."

Plucking a thermos from her wicker bag, Mrs O'Shea jiggled it with zeal. "Right-oh, well I thought I might drop in for a little chinwag and a drinky-poo!"

"Knock yourselves out," he said, slamming his foot on the accelerator and reversing down the drive.

♣ ♣ ♣ ♣ ♣

In the absence of Mrs Begley, Miss Colic and, more understandably, Mrs Breslin, and with the principal limited to guest appearances only, the master classes in 4C were a vacuum of culture and higher learning. In fact, their temporary surrogate had become into a permanent stand-in. Sadly, the old cathode ray tube was beginning to buckle under the strain and eventually fizzled out during a pivotal scene in *Murder She Wrote*. The minor fireworks display was greeted with an ovation, but soon, the sixty-odd students grew restless again.

"That's it!" Owen bemoaned. "Now we're truly sunk!"

Fate made a mockery of his words, when another substantial burden literally sunk itself on his lap. "How are ya' puddin', I thought ya' might appreciate some company?"

"Ashley!" he yelped. "Ah ah-aren't there p-plenty of other fr-free chairs available?"

"C'mere to me," she said, smouldering with the eroticism of a double decker bus. "I overheard your friend yesterday what's-his-name, Kerrin? mention that it's your birthday tomorrow!"

Owen glared unappreciatively at the unwitting turncoat.

"So, we'll have to organise a special treat for the birthday boy, won't we?" she said.

"What? No! There's no need! Honestly! I won't even be around!"

A nudge, courtesy of Kieran, interrupted their delicate courtship. "I think this may be a good time for our chat with the principal?"

"Too right it is!" Owen squirmed free from his captor.

Luckily, a debilitating fit of coughing took hold of Ashley, leaving her in no position to object.

As Kieran and Owen rounded up their third Musketeer, they encountered the usual dragging of feet. "I'm still not convinced that a confrontation will bear much fruit," Rory groused, before a large pineapple collided with the back of his skull.

With upped stakes, a brutish new tournament of 'pass the fruit' had erupted, while as always, the studious Rory remained a favourite foil. Picking up the pineapple, Kieran contemplated eating it, but deliberated too long and lost it amid a frenzied scrum. "Come on, let's get out of here!" he said, brushing a footprint from his chest.

With fresh enthusiasm, Rory fled the fracas with his comrades.

♣ ♣ ♣ ♣ ♣

Placing his ear against the office door, Kieran O'Dowd submitted a gentle knock. "Mr Begley? Hello? Sir?"

"Are you lads looking for me?" hailed a voice from further down the corridor. A lone figure, with a large cardboard box in his arms, stood in the staffroom doorway.

"Eh yes, we'd like a word please. It's very urgent!"

"Right, I'll be with you in a moment," the principal said, mulling over his sizeable load. "The office isn't locked, so you can wait inside if you like?"

"Okay, thanks!" Kieran acknowledged.

As soon as they were inside, Rory obediently sat in one of three chairs facing the principal's desk, a sense of discipline lacking in his two counterparts.

"Let's have a quick shufti before the old man gets here!" Kieran pulled open a filing cabinet drawer. "Teachers always have a decent stash of goodies on hand!"

But the only thing Kieran uncovered was some disturbing news. "Here, check out the timetable for extra curricular activities!"

And as Owen ran his finger down the schedule, the fear welled up in his eyes. "Crap on a stick! It's wall to wall *céilí*s, for the next two and a half weeks! And get this, it's double *céilí* tonight, tomorrow *and* Sunday! And every other weekend too!"

"One night per week isn't so bad!" Kieran cried. "But this is seriously messed up!"

"I shudder at the thought of another one! My ankles are blue and my feet are so covered in blisters that I can barely walk! And these new shoes are no picnic either!"

"It's the music that disturbs me! You'd have to be on drugs to enjoy that garbage, day in and day out. Every tune is exactly the same, diddle-e-eye, diddle-e-eye and fiddle-e-eye!"

"At least *you* don't have to dance with a gas boiler, every evening!" Owen grimaced.

Out of the blue, Rory cleared some phloem from his throat. Startled by what he thought was a warning signal, Owen hastily slammed the filing cabinet shut, failing to consider Kieran's ailing hand resting on the drawer.

"Aaaagggh! You idiot!!!" he howled.

"What? What have I done?

"You've mangled me!"

"S-sorry I-I didn't realise-"

As the dishcloth-covered hand was bandied about, Owen flinched in revulsion. "Dear God, it's that same stench I caught earlier in the dorm! It was coming from *you* all along!"

Kieran was in denial mode. "No it isn't!" he retorted, before a brief waft of the festering stump almost struck him blind.

"Oh it's fine, is it? There's nothing wrong with it, is there?" Owen jeered.

"Maybe it does need a f-fresh dressing," Kieran gagged.

"Or a fresh hand, by the smell of it!"

"If you two are finished arguing, it may interest you to know that there's a telephone over here," Rory interjected.

The inquisitors almost tripped over themselves as they scrambled towards the principal's bureau. There, nestled snugly amongst the clutter, was an antiquated apparatus with an old-fashioned dialling mechanism. Sadly, another obstacle proved to be their undoing. "What's this silvery thing?" Kieran pointed to a cylindrical object secured to one of the numerical cavities.

"A lock, I should imagine," Rory shrugged.

"That figures, the sneaky beggars. And I suppose it needs a key?"

"I expect so."

The echo of footsteps in the corridor locked the gang into position.

"Sorry to keep you waiting," Matthew Begley ripped through the office, "But it's just been one thing after another, this morning, what with looking after our distinguished guests and tending to the candidates in the exam hall!"

Flumping into his swivel chair, the principal proceeded to share his seemingly trivial inconveniences. "*Then* I had to rush home again to take the young nippers to school, before making another pit-stop at the wholesalers on the way back here!"

Observing Begley's twitching nose and probing eyes, Kieran did his utmost to stifle the errant hand.

"And that takes me to you gentlemen. So what's on your mind?"

Owen immediately set the ball rolling. "Our *Bean An Tí*!" he declared.

"Listen! We demand either a transfer or a ticket home!" Kieran cut straight to the chase.

Straight away, Matthew had an inkling of the troublemaker in question, but nonetheless consulted his trusty organiser, for reference. "Ah now lads, isn't that a bit drastic?" he said, leafing through its pages, "And your names are?"

"Owen O'Brien!"

"Kieran O'Dowd. And uh- Rory Waters," Kieran added, for the benefit of their third member, who's brain had taken a short sabbatical.

A brief annotation in the file confirmed Matthew's suspicions. "Ah yes, I see you're with Mrs Evelyn- I mean Peig Sawyer." Though he prayed it wouldn't happen, based on the woman's execrable track record, he knew such a visit was inevitable. Damage control was normally Catherine's division, a department with a huge remit, thanks to a certain firebrand. Now, Peig Sawyer was back with a vengeance and *he* was the last line in defence. "All right," he braced himself for impact. "Is there a specific complaint against Mrs Sawyer, you wish to relay?"

"A *specific* complaint?" Kieran said, looking in earnest, at his friends.

"She clobbered me!" *"She torched my clothes!"*

"She stole my medicine!" *"She swiped my shoes!"*

"My bed collapsed!" *"His bed crushed me!"*

"Sock in the butter!" *"Eating from the floor!"*

"Scurvy!" *"No Television!"*

"No amenities!" *"No phone!"*

"No phone signal!" *"Creepy crawlies!"*

"Making me eat corned beef!"

Inundated, the principal placed a finger on his pounding temples, to stem a vein rupture. "Gentlemen! Please! Take it easy! I'll take everything you say on board, but please, just one at the time!"

And so, one by one, the students recounted and chronicled their landlady's repertoire of crimes against humanity. When all was said and done, Matthew slumped back into his chair, cracked a few knuckles and drew a long contemplative breath.

"I can appreciate how daunting this must all seem, but it's still quite early in the game. By now, I'm sure you'll realise how vastly different the pace of country life is. But from here on in, it's a matter of settling in and simply enjoying the ride."

Kieran and Owen were stunned; quite unable to fathom how their counsellor could defend such a horrendous chain of events. Even more astonishingly, it was Rory who finally hammered the nail on the head. "Mr Begley, you appear to be merely sounding off an assortment of platitudes foisted upon us almost a week ago. Perhaps you wish to avoid the subject, or perhaps you are genuinely delusional, but I assure you, this is not a game and the terror we have experienced is very real."

"Yes, what h-he just said!" Kieran added, with a new-found respect for his friend.

Matthew, of course, was fully aware that he had been skirting the central issue, but it was a shroud to hide the fact that his own position had been compromised. Moreover, as he tried to compose an appropriate reply, the omnipresent overlord herself marched straight into the office, unannounced, unsolicited and unwelcome. Horror-struck, the three juveniles looked on as she heaved straight towards the principal's bureau.

"Look here lad," she began, "I've just been down to the canteen for my tea-"

"Oh yes and you found the biscuits, all right?"

"I found them all right, the very ones I told you *not* to get!"

"But I thought you specifically requested that variety?"

"No, I told you! I hate those! They're too hard on my teeth!"

"Oh, I see."

"So tell me, what in the blazes am I to do with fifty packets of Ginger Nut?"

"Fifty packets? Well I'm sure there are others who would appreciate- Just a minute Mrs Sawyer, who's keeping an eye on the students in the exam hall?"

"Ara they're fine! Sur' amn't I just on my way back there now. Only I needed to air my disapproval with your lackadaisical efforts in the catering division!"

As she made her way towards the exit, Peig gave a cursory glance to the three superfluous bodies sitting opposite the principal. Oddly enough, there wasn't hint of recognition. Had she failed to distinguish them outside their usual environs? Or was she simply being discourteous? More than likely though, she just didn't give a damn.

"I'm afraid it'll be Monday before I can make another trip to the wholesalers, Mrs Sawyer," Matthew grovelled.

"*Monday*?" she huffed, "Sur' I might be dead by then!"

All four flinched as the door slammed shut behind her.

"God willing!" he groaned reproachfully as a tuft of hair came away in his hand.

Slowly and evocatively, Kieran arose from his chair. The measure of white visible in his eyes was a fair indication of looming insanity. "I see it all now! You're in collusion with the devil herself aren't you? Go on! Admit it! What else would she be doing here?"

The principal mirrored Kieran's movements, to exceed his height. "Peig Sawyer is here today in her official capacity as an exam invigilator, an affiliation that was pre-arranged long before your arrival on the scene!" he declared.

Although something of a revelation, this was incidental to their case.

"And isn't the important thing that you all have your health?" Matthew attempted to moderate his tone.

"Look at us!!!" Kieran flashed his putrefying hand. "We're teetering on the brink of extinction here!!!"

The principal struggled to keep his breakfast down. It was clear that the gravity of their situation was worse than previously imagined, though he had hoped the old reprobate might have made some effort, this time around. Intriguingly, Matthew prowled over towards the door, opened it a crack, glimpsed briefly into the corridor and closed it again before returning to his bureau. There, he reached to the inside pocket of his tweed blazer and produced his pocket diary. "Now tell me, at what time do you have your dinner in the evenings?" he enquired.

"About six, I guess. Why?" Kieran frowned.

"If you could call it *dinner*," Owen muttered.

"Right, I've an important house-call this evening," Matthew noted. "But tomorrow is, let me see, Saturday, yes, why not? Perfect!"

Still in the dark, the students exchanged inquisitive shrugs.

"Now occasionally surprise inspections are carried out in certain households," Matthew elaborated, "Though normally it's to monitor student behaviour. But let's say, just between *you* and *me*, that I may happen to be in your area around dinner time tomorrow evening? I'm not promising anything, mind, but if conditions are as bad as you say, we shall have to pursue some course of action. Is that fair?"

Though his confidence was uninspiring, the proposal was met with approval.

"Remember now, mum's the word. Any questions?"

"Yes, is there any postal service around here?" Owen enquired.

Matthew furrowed his brow, but glancing at their file again, it suddenly clicked. "Ah, come to think of it, it's probable that your post may have ended up over at Evelyn Schalplatten's. I, or rather, the Academy ought to have re-directed your mail after that lady dropped out of the running."

"Don't you mean dropped dead?" Kieran amended.

"Oh, you've heard?"

"Yes, and frankly, we'd rather have taken our chances with a corpse."

"Not this particular one," Matthew murmured. "But rest assured, if there's any post for you, I'll have it sent on."

With a conclusive hand clasp, the principal drew a line under his arbitration. "So if there's nothing else gentlemen, thank you for coming and I'll see you all very soon!"

Everyone arose, apart from Rory who was still hooked on the telephone.

"There is one thing," he declared, "Might we be allowed a quick call home?"

Looking back towards the bureau, Begley bit his lip. "I'm sorry, but it's locked, I'm afraid."

"I'll gladly pay, of course!" Rory added, fearing this might be a contentious issue.

"Well it's *Mrs* Begley, you see. She's got the only key."

With another glimmer of hope snuffed out, Rory dragged himself to his feet.

As Matthew opened the door, they were hit by the escalating clamour emanating from 4C. "What's going on down there?" he gasped. "Don't they realise we've exams going on just down the hall?"

"Oh yes, your telly blew up." Kieran gently broke the news.

"Oh no! I'd better fetch some Plasticine or the Snakes and Ladders, to keep them occupied!" Matthew cried, clutching his keys as he galloped down the corridor.

Chewing over their negligible victory, the boys turned in the opposite direction.

"I suppose our hands are tied, 'til tomorrow!" Owen concluded.

"Ho-ho-ho-hoooo!" Kieran chuckled mordantly. "That money-grabbing, thieving, scheming, two-faced, two-timing, whoring cow!"

"You mean Peig?"

"No, Rory's mother. Yes, Peig! Who else? Her greedy hoofs are stuck in every pie! She's making a killing all over town! Jennifer mentioned her crackpot invigilator a few times, but I never imagined-" Kieran trailed off as they approached a large wooden panel door, with a poster of The Department of Education's rules and guidelines for state examinations. "That's the exam hall!" he whispered, sniffing and pointing feverishly towards the door. "Yes, she's in there all right, I can smell her!"

"Are you sure it isn't just the hand?" Owen rolled his eyes.

As an act of retaliation, Kieran exerted his injured fist at the door, but was dealt a harsh comeuppance, when the door abruptly swung out, thrashing his hand and compelling him to his knees. Aptly, the perpetrator was none other than the invigilator herself, entirely oblivious to the havoc she had wreaked, while traversing the corridor to the ladies'. Seconds later, Jennifer emerged from the hall, muttering some profanity under her breath, though mellowed, as she spotted Owen and Rory.

"Hello, what are you up to?" she whispered.

Closing the door, she encountered Kieran directly behind, writhing in agony.

"What's wrong with him?" she cried.

"Septic hand," Owen explained.

"Oh for goodness sake!" Throwing her bag over her shoulder, she grabbed Kieran's arm. "Come on, you're going down to the infirmary with me!"

Owen and Rory instinctively tagged along, but found themselves consigned to the corridor, as Jennifer shut the infirmary door in their faces. "You two wait outside!"

Inside the medical centre, Jennifer dashed about gathering cotton wool and disinfectant, while Kieran tendered his paw and whimpered helplessly.

"You shouldn't have left it go so long!" she scolded.

"It was all right until the wicked witch gave it the kiss of death!"

"Right show it here to me- ah look! Who in their right mind would wrap an old mutton cloth around an open wound? That thing is a breeding ground for bacteria! And a rusty safety pin, too! No wonder you're delirious!"

"I'm not! It's that invigilator of yours, she's-"

"This is going to hurt *you* more than it hurts me!" Jennifer exclaimed, as the cotton wool doused in antiseptic loomed large.

"Shouldn't that be the other way 'round?" Kieran gulped fearfully.

Seated on a bench in the corridor, Owen and Rory had been listening attentively to the audio presentation. Just as they were contemplating a momentary lull, Kieran's status was updated with a gut-wrenching roar. Fortunately, Kieran survived and moments later, emerged from the infirmary with Jennifer, by his side.

"This is fantastic!" he grinned. "I can actually move my fingers again! Here, you really ought to go for medicine, Jennifer!"

"Yes, I really fancy my chances in this kip," she griped. "Oh well, never mind. If I cram a bit more by this afternoon, I may get tenth choice on my college application form."

"I'm certain you'd make a very good doctor anyway!"

"Thanks for the vote of confidence!" she bestowed him with a peck on the cheek. "Now was there something else, you were going to say?"

"Was there?" Kieran said gormlessly, raising his hand to touch his face.

"No? Right, I'll see you later at the *céilí*!" she said, heading down the corridor.

"See you," he hummed dreamily.

"Oooo! There you go!" Owen joshed. "Private consultations now? Eh? Lucky you!"

"Stop that!" Kieran retorted. "Jennifer is the one shred of decency you're likely to find in this nest of scorpions, thieves and beggars! Now come on, let's go!"

But Kieran's sense of direction left the others bewildered.

"Where are you going? The classroom's the other way!" Owen declared.

"Stuff that! I'm heading down to the teacher's lounge to fill up on Ginger Nuts!"

11. Pillage Of The Damned

The general ambience in Peig's cottage provided an excellent stimulus for a brisk walk immediately after dinner, and often during. Thus, following their evening collation, Kieran, Owen and Rory opted to idle away an hour on the banks of the River Sualach. Although little more than a glorified stream, its gentle trickling was blissfully therapeutic, something these laden students needed in abundance. Seated on the grass verge, Owen removed his ungainly footwear and plunged his feet into the cool water. "Ah, that's a relief," he sighed.

Kieran, who had been washing his face only inches away, looked on in disapproval. "It's contaminated now!" he sneered.

"Actually, water purifies very quickly," Rory said, listlessly flinging in a pebble.

Twitching an eyelid in half-acceptance, Kieran dunked his comb in and moistened it to slick back his hair. "It must be nearly *céilí* time, I suppose?" he sighed wearily.

Owen, however, was far from enamoured at the prospect of yet another shindig. "No more bloody *céilí*. I'm whacked!"

"Can't you just sit it out in the toilets again?"

"Is it me, or does it reek of sour milk in there?"

"It's definitely you!"

"Well forget it! Because no matter how long I wait, the human vice-grips will be ready to snare me, the second I emerge!"

Kieran stood up and dusted himself down. "Sur' that Ashtray is a fine lump of a girl!"

"You marry her so!"

"What the hell is she up to now?"

"Something drastic, I expect, thanks to your mouthing off about my birthday tomorrow!"

"No, the old bag I mean. Look!" Kieran pointed upstream to where Peig was pitching the contents from an old white bucket into the water.

"God! I hate to think what might be in that!" Owen gasped, swiftly withdrawing his feet.

"I shouldn't worry," Rory affirmed. "As I said, water does purify very quickly."

"Not quick enough!" Kieran hastened to add. "Any fallout from that old goat will have a half-life of ten thousand years!"

♣ ♣ ♣ ♣ ♣

By the time our friends arrived back at the village, the *céilí* was already underway. The repetitive strain of 'diddle-e-eye' could be heard blaring away, quite a distance from St. Millipede's hall. And it wasn't just beginning to grate on Kieran's nerves.

"I'm not up to this!" Owen paused in the foyer. "I've a splitting headache and my feet are screaming blue murder!"

Alarmingly, the horde inside had reached a record level of boisterousness; unsurprising, given the absence of Mr Begley or any other senior staff member. The only semblance of management was the principal's daughter, seated on the stage steps, casually filing her nails on an emery board.

"Hi! They're a bit wild this evening, aren't they?" Kieran greeted.

Astonishingly, Jennifer failed to acknowledge him, but arose and handed her cassette player to Owen. "Would you mind this for me, please?" she formally requested. And with one swift lunge, she struck a devastating blow to Kieran's solar plexus, before storming out of the auditorium.

Bowled over, in every sense of the word, her hapless victim tottered about clutching his abdomen, panting desperately, as he tried to regain his breath.

"O'Dowd, you filthy pig! What have you been up to?" hailed a glib voice.

Still reeling in agony, Kieran looked up to find Dave Keogh, towering above him and grinning mischievously. "Go away!" he retched.

"Here! That girl that just left, her name's Jennifer, isn't it? Listen, I thought you were only spoofing about those dancers, but she's a stunner!"

Suddenly, it clicked. Dave and Ambrose had been spilling the beans on his alleged nocturnal exploits. Unfortunately, the last thing he had wanted to do was to alienate the only compassionate soul in this pitiless corner of the universe. *Oh my God! What have they been saying to her? What have I done?*

"Come on, you can tell *me*! She's one of those dancers, isn't she?" Dave persisted.

Kieran thinned his lips. "Back off, I said!"

Dave retreated, but as usual, remained collected. "Damn it, O'Dowd, always a scab."

As Kieran regained his composure, he turned on Owen. "This is your fault!"

"What? *Me*?"

"You and your cockeyed stories about lap-dancers! I mean like, what possessed you to name Jennifer as an accomplice?"

"Now look, *Jennifer* was just a random name that sprung to mind! Besides, you were the one egging us on, to boost your precious ego! Isn't that right, Rory?"

"Keep me out of it," Rory repudiated.

Utterly drained from an unrelenting series of disasters, Kieran was in no frame of mind for further quarrelling. "Forget it! I'm heading out for a while."

"Oh right," Owen set down the cassette player. "I'll just leave this here, so."

Kieran swung around again and lorded over his disciples. "Alone, if you don't mind! Contrary to popular belief, we're not joined at the hip! So please, just stay here and have some fun by yourselves, for a change."

"Fun?!!" Owen pouted incredulously, as Kieran hobbled towards the exit.

A tap on the shoulder roused him from his momentary stupor. Already fearing the worst, Owen reached for his liniment. But as he turned around, he merely encountered Ashley's two cronies, Natasha and Sharon. "How are ya, love?" Natasha croaked, between drags of her cigarette. "Ash says she can't make it this evening, cos' she's sick."

A smile began to form. "Sick, you say?"

"Yeah, doctor says she's got 'cute bronchitis."

"Thank heavens! I needed some bit of decent news!" he said, relaxing on the steps.

Noting their friend's malady was a font of rejoice, the girls were slightly disgusted.

Out in the foyer again, Kieran found himself buttonholed by Ambrose Cleary.

"Hey! Have you asked your landlady yet if we can call down to watch a film some evening?" he enquired.

"Eh? Oh eh, no, she's still in Carlow for the ploughing championships."

"But you said earlier she was potato picking in Sligo?"

"Did I? Uhm, yeah, same difference," Kieran backed towards the exit.

As he turned into the yard, Kieran found Jennifer sitting on the outer wall, facing the road. Unsure, precisely, of how to proceed, self-vindication was his top priority.

"Take a hike, jackass!" she said brusquely, on hearing his crunching footsteps.

"Come on now, you haven't even heard me out yet?"

"I've heard plenty!"

He paused briefly for the cathartic outburst. "I thought you were decent!" she inevitably blurted. "A notch above the other Neanderthals!"

"But I am! Nothing's changed!"

She finally looked at him, but only in condemnation. "Oh really? Well how do you account for the rumours that you've been carousing with lap-top-dancers every night?"

"You mean *lap*-dancers? And that's all they are. Vicious rumours!"

"The next thing I know, all kinds of lewd proposals are being hurled by friends of yours who are under the impression that I'm some sort of stripper!"

"They're no friends of mine!" he avowed. "And those stories are completely bogus! Can you honestly believe that I'd want to go clubbing after mincing around here, for two or three hours every night?"

"Don't not knock the *céilí*, it's traditional and it's fun!"

"I'm simply pointing out that I wouldn't have the energy for anything else!" *Given that I've also been running on empty for the past five days.*

Jennifer weighed up the facts. "That part did seem a bit far-fetched. But still, offering me chump-change if I'd strut my stuff for them!"

"Look, I'm dreadfully sorry, but this all began as an innocent lark just to impress the lads. Owen suggested, for a laugh, that our landlady had a night club down in her basement and that her daughters were, you know, exotic dancers-"

"They fell for *that*?"

"Hook, line and sinker! The rest they just assumed! You have my solemn oath that you weren't deliberately implicated in any of it."

"Hmm, well-"

"Anyhow, to my knowledge our *Bean An Tí* doesn't even have any daughters, nor a basement for that matter. In fact, Mrs Sawyer barely has room to swing a cat in that god-awful bungalow of hers."

Jennifer's demeanour segued from one of frustration to one of incredulity. "Mrs *Sawyer*? *Peig* Sawyer?"

"That's ri- oh *yes*, that's what I meant to say earlier on. I figured you know her, since she's your exam invigilator!"

"In a small town, Kieran, knowing everyone and every intimate detail of their business is a matter of civic duty! Especially a cretin like Pig Sawyer! But how did she end up as your hostess? The last I heard she was struck off the roster after some major upheaval last year!"

"Eh? Well I assume it was because Mrs Schal-thingy kicked the bucket?"

"Ah right! Maybe so! Oh, but listen, I'm so sorry about that battering! You've really been cutting out a rough time of it, lately!"

"You don't know the half of it!" Kieran clutched his gut. "Come on, let's go for a walk! I wouldn't mind giving my ears a break from that din, if at all possible?"

Having established his innocence, Jennifer was eager to make amends. "Absolutely!" she said, extending her arm. "So tell me, what kind of music do you prefer?"

"Anything, so long as it has more than one note!"

Setting some distance between themselves and the community hall, Kieran quizzed Jennifer on his monstrous adversary. "So you say the old bag was struck off? Had this anything to do with two girls who stayed with her last year?"

"Where on earth did you hear about that?" she gasped.

"Are they dead? Did she starve them to death?" he frenetically suggested.

"Funny you should mention it," Jennifer said pensively. "But a rumour circling the school last September suggested those two girls ate each other to stay alive."

Kieran pounded the air with a clenched fist. "I knew it! I just knew it!" But in few short steps, he lurched to a halt. "Just a minute, how's that possible?"

Jennifer's impish smile told all.

"Oh, *Et tu Brute*?" he said, slightly mortified.

"Others say they were so cold and hungry, that they killed a cow for its meat and crawled inside its guts for warmth. Unfortunately, they all ended up in sausages after the cow was taken away to be slaughtered!"

"Go ahead, make light of the situation!" Kieran said grimly. "But she really *is* an absolute tyrant and we really *are* bordering on starvation!"

Jennifer puckered her brow. "What? What are you talking about?"

"Let's just say she's dipped her hand in our bags so often that she must be suffering from repetitive strain syndrome. And after the goodies ran out she helped herself to the actual bags!"

"No way?! We all know she's as mean as dirt, hence the stories, but that's sacrilege! Did you try hiding the stuff?"

"Where? There are no cupboards, no drawers, nothing!"

"What about burying it in the garden?"

"Yes, a pity we didn't think of that in time!" Kieran conceded.

Jennifer shook her head at the audacity of it all. "This is madness! Did you mention this to my father?"

"Of course."

"And?"

"The U.N. envoys aren't exactly rolling in with the humanitarian aid."

"That bad?"

"There are whispers of a surprise inspection tomorrow evening," Kieran said, stroking his nose. "So we'll have to wait and see how that pans out. You don't suppose she's got some kind of a hold over him?"

At first, Jennifer resented the family slur, but having been privy to a portion of some very odd behaviour, was forced to give credence to the idea. "You couldn't find a worse exam invigilator! Up and down like a Jack-in-the-box, she goes, never sits still! And if she isn't peeling vegetables, she's running out to the toilet every five minutes. Sometimes, she's gone for a whole hour, before returning with a suitcase filled with potatoes."

"That explains a lot!" Kieran growled. "So, those two girls, you've no idea?"

"All I know is that they disappeared mid-way through the course last year and there was a big hush-up afterwards. If you like, I can ask my parents about it, though I'd be surprised if they told me anything."

"Please do! The sticks are awash with savages! And I don't want to be joining the ranks of the disappeared."

"Hey that's not fair on some of us!" Jennifer objected.

A low hum of multiple voices from a nearby garden diverted their attention. On looking around, they spotted several animated heads jutting from an overgrown hedge. "What's going on over there? A garden party?" Kieran probed.

"That's- oh God! That's Mrs Schalplatten's house. And it's a party, all right," Jennifer glimpsed at her watch. "A Plunder Party!"

"Eh?"

"A Plunder Party, alas, is one of our finest and proudest traditions, one I'm sorry to say, that gives weight to your *savages* theory."

"But what is it?"

"Well to truly understand a Plunder Party one needs to experience a Plunder Party. Come, you may as well have the grand tour." Taking his arm again, Jennifer casually escorted Kieran through the gate and into the late Mrs Schalplatten's garden.

The front lawn was ablaze with excitement. A gathering of fifty or sixty people were roaming around and chatting agreeably. They all appeared to be waiting in anticipation, though for what, remained a mystery. The garden itself was bordering on unkempt, though a neat row of begonias alongside the garden path, suggested that it had been cultivated until fairly recently. Jennifer ducked as she spotted her father chatting to the O'Sheas, or rather, Candy O'Shea appeared to be burning his ear about something.

"There's my Dad! He skipped this evening's *céilí*, to come to this! And I'm supposed to be back there running the show. Well tough luck, buster, I'm here now."

"All the same, we should try to keep out of his way," Kieran urged.

"Yes, you're probably right."

The pair skulked over to a relatively secluded part of the garden in the hope of remaining inconspicuous. "So what's it all about?" Kieran probed.

"As you know," Jennifer began, "Mrs Schalplatten doesn't get about as much as she used to-"

"Yes, I gathered that much."

(As it happened, being metabolically challenged was no impediment for Evelyn Schalplatten, who was on a leisurely cruise down the Ganges River, at this moment).

"Right, and when a villager like Mrs Schalplatten, who has no known relatives, passes away, all her worldly belongings are dispersed among the local populace."

"Ugh, that sounds a bit sick!"

"Naturally, there is a grace period as a mark of respect, after which a time and date are set for the Plunder Party. Around here, that usually amounts to about thirty minutes after the funeral."

"Oh man, that's low!"

"Otherwise, the state cleans up and nobody gets squat!"

Despite being revolted by such ruthlessness, it didn't take Kieran long to consider the practicalities. "It all seems so civilised, who decides who gets what?"

"Ah! This is where it gets exciting and where the plunder element enters the equation. Once the starter pistol goes off, it's a free for all. First-come, first-served, every man, woman and child for themselves!"

"These shenanigans can't be on the up and up!" he surmised. "What would happen if the *Gardaí* stumbled upon this little caper?"

"See for yourself!" Jennifer pointed towards the gate.

Kieran observed in slack-jawed bewilderment as a uniformed member of the *Garda Síochána* plodded into the garden. Furthermore, the accoutrements on his tunic alluded to his seniority. "That's Superintendent Leo O'Meara," Jennifer confirmed.

Kieran kneaded his eyelids, as he tried to get to grips with a chain of corruption that branched right to the top. "Crooks!"

he whispered frenetically. "Nothing but a shower of conniving crooks!"

"Leo's my uncle, actually," she revealed.

"Eh? Oh no! Sorry! I didn't mean him personally," he dithered, neurotically kneading his entire face.

"Don't worry, I agree!" she corroborated, "I think the whole affair stinks."

The next plunderer to grace the party, truly sent a cold shiver down Kieran's spine.

"Oh would you credit it? Look! It's Queen of the Pixies, Lady Godiva herself! Never misses a trick, does she?"

Peig Sawyer bulldozed her way through the crowd, lugging a cumbersome silver box, half-a-dozen iron rods and some coiled auburn wire. Casting a suspicious eye over this paraphernalia, the policeman accosted the elder on her way up the garden path.

"Now Mrs Sawyer, I hope we haven't been helping ourselves to a sneak preview?"

"Not at all lad, I've only just arrived, and these are a few bits 'n' bobs I've brought with me."

"Oh right, well carry on," O'Meara granted, looking away as the old woman submitted the most grotesque of scowls.

Nearby, Candy O'Shea was getting into a flap over punctuality. "It's gone half past now! Why doesn't he give the all clear so that we can get on with it and go home?"

"I expect it won't be long now," Matthew affirmed.

"Still, isn't it great crack Matty? They really should have more of these. I've a second cousin getting married in July, and I'm half hoping to pick up something for the wedding while I'm here. I'm really beginning to hate shopping! Now I do know she had a nice silver tea service, from the few occasions I called around. Indeed, I've had my eye on that, this long time. Worth a pretty penny too, I should imagine!"

"Now Candy, I wouldn't raise my hopes too high," her husband, Bernard interjected. "Old Buckley there may well have already got his mitts on it!"

"How do you mean?" she frowned, measuring up her competitor who was casing the parlour window. Undoubtedly assuming nobody else was watching him, Curly Buckley was stealing the occasional and discreet glance inside.

"Sur' wasn't one of his young-fellas the first on the scene? And if the father got wind of anything like that, he'd have been around in a shot, to get it," Bernard hypothesised.

"I don't know about that," Matthew said broodingly. "If he's already had his share of pickings, he'd hardly be sniffing around for sloppy seconds."

The enlightened O'Shea's hummed in harmony.

"So are you in the market for anything, yourself, Matty?" Mrs O'Shea enquired.

"Not really, although the wife asked me to keep an eye out for a lamp, if I see one."

"Oh yes? There's a lovely brass lamp inside all right. A fine antique one, just on the right hand side, as you enter the parlour."

"Okay, well, ehm, thanks very much-"

Two shrill blows of a police whistle brought an immediate hush over the crowd.

"Good evening and thank you all for coming!" Superintendent O'Meara announced. "I promise not to delay you much longer, only to apologise for the general hold up. You might say we experienced a few technical difficulties!"

The crowd chortled charitably, though a little nervously, given the strange disappearance of the former resident. Nevertheless, they were all poised for action. "But from what I hear, this one promises to be well worth the wait! And so, without further ado, let's get the festivities underway!"

Verifying the correct time, O'Meara raised the starter pistol. "On your marks, get set."

With a thunderous crack, a ravenous horde descended upon the dormer cottage. The force unleashed by the mighty rampage made instant kindling from the front door; though the astute bypassed that, making their way through the front window, courtesy of Curly Buckley and a wayward brick. Within a matter of seconds, looters were already fleeing the house, hauling tables, chairs, sideboards, fireplaces and indeed, the kitchen sink. Flabbergasted by such a radical display of collective voracity, curiosity still got the better of Kieran O'Dowd and he ventured over for a closer look.

"Where are you going?" Jennifer enquired.

"In for a quick peek?"

"Oho! You're on your own then and watch your back! There've been fatalities at these events before!"

"Thanks for the tip!" he gulped.

Inside it was sheer mayhem. Everywhere, people were grabbing, thumping, tearing, thrashing, trashing and literally ripping the heart from this homestead. Polarised in the battle to pocket the plumiest pickings, it was a startling metamorphosis, from a paragon of civility, to the epitome of impropriety. A pair who began stripping the carpet from opposite ends of the stairs, quickly found themselves in midst of a tug of war, as they met in the middle.

Armoured with a mahogany coffee table, Curly Buckley almost gouged Kieran's right eye, as he cleaved across the hall. Deeming this to be a man of discernible taste, Kieran trailed Curly into the kitchen where straight away, the linoleum beneath began to levitate. Soon, the actual floorboards were rising, either for the want of timber, or in the expectation of finding some vast fortune beneath. Amidst the mêlée was Mrs O'Shea, rifling through cupboards and drawers, despite the fact, that her wicker basket was already brimming with silverware. Curly Buckley filled his trouser pockets with cutlery and spotting an old biscuit tin above the refrigerator, made a dash for that too. On the verge of opening of the tin, the tycoon was sidetracked by some high jinks in the back garden. "What's that Sawyer woman doing prowling around out there?" he roared.

Suddenly, half a dozen others also dropped what they were doing and swarmed around the window to investigate. "You can be full-well sure that one is always on to a good thing!" Mrs O'Shea declared.

Rising to his tiptoes, Kieran could just about decipher the old codger pottering about outside, with her iron rods, auburn wire and silver box.

"We'll soon see about that!" Curly bellowed, thrusting the back door open and bearing down on his archenemy. Several curious bystanders, including Mrs O'Shea, followed him out onto the patio, while Kieran opted to observe from the relative safety of the kitchen window.

"What's all this about?" Curly Buckley demanded, though realisation was already beginning to dawn. Seemingly, the crafty sprite had been using her tools to erect an electric fence, effectively annexing the large field above Mrs Schalplatten's house.

"Keep back, if you know what's good for you!" she snapped. "This is my property now!"

Curly's chest swelled in defiance, he didn't take kindly to orders, least of all from a stunted little runt like Peig Sawyer. Unfortunately, Peig's electrically charged barrier wasn't quite so pernickety about its victims and as Curly veered too close, his groin became the beneficiary of an unpleasant jolt. "Agh! Damn and blast ya!" he howled, hobbling back several paces. "Now look here woman, this is the height of nonsense!"

"Go on away home lad, sur' it must be way past your bedtime!" she sneered.

Some tittering at the rear caused his blood pressure to soar. "Oho! You listen to me here, now," Curly quivered haughtily, brandishing an index finger for emphasis, "You won't get away with this!"

Before the spat grew uglier than these two old rivals, Leo O'Meara arrived on the scene. The Superintendent sported a large purple bonnet on his head (a gift for his wife, perhaps), though even more ostentatious was the full-length fur coat draped over his uniform. "Is there a problem here?" he enquired.

"Hah?" Curly grunted, briefly preoccupied by the disturbingly fetching ensemble. "Oh yes! Look! This auld shleeveen here has cordoned off that field below!"

"A land grab?!" O'Meara frowned, surveying the solid acre. "Begod! I wish I'd thought of that myself!"

His crimson countenance besieged with bitterness, Curly Buckley appeared to be on the brink of a cardiac arrest. "What? Surely that's illegal?!"

"And your point *being*?" the Superintendent observed, with a piercing glare, immediately forcing the objector to concede defeat. "As far as I'm concerned, there never *was* a field behind this house!" the official mediator ruled. "Only a front garden, for the sake of appearances."

Peig allowed herself a rare smile. "Thank you very much Superintendent!"

"Not at all. Just doing my duty, and maybe you can take me for a spin in your new aeroplane, one of these days!" he quipped, with a nod towards the corroding World War II aircraft, converted to a chicken coop, in a corner of the field.

"Oho yes! I will just!" she teased. "And for the benefit of those who may be interested, this field and all its riches are now on sale to the highest bidder!"

The only feedback was a murmur of indifference from the cluster, as they dispersed to resume their pillaging. Envious, perhaps, that the woman had done her homework, Curly Buckley hurled his biscuit tin onto the patio in abhorrence and stormed off with his mahogany coffee table and jingling cutlery. Unbeknownst to him, as the tin hit the ground, its contents unfurled at the feet of his opponent. Peig Sawyer's eyes bulged as they homed in on this beacon, a rolled up wad of banknotes. Promptly snatching the roll, she kissed and winked at it before stuffing it down her blouse. From the kitchen window, Kieran O'Dowd watched in utter dismay, quite unable to fathom how Lady Luck could persistently smile upon such an abominable wretch.

At the front of the house, Jennifer had been patiently awaiting his re-emergence, when her father opened the parlour window, despite it no longer holding any glass. Sliding an elegant antique lamp onto the lawn, Matthew inevitably spotted his daughter sauntering aimlessly about the yard. "Ah Jennifer!"

he beckoned. "Can you come in a minute? There's a grand colour television in here, practically new and just perfect for the school!"

As he closed the window again, an alarming disparity suddenly struck him. "Hang on!" he yelled, cropping his head through the empty frame, "Why aren't you down at the *céilí*?"

"Don't worry. It's in good hands," she affirmed.

♣ ♣ ♣ ♣ ♣

Slumped lethargically across the stage steps, Owen O'Brien's fingernails were providing the famished teenager with his most reliable source of nutrition of that day. Equally indolent, Rory, seated at the platform's edge, had created a makeshift ear muffler from the hem of the velvet curtains. Ten minutes earlier they had fallen foul of a group of rogue dancers who, recklessly, knocked them to the floor. With their strength sapped from the lack of proper food, neither had the remotest inclination to rejoin this sadistic brawl.

As they plucked wooden splinters from their palms, Owen and Rory noted the impeding approach of Damien Nolan, ringleader of the 'intelligentsia' circle (aka, the scumbags). Short in stature, and even shorter in temperament, Daimo's permanent frown was surrounded by a mountainous expanse of acne. As per usual, he was flanked by his faithful cohorts, the tall Jason (Locko) McLochlann, renowned for his agility, but lack of intellectual prowess, and the heavyset Sean (Higgo) Higgins, renowned for his lack of agility *and* lack of intellectual prowess. The intelligentsia had rode in late, and as such, had missed out on much of the unsupervised revelry. Spotting the cassette player at Owen's feet, led the posse to the assumption that he had been deputised. "Where's de headmaster?" Daimo grunted.

As one never knew what to expect from the chief instigator, Owen instinctively went on the alert. "I haven't seen him all evening!" he replied.

Daimo swept the auditorium with his usual derogatory squint, before focusing on the cassette player again. "Well enough of this bleedin' garbage, for starters!" he picked up the tape deck. "It just goes on and on and on and on!"

Once the music stopped, the entire *céilí* collapsed, and a chorus of condemnation arose from the floor. "What's *this* thing?" Daimo ejected the cassette.

Owen and Rory exchanged bewildered glances. "It's uhm-an audio cassette?" Owen ventured hesitantly.

"A what?"

"It's what they used before CDs," Rory suggested.

Yet, there was no hint of recognition in Daimo's intimidating stare.

"Somewhere between eight-track and *iPod*?" Owen offered, with bated breath.

Finally a flicker. "Oh right!" he said, allowing the tape to slip through his fingers and drop to the floor.

"Careful!" Owen protested. "Brake it and you'll land us all in trouble!"

Daimo clicked his fingers at Higgo. "You heard what the man said!"

But instead of retrieving the tape, Higgo dropped a large Doc Martin on it, not once, but ten times. After it was well and truly pulped, he kicked it over to Locko who picked it up, un-spooled it and thrashed it about like a lunatic for a few moments. The unravelled heap was returned to Daimo who stuffed it into the open cassette player and ultimately landed the completed masterpiece in Owen's hands.

"There you go, as good as new," he squinted.

"Thanks," Owen peeped nervously.

"Oh, and breathe a word of this to anyone and I'll hammer ye!"

"My lips are sealed," he quivered.

Silence reigned as Daimo swaggered to a nearby microphone and switched it on. Following a tap to make certain it was live, a pair of headphones and a small device, were produced from his tracksuit pocket. Using the lead from his headphones as a coil, Daimo attached the apparatus to the microphone. With the flick of a switch, St. Millipede's hall was teeming with the strident reverberation of heavy metal. Following a euphoric ovation, the *céilí* resumed with a traditional dance, *Baint An Fhéar*. It was a jarring juxtaposition, but nobody seemed to care.

"Make sure that player doesn't fall off the mic!" he warned.

"Yeah sure," Owen replied, eager to see the back of them. Allowing the philistines a moment or two to dissolve into the rippling mass, he breathed a sigh of relief. "Isn't it clever how they replaced one type of mindless repetition with another?" he said wistfully. "Daimo, Higgo and Locko, why do all scumbag names have only two syllables and always end in 'O'?"

"I expect the similarity is less taxing on their brain," Rory shrugged.

12. The Spoils Of War

With the dormer cottage stripped of its assets, all that remained was an empty shell. The Plunder Party had past its peak and the majority of looters had bolted with their prizes. Jennifer Begley, tiring of waiting, deemed it safe enough to venture indoors. But as she prepared to step inside, her father bounced forth, heaving a black bin liner, bursting at the seams with tacky trinkets. "Look Jennifer!" he said excitedly. "I've collected all these old biros and note pads she had lying around the house. It'll save a packet come next September!"

"Gosh! You've hit the mother-load there," she facetiously replied.

"Indeed I have!" he accepted the remark at face-value. But as Matthew wandered over by the parlour window to reclaim the lamp, his face sank. "Where's the television? Don't tell me you didn't get the television?!"

"Fine, I won't!" she sneered.

"Ah no! I told you I needed that for the school!"

A heated diatribe was circumvented by the emergence of the O'Sheas, Mrs O'Shea lugging a fortune in silver and Mr O'Shea embracing a twenty-four-inch colour television, confirmation that Matthew's trophy had been lost. Right away, Candy cast an eye over the brass lamp. "There you are Matty. I see you got your lamp and like I said, isn't it a grand one?"

"I see you struck uhm, silver too," he eyed up the contents of her wicker basket.

"Oh would you believe it," she rolled her eyes in disenchantment. "The set was incomplete! A lovely little pepper shaker, I remember it as clear as day. But there was neither trace nor tidings of it! It's heartbreaking! Absolutely heartbreaking!"

Matthew rummaged through his blazer pocket. "I found a pepper shaker, as it happens," he yielded a small slightly tarnished cylinder.

"That's it!" Candy avariciously snatched it. "Where did you find it?"

"Hey, now just a minute! On the parlour table, if you must know, but that's mine, fair and square-"

"All right, let's deal! What do you want? Anything at all!"

Matthew's telling glance towards the television set, tipped his hand and Mrs O'Shea instantly pinpointed a bargaining chip for her beloved shaker.

"Bernard! Give Matty the television there!" she snapped.

But the speedy negotiations had gone over her husband's head. "What? But I thought you wanted this for-?"

"Give it to him!!" she screeched.

"Fine!" he surrendered.

Matthew, naturally, didn't want to appear overly enthusiastic. "Fair swap, I suppose, although I am a bit weighed-down at the moment?"

"No problem, Bernard will drop it down to the house for you!"

"I will?"

"Yes, you *will*!"

"That's great, thanks a lot," Matthew twittered contentedly.

"Isn't that what good neighbours are for?" Mrs O'Shea winked.

The O'Shea's departed with waves and smiles, though as soon as they were out of sight, Matthew dropped the façade. "Sorry Jennifer, that pepper shaker was intended as a graduation gift for you. But sur' who knows, we might be seeing it again, one of these days."

"What would I want with- hang on, what do you mean?"

"Well the O'Shea's are getting on a bit."

Jennifer suspiciously eyed her father. "You can't be suggesting- ah now! I know they don't have kids of their own, but they *do* have nieces and nephews for goodness sake!"

"Hey look, as far as I know, Mrs Schalplatten has some bigwig son and daughter-in-law living in Brussels and yet, nobody bothered their backsides to contact them!"

Utterly nauseated, Jennifer raised her arm in protest. "Not another word! Or I'm calling the Criminal Assets Bureau!" she said, stepping inside the house.

Pondering on his motley collection of ill-gotten gains, Matthew sensed a smattering of guilt as he spotted Mrs. Shalplatten's begonias crushed to a pulp in the stampede. Frowning as yet another pair of feet added to the carnage, he looked up to discover that they fittingly belonged to the local plod. Although the hat and fur were gone, the superintendent had acquired a box of ladies' shoes.

"How do' Matt?" the policeman hailed. "I see you've cleaned up nicely!"

"I suppose I have," Matthew acknowledged, deciding to steer clear of remarking on his brother-in-law's variation of a recurring theme. "Actually, I wonder if she's any decent bath taps? All my own are corroded to feck."

As Jennifer traversed the hall from the parlour, she was almost mowed down by her father, as he dashed towards the stairs. Her brief exploration culminated in the kitchen, where she found Kieran gazing vacuously into the yard. A cupboard door dropped off its remaining hinge, crashing onto some broken glass, giving them both a start. As she hobbled across the razed floor, Jennifer noticed the old crone patrolling the back garden, scratching herself in a most un-effeminate manner.

"Dear God! There's your friend outside!"

Kieran shook his head in despair. "I have never ever seen such a shameless exhibition of greed, debauchery and wilful destruction."

"Did you get anything for yourself?"

"A tin of spaghetti," he sighed.

Upstairs, the thumping and crashing reached a pinnacle with an alarming and ferocious roar. "What's going on, up there?" Kieran looked towards the ceiling.

"I dunno, but it sounded like my father," Jennifer grimaced.

Within a flash, Matthew came pounding down the stairs, trailed by a bathtub containing both James and Jeremiah Buckley. Clearing the front door by a whisker, he ploughed straight into the nettles, luckily escaping the torpedo. Amid flying sparks and debris, the bath screeched to a halt halfway down the garden path. Kieran, Jennifer and the remaining looters cropped their heads from an assortment of crevices to investigate. "We'd better go, before it all comes crashing down on our heads!" Jennifer decided, observing smouldering burn marks on the hall floor.

"Back to St. Millipede's?" Kieran said anxiously.

"We could go to the beach?"

"Is that not miles away?"

"I know a short cut. But if you'd prefer the *céilí*?"

"The beach! The beach!"

Having decided to quit while he still had a pulse, Matthew gathered his booty. As he approached the front gate, he spotted a partially concealed post box in the undergrowth. Had it not been for the dense foliage, this too would have been lifted during the raid. Bound by a promise to a trio of students, and oblivious that one of them was cutting across fields to God-knows-where with his daughter, Matthew raised the flap. All letters and parcels for Kieran, Owen and Rory were collated into his perforated plastic bag, while anything that looked remotely like a Belgian postmark was given a wide berth.

Unfortunately, Matthew met his Waterloo on his route home, via the parish presbytery, where he unavoidably encountered the Parish Priest, clipping the outer perimeter of his hedge. An absentee at the Plunder Party, Fr. Tom Buttimer undoubtedly frowned on such illicit activities, placing Matthew in an embarrassing position.

"Hello Matt," Fr. Tom ceased shearing. "You've been up at the blitz, I see?"

"Oh, you've heard about that?" Matthew said, making a ludicrous attempt to obscure his swag.

"Yes, I saw the Antiques Roadshow rolling out with their sideboards, chairs and whatnot. Speak of the devil, here's another of our venerable parishioners now!"

Looking over his shoulder, Matthew suddenly sensed his lunchtime binge of whiskey and Ginger Nuts threatening to resurface. In his estimation, Peig Sawyer was anything but venerable.

"May God forgive me for saying so," Fr. Tom whispered, "But I'm surprised that she of all people would emerge without some few knick knacks!"

"Humph! She's not leaving empty handed," Matthew murmured, no doubt having heard the news of her conquest.

"Good evening all!" Peig declared.

"Hello Mrs Sawyer, and isn't it a lovely evening too?" Fr. Tom said cordially.

"Ara, it's too hot, it is!" she grumbled. "About time we had a drop of rain again, to water the crops!"

Deeming this as an ideal opportunity to lighten his load, Matthew plucked a fistful of correspondence from his bag. "Actually Mrs Sawyer, I have some packages here for your lads and I was wondering if you wouldn't mind distributing them?"

"What do you think I am? The Pony Express?" she groused.

"If it's too much trouble-"

"Oh all right so," she glanced briefly at the priest, "Give 'em here to me."

"Ah good on you!" he said, entrusting her with the delivery.

As Peig wandered off with the stack of mail, the sound of screeching tyres cast their heads back in the opposite direction, where a Volkswagen Beetle was hurtling chaotically towards them. Matthew ducked into the grass verge, his second near-miss in one evening, as a yellow blur raged by. Inside, he caught a brief glimpse of Curly Buckley laughing manically, signalling his jackpot hit with Mrs Schalplatten's pride and joy.

And as Matthew straightened up again, he discovered that his plastic bag had spilled its many keepsakes all over the road. Exposed wholesale, he scrambled about trying to retrieve them. "I-I just got s-swept away in all the excitement," he said, guiltily. "Innocent curiosity, that's how it starts out, but before you know it, you're filching the remnants of a forgotten life!"

Fr. Tom mopped his brow with a wrinkled handkerchief. "We leave as we enter this world; free of material wealth. And given that thought, maybe you'd consider returning that nice lamp, at least?"

"And let some other clown get his filthy hands on it?" Matthew baulked, "Hell no! Besides, how can anyone make restitution to the dead?"

A salient argument courtesy of the cleric was stymied before it could begin.

"Dear God, I just don't know myself anymore!" Matthew suddenly revolved. "Life these days is like pulling teeth! All I ever wanted was to be was as an astronaut, hundreds of miles away in outer space. My father, who was a woodwork teacher, gave me a right pasting with a set square when I shared this dream. Eventually, I had no choice but to go for teaching and I even made principal and a damn good one too. Although, my father was still desperately bitter when I didn't focus on woodwork, like him. Still, I wonder; did I make the right choices?"

Matthew gazed at the silhouette still visible on the horizon, a key contributor to his melancholia, though not exclusively so, Fr. Tom concluded.

"Look to the present Matthew," he choose his words carefully. "You've a roof over your head, a good job and a loving family. There's no gain in building a life on regrets!"

"That's true, I suppose." Matthew reflected. "No doubt you've done your family proud with your chosen path?"

"Actually, my parents were devastated when I told them of my vocation."

"Why? Nobody to carry on the family business?"

"No, they were both Protestants."

♣ ♣ ♣ ♣ ♣

A few hours at the beach had been a refreshing diversion, but with twilight falling, it was time to call it a day. Among the curios encountered by Kieran and Jennifer on their return journey to Rossbladderburst, was a Volkswagen Beetle wrapped around a telegraph pole, though the only casualty appeared to be the car itself. In the interim, Kieran had been regaling Jennifer with the wacky exploits of his landlady. "The *next* I know she's demanding presents from the lot of us! Of course I immediately figured, perfume, but I couldn't find a chemist shop that carried Abattoir Garnier!"

"Yes, because she's *worth it*," Jennifer added.

"Anyway thanks for everything." Kieran said, realising the end was nigh. "The beach was incredible! No crisp packets or hypodermic needles! Just surf and sand."

"If you like, we can drop down again tomorrow?"

"I don't know yet, Fr. Tom Buttermilk is giving us a lift into town in the morning, hopefully enabling us stock up on some much needed munchies."

"Listen, I can't imagine how awful things are in Camp Sawyer, but if you like, I could try and forage a few bits from home? Now, granted my mother isn't the best cook in the world, but maybe-"

"Anything, so long as it isn't potato. Mind you, things should improve once our tuck is topped up and with any bit of luck, get to eat it before it disappears!"

"I still think you ought to consider burying it!"

"Yeah, or maybe leave it in a safety deposit box, at the front desk!"

Bad vibes swathed the pair as they reached the gate outside Peig's cottage. With its charming yellow thatch, its whitewashed walls, its outer stone walls and the old front door with its layer upon layer of green paint, it must have seemed like a rustic dream to the casual bystander. But for Kieran it was the stuff of nightmares. The rabid butterflies were gone, having been devoured by a giant tape worm, he now suspected was gnawing on his innards. "Anyway thanks again and if I make it through the night, we may see each other sometime tomorrow afternoon!"

"Don't talk rot!" she said, wringing his hand.

He turned and looked at her, and as their eyes met so eventually did their lips, and for one blissful moment all feelings of anxiety subsided. But all too soon Kieran and Jennifer drifted apart. He watched as she glided to the stone bridge, where spurred by an extrasensory bond, she looked back and waved. "Cheer up! It may never happen!" Kieran feebly returned the gesture, but a hair's breadth later, the green door swung open and there it was, a dinosaur dressed in his navy blue robe, brandishing a rolling pin in her hand. Since she was not predisposed to baking, this blunt object almost certainly held a more sinister function. "Well-well-well, if it isn't Johnny Come Lately, the prodigal son himself!" she roared.

The old woman was incandescent with ire, though possibly with something else too.

"I'm sorry?" he blinked repeatedly, as some obscure fumes began to sting his eyes.

"Have you any idea what time it is?" she barked.

"It's only about eleven?"

"Oho! You're not pulling the wool over my eyes! It's well after it, I assure you! What's more, supper finished hours ago!"

"I'm sorry, but I honestly didn't think you'd mind."

"You'll get nothing to eat now! Do you hear me? Nothing!"

Folding his arms, Kieran adapted a cavalier attitude. "That's all right, I couldn't care less anyway!"

"And you can cut out that slish, right away! And don't think that I'm not wise to your other little capers either! Who's that girl you were with, just now?"

"I don't see how that's any of your business?!" he retorted.

"Oh you're the devil's disciple, all right! I know what you need! Work! And plenty of it! In the meantime, I think you need to cool off and think about what you've done!"

"But I haven't *done* anything!"

"And since you've breached the curfew I can't let you in. You'll have to stay out here for the rest of the night!"

"Curfew? What curfew? You never mentioned a curfew before!"

"My house, my rules!"

"What? You can't be serious!"

Like a mallet to the cranium, Peig slammed the door in his face. "And may God forgive you!" she bellowed, through the letterbox.

Dazed and confused, the condemned teen wondered which way to turn, when a tiny flicker of candlelight offered a beacon of hope.

"Psst! Over here!" Owen O'Brien beckoned from the bedroom window.

Wasting no time, Kieran scuttled straight over. "Did you hear that?" he cried.

"Shhh! Yes! She's rat-arsed!" Owen whispered.

Kieran looked towards the front door. "I caught a whiff strong enough to kill a horse!"

"Rhubarb home brew, I suspect. I'm surprised she didn't go blind with the copious quantities she was throwing back all night. But first of all, let me tell you; after arriving back from the *céilí*, she was in powerful form, laughing and chatting away without a care in the world! Every so often she'd nip into her room for a refill, and once I even managed to catch a glimpse of a large glass cylinder with a clear pink-tinted liquid. She must have a distillery in there. Anyway, as usual, we sat at the table for our supper, in fact, *you* weren't even mentioned, and it was only when Rory accurately pointed out that she was serving *air* instead of actual *food* that she went completely crackers! After that, anything we said or did, was all wrong. She kept barking at us, saying that we should be ashamed of ourselves, forcing us on our knees where we spent the best part of three hours praying for our sins. Of course, that wasn't nearly good enough, so we were eventually packed off to bed, shortly before you arrived!"

Relieved at first, that her alcohol fuelled ravings weren't part of a personal vendetta, Kieran was quickly angered by what was, under no circumstances, justifiable behaviour. "Stark raving mad!! She ought to be thrown up against a wall and shot. Well if there's one sure thing, I'm not standing out here all night on the whim of a drunken nut-bag! Stand back and let me in."

Owen duly complied, allowing Kieran to get his leg through the window, but the overly cautious Rory threw censure on this illicit undertaking. "You can't let him in!" he griped. "She'll have our hides, if she discovers we've been harbouring him!"

"Shut your trap, you moron!" Kieran snapped, as he climbed in the rest of the way. "If push comes to shove, there's only one of her and three of us- well, *two* anyway!"

Having gained unlawful entry into the dormitory, Kieran paused for a breather on the window sill. Though he was innocent of any wrongdoing, his heart was racing from the stress of it all.

"What've you been up to?" Owen enquired. "We were expecting you back ages ago!"

Kieran drew another long despondent breath. "This *wretched* hive of scum and villainy makes Mos Eisley look like the Vatican."

"Where?"

"Never mind. Look! I managed to get us some spaghetti, at least!"

But as he submitted the tin, Owen remained sceptical. "Uhm, I hate to throw a spanner in the works, but you need a tin opener for that."

Kieran bowed his head in defeat. "Stands to reason, doesn't it? Have we *anything* at all? Or shall I just start tearing strips from my shoes?"

"There's still plenty of Ginger Nut!" Owen said optimistically.

This merely caused Kieran to slump even deeper into the pits of depression. "My ginger-battered taste buds salivate at the prospect!" he groaned bitterly.

"That's too bad," Owen helped himself to another, "They're my favourite, as it happens."

13. Fresh And Green Are The Pastures...

Given the mutinous escapades of the night before, the students were predictably slow in rousing from their dormitory protectorate. Outside the cottage limits, however, a red Mini had rolled up, from which the man in black emerged. As he approached the front gate, Peig came lumbering around from the side of the house, with a bundle of rhubarb beneath her arm.

"Good morning Mrs Sawyer!" Fr. Tom Buttimer vociferously greeted.

The onset of a prowler put a sudden crease in her stride. "Ah 'tis yourself," she squinted warily. "To what do we owe the pleasure?"

"I'm heading into town and I promised your lads a lift in!"

"Oh is that right?" she said pensively.

Pausing at the pillar and leaning on it for support, Fr. Tom leisurely regarded Peig's front yard. "Isn't that a grand looking garden! It really is a credit to you."

Peig reallocated her cradle, to alleviate the burden. "Eh? Oh yes, and to be sure, it gets harder and harder every year."

"And that's some prime rhubarb you've got there. Tell me, what sort of fertiliser do you use?"

"Ah, whatever's at hand really. Here, why don't you take a few sticks of it with you? It's very good!"

Since he hadn't actually been petitioning for a free sample, Fr. Tom became a little flustered. "Ah no-no-no, you're all right!"

"Oh yera, take a little bit of it anyway."

Half a dozen sticks were dropped on the pillar, making it seem rude to decline.

"And isn't there plenty more where that came from?"

"All right so, thanks very much," he assembled the cluster.

"That'll be six Euro now!" the old woman snapped.

"What?"

"Yera, we'll call it five, seeing as it's your good self!"

As she was hardly renowned for her sense of humour, Fr. Tom numbly reached for his wallet. But as the banknote was tendered, Peig suddenly clutched his wrist.

"Wait a minute now," she stood firm. "Put that away! There may be another little job you could do for me, instead."

Fr. Tom was suddenly beset by a suspicion that he was about to become embroiled in one of her devious machinations. Indeed this could possibly emerge as the most expensive bundle of rhubarb he had ever bought.

♣ ♣ ♣ ♣ ♣

After ninety minutes of incessant hammering against his bed post, Owen O'Brien could no longer moderate his temperament. "Oh for the love of God!!!" he cracked.

"What?" Kieran huffed resentfully.

"Would you please shut-the-hell-up with that damn tin! You'll never bust it open, in a month of Sundays."

"But I'm hungry!" Kieran pined, resignedly rolling the assaulted canister of spaghetti into the centre of the floor.

Once the clamour desisted, the murmur of voices could be heard drifting in from outside. Arising from his shabby mattress, Kieran shambled over to the window. The red car immediately caught his eye, followed, inevitably, by the old vulture digging her talons into the parish priest. "He's arrived!"

Brushing a surfeit of crumbs from his chest, Owen stirred from his bunk. "He's early! It's not even ten to yet!"

"Right, we'd better look lively," Kieran urged. "This could be a one-off opportunity! Come on Rory, time to get up!"

Rory groaned apathetically.

"Hello?! Telephone?!! Food?!!!" Kieran prompted.

Fittingly motivated, their taciturn comrade coiled into motion; and recalling the significance of this special day, Kieran dealt Owen a good thump in the arm.

"Ow! What have I done now?" he cried.

"Happy Birthday!"

"You already gave me my beating yesterday!"

"Did I? Oh right, yes, it slipped my mind!" Kieran noted with mock sincerity.

Eager to avoid another confrontation with his landlady, Kieran cropped his head from the window before venturing into the yard. During the time it had taken to get ready, she had apparently slithered out of sight and only the easily detectable Fr. Tom stood in plain view. Erring on the side of caution, Kieran lithely exited through the window, while Owen and Rory needlessly aped his callisthenics. Scanning the outskirts like a trio of escaped convicts, the unit advanced down the garden path. The subtle vibration of the gate as it opened, alerted Fr. Tom to their presence. "Oh there ye are lads! I'm really sorry about this, but-"

One look at the priest's sombre expression and Kieran's heart sank; it was a sure-fire bet that he was going to renege. All that left to do now, was measure each of them for a pine casket, or oak if they were lucky. "Don't tell me you're not going?"

"Oh I'm still going all right! But it'll be a tighter squeeze than expected."

The cleric's reprehensible secret was revealed as he stood aside, and there it was; as bold as brass, nestled snugly in the back seat; kitted out in her coat, scarf and a wicker shopping basket on her lap. "Isn't this great, lads?" Peig cackled. "We're all going for a spin in Fr. Buttimer's car, together!"

Before anyone could revel in the joy of sharing cramped quarters with someone whose body odour made fresh silage smell like Pot Pouri, a lime coloured Fiat Punto juddered into the foreground. As the vehicle braked, it scraped agonisingly against the briars at the opposite side of the road. Seconds later, a homely but well-attired woman with a shock of pure white hair surfaced and greeted the bunch with a friendly wave.

Kieran and Owen recognised the phantom as one who frequently haunted the corridors of their own school, back in Dublin. It was auspicious timing, not least because if ever there was the need of a school counsellor, it was now.

"Well-well-well, you're a hard bunch of lads to track down!" Mrs Waters beamed as she stomped across the boreen in her two-inch high heels. "I might have been here sooner had I not turned up at the wrong address this morning, an awful wreck of a place too!"

Straight away, she bore down on Rory, smothering him in hugs and kisses. "Oh my precious little lamb! How are you at all?"

Under normal circumstances, Kieran might have creased up at such antics, but found himself too emasculated by malnourishment to care.

"Where was I?" she continued, "Oh yes, one of the locals pointed me towards the principal's house, and *he* explained all about poor Mrs Schalplatten. Although I can't say I'm surprised. How could anyone live in such appalling conditions? Imagine, a bath in the front garden? And you were all very lucky to find a last minute replacement, I understand?"

Rory squirmed free from his mother's embrace; in the company of his peers he didn't care to indulge in her affection for too long.

"Eh yes, ehm, this is my m-mother," he mumbled bashfully.

Fr. Tom raised a single eyebrow. "Oh I see! Hello there, delighted to meet you! I'm Father Buttimer, Father Tom Buttimer!" he extended a robust hand.

"Hello, I'm Mairéad Waters, *Scoil Gailseach's* counsellor. I'm just down for a flying visit, although my own mother hails from Knockyadown!" she said, flexing her digits once the priest released his mighty grip.

"And, uhm, this is our *Bean An Tí*, Mrs Sawyer," Rory quivered nervously, with a nod towards the Mini.

Stooping over slightly, Mrs Waters proffered her hand through the passenger door.

"Hello Mrs Sawyer, lovely to meet you-"

The reigning matriarch greeted the interloper with only the coldest of smiles and a token nod. Immediately detecting a distinct chill, Rory's mother retracted her hand.

"I hope they haven't been too much trouble anyway!" she chuckled, trying to maintain a sense of conviviality. But Mrs Waters' cheerful outlook wasn't to last.

"Have you lost weight Rory?" she frowned. "You *have*, haven't you?"

Petrified of retribution, Rory's eyes remained fixed on the back seat of Fr. Tom's car.

"Shh! Not here Mother, please!" he trembled.

Such an allegation could not be allowed to slip by unchallenged. "Oh, I'm afraid they're only poor enough eaters!" Peig redirected.

"As if we had a choice," Kieran grumbled.

"Well Rory," his mother continued, "I was going ask if you'd like to go and-"

"Yes, let's go *now*!" he snapped.

"Okay and what about your friends? Would they like a whirl around the countryside?"

Whirling stomachs kept the other pair focused on their primary mission.

"I'm fine anyway!" Kieran declared.

"Thanks Mrs Waters," Owen added, "But we have plans."

The relief on Rory's face was almost insulting.

"Right-oh, we'll see you all later," Mrs Waters bid, escorting her son across the road.

"Do you want to flip a coin, for the front seat?" Owen whispered.

"Not bloody likely!" Kieran retorted, grabbing his friend's shoulder and shoving him into the back. Rapidly thrusting the passenger seat into its upright position, he pinned his housemate down beside the old woman. There was little Owen could do but cower and hold his breath for as long as possible.

As Fr Tom lodged himself behind the wheel of his Mini, a casual glance towards the Fiat Punto induced a sensory overload. "Ah for goodness sake! Did that woman say she was a *counsellor*?!" he gasped.

Kieran matched his eye-line, only to have his retina burned by a mawkish imprint, bordering on indecent. "Uhm, yes."

"A lad his age, that *can't* be healthy? Still, I suppose he isn't out robbing banks?" Fr. Tom endorsed.

A long-standing witness of Mrs Waters' cosseting, Kieran didn't bat an eyelid. Far more gobsmacking was the sallow and emaciated complexion that greeted him in the vanity mirror above. Tracing the furrows of his gaunt cheeks, Kieran also noted Owen cringing in the back seat, still scowling and gritting his teeth.

Wisely allowing some distance between themselves and the Punto, Fr. Tom turned the key and embarked on his errand of mercy. Within minutes they were clear to the other side of the village, though owing to some unsavoury company in their midst, a prickly silence hung in the air, something the loquacious Fr. Tom found impossible to uphold.

"So Mrs Sawyer, I hope these lads haven't been too much bother?" he said, half in jest.

"Not at all," she replied. "Sur' they're almost little angels!"

True enough, Kieran mused, and they would be soon fully fledged angels, if he didn't find something to fill his craw.

Duly noted was her cordial, if abominably self-serving, reply. On the plus side, the lack of any reference to the big lockout, led to the belief that the phenomenal effects of alcohol had wiped the slate clean. Then again, it did seem wrong that an evening of bedevilment had left her none the worse for wear.

"Nothing from the west!" Peig said, peering through Owen's window as they reached the hazardous T-junction leading onto the Rossbladderburst bypass.

"We'll need to stop off for petrol before we get to Knockyadown," Fr. Tom apologetically tapped the fuel gauge. And once they turned the corner, the anticipated service station fell into view.

In addition to the pumps, garage, carwash and adjoining house generally attached to such a facility, this outlet had the bizarre distinction of being swamped with tumbleweeds. While befitting the relative wasteland, it was doubtful that they were indigenous.

"I expect you're wondering about those fellahs!" Fr. Tom chuckled as he veered into the yard. "Domingo imports them to amuse the tourists!"

"Domingo?"

"Yes, Domingo Murphy. He and his wife Dominga moved here from Argentina three years ago, he's a real character, you'll love him!"

"*Murphy*?!" Kieran frowned.

"Yes, his grandfather was an Irish emigrant."

As the cleric wrenched the handbrake, a gentleman in a straw hat and oily overalls came scuttling forth. "Ah Buenos dias, Padre! Buenos dias!" he beamed, wiping his oily hands on an even oilier rag.

"Good morning Domingo! Can you fill her up for me, please?" Fr. Tom gesticulated inanely towards the gas tank.

"Sí Padre, Sí Padre!" he replied, springing into action.

"Oooh! Ow! Ah!" Owen suddenly cried.

"What's wrong?" Kieran said, glancing in the vanity mirror.

"It's my leg! I've got a terrible twinge in my right leg!"

"Ara hold your whisht lad, sur' we'll all be getting off in a minute," the old woman growled unsympathetically.

"All the same, it might help if I got out and stretched for a minute. You know, just in case I get leprosy uh, I mean, gangrene. So Kieran, can you uhm-?"

Kieran naturally suspected a ploy, but since anything less would have been inhumane, he arose and tilted the passenger seat forward. Owen sprung like a greased pig, immediately filling his lungs with the heavenly aroma of gasoline. Almost at once, his twitching nose caught the faintest whiff of cigarette smoke, a smell inextricably linked with danger. On looking around his prophecy was fulfilled, by a familiar gasping-choking-colossus galloping mercilessly towards him.

Dear God, no! It can't be! Not Ashtray!

"How are ya' gorgeous!" she wheezed breathlessly, fuelled by a long drag from her cigarette.

Owen swallowed nervously. "Hi, eh, wh-what are you doing here?"

"As if you didn't know you little scamp!" she ruffled his ginger hair. "This is where I'm staying!"

"Oh sure," he grinned gingerly.

"How thoughtful of you to come and visit! So tell me, what did you bring the patient?"

The Patient?! Oh yes, of course, the bronchitis!

"Uhm?" Spotting the rhubarb on the dashboard, he promptly lifted a single stick and surrendered it. "This! It's very good for- eh, for-for what *ails* ye!"

Ashley threw her arms around Owen, locking in a powerful clasp. "You're *so* considerate! And don't worry, I've haven't forgotten about the birthday boy!"

A multitude of wet slobbery kisses were garnished all over his cheek, sprinkled with coughs and splutters. It was a fate worse that death. Her open door policy on germs illustrated a barefaced disregard for, not only herself, but all humanity. Writhing free, Owen scoured his face with his sleeve. "Listen, I hate to be a wet blanket, but should you be smoking in your current state? Come to think of it, it may not wise to smoke around a petrol station, full stop!"

"So what's your point?" she chugged.

"Uhm, well-"

"Are we all set?" Fr. Tom interjected, having just settled up with Domingo.

"Sorry, but I must dash! We've got to rush my g-g-grandmother to the hospital for a hip transplant! It's a matter of life and death, which is *why* we have a priest on hand," he backed away.

With Peig, for once, being the lesser of two evils, Owen hastily took refuge in the back seat. As the Mini pulled away from the service station, the prying the old mare gawped out the back window.

"She seems like a very nice girl!" she whinnied, nudging his arm.

"A class act," he shamefully bowed his head at the litany of lies.

"Here, I think she has her eye on you," Peig enthused, nudging him almost to the point of brutality.

"Oooh, ow! Eh, lucky me!"

♣ ♣ ♣ ♣ ♣

Civilisation appreciatively loomed in the shape of Knockyadown. A host of colours on the sprightly terraces formed the appearance of being constructed from Lego. As one might expect on a Saturday morning, the streets were choked and parking was difficult to find.

"Look Father, there's a grand little spot over there," Peig eagerly suggested, while impeding his rear view by horsing around in the back seat.

"That's somebody's front garden, Mrs Sawyer," he groaned wearily.

"Sur' what does it matter? Or look! You could easily squeeze in over there!"

"No, that's a *laneway,* Mrs Sawyer," he added tersely.

"All right lad, keep your head cool and your foot dry and you'll be fine! Quick-quick-quick! There's a grand spot just there! Ara blast ya! Some other auld *lúbán* has gone flying in! Come on now, you're far too slow altogether!"

Unlike his backseat counterpart, Fr. Tom proved a competent driver, soon locating a space, not far from the main thoroughfare.

As the agitated cleric alighted, he verified the time. "I need to get the parish newsletter printed now, but if we meet back here around one? That should give everyone plenty of time to go about their business."

"That's great, thanks a lot Father," Kieran said, straightening the passenger seat, once Owen and Peig had emerged. But as he looked up again, the priest was nowhere to be seen. "Where'd he go? He forgot to lock the car!"

Peig slammed the passenger door shut, almost clipping the tips of his fingers. "This isn't Dublin lad!" she snapped. "There's no crime here!"

No Crime?! Talk about the pot calling the kettle black! As far as Kieran was concerned, he had seen more criminal activity in the past week than during his whole lifetime back in Dublin. In fact, with Peig Sawyer in the vicinity, it was no wonder that Fr. Tom didn't dawdle.

"So lads, which way are ye headed?" she sandwiched herself between the pair.

Kieran grew very anxious. The presence of a chaperone, scrutinising their every purchase, was by no means required.

"No doubt ye'll be off throwing yer money away at the amusement arcades or the likes?" she posed.

Amusement Arcades? Kieran pondered incredulously. *It's food we want!*

Fortunately, starvation hadn't numbed the senses entirely. "Eh, which way are *you* headed Mrs Sawyer?"

"I must go down to O'Donovan's first, to buy a new knickers elastic," she nodded to her left.

"Okay, well, we're actually headed *this* way!" Kieran pointed to the right.

Without further ado, Kieran and Owen discharged their unwanted baggage.

"There now, not just a pretty face, am I?" Kieran said smugly, as they sauntered down the street.

"You're a louse, that's what you are!" Owen moped.

"What? Why?"

"Chucking me down beside that old compost heap, and on my birthday too! Everywhere I go, it seems, I'm being poked, pawed and mauled!" Owen scratched himself in a harried manner, particularly in the arm where Peig had being needling him. "I'm beginning to feel so unclean!"

"Tell you what, I'll buy you a nice cake when we get to the shops!" Kieran offered.

"What? Mr O'Dowd has money?"

"Well, at least she didn't manage to lay her hoofs on *that*. Plus we still have the twenty quid from Fr. Buttercup."

"And where have you been hiding it?"

"Never mind!"

"Ah, I wondered about your funny walk, of late."

Ignoring that last comment, Kieran scanned the locality. "Where are all the decent stores? It's all mobile phone shops and insurance brokers!"

"Oh no!" Owen cried, "I forgot to bring my mobile!"

"Don't worry, we'll find a kiosk, after we've done our shopping! Now, there's a likely suspect," he pointed to a decrepit edifice on the opposite side of the road. "*S- oriarty, Sweets, Tobacconist and Grocery*. Soriarty? What the hell kind of name is Soriarty?"

"No, look," Owen gestured. "You can just about see the outline where the 'M' used to be. It's meant to read *S. Moriarty*! But I dunno, Kieran, the awnings have more holes than Swiss cheese."

"Well the door is open, which means they're open for business," Kieran asserted. "So come on, there's no harm in looking, anyway!"

Their initial scouting proved disappointing, as the only item on display in the shop window was a solitary sun-bleached biscuit tin.

"It all looks a bit dodgy to me," Owen said anxiously.

"Maybe they're stocktaking?" Kieran responded with blind optimism, marching straight inside. Owen remained hesitant; much of the town had yet to be explored and this seedy looking establishment would not have been his first port of call. As he wavered by the window, a small hatch in the display area slid open and a sinewy old lady, with large bulbous eyes, peered inquisitively at him. Pretending not to notice, Owen hastily scampered into the shop.

Unfortunately, the dull and dreary outer façade extended to an even gloomier mausoleum inside. Everything harked back to yesteryear, from the old Irish Sweepstake stickers glued to the counter, to the ancient timber shelves behind, all of which were bare. Most disquieting, was the old lady's hypnotic stare. A stare capable of penetrating souls, or so Owen believed.

"Good morning lads, another lovely day isn't it?" the doddery old dear quivered.

"Come on Kieran, there's nothing here. I think we should just leave," Owen said restlessly.

But a palpable deficiency of stock wasn't enough to deter Kieran from making some baffling enquiries. "Uhm, have you got any bread?"

The old woman slowly turned to appraise the empty shelves behind. "Eh no, we-we- I don't think we've had any in today, yet."

Suspecting that he had been overly ambitious on initial request, Kieran set his sights on something a little more tangible. "Eh, what about biscuits? Have you any biscuits?"

"Biscuits? Oh yes-yes we do!" she rattled excitedly towards the window.

A dusty 1982 calendar with some faded illustrations of Killarney National Park, added to the feeling of temporal displacement. Fearing they had fallen into a time vortex, Owen tugged at Kieran's shirt. "Forget the biscuits," he whispered, "I really think we ought to go."

"Shh! In a minute!" Kieran averred.

Opening the hatch again, the wiry old lady retrieved the tin and blew some dust from it as she placed it on the counter.

"And are they the only sort you've got?" he enquired.

Has he lost his marbles altogether? Owen ruminated, *Of course they're all she's got! That's all there is in the whole shop!*

She deliberated for a good moment before reaching her conclusion. "I think that's all we've in at the moment."

"Right, and how much are those?"

"Eh, te-ten pounds."

"Don't you mean Euro?"

"Who?"

"*Euro*?"

"Oh yes it's the auld *Euro* now. Eh, ten Euro, no, eh, twenty Euro!"

"But you just said ten!"

"*Ten* Euro so."

"Right Owen, do you want to go halfsies on these?"

"Are you touched?" he gasped. "See the date on the tin; it's there in plain lettering; *expires October 1991!*"

"Look, I honestly don't think I can hold out much longer so I suggest we make hay while the sun shines! Besides I read somewhere recently that those expiry dates are just a scam."

"No, I don't think- *look*, you still haven't considered the other side of town?!"

An ominous figure suddenly filled the doorway, casting our friends into a penumbra. But far from the coming of the apocalypse, it was merely Fr. Tom with a friendly word of recommendation. "Oh lads, lucky I spotted ye there! Only I forgot to mention earlier that there's a grand supermarket just around the corner from here!"

"*Amen* to that!" Owen praised with incalculable relief.

Avoiding further eye contact with the aged merchant, the pair surreptitiously edged towards the door. "What about the biscuits?" she cried. "Don't ye still want them?"

"Sure, we'll, ehm, drop in again later," Kieran shrugged.

The old dear shook her head, and restored the box to the window display where it was likely to remain a while longer.

♣ ♣ ♣ ♣ ♣

Spellbound by the prospect of a bountiful paradise, Kieran grappled unscientifically with the store's turnstile. "Food! Glorious food!" he drooled, tearing straight across to the bakery section. Straight away, he began hugging and fondling multiple rows bread and buns, as if they were his long-lost brethren.

Owen, still retaining some modicum of dignity, was astounded by his primordial regression and positively mortified when bystanders began to mutter in revulsion. "Come on, Kieran," he chuckled nervously, "Other people shop here too, you know."

Kieran responded by taking a gargantuan bite from a sliced pan and dropping it into his basket. Clearly beyond reasoning, Owen chose not to meddle, until his friend had ingested further nourishment.

♣ ♣ ♣ ♣ ♣

Some forty-five minutes later, the pair re-emerged lugging half a dozen bulging shopping bags between them. Both had large ice-cream cones; though eating them was a gruelling task, as they had to elevate their bags with every bite.

"Rife, aw we gneeg coo goo ich coo chynd a keghechone gox ngow!" Kieran gurgled, as they exited the supermarket car park.

"I haven't the faintest idea what you're on about!" Owen frowned.

"Gere's one ngow!" Kieran hobbled down the street.

"Hey, what's your hurry?"

But observing that his friend was heading towards a telephone kiosk, Owen gorged his ice-cream and sprung into action. "Oh ngo you gon't!"

When Kieran made it to the kiosk first, Owen threw himself and his bags on a nearby public bench and awaited his turn.

Two protracted torrents of belly-aches and bile gushed back to Dublin, the outcome of which proved unrewarding and astonishingly frustrating. Crestfallen, Owen lurched from the kiosk and joined Kieran, who was sprawled flaccidly across the bench.

"Well?" Kieran said, while polishing off the remnants of a fruit Danish.

"Well what? Nothing! I tried to explain that we were living in abject poverty all I got in return was a chorus of Happy Birthday and a pile of old guff about sticking it out a while longer. They couldn't seem to grasp that we were being brutalised, tortured and starved, telling me that if things had been so bad, why hadn't I bothered to contact them sooner!"

"Yeah, I got a similar earful from my auld fellah. He just ranted on about how much this trip had cost him; saying that I'd *better make the most of it* seeing as it would be my last holiday in a long-long time. Like, a *holiday* he called it!"

"That's it, then!" Owen concluded. "We're definitely stranded here for the next fortnight! Well, at least now, we've a few goodies to fall back on, I suppose."

Kieran licked his fingers before dipping them into one the bags for another pastry.

"Sheesh! This heat is brutal!"

"Remember now, that stuff may have to last us a while," Owen warned.

Fortunately, an influx of sugar had rendered Kieran fairly amenable again.

"Which is why I bought these," he retrieved two moderately large Tupperware boxes from another bag.

"Oh and another thing," Owen continued, "My Mum mentioned that she'd sent a small fruitcake in the post, along with a card and some cash for my birthday."

"Right, well, maybe Begley will have some news on our post, this evening."

Owen rose to his feet again and sighed. "Listen, my heels are ready to fall off from these shoes. I think I'll shop around for a new pair of runners- *cheap* ones."

"Yes and maybe I can pick up a few new shirts, seeing as that parasite burned half of them and made rub-rags from the rest," Kieran resolved.

14. Fit To Be Laid Out

On completion of their shopping expedition, Kieran and Owen arrived at the rendezvous point with a good ten minutes to spare.

"Here, you're not throwing those out?" Kieran baulked, as Owen casually flung his old footwear into a nearby dustbin.

"Why, did *you* want them?"

"No, on second thoughts, go right ahead!"

As they wearily dropped their bags beside the Mini, their flaring nostrils caught a waft of something agreeable for a change. "Where on earth is that coming from?" Kieran said, darting his head about like a chicken, trying to isolate its origin.

"Look, it's probably that restaurant behind you," Owen replied, "*Chateau Monsieur Duffy*-"

The enthralling and almost maddening aroma, lured the lean and hungry teenagers over to the window. Notwithstanding its escod-French title, Chateau Monsieur Duffy was a respectable establishment, judging by its white table linen and plush furnishings.

"It looks expensive," Kieran bleated.

"It *is*," Owen confirmed, as he studied the *Carte du Jour* posted on the window.

Kieran crouched over for a quick assessment. "Would you look at this?!" he exclaimed. "*Monsieur Duffy's La Porter House Steak: Prime fillet of char-grilled beef!* Mmm, *topped with sautéed onions and herbs, served on mound of garlic mash potatoes.*"

"I wouldn't mind sampling the *La Pork Grillée,*" Owen moistened his lips. "*Marinated medallions of pork, served with homemade apple sauce, mashed potatoes and fresh spinach.* Mind you, some options do sound a bit dubious: *La Pigeon Grillée* anyone? *La Verminée de Terre*?!! Still, the others don't look bad; *La Rack du lamb*, *L'Atlantic Salmon Steak* and *La Roulade du Chicken Breast.*"

"Yes, but those prices," Kieran jingled the change in his pocket. "Maybe buying those shirts was a mistake, when what we truly need is a good feed! Here, what's your current cash situation?"

A glance into Owen's wallet confirmed their depleted capital. "I'm not down to my last cent yet, but it's a dead cert that a kip like this would break the bank. The best *we* could hope for would be a croissant and a glass of tap water."

"Well hello again lads!" greeted a familiar voice, scotching their gastronomical fantasy. Kieran and Owen spotted the reflection of old Mother Hubbard and her dumb mutt in the restaurant window. "Well-well-well, isn't it small world? Have ye been out shopping?" she beamed, with a nod towards the bags.

Too small, Kieran mused. "Eh yes, that's right Mrs Waters."

"And we're just waiting for our lift from Father Buttimer," Owen added.

"Oh right? We were just out for a drive too, when my little lamb here said he was feeling weak with the hunger. So I thought we'd better get something for the child before he wastes away altogether!"

Mrs Waters squinted at the sign above the restaurant. "*Chateau Mou-rier Duffy.* Tell me, is this place any good, do you know?"

As if, Kieran pondered. "I dunno, it looks f-fine," he murmured.

"We'll give it a try anyway," she said, grabbing her son's arm and hauling him through the door. "Come on child, let's get some food down you!"

A gargoyle laced with spite and malice swallowed Kieran's face. "Oooh! Little Rory was feeling hungry! Then why the hell didn't she just mash up a banana for the *child*? A place of this calibre is wasted on that arsewipe!"

"Ssshh! They'll hear you!" Owen whispered anxiously, albeit with a slight grin.

"Who cares? I expect the staff will have a job finding a bib and high chair to accommodate him anyway!"

As if to rub Kieran's nose in the dirt, Rory and his mother were ushered into a window cubicle, with Mrs Waters adding insult to injury by smiling and waving from her lofty heights. Even so, Kieran simulated a courteous nod in return

Despite the badmouthing and vilification, Mrs Waters wasn't unmoved by the long, sad faces and doleful eyes peering in from outside. "Maybe I should've asked them to join us?" she said repentantly. "They do look a bit half-starved."

"I'm sure they're fine," Rory shrugged, in a response stemming not so much from parsimoniousness but from five days conditioning at the Peig Sawyer Academy of Indifference.

"Go out sweetie and ask them if they'd like to join us for a bowl of soup or something."

"Ooooh!" he groaned grudgingly.

"Never mind, I'll do it myself."

Rory observed as his mother stepped outside to extend an invitation to his housemates. The ignition of a sparkle in their eyes was instantaneous, though the flailing and pointing to watches hinted at some reservations. Nevertheless, Mrs Waters appeared adamant, eventually coaxing the shy and unassuming teenagers into the restaurant. "And sur' he's only parked outside the window, so you'll see him when he arrives!" she avowed, as they entered the premises. "Now sit down there and we'll order you a snack!"

After a ninety-minute jaunt around Knockyadown, the cool air conditioned restaurant was a pleasure for Kieran and Owen. Securing their bags in an unobtrusive position, the pair sat quietly at one side of the table, while Mrs Waters joined her son at the other. Hot on their heels, a maître d', with slicked back hair greeted the quartet, offering them each the bill of fare. "*Bonjour* mates! I'm Ricky and welcome to Monsieur Duffy's! Here are your menus, and today's special, which comes highly recommended by our accountant, is *Anguille et Frites*."

The waiter's glossy appearance was offset by his informal, albeit friendly manner and a telling antipodean accent.

"Angry feet?" Owen raised an eyebrow.

"That's eel and chips to you and me, mate!"

"Ugh, no thanks, I've already had one bad experience with seafood this week."

"I might have a salad anyway," Mrs Waters skimmed though the menu. "What'll ye have lads? Soup? Sandwiches? Do ye do sandwiches here?" she turned to the waiter.

"Yes ma'am, we've a choice selection," he nodded agreeably.

Kieran, who was hacking vigorously through the complimentary breadsticks, could not focus beyond the tantalising Porter House Steak listed on the main course. "Well to be honest, I wouldn't mind trying the- oh don't bother, it's too late, now!"

Directly outside, Fr. Tom was loading some shopping bags into the boot of his Mini, whilst scanning the locale for his elusive passengers. Owen groaned dejectedly and tossed his serviette onto the table. "Thanks Mrs Waters, but there's our lift now."

"Don't be ridiculous!" she cried. "Sur' I'll drop you all back myself, later on. Now you stay there and order whatever you like, while I go out and explain the situation to Father Butters."

The unexpected boon caught the duo by surprise. In fact, both were almost afraid to get too exited, lest they would wake up and discover it was the cruellest of all dreams.

"Oh right, yes, that would be g-great!" Owen quivered, with a meaningful glance at Kieran, as Mairéad Waters dashed towards the exit.

"Whatever we like, eh?" Kieran salivated in anticipation.

"Perhaps you folks need more time to decide?" the waiter suggested, taking a step back.

"Hell no! Don't go!" Kieran cried, terrified that even the slightest delay might hinder their chances. "I know exactly what I want; one of those *La Porter House Steaks*!"

"Oh yes, the *Porter House*; that's really choice, and would sir care for an appetiser?"

"No, I don't need appetising. I'll eat one later, if there's time. All I want now is a nice big steak, just smothered in onions!"

"Choice bro."

Jotting the order into his notebook, Ricky centred his attention on Owen. "What I can get you, mate?"

Broodingly stroking his chin as he studied the menu, Owen's response appeared spontaneous to everyone but Kieran. "Yes, I think I'll have the, uhm, *Pork*."

"Choice bro!" Ricky repeated.

"But no potatoes please!"

"Oh yes, don't give me any flipping potatoes either," Kieran said. "If I see another potato, so help me God, I'll strangle someone!"

Unperturbed, Ricky pencilled down the annotation. "Okay, no problem, or perhaps you'd care for some French fries instead?"

"Chips, Owen?"

"Mmm!" he concurred with wide-eyed glee.

"Yeah, grand, and maybe some wedges too? And onion rings? Oh! and while you're at it, another bowl of these toothpicks?" Kieran said, returning the ceramic dish now stripped of bread sticks.

"No problem mate- and what can I get you, sir?"

With his forehead resting in his palms, Rory appeared to be at a loose end.

"With so many salads here, I barely know where to start."

"Well the *Caesar* is my personal favourite."

"Right, two of those- no, better make it three. Mother wants a salad too."

And when the waiter uttered 'choice bro' for seemingly the millionth time, the mischievous glint in Kieran's eye denoted his hilarity at such trite repetition. Pocketing his notebook and pencil, the waiter assembled the menus and placed them under his arm. "And can I get you folks anything to drink?" he enquired.

"I'll just have a glass of water- Wait *no*! *Cokes* all 'round!" Kieran proclaimed, with a magnanimous gesture at someone else's expense.

"Right, I'll have those over to you in a jiffy."

Once Ricky was out of earshot, Kieran sounded off some of his usual glib banter. "Yes Owen, I think that pork you ordered was definitely a *choice* selection!"

"Ooh, thank you very much! Although your Porter House sounds extremely choice-y too!" he replied, in a similar patronising tone.

"And two salads Rory?" Kieran exclaimed. "That's very *choice-y* indeed!"

"Shut your hole!" he snapped, failing to see the irony and taking the comment as a personal affront. His visceral retort was a probable indication that Rory had now regressed to the primordial stage, signifying to Kieran that he should ease off the repartee for a while. Curious to know what the delay with 'Mother' was, he looked outside to find her still nattering to Fr. Tom. The old bag had since arrived on the scene and appeared to be scrutinising the restaurant with her customary air of contempt. In a superstitious attempt to deflect her evil rays, Kieran shielded his eyes. It was only when Mrs Waters returned some moments later, by which time it was safe to assume the threat was over, that he dared lower his defences again.

"Now lads, that's all sorted out," Mrs Waters confirmed, as she reclaimed her seat. "Have ye ordered yet?"

"Done and dusted," Owen declared. "Rory's ordered a Caesar for you."

"Oh great! I'm so hungry, I could eat a Rhinoceros!" she quipped.

Just then, their cubicle was invaded by the shrill chords of a mobile phone.

"Eh? Oh, my phone's just kicked in," Rory plucked the device from his pocket.

But as he tussled with the key-pad, a look of surprise took hold. "Seventy-four new messages?"

"Yes darling, I was worried when you weren't picking up so I sent you a few texts every day, in case you might be lonely," Mrs Waters confessed.

Kieran and Owen bowed their heads and twiddled their thumbs; both striving to keep a sudden attack of biliousness under wraps.

After a torturous thirty minute interlude, in which Kieran inserted bread sticks into every orifice in his head and Owen agitatedly defiled a table candle; and in which Rory verified aloud all seventy-four 'I love you' messages from his mother; Ricky, accompanied by an assistant, arrived on with their meals. Naturally, the scale and quantity of the dishes was a surprise for Mrs Waters, who, for whatever reason had been expecting sandwiches. But unlike some, Mairéad was not one to get into a lather over such trifling details. Indeed, their want of food was so tangible that one could almost smell the desperation.

"There's your Porter House, mate," the waiter placed a large steaming plate in front of Kieran.

"Mmm! Choice!" he responded risibly.

"Yes, that really is a choice cut!" Ricky stated, oblivious to the undercurrent irony.

Soon, the remaining meals were circulated around the table.

"Your pork and your salads, sirs and madam, and if there's anything else, just give us a holler," the waiter pledged, submitting a deferential bow on his departure.

Snacking on pastries and breadsticks had done little to diminish Kieran's cavernous appetite. Relishing every moment of this ritual, his blade carved gently through the tender, succulent flesh, and once the savoury juices doused his parched pallet, he knew that he'd been rescued from the precipice of annihilation.

"I swear to God, Rory, I promise never to slag you, ever again," he expressed his gratitude in, perhaps, not the most judicious manner.

Mrs Waters glanced up from her Caesar salad, evidently a little dismayed by Kieran's chance admission. "Chew your meat well lads," she advised nonetheless, "I had to forbid Rory from eating it after he nearly choked on a piece!"

"When I was *two*," he huffed.

"Anyway," Kieran cut in, "Just to let you know, we've stockpiled enough grub to last us 'til the end of next week and as I'm sure Owen will agree, there's plenty to go around."

"You can keep it!" Rory rejected. "Because there's no way I'm heading back to that hovel. Rest assured, I'll be going home with Mother this evening."

"But you can't Honey-Bun!" Mrs Waters declared. "As I've already explained, I've got to drive to Galway this evening, for an I.C.A. seminar."

"What's that? The Irish Dyslexic Association?" Owen said dryly.

"No," she frowned. "It's the Irish Country-*Ladies'* Association!"

"Well in that case, I'll just have to come with you!" Rory persevered.

"But petal, it's a three day assertiveness course, for women only!"

"Well that's all right, isn't it? Rory's practically a woman anyway," Kieran jibed. With his steak barely touched, he'd had already reneged on his oath. Censorious stares abounded, even from Owen. Rapidly realising which side his bread was buttered on, Kieran blurted a retraction. "Sorry-sorry!" he mumbled contritely, before proceeding in silence with his meal.

"Okay, look," Mrs Waters continued, "If by Tuesday afternoon you still want to leave, then I'll drive straight down here and collect you. In the meantime, I'm sure my little Schnookums can stick it out just a few more days?!"

"And I suppose you've already paid for the course anyway," Kieran warranted, now looking for an angle to assist his generous benefactor.

"What? No! I'm the one giving the course!"

"Oh," he cowered, in wide-eyed astonishment.

"It's discrimination! That's what it is!" Rory sulkily tossed the salad around on his plate.

"Sur' you won't starve, now that we've stocked up on munchies," Owen sugar coated.

As they scythed their way through an expanse of food, it wasn't long before their cadaverous complexions were supplanted by a healthy glow. Undoubtedly detecting the empty platters on his radar, Ricky, their genial waiter, emerged from the shadows.

"Bonjour again folks! And how was the cuisine?"

Kieran flexed his arms with feline contentment. "Faaaantastic!" he purred.

"And would you care to order dessert now?"

"Why not?" he declared, failing to consult their sponsor on the matter. "After all, it *is* Owen's birthday, so I believe a little celebration is in order. Isn't that right, Owen?"

"Uhm yeah," Owen murmured hesitantly, clearly trying to avoid the fuss Kieran was so intent on making.

Once the dessert menus were distributed, Kieran was the first to amplify his preference. "What's the *La Tiramisu* like?"

"It's really choice, mate!"

"Yes, I suspected as much. *Italian Mousse with Mascarpone Cheese? Lady Fingers, marsala and coffee liquor; with lashings of whipped cream and Belgian Chocolate.* Mmm, I think I'll give it a try."

"Same here!" Owen decreed.

"And for you, sir?"

Still a far cry from a butcher's dog, Rory was beginning to thaw. "Let me see, *La Hot Fudge Sundae*, maybe?"

"Choice bro."

"Are you sure you wouldn't prefer a few rusks, Rory?" Kieran joshed, before realising he had, yet again, stumbled into perilous territory. "Eh, but the sundae is definitely an *inspired* choice, if I may say so."

"And for you ma'am?"

"I'll just have an Americano, thanks very much," Rory's mother whispered.

"No problem."

"God bless your appetites," Mrs Waters smiled at the cluster of lustrous faces. But with the arrival of a steep bill some twenty minutes later, came a dour expression suggesting her benevolence had reached its zenith.

♣ ♣ ♣ ♣ ♣

Although Kieran was in no hurry to see his landlady again, he couldn't help but notice that the Punto's speedometer dial had barely budged since its turbulent take-off in Knockyadown. Speed, however, wasn't the only worrying factor. "Uh, you seem to be driving on the hard shoulder there, Mrs Waters?"

"You mean the slow lane?" she replied, "Yes, it's best to take it easy when the car is full. At any rate, what with all these speed traps and penalty points they have now, one needs to be extra vigilant."

With deep vein thrombosis taking root in the back seat, Mairéad Waters' concern for their health and safety was in danger of backfiring. Furthermore, Kieran could have sworn that this was not the road taken by Fr. Tom earlier that day.

"Eh, are you sure we're headed in the right direction?" he hazarded.

"This is the way we came!" Rory huffed with aplomb, from his front seat stronghold.

"Sur' I know these roads like the back of my own hand," Mrs Waters boasted. "It's many a time I used to come down here on holidays, when I was only your age."

"Isn't that penalty points system ridiculous, though?" Owen said wistfully. "These days if you so much as look sideways at a Garda, Bang! Three points on your license!"

"Four if you hit a cyclist," Kieran added, observing a bicycle overtaking them.

"Penalty points?"

"No, bonus points."

"Oooh! I'm fit to be laid out, after that feed," Owen loosened his belt a notch in order to alleviate his expanding waistline.

Disenfranchised, Kieran took a leaf from Owen's book and tried to relax. In truth, there was nothing such as a free meal and this was the price to be paid. The thought had occurred to ask Mrs Waters where she kept Rory's baby seat, but Kieran thought better of it.

♣ ♣ ♣ ♣ ♣

Oddly enough, their crotchety hostess failed to greet the trio, now accompanied by Rory's mother, as they sauntered up the garden path. "I'll just have a quick word with Mrs Sawyer before I leave," Mrs Waters declared.

"Yes, take your time, there's no rush," Rory clingingly urged.

As it happened, the front door was unlocked. Accordingly, all four proceeded into the kitchen, where Peig was curiously absent.

"Hello? Mrs Sawyer?" Kieran hailed.

An array of squeaking, creaking and bleeping noises drew their attention towards the dormitory. Meandering over to investigate, they cautiously pushed the door in. Inside, to their bewilderment, Peig Sawyer was sprawled across Rory's bed, dressed yet again in Kieran's robe, wearing Owen's Reeboks and groping the portable computer game that had gone 'missing' several days ago.

"Uh, Mrs Sawyer?" Kieran peeped.

Her head jerked suddenly, as their arrival had caught her unawares. "What do ye want?!" she screeched, promptly stuffing Owen's game beneath her hide.

"Uhm, well, this *is* our room," he gestured.

"And that's our stuff!" Owen protested.

In a fiery rage the demon soared into the air before bearing down on the intruders.

"This is my house and therefore *my* room!" she bellowed, justifying her incursion while poking Owen in the chest with her index finger.

"Mrs Sawyer!!!" Rory's mother exclaimed. "When my son spoke of your untoward conduct, I never imagined anything quite as despicable as this. Let me tell you here and now, that this kind of behaviour is just intolerable!"

"Ara, away back to Dublin with ya' or whatever auld gutter you crawled out of!" she roared. "And take that snivelling little weasel with you!"

"My son," Mrs Waters quivered, "Is the apple of my eye. Anyone who degrades him will feel the brunt of my wrath!"

As the confrontation spilled into the kitchen, Peig wrenched a red hot poker from the fire and brandished it at her accuser. "Ara don't be annoying me with your auld slish! Now go on away, before your face feels *burnt* with my poker!"

While the conflict grew more caustic by the millisecond, its culmination knocked Kieran for six. Fumbling momentarily in her handbag, Mrs Waters whipped out a sawn-off shotgun and wielded it at her assailant. Stopping dead in her tracks, Peig Sawyer's eyes glazed over. "You wouldn't dare!" she hissed.

Astonishingly, Mairéad Waters called her bluff and pulled the trigger.

As the shot sounded, Kieran jumped and hit his head on the ceiling of the Fiat.

"What are you playing at now?" Owen frowned.

"Hah? What?" Kieran croaked, observing the tranquil countryside passing them by at five kilometres per hour. "Uhm, nothing, wh-where are we?"

"I've no idea. But I'm almost certain the last signpost I spotted, read Dunmanway and Skibbereen."

"What?!! But they're in *Cork*, aren't they?"

"Are they?"

"Mrs Waters! I definitely think we're headed in the *wrong* direction."

"Yes, I realise that now," she responded peevishly. "So I'm just waiting for the next roundabout, so that I can turn around again!"

Kieran massaged his crown. "Oh-ho-ooh!" he groaned, wishing he hadn't woken from his nightmare, especially given this one's promising ending.

After wandering around the wilderness for four hours, taking in two toilet stops, during what should have been a simple fifteen minute journey, St. Millipede's church eventually loomed. "What time is it, now?" Kieran whispered.

"Six-twenty-five," Owen replied.

"Oh the agony! And if last night is any indication, she'll go bonkers if we're late for dinner."

"Surely you can't be hungry?"

"Stuffed! But you're forgetting you-know-who's surprise visit, this evening!"

"Oh wow! I had forgotten!"

As the vehicle came to a rambunctious halt outside Peig's cottage, Kieran caught the reflection of Rory's quivering bottom lip in the wing mirror. It had been a swell spree, but anticipating a toe-curling, mother-and-son farewell, he and Owen thanked Mrs Waters, grabbed their shopping bags and bolted.

The clink of the gate latch announced their arrival, though it was Matthew Begley, weirdly, who opened the front door, extending them a sheepish wave as they lumbered up the garden path.

"Quick Owen, take the bags and hide them 'round the side of the house," Kieran whispered frantically.

"What?"

"Just do it!"

Entrusting the diversionary tactics to his comrade, Owen obliged.

"Mr Begley, ah hello, eh, what a surprise," Kieran suitably instigated the theatrics. "Sorry we're late."

Matthew's performance was lamentably stilted. "Yes I was just, uhm, in the neighbourhood, and I thought I might drop in to see how you were all getting on," he said, with an expressive wink, indicating herself was inside, clinging to every word.

The principal took a step back, permitting Kieran to step through. But the exposition that enfolded before the teenager, served only to confound and exasperate. In contrast to the flimsy supper he had anticipated, the dinner table was overflowing with haute cuisine. To all intents and purposes, it was on par with the standard they had seen that afternoon at Chateau Duffy's. Among the luscious delicacies awaiting their pallets were; roast turkey and ham, cranberry sauce, sautéed vegetables, gravy and onions and of course, mashed potatoes. A floral motif cloth veiled the table, while the skip-salvaged crockery had been ditched in favour of a dinner service devoid of defects. The addition of a Christmas cracker on each plate was a charming touch, even if it smacked of overkill. As Peig spun around, she placed what appeared to be a large cheesecake on the table, before looking up to greet the first of her arrivals.

"Well-well-well, there you are, Kieran!" she grinned. "We were getting worried about you. Are Owen and Rory on their way?"

Kieran, *Owen* and *Rory*?!! What supernatural phenomenon had triggered the sudden recollection of their names?

"Ehm yes, th-they-they're just outside!" he stuttered.

It wasn't just her personality that had undergone a major overhaul, but her appearance too. Gone was the filthy disease-infested apron. In its place; a brand-spanking-new one, inscribed with the most dubious of all slogans; 'Kiss the Cook'. So wholesome and jovial was the renaissance, that Kieran found the need to pinch himself, to confirm it wasn't part of some delirium. Certainly, Saturday had been tipped as bath night, but this was no superficial scrub up. No, this bore all the hallmarks of a conspiracy. The only plausible explanation was that the principal had sold them out. Heaving a chair from the table, their vivacious hostess invited Kieran to sit down.

"Come on, tuck in before it gets cold!"

"That's a fantastic looking spread, Mrs Sawyer," Matthew enthused.

"I do my best for them anyway," she solemnly declared.

In taking his seat, Kieran was allotted some generous portions.

Seconds later, Owen sauntered in, lurching in mid-stride as he too eyeballed this veritable feast. Right away, he glanced over his shoulder to confirm that he had entered the correct house.

"Aaah! There's my other little cherub, now!" Peig grinned, extending him a chair. "Come in and sit down!"

Mystified by her transformation, Owen simply gawped at Kieran, who himself, shrugged back in bafflement. As some equally liberal portions were meted out to Owen, the principal began to drool. "These braised carrots are top notch!" Matthew said, daring to sample some of the appetising titbits on display.

"Oh right? All the more of a shame then, that you can't stay and join us," the old woman remarked, while betraying a slight frown.

"Well maybe I could stay for a little bite-"

"Ah-ah-aaah! You wouldn't want to spoil your appetite for when you go home now?"

Although Peig had retained a civil tongue, she was most anxious to see the back of this interloper. "Ahh, here's my other good friend now!" she declared, with open arms. "Come in my dear and sit down!"

Having bid adieu to Mother, Rory slouched into the kitchen with the zeal of a death-row convict. It wasn't until he spotted the Christmas cracker on his plate, that his eyes were inevitably drawn to the remainder of this exquisite banquet.

"Now lad, extra vegetables for you, isn't that right?" Peig said, unloading vast sums onto his plate.

With her brood now provided for, the enchanting elder dabbled about by the dresser for a moment, before rolling up with a freshly iced fruit cake and a lighting candle.

"Now mister," she placed the cake in front of Owen, "A little bird told me it's your birthday, today. So I thought a little memorial might be in order. In my day, we never had sweet cake-but sur' sweet sixteen comes only once in a lifetime."

Following an eerie rendition of Happy Birthday, Matthew Begley grew weary of their company. "Ye-es, I'd better be off," he buttoned up his blazer.

"Ah no! Already? Are you sure you won't stay for some pudding?" Peig suggested.

"Well perhaps-"

"No, I suppose Mrs Begley will be waiting for you at home," she pre-empted, sensing his answer would be the wrong one.

"No doubt," he added abrasively.

Flummoxed by these insidious developments, Kieran racked his brain in an attempt to get his priorities in order. "Right then, I'll eh, see you out."

Arising and following the principal towards the door Kieran recalled his intended questions. "So, did you manage to pick up our post?" he whispered, in view of the champion ear-wigger nearby.

Matthew, at least, had the good sense to match his intonation. "Oh yes, I handed several packages to Mrs Sawyer last night."

"Mrs Sawyer? Last night?!"

"That's right- eh, *Mrs Sawyer*?" he said more volubly, "Have you got those bits and bobs I left with you yesterday evening?"

"What?"

"You know, those letters and packages for the boys?"

A cross examination on the subject hadn't been anticipated. "Hah? Oh eh, yes, I'll eh, sort those out in a few minutes."

Reasonably satisfied, Matthew opened the front door and stepped outside. "I fail to see what all the commotion is about. You've obviously been conjuring up things, in your own head. The truth is, you all seem to be doing jolly well for yourselves."

"But it's not like this!" Kieran avowed. "Every other day, the food is fatal!"

"Look, I don't know what sort of fare you're used to getting at home, pizzas and microwaveable salmonella, I expect. But that, to me, is the best of food. In fact, I wish I had it that good, myself. So, unless there's something truly drastic afoot, like mass genocide, your grievances seem utterly groundless. Now it's getting late, I'll see you all soon and don't worry, I'm sure you'll be fine."

As Matthew Begley hastened down the garden path, there was little doubt in Kieran's mind concerning his treachery. His reflective pause abruptly ceased as Peig kicked the front door shut, again, without consideration for Kieran's fingers.

"Enough maggoting! Sit down and eat!" she bellowed.

Surprise, surprise, with Begley barely out of earshot, her tongue had instantly regained its sharp edge. Kieran, nonetheless, re-joined the others, who were now slogging through their grand meals. This surely had to be the cruellest of all ironies, to arrive back to a full buffet on the evening they were positively sated.

"Like clockwork that man is," she blethered, "Always gandering about on every first Saturday for one of his so-called surprise visits. *Always*, the first Saturday!"

Kieran and the others couldn't believe their ears. Evidently, she and Begley were *not* in cahoots, but rather, this scheme had been the result of meticulous calculation and planning. Every minute detail, from the lavish spread to her cosmetic performance as a paragon of virtue, had been purely for the benefit of the principal.

"Now listen up, I've a card game over at Teddy Holland's this evening, so I want the lot of ye out and gone by a quarter to!" she decreed.

"That gives us barely five minutes to finish our food!" Owen whimpered.

"Well, ye should have thought of that, before ye went out gallivanting 'til all hours!"

The removal of her apron saw the final trace of their bogus landlady laid to rest, not that anyone was remotely tempted by the apron's slogan.

"May we have our packages now, Mrs Sawyer?" Rory ventured.

"Can't you see I'm busy," she said, avoiding eye contact, while draping her apron over a chair.

"Please?" Owen petitioned.

With a petulant sigh, she eventually ceded. "All right so, I'll see if I can find them."

Stepping into her private chamber Peig purposefully closed the door behind her. Following an abnormally long intermission she re-emerged with a few crumpled pieces of paper and tossed them onto the table; items so severely damaged that only the most naïve could accept without question.

"What's this?" Kieran gasped, while straightening out the frayed scraps.

"Letters from your parents!" she replied curtly, while 'casually' resuming her duties.

"What about envelopes and all the other trimmings?"

"Oh yera didn't they fall into a pool of water on the way over, and weren't they all covered in muck and dirt and that was all that could be salvaged!"

All were convinced that this account was complete fabrication and that any trimmings had been shaven off by a two-faced bandit. The only thing sullied about the mail was that it had fallen into her hands. Promptly identifying the letters, Kieran distributed them accordingly. Owen, however, remained extremely disappointed. "There wasn't a birthday card among the bunch?" he said glumly.

The barrage of inconvenient questions agitated the old woman. "A card?" she frowned, while irritably scratching the back of her neck. "Maybe, I'll just check-"

Scurrying back into her room for a moment, Peig resurfaced once more, holding a card inscribed with the standard 'Happy Birthday' tag and an illustration depicting Formula One motor racing.

"Here!" she gruffly surrendered the item. "I didn't know whether you'd want it or not!" Not only was the back of the card missing, but its serrated edge signified that it had been freshly torn in half.

"Is that it? No inscription? No message from my parents?"

"No! The rest of it was destroyed!"

Just how stupid does she think we are? Owen pondered in disbelief. "What about-?"

On the verge of asking about his mother's fruit cake, he regarded Peig's so-called birthday slab. This could only be the same cake, thinly disguised with some fresh icing, to give it that spur of the moment homemade look. As for his birthday money, well, that probably had 'fallen' into her private coffers.

The seditious topic was terminated by a rap on the door.

"Now, who in the blazes is that?" she heaved towards the window. A puzzled frown, as she raised the net curtain, suggested that it wasn't an acquaintance. Thus, wrenching the door wide open, Peig extended her customary salutations. "Yes?!!"

"Hi, is eh, Kieran there?"

The trio seated at the table were well acquainted with the party standing in the doorway, but couldn't fathom what warranted a visit from Daimo and his fellow delinquents, Higgo and Locko.

"Who are you? What do you want?!" she spat.

"Could you just ask him if the girls are in this evening?" Daimo continued.

Kieran's face immediately fell into his hands. Once again, their disgraceful deception had returned to haunt them.

"What are you on about? What girls?"

Locko pushed his way into the fore, pitching a two litre brown bottle in her face.

"Look, we've brought cider!" he grinned guilelessly.

"Yeah come on missus, let us in, just for a bit!" Daimo persisted, sticking his foot inside the door. "I swear we won't get in the way!"

"What do you think this is? A flophouse?" she bellowed, kicking his foot back outside. Winching a slop bucket containing all the peelings and drained fat left over from the preparation of dinner, Peig hurled the lot over these gatecrashers before slamming the door in their faces. Curiously, the door was re-opened, but only to snatch the cider bottle from Locko's clutches. "You little scuts are far too young to be drinking the likes of this!" she hissed, before slamming it shut again.

With the empty bucket still in her hand, Peig stampeded towards the table. "Right, I think ye've had enough now."

Rory's plate was suddenly ripped away and its contents scooped into the bucket. Kieran and Owen reacted immediately and began wolfing down as much as possible.

"Aren't you going to save the leftovers for supper?" Owen gurgled, as his plate was seized and scoured.

"No! Those bits I just threw out were intended for Teddy Holland's pigs. And since I promised to bring scraps, your leftovers will have to do."

"Here! There was ham on that plate!" Kieran remonstrated, as his own dish was hauled away. "Surely, that can't be healthy for pigs?"

"Pigs will eat anything!" she scowled. "That's why they're called *pigs*!"

"Well, I'm going to take some of this cheesecake anyway," he exclaimed, while frantically hacking into the dessert. Lobbing a cosmic portion into his mouth, Kieran quickly found his pudding somewhat less palatable than anticipated. "Goooch!" he sloshed, "What the bloody-hell flavour cheesecake is this?"

Assuming none of her brood was looking, their slippery hostess covertly concealed the fruit cake in the dresser drawer. "What cheesecake?" she looked over her shoulder. "Ara go way! That's no cheesecake! It's carrageen, and the best of food too!"

"W-what's that?" he said fretfully.

"Boiled seaweed!" she declared.

On hearing this, Kieran began to expel a series of disconcerting guttural chafes, much to the vexation of the Peig.

"Get out!" she roared. "Go to your auld *céilí* or whatever it is! I won't have you getting sick all over my nice clean floor!"

Once again, the trio were turfed out, punctuated, as usual, with the door being slammed shut behind them. Outside, Kieran found himself gasping for air.

"You're not choking, are you?" Owen worriedly enquired.

"Acchh!" he rasped. "There's a bit of grape from that cheesecake, stuck in the back of my throat!"

A hearty slap on the back, courtesy of Owen, saw the wayward article expelled into Kieran's palm. "Hang on, this isn't grape!" he quivered. "Look! It's one of Rory's cough lozenges!"

"So, that's what happened to them!" Owen gleaned.

15. A Grave Error

Three pairs of eyes blinked synchronously. The thud of the front door was the anticipated signal that their nemesis was on the move again. Patiently waiting for the old woman to take her leave, Kieran, Owen and Rory had concealed themselves at the gable end of the cottage. Cropping his head from around the corner, Kieran observed her trudging towards the gate, with her swill and cider in hand. Everything was spot on until Owen vented a tremendous, flower-wilting belch. Her finely honed senses mechanically activated, Peig Sawyer ground to a halt to scan the locale. A passing vehicle fortuitously threw her off the scent and the behemoth proceeded on route. Kieran looked daggers at Owen for almost foiling the entire operation.

"S-s-sorry," Owen bleated remorsefully, "All that rich food is a shock to the system!"

"So why is it we're *not* heading down to the *céilí*?" Rory contested.

Kieran hoisted a shovel and spade that had been propped up against the white-washed wall. "To safeguard our survival for the next week or so, I've decided we should bury our food at the bottom of the garden."

Owen's demeanour brightened considerably. "Capital idea!"

"Yes, well otherwise it'll be capital punishment for the lot of us," Kieran stated grimly.

The discussion was adjourned until the students and their garden tools had relocated to the end of Peig's back garden, where the search began for an ideal burial spot.

The area itself was a diverse mix of grass, tilled soil and crops consisting of mostly rhubarb.

"Check that out!" Owen pointed to the roof of Peig's cottage. "Corrugated iron!"

Kieran looked on, but failed to see its significance. "So?"

"So, the thatch only covers one side!"

"Ah yes, everything by half measures."

"I hope we don't get into trouble for missing the *céilí*," Rory whined.

Such adherence to duty in the face of adversity was now truly grating on Kieran's frayed nerves. "Look!" he snapped, "I don't know about the rest of you, but I'm in no fit form for the hick version of Dance of the Sugar Plum Fairy, this evening!"

"Same here," Owen patted his paunch.

"Good, you can work off some of that, right now," Kieran handed him the spade. "Rory, you take the shovel and give him a hand."

"Hey, why should *we* do all the hard graft?" Owen huffed.

Kieran picked up the shopping bags. "You see, in this world there are two kinds of people, my friend; those with loaded Tupperware boxes and those who dig. *You* dig."

With a doleful sigh, Owen capitulated. "So how far down do we need to go?"

"I dunno, five or six feet should do the trick."

"Five or six?! That's ridiculous!"

"It doesn't matter, so long as it's deep. You know what she's like; she can sniff out a box of jam tarts at fifty paces. I suggest you use the back wall there as a reference point for easy return access. And you'll need to maintain a safe distance from the rhubarb, otherwise she'll unearth our goodies for sure."

"Yes your honour, and if it pleases your honour would three feet from the back wall suffice?" Owen whimpered, in pseudo subservience.

Meticulously advancing three steps from the stone wall, Owen sunk his spade into the soil. The ease and pace at which he laboured surprised even him, leading to the startling conclusion that walking and dancing actually paid dividends. It wasn't long before a substantial crater had formed and their deposit was made. Once the hole was refilled, the tools were restored to their original positions, in the hope that her ladyship would be none the wiser.

"What's going on?" hailed a voice from beyond the garden. "I hope you lot haven't been digging your own graves?"

For one horrifying moment, the trio thought they had been caught behind enemy lines, but thankfully it was their ally, Jennifer Begley.

"Don't tempt fate!" Kieran quipped, striding up to the front wall to greet her. "Actually, we've just been following your advice and our rations are now safely buried in the field below."

"R-right, so you haven't been down at the hall, yet?"

"No, why?"

"Tonight's *céilí*'s was cancelled after our only music cassette went AWOL."

Owen cast his face at an angle, while awkwardly making circular patterns in the dirt with the tips of his new runners.

"Plus, Dad threw a wobbly when he found out that yesterday's unsupervised session yielded several broken limbs. Anyhow, I thought I'd come down here on the off chance of meeting you."

She plucked a neat bundle from her shoulder bag and extended it to Kieran.

"Surprise! I've brought you sandwiches!"

But since Kieran and company were royally stuffed, it was a struggle to muster much enthusiasm. "Oh lovely," he nonetheless replied.

"They're corned beef," she added.

Owen patted Rory on the shoulder. "Your favourite, eh buddy?"

"Thanks," Kieran graciously acknowledged. "We'll eh, we'll *save* them for later."

Jennifer sensed the prevailing air of angst. "So how did it work out with the surprise inspection?"

"We crashed and burned! The old bag had insider information!"

"Oh dear. Well I did ask my parents what happened to those two girls last year-"

"And what did you find?"

"A brick wall, I'm afraid. But foodwise, I didn't forget to bring you afters!"

Whipping out a packet from her bag, Jennifer landed the item in Kieran's hand.

"Ooohooo! Ginger Nut biscuits!" he quivered. "They're *sure* to go down a treat!"

♣ ♣ ♣ ♣ ♣

Sunday morning had arrived and our friends had survived another night under the heel of the Sawyer Administration. "Oooooh! I'm absolutely shattered," Kieran groaned, as he heaved himself to the edge of his marginal bunk.

Rubbing his eyes to the extent of doing more damage than good, he eventually tottered to his feet. The others were still horizontal, Rory in his single-layered bunk bed and Owen, half-dozing away in his termite-infested canopy.

"That funny tasting cocoa she gave us last night was a real knockout and now my head is spinning. Rory, have you any paracetemol left?"

"No!" he growled. "All my medicines are gone, apart from one new inhaler purchased by Mother, yesterday. For anything else you'll have to ask Mrs Sawyer."

"I may have to," he said broodingly. "I've an absolute migraine now."

"That's odd," Owen croaked. "So do I. Here, you don't suppose she slipped us a Mickey last night?"

Kieran moistened his tongue. "Probably."

"Yes, well, if you're going to stick your neck out, see if you can fetch something for me too," Owen appealed.

Looking even more dishevelled than usual, Kieran entered the kitchen, yawning and scratching his head. With a wire-mesh guarding the hearth, it was safe to assume that the ogress hadn't yet stirred from her den.

The stingy cow probably burns those same ashes time and time again, he hypothesised while gazing into the smouldering embers. His roving eye unavoidably wandered towards the forbidden door. There was nothing quite like tagging the old forbidden label on something to rouse one's interest. What had she been so hell-bent on protecting? A chop shop?! A dead husband?!! The Ark of the Covenant?!!! Furthermore, what harm could there be in stealing a quick peak inside? And by gum, there was no time like the present. Slowly, his hesitant hand reached for the handle. Petrified his palpitating heart would betray him, he regarded her chamber again, to ensure the perimeter was secure. So far, so good. Infuriatingly, his efforts were in vain, as the door, predictably, was locked. It stood to reason that the crafty old beggar would have taken security measures, especially if she had something to hide. Undeterred, Kieran crouched in front of the keyhole in the hope of catching a glimpse inside. But as he squinted into the recesses of obscurity, a shadowy sensation beset the teenager. Fearfully turning his head, he encountered a pair of bulbous eyes, perilously close to his own. "God almighty O'Brien!" he roared, reeling backwards. "You nearly gave me a stroke!"

Worried that Kieran's cry had raised the living dead, all eyes immediately darted towards her crypt, where silence still reigned.

"Shh!" Owen whispered.

"Oops, sorry."

"Well?"

"Well what?"

"Did you see anything?"

"Yes, it was horrible, just horrible. First I heard a child crying and then, the rattling of chains," Kieran divulged.

Owen's eyes bulged in terror. "What? Really?"

"Followed by the sound of Jacob Marley's ghost groaning Oooaaahh!"

Owen's expression skewed from trepidation to scepticism. "Yes, come on, let's make ourselves scarce before old Scrooge wakes up." But as he turned to leave, a puckish look briefly swabbed his countenance. "Hey, I've just had an idea!"

Rising to his tiptoes, his fingers probed the architrave above the door and midway across Owen found a single key.

"Well done Mrs Fletcher," Kieran whispered in wide-eyed awe.

Deftly and silently, the key entered the lock. It clicked 180 degrees. This was it. Finally some answers. As the handle turned, both braced themselves for the worst; the likeliest scenario: a room littered with corpses. But damn the consequences; they were compelled by a sense of duty (and self-preservation), to proceed. Horrifically, as the door creaked open, several dozen saucepans, frying pans, kettles, colanders and decanters came crashing down over their heads and all around them.

Knee high in aluminium and iron, it didn't take a genius to deduce that they had merely stumbled upon a cubbyhole for worthless clutter. Shocked and literally crippled by their blunder, Kieran and Owen received a further jolt when the front door almost blew off its hinges. There she stood, staring scornfully at the quarry trapped in her snare. "What in-the-name-of-God do ye think ye're doing?" she methodically began.

"I was looking for- ah-ah, an aspirin," Owen ventured, following a weighty pause.

"The devil finds work for idle hands!" Peig roared, bearing down on ground zero. "What did I say? Out of bounds! Forbidden! And for your own good too! I've a good mind to give ye a good hiding, for this!"

Kieran stooped down and began gathering up the detritus. "Sorry, we'll eh, we'll put it all back," he stuttered.

The old woman slammed a large battery-operated torch on the mantelpiece. "Just leave it! I'll put it away myself! Only I'm sick of looking at ye! Sick of ye! And what are ye doing up at this unearthly hour, anyway?"

Owen checked his wristwatch. "It's twenty past eight Mrs Sawyer, breakfast time!"

"Breakfast? Well it's self-catering today!" she huffed imperiously, "Sunday is a day of rest and my day off!"

A day off? From what?!! Owen pondered incredulously.

Equally astounded, Kieran considered raising the issue of where precisely his three thousand Euro had been implemented, but recalling the futility in doing so previously, simply saved his breath. In any event, their culinary skills, or lack of, were unlikely to be tested, given the absence of compatible raw materials. Fortunately, they wouldn't go hungry, now that they had secured ample provisions. Or had she somehow sussed that? Moreover, where exactly had *she* been at this unearthly hour? And what nefarious task necessitated a torch? And *why* were her boots dusted in soil?

As if trying to resist the ravages of fatigue, Peig placed a finger on the bridge of her nose and closed her eyes for a moment. She seemed more bleary-eyed and bushed than usual. "I need to lie down now, for a while," she said, edging towards her private quarters.

With his temples still throbbing, Owen made one final attempt to acquire something to ease the pain. "Mrs Sawyer? You wouldn't happen to have some paracetemol to spare?"

"Your birthday was yesterday lad!" she sneered.

"Y-yes, I realise that," he added guardedly.

"So don't go expecting any special treatment, again today!"

Special treatment? With a bedside manner like that, she'd make a worthy recruit for the Health Service Executive, he surmised.

As Peig prepared to retire, she fobbed them off with more of her clichéd and crass remedies. "Ye can go out now and bring in a bucket of water and start washing down the walls and scrubbing the floors. That'll soon give ye plenty to think about! Now get to it, before I lose my rag with the lot of you!"

While Owen didn't doubt that she had lost her rag long ago, Kieran would have preferred seeing the proverbial garment being used as a noose. Unmistakably, neither had a penchant for manual labour and once their landlady was out of sight, both waded through the metallic deluge, back towards their sweat box.

On their return, Kieran caught Rory peering out through a fissure in the doorway. 'Goggles Boy' made no secret of his eavesdropping and opened the door as they approached. "I suppose you saw that," Kieran declared. "Or half of it anyway, there's a lens missing from your glasses!"

"Yes, I had noticed," Rory pouted.

"Broken?"

"No it's gone."

"Lost?"

"No, it's just gone! Okay?" he said, eyeing the miscreant's chamber across the way.

Kieran promptly grasped the situation. "Agh no! Don't tell me we've been burgled again last night?!!"

♣ ♣ ♣ ♣ ♣

It was corned beef sandwiches for breakfast that morning, while Rory's vegetarian option, fingernail clippings and toothpaste, was only marginally more appetising. Fr. Tom Buttimer's heartfelt Sunday sermon on the ills of greed and covetousness saw much squirming in the pews, though Kieran, a victim to a voracious rash of thefts, found it strangely poignant.

Strolling casually through the village with their hands in their pockets, it wasn't long before food began to consume the conversation, once again. "Is anyone else here feeling a bit peckish?" Owen enquired. "I say we nip back to the house and dig up some snacks."

The team was sidetracked before an agreement was reached. Dead ahead, just beyond the thoroughfare, a sizeable throng had amassed at the gate of a large field. A row of mature Leylandii obscured the site, prompting our inquisitive friends to amble closer. Once the swarm filtered through, Kieran, Owen and Rory encountered a makeshift sign. "Look! *Sunday Mar-*

ket: 10am - 5pm," Kieran decoded from the lettering, barely legible from the perennial weathering. "It must be a car boot sale or something?"

Just beyond the gate, however, the trio were accosted by an elderly gent in a peaked cap. "That'll be four fifty each lads," he slurred, with an open palm.

After their taxing seven days, this was a tariff too far. "Four fifty?! *Each*?!" Kieran gasped, "That's the equivalent of three packets of biscuits! And chances are we won't be buying anything! Come on, Owen, let's go. We're not forking over good money just to be insulted."

Owen, on the other hand, was already scouring his wallet. "Uh, you wouldn't take ten for the lot of us?" he tendered.

Tilting his cap backwards, the wily old codger wistfully scratched his clammy forehead. "All right lads, work away," he winked, pocketing the bill.

Scattered across the length and breadth of the field, the natives peddled their wares, while little clusters huddled around the stalls, poring over the merchandise on display. It was an archetypal rural fair, featuring an assortment of livestock, fresh produce and agricultural machinery. The line-up also included members of the Buckley clan, James and Jeremiah, conscripted into selling jars of honey and sacks of turf by their father, but on the whole, there was very little to enthral the average Dublin teenager.

"Crap! Absolute crap!" Kieran bellowed, eyeballing a nearby attraction with a sign reading; *Madame Cashmere, Clairvoyant - Consultations half-price, today only,* €9.

"My fortune for the next fortnight is a forgone conclusion! And all I can say is that it looks bleak! But four-fifty for *this*? *Four*-fifty! I mean like I ask you. Four fifty!!"

"Okay!" Owen snapped. "You've made your point abundantly clear, now!"

Surprised by his friend's abnormally sharp retort, Kieran buttoned his lip, and as they meandered along, a Khaki jacket sprung from the crowd. "Oh no! Here's Colonel Mustard and

Ambrosia Creamed Rice," Kieran bemoaned. "That pair are really getting on my tits!"

"Yeah, me too," Owen concurred.

As their privileged pals converged, duly noted was the periodic decline of their destitute counterparts. "What's with Lord of Flies there?" Dave hinted at Rory's compromised optical status.

"Mind your own business!" Rory hissed.

"Ah there's no *flies* on Rory," Owen quipped.

"So are we just out window shopping or are we looking to cadge a nice bale of straw for our supper, this evening?" Dave gestured.

"Actually, *straw* is more commonly used for bedding, while hay is for feeding," Rory amended.

"Gone native, are we? Still, with the stuff growing from the roof of your crummy gaff, I expect you won't go hungry at teatime!"

Visitors soak up the carefree atmosphere at the local farmers' market:

This time around, Kieran was less inclined to take the bait. "Just having a look around. We may as well get our money's worth for that hefty admission charge at the front gate."

"Admission charge? What admission charge?" Dave frowned.

"Didn't you pay four-fifty, coming in?"

"*Four-fifty* to see this rubbish? What are you on? Reality check, mister! Admission was free! And even that was a stretch!"

Kieran glared at his housemate, who in turn, scanned the area surrounding the main entrance, where the culprit had absconded, probably on his way to one of Rossbladderburst's six pubs to dispose of the evidence.

"I don't understand," Owen whimpered. "Then who did I give my money to?"

Realising they had been hoodwinked, Dave and his underling guffawed heartlessly.

"Oh but listen," Ambrose chuckled, as he dried a tear from his eye, "About coming down to watch a film some evening-"

"Look!" Kieran barked, "I still haven't asked the old heap yet if it's all right to-"

"No-no-no! I was just about to say that Mr Buckley made a packet at the track yesterday and bought us a new satellite dish, including a full subscription to the movie channels, to celebrate! So really, you needn't bother, now!"

Numbed to the extent of having downed a pitcher of local anaesthetic, Kieran contrived a feeble smile. "Oh right, that's just- terrific then, isn't it?" he murmured.

Still smarting from his big sting, Owen was further riled on recognising an object jutting from the pocket of Dave's khaki jacket. "What have you got there?" he enquired, pointing knowingly to the rectangular bulge.

"*Death On A Chairlift 9000*. The same as yours, actually," Dave proudly proffered the portable games console.

A brief inspection of the article confirmed Owen's suspicions. "This *is* mine!"

Dave brusquely withdrew his acquisition. "How could that be? I only bought it less than five minutes ago!" he said, polishing its casing with the hem of his sleeve.

"Where?"

"For a song too. Obviously the daft old biddy had no concept of its real value!"

"But *where*?"

"Over *there*!" Dave nodded irritably to his right.

All eyes immediately pinpointed the familiar wind-burned jowls sandwiched between a mountain of rhubarb and multiple cartons of 'free range' eggs. More incensed than anything else at their inability to elude this ever-present wretch, the unit abandoned Dave and Ambrose and marched over to inspect the remainder of her wares.

Noting their impending approach, the eagle-eyed woman swiftly draped a tea towel over a cardboard box, beneath the table. This, needless to say, provoked further suspicion. "Hello lads, I'll be wit'ye in a second," she declared, while counting out several sticks of rhubarb for a customer.

Deeming her actions to be a tardy, if uninspired, attempt to cover her tracks, Kieran boldly raised the screen. Inside, exasperatingly, was nothing more than a pair of chequered boxer shorts and the tea-cosy Rory had given her on the day of their arrival. Scant evidence indeed. Either they'd been thrown a red-herring or the manipulative mastermind had already sold on any other misappropriated effects. Having concluded her business, Peig homed in on her young wards. "Well, good afternoon lads," she said with her usual poker face, "See anything that tickles your fancy?"

"Tickles my fancy?!" Owen blurted, as he gawped into the box. "What are my shorts doing in there?"

"Oh my, yes indeed!" she cried, amid wide-eyed astonishment. "Yes, they must have fallen in when I was packing up the rhubarb earlier this morning."

Owen swiftly pocketed the embezzled briefs, one down and only seventeen pairs still unaccounted for.

♣ ♣ ♣ ♣ ♣

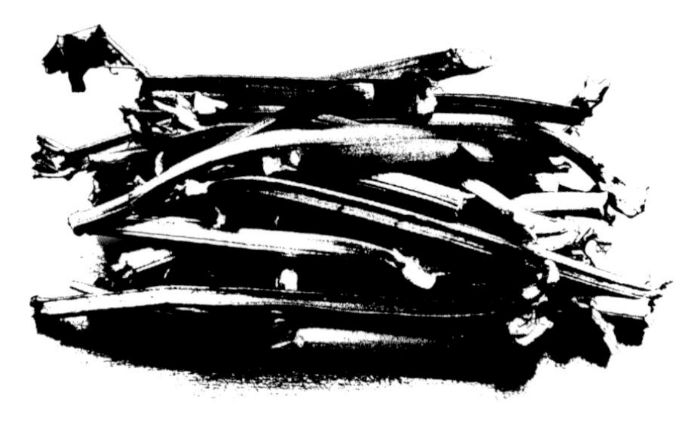

Back at the cottage, sometime later, our intrepid friends were poised for a spot of furtive undertaking. Armed with a shovel and spade they pottered about Peig's garden, trying to decipher their bearings.

"Another day of non-stop merry-go-round pure hilarity," Owen grumbled. "First I get fleeced for ten Euro and then I discover the old buzzard has flogged all our gear!"

"She didn't exactly cherish Rory's cosy-thing either," Kieran added sceptically.

Beyond insulting, Rory was too busy counting down the days, hours, minutes and seconds until his mother's return to the village.

"Now where exactly is this stuff buried?" Kieran scratched his crown.

With the spade in hand, Owen strode three paces from the back wall.

"Well it ought to be about here, I think."

"*Ought* to be? You *think*?"

"Uhm, yeah, the area looks kind of bare or something. Perhaps it's because she's ripped out half the rhubarb since last night."

"Well let's pray we haven't been ripped off again, because right now I could massacre a Kit-Kat!"

Abandoning the hierarchy this time around, Kieran grabbed the spade and began the excavation with gusto. But it wasn't long before an inkling of insecurity began to hamper the proceedings. "Are you sure we're in the right place?" he gasped. "The soil here does seem fairly compact!"

Owen too had his doubts, but was afraid to come clean. "Mathematically speaking, you're definitely in the right spot, although-"

"You haven't a clue, do you?!" Kieran exclaimed.

"Well geographically speaking, that area where Rory is standing now, looks more like the spot where we were digging yesterday," Owen clarified.

"But *that's* at least another three paces down the garden!"

"But maybe the measure of my steps were *longer* yesterday-"

"In that case, you just take the shovel and begin on another hole. Meanwhile, I'll continue on here and at least then we'll stand a better chance of finding it sooner."

Alas, hope turned to despair, as Kieran continued to plummet deeper and deeper into a seemingly barren trench. "I've got a wretched feeling about this," he panted, "Did you see the earth on her shoes this morning? It's a safe bet that she was mooching around here last night. Now I'm beginning to suspect she may have exhumed our secret cache and just when you think she's hit rock bottom-"

On these words, Kieran's spade scratched the surface of a pale coloured object below.

"Wait-wait-wait! I have it, I have it!" he declared.

Owen cropped his head from the second pit. "What? How can that be? *I've* just found them!" he yielded both Tupperware containers.

"Eh? Well, what's *this?*" Kieran frowned, as he brushed aside the earth with his fingers.

"Oooohooooohohohohooho!" he shuddered, instantly recoiling and scrambling manically to the embankment. The depravity of what unfurled saw the realisation of all his suspicious and fears, proof positive that they hadn't been suffering from collective paranoid delusions. Indeed, the horror intensified as Kieran became cognisant of a palpable threat to their very existence.

"W-what? W-what is it?" Owen stuttered, as he and Rory scuttled over to investigate.

Both were thunderstruck. Low and behold, peering eerily from the abyss was a skull; human, in all probability. At long last, the old woman's deepest, darkest secret had been unearthed.

16. Skulduggery

If Catherine Begley's industrial action was a blow to her husband, it was even more detrimental that Sunday brunch was *not* on her list of affected duties. Fortunately, the chiming of the doorbell provided Matthew with a stay of execution from the dinner table. As he opened the door, alas, the calibre of his visitors caused his upward crescent lips to capsize. "Oh! Mr O'Dowd, 'tis yourself," he said, subtly discarding a murdered parsnip into some nearby shrubbery. "Is ehm, is everything okay?"

Cautiously raising a blue plastic carrier bag and holding it at arm's length, Kieran issued a unique doorstep challenge to the principal. "Something *drastic,* I believe you said? Well, feast your eyes on the baubles she's been planting in her back garden and tell me everything is still *fine*!"

Baffled by the cloak and dagger pitch, Matthew swabbed his fingers on a paper napkin and peered into the bag "Ah come on lads!" he chortled. "April fool's was months ago!"

But noting Owen and Rory posted by the front gate, both clutching Tupperware containers and both seeming equally jittery, Matthew had a sickly feeling that something genuinely lethal was brewing.

"It's not something that merely tumbled out of the cereal box this morning, if that's what you're implying," Kieran warranted. "And I bet there's *more* where that came from!"

Matthew swiftly switched gears. "Ooooh! I knew it! I just knew it!"

A curious Jennifer Begley joined her father at the doorway. "What is it? What's going on?" she hovered over his shoulder.

"Nothing!" he snapped the bag shut. "Go and get your mother. Quickly!"

The mother hen was inevitably summoned and in the frenzied blur of events that followed, so too was her eminent brother, who, upon learning the news, ricocheted through the glens in record time. Before long, an impromptu preliminary hearing had convened in the Begley lounge. Flanking Leo O'Meara on the sofa, were his sister and brother in-law, while to their right, fidgeting restlessly in an armchair, was Kieran. Rounding off the conclave, Owen and Rory sat rigidly in a pair of kitchen chairs, still guarding their Tupperware. Young Derbhla and Daniel had been banished to the garden, while all efforts to dispel their older sibling, leaning against the back of the sofa, simply misfired. "Are you sure you haven't more study, Jennifer?" her mother suggested one last time.

But having already sneaked a glimpse into the blue carrier bag, the clued-in teenager had no intention of bowing out. "Wow, thank you for your belated concern!" she stated glibly. "But I'm all done, for now!"

With a weary nod from Catherine, her brother proceeded with the unveiling of Peig's magnum opus. A hush descended as all attempted to absorb the enormity of Kieran's landmark discovery.

"So, buried at the end of Sawyer's garden, you say?" Superintendent O'Meara probed.

"Yes, and as I said, you'll probably find the rest there, too," Kieran replied.

"No fear, we'll soon be scouring that garden with a fine-toothed comb. However, in all fairness, it's not the done thing to remove human remains from the scene of a possible homicide!"

Considering they had been on the endangered species list themselves, Kieran grew frustrated over the superintendent's nit-picking over protocol. "Yes, I'll bear that in mind, the next time I stumble across a stiff," he enunciated. "But given the circumstances, I thought it best to just grab the evidence and get the hell out of there!"

"You're dead right!" Matthew concurred. "After all, it wouldn't do for *us* to be sending your bones back to your parents in a jiffy bag."

"Uhm yeah, something like that," Kieran winced, drawing little comfort from the principal's espousal.

Catherine squirmed at her husband's gauche remarks, but held her tongue as her brother, once again, took centre stage. Inserting a biro into the eye socket, O'Meara hoisted the relic for a closer examination. In truth, he barely knew what clues to look for, but wanted to give an impression of being reflective, as it was expected from a man of his standing. "Yes, it's definitely been underground for quite a while," he wistfully stroked his chins. "Maybe even as long as a year. But tell me this much, what prompted ye to go mucking about there in the first place?"

"We'd no choice!" Owen exclaimed. "It was the only place left to hide our grub."

"That gluttonous gannet was pilfering all their food!" Jennifer interjected.

"Jennifer!" her mother shrieked.

"No! That's pretty much the sum of it all right," Kieran corroborated. "Every time we'd arrive back from a *céilí* or whatever, we'd find the dormitory ransacked. That, we figured, was the only option left open to us!"

Catherine folded her arms at the ignominy that had, yet again, besmirched the fine reputation of her summer school conservatory. "Didn't I always say she was a bad sort?! Isn't that what I've been saying all along, Matthew?"

"Something about owing her a debt of gratitude was how you put it, the other day," he murmured candidly.

"What I can't understand is what possessed you to rope her in again, after last year's fiasco!" she deflected.

Matthew grew hot under the collar. "Yes, you see, when Mrs Schalplatten died we- ah, the- uhm-"

"Yes, things start falling apart, once I'm out of the picture!" Catherine retorted. "Still, lads, ye shouldn't have let things get so bad before coming to us?"

Kieran opened his mouth to explain, but was brusquely pre-empted by Matthew. "Look, the important thing here is that nobody got hurt."

"Just in case it has escaped your attention, Bozo, there's somebody's head on our coffee table," his wife elucidated.

"None of *us*, I meant," he underlined.

Indeed, Matthew felt greatly reassured that his pandering had prevented *his* dismemberment. It was a tragedy, of course, but the sacrifice of some poor beggar meant that lazy days were back on his curriculum.

"Listen, for all we know, she could be still running amok," Kieran urged. "So will you be caging the old bird or not?"

"Oho! She's got plenty of explaining to do, all right," O'Meara advocated. "But first things first-" Groping around in his trouser pocket, he produced a mobile phone, though suddenly recalling the limited bandwidth, cast it aside. "Ara listen, do you mind if I use your telephone?"

"Is it a local call?" Matthew enquired.

"Yes, damn it! It's local! And this could be a murder inquiry we're dealing with now! So I'll be needing full cooperation from everyone!"

"Yes, of course Leo! You don't have to ask," Catherine gestured in the direction of a decorative table under the stairs.

Silence fell as the Superintendent picked up the earpiece and punched in the numbers for Knockyadown Garda station. "So lads, where and when did ye see her last?" he asked, while pausing for a reply.

"Over at that car boot sale thing, a couple of hours ago," Owen declared.

"Oh yes, I might have guessed," he huffed. "Hello? Yes? Is that you Leonard? Oh sorry, Alicia, yes, put Boyer on there. He's what? Fishing somewhere along the Blackwater?! Yes, I *do* know today is Sunday! Just reel him in and tell him to meet me down at the station A.S.A.P!"

O'Meara slammed down the receiver and turned to address the three orphaned students. "Now lads, there'll be no going back to that house this evening-"

"There's no question of them going back to that den of iniquity!" Catherine decreed.

"But what I *can* do," he averred, "Is to have a Garda pack your bags and bring them over here."

"What bags?" Kieran gestured.

"For your clothes and what-not?"

"See here!" Kieran flailed. "All I have is the shirt on my back! The same applies to the others. Everything else has been burned, torn, pilfered or flogged! So save your precious manpower for collaring the *bag* who robbed us blind!"

Tucking his shirt into his trousers, an infinite task, thanks to a substantial overhang, O'Meara swaggered towards the front door. "Rest assured lads, we'll be pulling out all the stops on this one. If there's so much as a wish bone in that garden of hers, we'll be down on her like a tonne of bricks. So you just sit tight and someone will be over shortly to take your full written statements!"

Leo was in his element. With retirement just around the corner, the superintendent had delusions of turning his career exploits into a best selling novel. Unfortunately, a history of self-indulgence over self-sacrifice left his memoirs a bit thin. But the capture of a wanton psychopath in his own back yard was the perfect opportunity to fill that void, and the bigger his input, the better the copy. Yet, before turning a page on this exciting new chapter, his sister highlighted a few basic ground rules.

"Leo?" she pointed to the coffee table, "Aren't you forgetting something?"

"Oh? Oh yes of course!" he doubled back, "Forensics might need to give the old noggin a quick once over."

♣ ♣ ♣ ♣ ♣

It was fast approaching tea-time, and at the Rossbladderburst farmers' market, operations were slowly winding down. Over at the Buckley stand, Curly was tallying the day's takings, while his retail division packed the leftover honey jars into the boot of his Rolls Royce.

"All the turf's gone, I see," Curly said, checking under the table.

"Oh yes, and we could have sold more too!" James boasted.

But rather than seeming content, with what was no mean feat for mid-June, the patriarch merely growled. "You two had better get back to the bar now and start cleaning out those toilets. But tell me, which one of ye did it last?"

Sensing, they'd somehow dropped another clanger, James and Jeremiah grew twitchy.

"Why?" the former asked.

"Well, when I said the urinals needed some fresh *cakes*, I didn't bank on spending half a day trawling the drains for blueberry muffins!"

Mercifully, Curly's begotten escaped a further rollicking with the blessed arrival of Fr. Tom Buttimer. "Greetings all!" he hailed piously, "I hope I'm not too late for some honey?"

"Not at all, father!" Curly beamed in a swift reversal of temperament. "You can have a crate, if you like?!"

"Oh no, just a jar, thanks. I do have to watch the figure you know," the priest patted his considerable girth.

"And tell me, how are you fixed for milk, at the moment?" Buckley enquired, as they completed the transaction.

"Grand! Perfect! Overloaded!" Fr. Tom hastily assured him, recalling several unbearable hours he had spent with a plunger. "Although, I *was* hoping for a quick word with the two lads, there?"

Wise to what he deemed was the cleric's not only pointless but egotistical mission, Curly quickly turned on the defensive again. "Look, they've more no time for playacting now. They're already a week behind with the turf cutting and there's at least another half-dozen jobs in the pipeline!"

"But Curly, we've still the unresolved issue of a missing coffin and I'm sure we'll all rest better, including Mrs Shalplatten, herself, once it's found!"

"Well at this stage, I hardly think her ladyship is going anywhere in a tearing hurry," Buckley warranted. (Ironically, the lady in question was, at present, hurtling through the streets of Manhattan; wreaking havoc in lunchtime traffic). "And wherever she is, I'm sure she's well out of harm's way. What's more, these lads aren't just a pair of skivvies, you know." Instinctively looking over his shoulder, Curly spotted James and Jeremiah creating facial contortions in the wing mirror of his car. "What are you eejits waiting for? Those toilets aren't going to clean themselves! Now go on! Skedaddle!"

Flushed with embarrassment, the pair scuttled off.

At that moment, the delicate equilibrium of this rural trade fair was shattered when a cavalcade of Garda vehicles came cascading through the front gate. Curious onlookers cropped their heads high as the squadron rumbled through the paddock. Assuming his own neck was on the block, one pirate-DVD vendor began frantically thrusting his wares into a suitcase, but slowed up again as the convoy moved farther afield in search of their true target.

The grand doyen herself barely batted an eyelid as the armada anchored alongside her stand; thanks to a mesmerising romance novel, with the compliments of Rory Waters' bag. Two plain clothes policemen alighted from the flotilla's flagship (an unmarked Ford Mondeo), to engage their suspect who was sitting on an overturned pail. Both reached for their identity cards, though it was the more senior and generously proportioned of the pair who cleared his throat to speak. "Ahem, Mrs Sawyer?"

As the old woman glanced up, a makeshift monocle dropped onto her lap.

"Yes?"

"I'm Superintendent Leo O'Meara," he flashed his card.

"Sur' I know that," she scoffed.

"And this is Detective Sergeant Boyer."

She did, however, adjust the monocle to assess this less familiar but tall, dark and handsome thirty-something officer, waist-high in waders.

"So?" she said, mentally dressing down his curious apparel.

"I'm afraid we'll have to ask you to accompany us down to the station to answer some questions!"

"I will not! I'm going nowhere 'til I finish up here for the day!"

Given her rancorous disposition, O'Meara took a step back to casually address his subordinate. "Sergeant, buy the auld rhubarb there and let's be done with it."

"What? Me?"

"Come on, time is money."

Groaning reproachfully, Boyer fished three two-Euro coins from his inner pocket. "All right, how much?" he said, flinging the currency on the table.

"That'll do," she siphoned off all three coins into her own coat pocket.

"Six Euro for three withered sticks of Rhubarb?!! That's daylight robbery!"

"Supply and demand, lad! Supply and demand."

With that, the superintendent signalled the 'all clear' to the remainder of his task force, who were standing by. An elected Bangarda emerged from the corps and escorted the elder towards one of the marked vehicles. True to form, Peig conveyed little emotion apart from some bewilderment and a general crabbiness at the inconvenience of it all. "What's all the to-do anyway?" she groused, while being bundled into the back seat.

Observing a plethora of bystanders, with their ears open and their tongues hanging out, O'Meara hedged his bets. "Why don't we discuss that over a nice hot whiskey down at the station?" he proposed, before closing the car door.

"Okay Boyer," he turned to his sergeant, "You go with them and keep an eye on things."

"Shouldn't I investigate the crime scene first?"

"Ara, I'll take care of it. I already have a team on the way- and I'll be heading over myself now, to set the ball rolling, as it were. So I'm leaving you to hold the fort, 'til I get back."

The detective was forming a hunch that his superior was on a power trip, but nonetheless accompanied the suspect in her designated vehicle. As the motorcade began to depart, O'Meara lingered behind to exert his authority over the crowd. "Please stand aside!" he gesticulated wildly. "There's nothing to see here! Everyone please, just go about your business as usual!"

Even so, the gaping throng couldn't help but wonder at the heavy handed tactics employed to detain one seemingly defenceless civilian. Nearby, a flamboyantly clad eccentric, festooned in tawdry jewellery and layers of make-up, folded her arms as the procession passed her by. "I saw this coming," she said, in a dry husky tone. "It was all in the cards this morning!"

"A fact you might have shared with the rest of us, Madame Cashmere?!" contested the perspiring gentleman, seen earlier stuffing DVDs into a suitcase.

Further along the ranks, Curly Buckley and Fr. Tom Buttimer were no less riveted by these astonishing developments. Peig's arch-nemesis stroked his bristled face, afraid to blink, in case he'd miss a fraction of this momentous occasion.

"Peig Sawyer is fettered, at last!" he declared, fluctuating between incredulity and euphoria. "I never thought I'd see the day!"

Fr. Tom, on the other hand, was fearful for those at the front line. "Heavens above!" he cried. "What about those poor young lads? I hope this isn't a repeat of last year's debacle. Here, I'd better call on the Begleys to see if they know anything about this."

Smelling an opportunity brewing, or if nothing else, some light amusement, Curly Buckley quickly jumped on board. "Ah sur' wait up there and I'll give you a lift!" he magnanimously offered, appreciating, no doubt, the need for a Trojan horse.

♣ ♣ ♣ ♣ ♣

The refugees had, for the time being, found sanctuary. Although Rory looked particularly heart-rending with his single lens repeatedly fogging up, Owen too had become progressively morose. The pair oscillated in their chairs, clutching their Tupperware containers as if their lives depended on them.

Kieran wasn't entirely unaffected either. "So what's the story?" he said, scratching the armrest, with a feral-like complex. "Do we need to write out our statements, or what?"

"Take it easy!" Jennifer advised. "Just tell them in your own words and they'll take care of the rest."

"Right, just so long as they bring enough paper."

Close at hand, Catherine Begley had been engaged on the telephone. "Okay, Rory," she replaced the handset, "I've tried calling your mother again, but still keep getting her answering service."

"Sh-she might be in the c-conference or something," he speculated.

"Oh I see, well I've left several messages anyway to say you're okay. Now what about you the rest of you?" she focused on the others. "Are ye sure ye wouldn't like me to give your parents a call?"

"No, you needn't bother, thanks very much," Kieran declined, knowing rightly she would be hard pressed to find a sympathetic ear at the other end.

Amid these trials and tribulations, Matthew Begley was stretched across the full length of the sofa, eating a marmalade sandwich.

"For goodness sake!" his wife protested, "Would you not let those poor lads sit on the sofa there, after the terrible ordeal they've been through?"

Nodding in accordance, Matthew relinquished his position.

"Now lads," Catherine gestured, "Make yourselves comfortable- and let me put those boxes aside-"

But a startling objection tackled her helping hand. "No! *My* food!" Owen barked, covetously intensifying his grip. Astonished stares encircled Owen, prompting him to realise that he had been gripped by paranoia. "Eh, no thanks, I mean. W-we're all right as we are," he politely rephrased.

"The *creatur's*," Catherine appraised their war ravaged faces, "Like death warmed up, they are!"

The slamming of car doors drew the couple's attention towards the window.

"Now who's *that*?" Catherine irritably responded.

Cagily positioning himself behind the curtain, Matthew peered outside. "Father Buttimer and *Curly Buckley* by the looks of it!" he recognised the carriage of the duo shuffling up the driveway.

"Buckley?! What does that auld ape want?!"

Sanctioning the function of porter to her husband, Mrs Begley nonetheless extended a warm welcome to both visitors. "Father Buttimer! Mr Buckley! Hello there! Come in, come in!"

First to set foot inside was the visibly harried parish priest. "Sorry, we eh, I- Hello! Eh, we uhm," he rambled incoherently for a moment, though trailed off upon spotting the cluster across the lounge, with their faculties seemingly intact.

"Oh! Oh good," he said, realising, perhaps, that the worst had not come to pass.

Rapidly deducing that new intelligence was pending, Catherine groomed her visitors. "Come in Father, sit down there and relax," she ushered him towards the available space on the sofa.

Swiftly latching on, a comparatively calm Curly Buckley squeezed in at the end, placing a jar of honey on the coffee table, as his ring-side ticket to the event.

"Ah you're very kind!" Matthew acknowledged.

Gathering his thoughts into a more cohesive framework, Fr. Tom rebooted. "Sorry, yes, you see, we've just come directly from the market and the place was swarming with Gardaí and Mrs Sawyer, you see, was-"

"Oh yes, we know all about it," Catherine said, shaking her head.

"You do?"

"Well no details yet, only to say that the lads here found a skull buried in her yard."

Curly Buckley's eyes looked set to explode. "A *what*?!!" he expostulated.

"Oh dear Lord!" Fr. Tom cried.

Allowing a token breather for assimilation purposes, Catherine filled in the blanks. "A big investigation is underway and from what I hear, there'll be no stone left unturned in that house below."

"That explains the fleet of JCBs we saw on our way over!" Fr. Tom gathered.

Whilst the cleric was recouping his equanimity, a simmering Curly Buckley was only now coming to the boil. "I knew that woman was no damned good!" he pounded the armrest. "It's all in the breeding, and I've always said, her lot were sired from only the poorest stock!"

"Ah Curly, haven't we all fallen among the thorns, at one time or another?" Fr. Tom implored.

Buckley, however, had no intention of dismounting from his high horse. "I hope they see to it, she gets the electric chair for this!"

"Ireland doesn't *have* the electric chair," Rory interjected.

"Is that right? Well, maybe an electric blanket, so!" he asserted. "Yes, that would do the trick!"

"So now, what are we to do with these poor lads?" Catherine said, trying her best to assuage the subversive tone. "I suppose the only thing for it, is to fix them up here for the night?!"

Kieran and Jennifer exchanged hopeful glances.

"Oh! I know what to do," Matthew dashed for the telephone. "Mrs O'Shea was adamant about wanting to keep more students! We'll give her a ring!"

"Do not!" Catherine snapped.

"What? Why not?"

"Candy O'Shea has enough on her plate! Didn't she spend the whole morning on the phone, griping about how obstreperous her own three lads were? And that according to Bernard, a crate of Port and umpteen bottles of cider have gone missing from the Tavern!"

"Oh?"

"I don't mind," Jennifer shrugged, "They can all stay in my room, if they like."

"Don't be daft!" her mother summarily discounted.

Curly Buckley, to everyone's surprise, volunteered an uncharacteristically generous solution to their accommodation woes. "Sur' why not send them down to me? It's no skin off my teeth?" he suggested.

Catherine could barely conceal her optimism. "Oh but Curly, I wouldn't dream of asking!"

"Nonsense! I've three rooms lying idle as it is, so no buts about it. And I don't want to hear so much as a mention of money!" he avowed, overstating his 'sincerity' with some animated hand gestures.

"We never mentioned it," Matthew foolishly added.

"Grand so! That's settled!" Catherine ever so swiftly clinched the deal. "Do ye hear that lads? Ye'll be leaving with Mr Buckley, this evening!"

While a venue change was far from earth-shattering news, it put paid to Kieran and Jennifer's short-lived aspirations. And with a verbal treaty in the bag, Catherine propitiously clasped her hands. "Now, who's for a nice cup of tea?"

17. A Bumper Harvest

In a sterile interrogation room, in Knockyadown Garda station, the suspect sat alone at a table with her arms folded. Growing weary of the limited frills on view, a map of Ireland on one wall and an enlarged framed photograph of their beloved superintendent on another, Peig Sawyer turned to her sole compatriot, on sentry duty by the window. "So what's your name, girl?" she enquired.

"Alicia, Ma'am," the Bangarda replied.

"*Liquorice-Man*?!

"No, just *Alicia*!"

"Oh, just Liquorice-"

"No! *A-li-cia*!" she volubly amended.

"Isn't that what I just said?!!" the detainee bellowed. "Although I can't, for the life of me, figure out all these silly names selfish parents inflict on their youngsters these days! So tell me Liquorice, how long more am I going to be cooped up here? Only I've three hungry lads, at home, waiting for their dinner!"

"Uhm, I'm certain that's been taken care of, Mrs Sawyer," Alicia anxiously bit her lower lip. "The sergeant should be along any minute."

Doubtless, the young lady's newly acquired facial tics were enough to suggest that Peig had a fresh recruit in her vast legion of devotees.

"So where is he, now?" she niggled. "At the toilet, is he? Surely it can't be taking him that long? What is he, suffering from constipation?"

D.S. Boyer's timely entrance, seconds later, elicited an inaudible sigh of relief from his colleague. Gone were his waist-high waders, having ceded to a formal dark-grey suit. "Now Mrs Sawyer," he dropped a dossier on the table, "Are they looking after you, all right?"

On the assumption that this young man was a soft touch, Peig attuned herself. "Well I wouldn't mind a bite of dinner, to tell you the truth," she bleated mournfully.

"Right, would you like us to send out for a curry, or something?"

"A what? Ara, I'd rather boil my own Wellingtons than eat that tripe!"

"Well there's always Duffy's around the corner, I suppose? Although they don't come too cheap."

"Oh lovely! Ask them if they'd do up a few crubeens for me."

Boyer waveringly stroked his sideburns while taking a seat opposite. "Right, perhaps I can ask someone to fetch a menu. But putting *that* on the back burner for a moment, Mrs Sawyer, let's you and me have a little chat. Now I half suspect you've already an inkling of why we've called you down here?" he manoeuvred skillfully into the raison d'être for their meeting.

Peig glanced briefly at the dossier. "If it's about the butter again-"

"No Mrs Sawyer, it's not about the butter. In fact, we need you to answer a few questions about a certain discovery made at the bottom of your garden, this afternoon?"

As if hit by a bolt from the blue, her craggy mug suddenly darkened, but this was a transitory portrait and all too swiftly, the blinkers came down again.

"What did you say your name was again?" she digressed.

"I'm Detective Sergeant Danny Boyer," he articulated.

"*Danny Boyer?*" she repeated.

"Correct. So now, back to the question of-"

But before he could forge ahead, the brazen hussy burst spontaneously into song.

"*Oh Danny Boyer, the pipes, the pipes are calling!*"
From glen to glen, and down the mountain side,
The summer's gone, and all the flowers are dying,
'Tis you, 'tis you must go and I must bide...

"Aha yes, very droll," he feigned the briefest of smiles. "But now, back to the matter at hand-" Despite his plea, the old crank defiantly augmented her voice by several decibels.

"*But come ye back when summer's in the meadow!!*
Or when the valley's hushed and white with snow!!!"

Several aborted attempts to interject followed. "Please, Mrs Sawyer, if we could just get back to-" and yet, the powerhouse showed no signs of letting up.

"*'Tis I'll be here in sunshine or in shadow.*
Oh Danny Boyer, Oh Danny Boyer, I love you-love you so..."

A shamefaced detective-sergeant despondently bowed his head, conceding that his interview had, for the moment, reached a deadlock.

♣ ♣ ♣ ♣ ♣

The Begleys' guests had gathered around a swish glass-top dining table, in the lounge window bay, having graciously accepted an invitation to tea. As the 'gallery' was off limits, save for special occasions *and* visits from the landed gentry, this was a rare privilege. Good food and stimulating conversation were all the ingredients sadly lacking in this social gathering. Squire Buckley, fittingly, dominated the discussion, progressing naturally from Peig Sawyer to 'worming' foals.

"So from the age of three weeks, you have to worm every three weeks until they are about twelve weeks old. It costs a pretty penny too. But of course, with the foals, the main worry is the tapeworm, although roundworm, which migrates through the throat, can be fairly problematic too-"

On the threshold of eating a mouthful of watercress, a truly nobbled Fr. Tom threw down his fork. While ingesting Curly's horrific homily on equine care, he and the others had to wrestle with Catherine Begley's doubly gruesome mixed-grill-cum-salad.

Leaning to one side, Kieran elbowed his associate. "Sheesh, I never thought I'd hear myself saying this, but even the old hag made a better cup of tea than this."

"Yes, burnt tea is a new one on me," Owen whispered. "And that apple tart wasn't exactly kosher, either."

"I couldn't even finish mine, especially having found that bacon rind in the pastry."

It suddenly twigged that a real banquet was just begging to be put out of its misery. Elbowing Owen again, Kieran nodded towards the Tupperware container on Owen's lap. Owen caught his gist and surreptitiously raised the lid.

Across the table, meanwhile, Jennifer Begley dithered over the black-leathery artefact that graced her platter.

"I hope those chops are done enough!" Catherine declared. "I don't know what happened to the end of yesterday's corned beef," she said, with a biting scowl at her husband, "So I threw those into the chip-pan at the last minute."

Jennifer bowed her head and kept quiet. The less her mother knew about her subsidies for the less fortunate the better. As her fork met with the dubious article, it was accidentally jettisoned across the table onto her father's plate. Luckily for Jennifer, he had been reaching for the salt at the time and failed to notice that his food had suddenly propagated, though predictably, was plumb horrified on making this hideous discovery.

Deeming this as a high time to repay a favour, Kieran passed around the tuck box beneath the table. Surprised at first when something nudged her, Jennifer's eyes widened on finding a box of Angel Cakes on her lap. Gladly helping herself, she tried not to laugh at the fact that Kieran's 'sleight of hand' went unnoticed below the transparent table-top.

"Of course with the mare then, one of the things you have to watch out for is neonatal septicaemia," Curly Buckley rattled on.

While failing miserably in home economics, Catherine fared marginally better in the hospitality sector, auspiciously pitching in as she spotted the priest floundering.

"Are you all right there, Father? You're not eating anything?!"

"What? Oh yes, I'm grand, thanks," he replied, gently beating his chest in an attempt to dislodge a frozen piece of sausage roll.

"How about a cup of tea?" she raised the pot.

"Eh no, thanks very much," he demurred, though it was already too late.

"And what about you Curly?" she veered the teapot in his direction. "Will you have another cup?"

"No-no-no!" he shielded the rim. "No more for me, thanks."

Just then, their soirée was ambushed by an unnerving hammering on the window.

"What on earth is that!?" Catherine jumped.

Tottering about outside, with his face turning an unhealthy lilac, her own brother was in the throttlehold of two young scallywags.

"Ara blasht!!!" Curly suddenly howled.

As Catherine refocused her attention, she realised that she had been pouring hot tea all over the back of Curly Buckley's hand. "Oh jeepers! Oh no! I'm awfully sorry, Curly! Quick! Let's run the cold tap over it!" she cried, grabbing his wrist and spiriting him into the kitchen.

Matthew was left to police the 'mugging' on his doorstep. "Stop that now! Your poor uncle is enough of a wreck, as he is!" he roared.

When this failed to incite, the mention of the word 'bedtime' sent the pint-sized attackers scuttling into the bushes. "Nothing damaged, I hope?" Matthew enquired, as his brother-in-law staggered through the front door.

"Of course not!" O'Meara squared his shoulders. "I'm used to all that rough-and-tumble!"

Before the superintendent could regain his breath, Kieran O'Dowd let fly. "Well, did you get her?" Loosening his collar a notch, the winded policeman collapsed into the chair vacated by his sister. His brooding glare suggested the imminent disclosure of a significant new development. "Yes, she's in custody all right. We picked her up long 'go!" he gushed.

"Well that's a relief, isn't it?" Kieran concluded.

"It's not exactly all good news, I'm afraid-"

"Oh?"

"It seems that a few complications have arisen, as it were, over at the site. You see, twenty minutes after our forensics squad rolled in, believe it or not, we actually uncovered a second body."

For some, this newsflash was literally jaw dropping, though for Kieran, it was the thrilling affirmation of his theory. "Aaah! I knew it! Isn't that what I said?!"

"And ten minutes after that," O'Meara sustained, "We found another-"

All too quickly, Kieran's conceit was thrown into obscurity. "Whoa, wait a minute, *two* more?!"

"*Three* more, to be precise."

"What?!!" Glancing down at his fingers, the befuddled youth began to tally up the body count.

"I believe that makes four?" Rory punctuated.

"Yes, thank you Mr Cyclops!" Kieran barked. "I can do the math!"

"But weren't there just two who disappeared?" Owen recapped.

Right away, the superintendent seized on what he believed could be a vital lead. "Disappeared? Who disappeared?!" he grappled for his notepad and biro.

Owen gawped at Kieran in a bid for support.

"Those two girls who dropped off the radar, last year," the elected spokesman clarified, with uncertainty. "Remember Father, you mentioned them earlier in the week? So we just assumed that's where they ended up after Mrs Sawyer finished with them."

"Good grief!" the cleric gasped. "No-no-no! That's not what happened, at all!"

Leo O'Meara dejectedly folded his arms. "Yes, perhaps you'd best explain that one, Father?"

Heaving a weary sigh, the parish priest finally unravelled a conundrum that had beleaguered our friends, night and day for a whole week. "Last year, unfortunately, I apprehended two young ladies walking away from St. Millipede's with a wheelbarrow of lead, which had clearly been lifted from the church roof. To cap it all, when the superintendent's inquires led him to Mrs Sawyer's cottage; not only did he find the girl's dorm stacked to rafters with lead, but he also found the church organ which had gone missing only three days before. Although I still can't fathom how they carted that colossal instrument across an entire village, let alone get it through the front door!"

"They had help, didn't they?!" Jennifer blurted.

"Peig Sawyer!" Kieran concluded.

"Apparently she was just as surprised as we were," Matthew shrugged.

"That figures," Kieran added sceptically.

"And the girls were the ones who were caught red-handed," O'Meara warranted.

"Ah excuse me," Rory intervened, "But didn't it occur to anyone that these students might have been coerced into doing someone else's bidding?"

Mortified shrugs abounded at the irrefutable cold-hard logic. In hindsight it seemed glaringly obvious that her ladyship was the linchpin.

"Her word against theirs," Owen suggested.

"She put the screws on them, I'll bet," Kieran surmised. "If like us, they were probably sentenced to death by potato. So is that *it*? All that song and dance over some crappy stolen lead and a church organ?!!"

"All?!!" Fr. Tom cried. "Not only were those poor girls expelled, but they each had to spend six months in a juvenile detention centre!"

"Right, but they're definitely not dead?"

"God forbid!"

"But if it's not them, then who-?"

"Exactly!" the superintendent declared. "So lads, since all my staff are working flat out this evening, I'll need each of you to drop down to the station tomorrow morning- say, at about eleven, to make your full statements. Matt, you'll be going with them, no doubt? And it mightn't hurt to ask Cathy to come along, too."

Matthew looked anxiously towards the kitchen. "Maybe you'd ask her yourself?"

"I'm completely snowed under now!" Leo glanced at his watch.

"Hey! Aren't there slates on the roof of St. Millipede's?" Owen cried.

"Yes," Fr. Tom sighed, "Ever since Monsignor McCashin was given that rather enticing appraisal for the lead."

Close at hand, Mrs Begley had the unappealing task of nursing Mr Buckley's burn. "Once that soaks in, you'll be fine," she deciphered, while lubricating the inflamed area with butter.

"Ah well in that case, I won't sue, this time around!" he quipped.

"Thanks a bunch!" she chuckled sardonically at his veiled caveat.

Their innocent tête-à-tête ended sharply as Matthew ploughed through the louvre doors, predictably lurching to a halt on finding his wife and his neighbour amid some questionable shenanigans. "What the devil's going on here?!!" he grimaced at the pound of butter lying ravaged on the table.

Startled by his overreaction, the intertwined glistening hands briskly parted company.

"Nothing at all!" Catherine replied, grabbing a towel from the rail, as she marched towards the door, with her greasy 'Lothario' in tow.

As Catherine re-entered the lounge, her brother was about to depart. "You're not leaving already, Leo?" she asked, while scouring her fingers on the cloth.

"I must," he reached for the latch. "But I'm sure the others will give you an update-"

"They've found three more stiffs buried in the old biddy's garden!" Jennifer hastily delivered.

"Lord save us!!!" Catherine cried, teetering back several steps. "*Three?!*"

These groundbreaking developments also furthered the cause of the right honourable Mr Buckley. "Oh, how the mighty have fallen!" he quivered imperiously.

Absent-mindedly throwing her towel across the sofa's arm-rest, next to Fr. Tom's blazer, Catherine bowed her head in remorse. "How could we have been so blind?"

With that, the telephone sounded.

"If that's for me, I'm not here!" she declared, as her daughter pounced to answer it.

Jennifer picked up the handset and extended a cordial reply. "Hello? Yes it is. Who? Uhm, hang on and I'll check-" Shielding the mouthpiece, she turned to the figure still hovering in the doorway. "Somebody called Boyer for you, Uncle Leo?"

With a consenting nod, O'Meara traipsed over to accept the call. "Yes Sergeant, what's the score?"

At the opposite end of the line, the aggrieved policeman was hunched over his desk, with the receiver at one ear and his index-finger wedged firmly in the other.

"She's singing like a canary, sir!" he declared.

Leo's demeanour brightened considerably. "Oh good! A full confession?"

"No, that's not what I mean, unfortunately!" Tilting backwards, Boyer extended the earpiece in the direction of the interview room, indulging his superior to a smattering of what *he* had endured for two and a half hours.

"And if you come, when all the flowers are dying
And I am dead, as dead I well may be
You'll come and find the place where I am lying

And kneel and say an 'Avé' there for me."

On that note, Boyer culminated the impromptu recital. "Did you get that?"

"Loud and clear!" O'Meara scowled. "Listen Sergeant, she's playing the fool, now that she knows we've yanked an ensemble of her clacking playmates, below!"

"Sir?"

"Oh didn't you hear? Three more exhumations!"

The detective glared at his garrulous guest whose vibrant lyrics suddenly took on a new meaning. Clearly he was dealing with a fanatic more treacherous than previously imagined. "Well hurry back," he urged. "She's becoming a right pain in the Derry-Air, if you know what I mean."

"Oho! Let's see how chirpy she is after spending a night in the cells!"

Leo O'Meara's own captive audience was attentively ear-wigging to one-side of this conversation. Hungry for more, Curly Buckley angled his head closer, while inattentively reaching for the towel, left by Catherine, to wipe the oily residue from his hands.

"Right, I've a few stops to make first," the superintendent resolved. "But I should see you in about half an hour! Oh and try and keep this under your hat, Boyer. The last thing we need is the media drumming up a ruckus, at least until we've got a proper handle on things!"

So rapt was Curly by these salacious and possibly useful titbits, that he failed to discern an unseemly indiscretion of his own. In fact, it was only after wiping the sweat and froth from his jowls, that he realised he had been using Fr. Tom's jacket as a face cloth.

O'Meara replaced the receiver and made straight for the door. "I must dash," he said, in haste, "but I'll see you tomorrow, at eleven, as arranged!"

"Right Leo, see you then and thanks a lot!" Catherine smiled, as she gently closed the door behind him. "See us for what?" it clicked after a brief pause.

"For interviews down at the station," Matthew clarified, "You, me and the three lads."

"At eleven o' clock in the morning?!" she cried, apparently detecting a fly in the ointment. "But tomorrow's Monday! And if we're in Knockyadown, then who'll be handing out exam papers over in the school?"

"Oh you're right there," he realised. "And I suppose Mrs Sawyer is definitely out of the running, now!"

"Evidently! So why didn't you make a later appointment?"

Matthew grew flustered. "Sh-shall I go after him?"

Before the recriminations turned nasty, Fr. Tom judiciously intervened.

"Listen, is there anything I can do to help?"

"Only if you've an hour or two to spare in the morning?" Catherine proposed.

"Ah sur' isn't it all part and parcel of the job, anyway?" the cleric said in earnest.

"Well, you're an absolute godsend!" Matthew beamed.

"Yes, thank you, Father," Catherine acknowledged. "But we've still the sixty-odd visiting delegates to consider. Who'll sit in on them, presuming Miss Colic is still indisposed?"

"That waste of space?!" Curly remarked, with disdain, "It's disposing of she needs. I saw her falling out the door of O'Shea's Tavern, this afternoon, hardly able to stand up, she was!" Across the room, Kieran and Owen marvelled in silence as yet more spice was added to the proceedings. Mindful, however, that all eyes were now trained on him, Curly grew restive.

"Eh Curly?" Catherine inevitably broached, "You wouldn't happen to-?"

"Oh begod! Is-is-is that the time already?" he peeped nervously.

"You wouldn't have a couple of hours to spare, yourself?" she persevered.

"Oh, eh, well, I don't know now?"

"No, of course not," she dismissed apologetically. "Forget I even mentioned it."

Yet, as it dawned on Curly Buckley that these were the very people he needed to impress, the philanthropist made an extraordinary u-turn. "But sur' seeing as it's an emergency, where's the harm, I suppose?"

"Ah, fair play."

"Yes, maybe I could even organise a field trip for them?" Curly mused, gradually warming to his new responsibilities.

"No-no-no!" Matthew baulked, "Keep them pacified, but keep it simple."

"Good, that's all sorted, so!" Catherine concluded. "And I must say, Curly, it's admirable the way you've taken those poor lads under your wing. I'm sure you'll reap great rewards for your efforts!"

"And isn't virtue its own reward?" Fr. Tom said, as he made for his jacket.

While Curly was banking on something a little more tangible, he didn't care to argue with the man whose coat he had just defiled. "Right lads, grab your bags and what not," he declared. "It's time we were making a move!"

"We've no bags," Kieran sighed wearily.

"What?"

"Yes, I'm afraid the lads' luggage went missing during their stay with Mrs Sawyer," Catherine diplomatically explained.

Curly, of course, read between the lines and the further his enemy fell from grace, the more inflated he became. "That lighting cow!"

"Wh-what time would you like us to drop by in the morning?" Fr. Tom enquired, while donning his blazer.

"Half-past-ten at the latest, I should say," Catherine suggested, while seeing him to the door.

"Don't worry, I'll be there long before that," he pledged.

As the priest turned to face the exit, duly noted was his sullied garb. "What happened to your jacket there, Father Buttimer? It's a right show at the back!"

"It's what?" he attempted to look over his shoulder.

"Yera nothing! It's fine! It's fine!" Curly rubbished, escorting him straight out the door.

Thanking Mrs Begley for her well-intentioned hospitality, Kieran, Owen and Rory also made for the exit. "Take it easy now, lads," she added. "Whatever time suits Mr Buckley is an early enough start for *ye* tomorrow morning."

"Okay, thanks a lot," Kieran said, happily basking in some long overdue sympathy.

As their new custodian followed on, he left Catherine with a parting wink that further roused Matthew's fertile imagination. Indeed, once the door closed, she faced the inevitable grilling from her husband. "What was all that about?" he huffed.

"What was *what*?"

"You and that great baluba there, one minute you're capering behind my back and next, it's all this, wink-wink lark!"

Catherine was intent on shirking the issue. "Jennifer! Clear off the table!"

The teenager made a mad tear for the stairs. "Oh, I just remembered, I've a few notes to revise for my French exam tomorrow!"

"So?" Matthew persisted. "Is there something afoot that I ought to know about?"

With Jennifer now out of the frame, there was no excuse for shilly-shallying.

"Ara, didn't you see that the poor man scalded his hand, for goodness sake!" she scoffed. "If I didn't know better, I'd think you were jealous!"

"What? Me? Don't be ridiculous!" Nibbling on his lower lip, Matthew pondered briefly on whether or not *he* was now on solid enough footing to resolve some contentious issues of his own. "So are we are all, uhm, feeling better now, or what?"

Catherine groaned as she contemplated the mouldering shrine that still dominated one corner of their living room. "Well I can't have you squandering *all* our savings on flowers, even if they *have* brightened up the place," she grudgingly yielded.

As this was tantamount to a pardon, Matthew plucked a red rose from the vast bouquet and clenched the stem between his teeth. Grabbing his wife in a passionate embrace he whisked her across the lounge. But Catherine's response to his frivolities was less than favourable. "Ah give over! Can't you see that everything is in a heap and there's people out there dropping like flies!"

18. It's A Turf Life

Hale and hearty, Peig Sawyer cleaved through her veal supper, unmindful to the escalating evidence that was entrenching her guilt. But the inscrutable sprite was about to be served with some 'just deserts' to complement her decadent appetite. Just as she was dabbing up the last of her gravy with a piece of bread, a bumptious Leo O'Meara barged into the interview room.

"It's about time *you* got here!" she sloshed. "I'm ready to go home now, if you don't mind."

"I'm afraid that won't be possible," he officiously declared.

Clicking his heels and broadening his shoulders, the superintendent adapted a dazzlingly formal deportment. "Peig Lacerina Sawyer?"

"Yes?"

"We have a warrant here for your arrest. You are not obliged to say anything unless you wish to do so, but whatever you say will be taken down in writing and may be given in evidence."

Wiping her face on a silk-lined serviette, Peig arose from the table. "Now look here!" she cried, "Hasn't this little joke of yours gone far enough? If you want something then speak up and I'm sure we can arrive at some accommodation, as we've always done before!"

Raucously clearing his throat, O'Meara struggled to keep a professional distance, while keeping a nervous eye on his sergeant, who was observing from the doorway. "Quadruple homicide is no laughing matter!" he handed her the charge sheet.

"Homicide?" she repeated.

"Yes! How can you possibly discount the four bodies we found buried at the end of your garden, this afternoon?"

The indictment threw a conspicuous crimp in the old woman's bravado and she slumped quietly into her chair.

"Well, Mrs Sawyer?" the superintendent pressed. "Is there anything pertinent you'd like to add in your defence?"

"Yes!" she snapped. "Where's that hot whiskey you promised me?"

♣ ♣ ♣ ♣ ♣

Under the patronage of Curly Buckley, our nomadic friends soon found themselves spinning from pillar to post. It began with the preordained diversion to Buckley's watering hole, where a pledge of 'I'll be only five minutes!' was grossly underestimated. In fact, the surplus baggage were kept twiddling their thumbs for a good hour and *ten* before his lordship re-emerged, smelling like a brewery. More intriguing was his 'slight detour' via the actual crime scene. Inside and out, Peig Sawyer's cottage was literally crawling with forensic investigators. Heavy machinery laid waste to vast tracts of Peig's precious rhubarb and since dusk had now fallen, enormous halogen lamps dominated the landscape, to ensure continuous progress. In view of the sheer scale of the operation, it was difficult for Kieran, Owen and Rory to recognise their part in setting this wrecking-ball rolling.

Undaunted by the police blockade, Curly Buckley surfaced from his golden chariot. He had no sooner reached the flapping ribbon barrier, when he was intercepted by the night patrol. Kieran too was curious and lowered his window to eavesdrop.

"Excuse me sir, this is a crime scene," the sentry forewarned. "Access is restricted!"

Astonishingly, there were significant grounds for Curly's snooping. "Ah hello there, how are ya' at all!" he ignored the standard brevity. "Listen, if by any chance you find a hoard of gold sovereigns knocking about, you wouldn't give me a call?" Irreverently dispensing one of his business cards into the policeman's pocket, Curly pleaded his case. "You see the collection actually belonged to my father, until that auld scrounger swiped the lot, along with the family silver, years back."

"I'm sorry sir," the officer declined, "But I can't personally authorise any such transaction. Anything we do find is automatically classified as evidence."

"Oh yes-yes, of course, yes, I understand perfectly! But sur' listen, thanks anyway," Curly extended his hand in friendship.

The Garda cagily reciprocated, but in doing so, came away with a large banknote in his hand. "Hey you!" he exclaimed, once it clicked that he had been tendered a backhander. "We're not permitted to take personal donations!"

But the warning went unheeded by the brass-necked monkey who was already scuttling back to his Rolls Royce. "What?" Curly said innocently. "Sur' that's only an advancement on your Christmas raffle tickets, and now don't you forget to keep an eye out for those coins!"

The leery Garda seemed intent on taking further action, but luckily for Curly, he was sidetracked by an almighty crash from within the cottage. As the patrol officer scrambled to investigate, Buckley ventured closer in a bid to satisfy his own curiosity. The trio seated in the back of his car, were far less interested, having swiftly reached their own conclusion. "The forbidden door strikes again," Owen sighed.

♣ ♣ ♣ ♣ ♣

In the Buckley manor, life remained rosy for Dave Keogh and Ambrose Cleary. Sitting comfortably on a large settee in the kitchen-cum-living-room, the pair were capitalising on their host's latest purchase, in the company of Steven Seagal. Alas, such extravagances were seldom afforded to Mags Buckley whose mind-numbing existence was sublimated in the pursuit of an immaculate abode. Adding to her burden was an accumulation of popcorn on the floor surrounding the settee. Chalking this latest task onto her everlasting rota, Mags dutifully advanced with her manual carpet sweeper. "Lift!" she commanded.

As the slothful pair perfunctorily raised their feet, the homespun housekeeper paused for a moment to stare as the on-screen action reached some bloody climax.

"So lads, no *céilí* again this evening?"

"Yeah, cancelled 'til further notice," Dave said unflappably, leaning to one side, in order to compensate for the large obstacle impeding his viewing pleasure. Once their popcorn deposits were swept away, Dave and Ambrose munificently brushed a fresh batch onto the floor.

On completion of her vacuuming, Mags, in passing, went to draw the curtains, and outside, illuminating the velvet blackness, a pair of oncoming headlamps heralded Curly's homecoming. A piping hot meal awaited her bloated brother, as he stepped inside the front door.

"Ah there you are Curly!" she greeted. "Your dinner's on the table-"

The slamming of additional car doors, however, suggested to Mags the advent of visitors. "Oh!" she cried. "Have we company?"

An answer manifested itself, as Kieran, Owen and Rory shuffled sheepishly into the kitchen. "Three more for breakfast tomorrow morning, Mags!" Curly declared, failing to elaborate vis-à-vis the procurement of these new recruits.

"Three?! Oh right, grand so," Mags noted, with slavish devotion.

The other residents, in contrast, were astounded by this incursion and promptly unleashed an inquisition, as they leapt from the settee. "What are *you* lot doing here?" Dave probed.

"Our gaff was raided this evening by the guards," Kieran clarified.

"The vice squad?" Ambrose gawped.

"Eh? Oh yeah sure, why not?" he shrugged, realising the other troupe were still under a certain misapprehension.

"Oh you jammy beggars! How come you lot always land the exciting gigs?"

"The luck of the draw, I suppose," Kieran said blankly, absorbing his cosy new surroundings.

Owen, too, was agog at the imposing LCD widescreen television, overshadowing much of the living room. "Where did *that* monstrosity spring from? NASA?"

"Nifty, eh?" Dave smirked. "That was another of old- eh, I mean Mr Buckley's purchases, yesterday."

"Here, I expect it's bigger than your titchy little sixty-inch effort?" Ambrose crowed.

"Yes, just- just a tad," Owen nodded.

While the accusations of hedonism being levied against them were based on a complete cock-and-bull story, the fact that so many of their rivals' whims were being pandered to, seemed all the more galling. Nevertheless, given that *they* were now about to share in this windfall, O'Dowd and company were undoubtedly prepared to let it slide. "So what are we watching?" the alpha male enquired, as he seized not only the remote control, but a prime spot on the settee.

"*Spine Crusher 2*," Ambrose frowned.

"Cool!"

Swiftly joining Kieran at either side, Owen and Rory made themselves equally comfortable. Dave managed to squeeze in at the end, while Ambrose, unfortunately, found himself relegated to the floor. "Uhm, I think that might be my popcorn you're eating," he whined, as Kieran siphoned the end of a bag he had found on the armrest.

But already too engrossed to discern anything untoward, Kieran dismissed his mild irritation with a 'shush' before amplifying the volume.

At the other end of the room, Curly flung a copy of the Golden Pages telephone directory onto the table.

"Don't forget to eat your dinner there, before it gets cold," Mags cautioned.

"Ah, give it to the dog," he frowned, while leafing through the pages, "I've deadly heartburn, this evening."

"Oho! That'll be the liquor causing your ulcer to flare up again!" she scolded.

"Tis not!" he snapped. "I had tea over at the Begleys' this evening and I swear that woman was trying to poison me!"

"Ooo?! Tea at the Begleys'? How did you manage to swing that?"

"Why?"

"Just wondering, that's all," she said casually.

Clasping the large tome beneath his arm, Curly made for the hall door.

"I'll explain later, but right now I've some important calls to make," he declared.

Taking the apparent snub in her stride, Mags busied herself in the kitchen and within minutes had produced five cups of hot-chocolate and a plate of Jam Rings.

"There ye are lads," she said, arriving with a tray, "A light snack before bedtime."

While all five eagerly accepted a cup, the new arrivals were most impressed with her top drawer hospitality. Owen, being first in line on the couch, found himself entrusted with the biscuits. "Oh wow, my favourite!" he grinned. "Thanks very much!"

Mags, on the other hand, was pre-occupied with Rory who, with his head buried in his lap, appeared to be in a state of acute anxiety.

"What's wrong with that poor lad?" she asked. "Is he exhausted?"

"Who? Rory? No, he's just a bit simple," Kieran scoffed.

"Shuddup!!" Rory barked. "I was only trying *not* to watch the film since it obviously must have an eighteen's certificate!"

"Gosh! And Mummy would be ever so cross, if she found out!" Dave ribbed.

Knowing he was in the minority, Rory strove to maintain his reserve.

"All the same, I think I'll go and fix up yer beds, for ye now," Mags said, leaving them to their own devices.

As the biscuit plate reached Ambrose, all that was left were mere crumbs. "Hey! What happened here?" he squawked, to which the automated grinding unit simply shrugged and chugged. "Scabs! That's what you are! Scabs!!!"

♣ ♣ ♣ ♣ ♣

Kieran O'Dowd awoke to find himself in a celestial temple. A shaft of brilliant sunlight penetrated his eyes; proclaiming not just a new dawn, but a whole new era of optimism. What a joy it was to be surrounded by crisp clean sheets and plump pillows; it was as if he was floating on a cloud. More palpably, it was a breath of fresh air from the ghastly rank and mildewed rags masquerading as Peig Sawyer's bed linen. As an added bonus, he no longer had to contend with chafing bedsprings, Owen's snoring, or Rory's incessant whining. Yes, the past seven days had truly been a feat of endurance. By no means either would he be shedding a tear for that other horrid abomination, who had justifiably spent her first night in the clink; the first of many, he prayed. It was his best night's sleep in ages and the mere idea of having to stir seemed loathsome. But an alluring aroma drifting up from the kitchen below was the perfect inducement. Over at the wash-hand basin, Kieran soon reacquainted himself with another long-lost friend. "Aaaah! Hot water!" he sighed, gently effacing his drowsiness with a light sprinkling.

Temporarily breaching the peace, however, an oppressive booming reverberation unexpectedly descended from above. While assuming it was a passing helicopter, Kieran couldn't verify this from the poor vantage point of his dormer window. Once the anomaly receded, it merited no further consideration, being from a bustling metropolis where such noise was commonplace.

Far more alarming was a mockery laid bare as Kieran prepared to get dressed.

"My clothes!!!" he howled. "Where the bloody-hell are my clothes gone?"

Apparently no longer on the floor where he had bunged them the night before, his sickly feeling of *déjà vu* intensified when a rummage through the wardrobe also proved fruitless. Was there no end to the treachery? "No-no-no-no-no, for the love of God, please no. Not again! Not my very last set of threads!"

Heaving a sheet from the bed, the toga clad teen clumped towards the door in a panic. Amazingly, it transpired that no crime had been committed. On the contrary, hanging directly outside were not only the missing garments; but they had been washed, dried and neatly pressed. Across the landing, a second door creaked open and from it cropped an anxious redhead sporting a duvet. Clearly having found himself in a similar quandary, Owen looked equally relieved and gratified, on being reunited with his only remaining clothes. Exchanging a brief nod, the pair grabbed their respective hangers and stepped back inside.

♣ ♣ ♣ ♣ ♣

The enticing bouquet of scorching fat hit critical mass as Kieran opened the door to the kitchen, where Owen, unsurprisingly, had beaten him to the breakfast table. Over by the cooker, Mags Buckley fished a Pyrex plate from the oven before glancing up to greet the new arrival. "Ah there you are," she beamed. "Are you for a fry?"

Bearing in mind her dissipated prototype, this landlady radiated a level of warmth that seemed utterly surreal. Truly, this was Peig Sawyer's antithesis.

"A-all right, y-yes please!" he said, holding back the tears of joy.

"Grand so, sur' sit down there and we'll sort you out!"

As Kieran took a seat beside his comrade, a scintillating dish of imperial diadem was placed on the table before them. Sausages, eggs, bacon, black pudding and white, and not a potato in sight, unleashed the full flow of his saliva ducts. Notwithstanding their calorie deficit, it was a coronary in the making,

"Mmm," Owen ogled. "Ta very much!"

"Thanks a million for sorting our gear too!" Kieran declared, as the waft of summer meadow freshness from his shirt sleeves added to the dreamlike ambience.

"Well isn't it a disgrace, lads?!! Mags cried, as she returned to her station. "After Curly explained what happened with Mrs Sawyer, I could scarcely believe my ears! And losing your clothes like that, I thought the least I could do was a bit of laundry!"

"Yes, well, after *she* made off with our clobber, they ended up being laundered too," Owen muttered in disgust.

"Fair enough, I knew she was a bit cranky," their hostess harped on. "But imagine, all these years, living next door to a murderer!! Shocking altogether!!!"

A moment of introspective silence ended as 'Mr Cyclops' trudged wearily into the kitchen. "Good morning sunshine!" Mags beamed, in the face of blatant evidence to the contrary. "Are you for a fry?"

"No thanks," Rory pouted.

"Oh right, what'll ya have, so? Corn Flakes, fruit juice and toast?"

"Hah? Oh! Eh, yeah- yes please," he perked up significantly. "Yes, that would be terrific!"

"Well have a seat and I'll be with you now," she bustled around the stove.

As if their good fortune was about to peter out at any moment, our hardened friends over at the table, were furtively making contingency plans. "Here, we ought to leave some for the others, I suppose?" Owen whispered, while cramming two sausages and a gammon steak into his shirt pocket.

Likewise, Kieran wrapped several pieces of pudding in a serviette. "Yeah, maybe. Although, it's their own tough luck if they miss out on the best pickings."

Foiling their miniature plot, a second Pyrex dish suddenly appeared before them. "There y'are now, tuck in!" their hostess declared.

Both were stumped. "I'm sorry, but *who*'s this for?" Kieran gestured.

"That's yours- Why? Is it not enough?"

"*Enough*?! No- I mean *Yes*, thanks!"

What they initially thought was a communal trough, delightfully turned out to be mammoth-sized individual portions.

"Now young lad," Mags focused her attention on their relentlessly cheerless third member, "Corn Flakes for you, isn't that right?"

What emerged from the cupboard was a box of Frosties, though Rory chose not to split hairs as she filled his bowl. He did, however, object as the landlady threatened to sprinkle an entire table-spoon of sugar over the pre-sweetened cereal.

"No-no-no!" he baulked. "No thanks!!"

"No sugar?"

"No, these are already sugar frosted!"

"Oh is that right? Sur' I'll leave you to it so, while I make the tea."

Lacking a decent bite since Saturday afternoon, the trio decided to seize the moment and devour with pleasure. Presently, and presumably with their noses still out of joint by the intrusion on their territory, their scowling rivals shuffled in.

"Ah there ye are, lazybones!" Mags teased affably. "Eat up or ye'll be late for class!"

"Yes, I'm dying to finish my Plastecine model of Miss Colic," Dave said dryly, as he took his seat. "Though so far, I've had only enough material to make her arse!"

Ambrose stubbornly parked himself directly behind Rory, with folded arms and a tapping foot. At first, his antics went ignored, though Kieran quickly grew vexed by such puerile behaviour. "Here, what's your problem?" he snapped.

"He's sitting in my place!" Ambrose scowled.

For the sake of harmony, the semi-bespectacled one meekly raised his bowl in a bid to relocate, but was vetoed by a compelling argument from Kieran. "Look here Ricey-Boy!" he spouted, his mouth replete with meat. "It's as plain as the snot at the end of your nose, that there are plenty of other good chairs available! It's living in the lap luxury you are, with the best of food at your fingertips!! So give over your auld whinging and sit down and eat!!!" Swallowing nervously, the muted rabble-rouser slouched into the next available chair and downed his breakfast without further protest.

A time for school drew near, Dave Keogh arose from the table again. "I don't know about you, but I'm raring to get my hands on Miss Colic's arse!" he said frivolously. And while his underling followed him to the door, the other three remained surprisingly leisurely. "Aren't you coming with us?" Ambrose enquired.

"Nah, I think we'll just rest up here a while longer," Kieran yawned, while casually pouring himself another cup of tea.

"You'll get a demerit, if you're late!"

"On the contrary, *we've* received an exemption from this morning's master-class," Rory divulged, with a certain understated pleasure.

"Yeah, right!" Dave squinted sceptically.

Rolling up with another basket of soda bread, Mags confirmed this bizarre deviation.

"Oh indeed they have!" she declared. "Those lads are needed down at the Garda station later on, to give statements! So ye needn't be waiting on them!"

Kieran smugly buttered another triangle of toast and stuffed it into his mouth, leaving an acrid taste in the mouths of the departing duo. "Can we give you a hand with anything there, Mrs Buckley?" Owen offered, as the landlady set about stacking the dishes.

"There's hasn't been a *Mrs* Buckley around here for many a year!" she chuckled. "It's just *Mags*! And anyway, ye're grand! In fact, why don't ye sit over there and watch a bit of telly, until it's time to go? Curly won't be up for another while yet, I expect."

Needing no arm twisting, the trio transferred to the settee, with their cups of tea still in hand. "Sweet justice, at last!" Owen beamed, as he reached for the remote control.

Meanwhile, still shaken from 'Spine Crusher 2', Rory decided to make a stand. "You ought to let *me* chose some responsible viewing for us this time," he said, picking up the television guide and casting an eye over the choices at hand.

"Let's see what's on first," Kieran said evasively, seizing the remote from Owen's apparently incompetent fingers.

"*Schindler's List 4: The Lost Years* is starting in five minutes, if anyone's interested?" Rory suggested.

"Number *four*? What's that about?"

"Oskar finds a time machine and grapples with mobsters trying to take over an orphanage in modern-day New York. Facile fantasy drama starring Tony Danza and James Gandolfini; Black and White, with strobe lighting. One star (1998)."

"Well I'm definitely not watching it, if it's in black and white!" Kieran avowed.

"Yes and I haven't seen the previous instalments, yet," Owen averred.

"Okay, what about *Revenge of Ben Hur?*"

"*Revenge?*"

"Yes, *Ben turns vigilante after his chariot is stolen during a shopping visit to Rome - Uninspired sequel, stars Charles Bron-*"

"No-no-no!" Kieran argued. "What we need is a good romp, something over the top with a heavy dose of comic-relief."

Out of the blue, Curly Buckley charged through the front door with the grace of a bull on steroids. "Quick lads!" he roared, almost deranged with excitement. "Turn over to the News!"

"Oh begod!" Mags blurted, "I thought it was still in bed, you were, Curly?"

"Sshh! Hold your whisht now!" he wheezed breathlessly.

As Kieran located the pertinent channel, a vaguely familiar panorama manifested itself across the cosmic screen. "Isn't that-?"

"That's an aerial view of Peig's cottage!" Owen gasped.

"And those pictures are live!" Rory gawped at the subtitle.

When the face of a female reporter suddenly graced the screen, Curly Buckley made a frenzied dash for the remote. "Quick! Quick!" he cried. "How do you turn it up?"

With his stubby fingers guided in the right direction, a startling newscast resonated loud and clear.

"*The rural backwater of Rossbladderburst in Co. Kerry, has been left reeling this morning following the discovery of eleven bodies buried in a pensioner's garden-*"

"What? Eleven bodies?!!!" Mags shrieked.

"Whisht up now!" Curly said excitedly.

"*While Gardaí are treating the mass grave as 'suspicious', they have confirmed that a local resident has been assisting them with their enquiries. As the investigation here gathers momentum, with as many as twenty-five officers assigned to the case, today's findings have sent shock-waves rippling through a small community. Some claim they are now afraid to step outside their doors, while others are demanding that justice be served-"*

"Damn right!" Curly spat vehemently.

"*It is believed that this may be the work of Ireland's worst serial killer to date. Further developments as they happen. Rachael Dowling for Éire News, in Rossbladderburst, Co. Kerry.*"

"Well lads, isn't it a good job ye made it out of there in time?" Mags gleaned.

But as she turned to face the settee all that remained of the students were three spinning teacups. "Bejapers! They left in a hurry?!" she cried.

"Sur' why bother with this contraption, when you can have proper high-definition over the road!" her brother declared, as he muted the volume.

"Still isn't it amazing how quickly the press catch wind of these stories?" she sighed.

"Isn't it though?!" Curly said wistfully. "Well, I'd better be making a move too. I've been roped into yet another baby-sitting assignment over at the school, this morning."

"What? But I thought you were going to sort out the turf today?"

"Don't worry girl, that'll all be taken care of too," he winked.

"Oh right, well what a about a bite to eat?"

"No, I'm grand. I've already had a couple of hot dogs from the van outside Peig Sawyer's cottage."

♣ ♣ ♣ ♣ ♣

As Matthew Begley hauled a television set into room 4C, shortly after nine o' clock, he was greeted by a sarcastic ovation. "All right, everyone!" he said, replacing the old set with the new and plugging it in, "Let's have a bit of consideration for those down the corridor!"

Gazing out the window, a curious Ambrose Cleary raised his hand. "What's with all the lorries and vans coming through the village, this morning, Mr Begley? Are they making a film?"

"Nothing you need concern yourself with, I'm sure," the principal dismissed.

However, it was only when he switched on the television, that Matthew himself became fully aware of the bigger picture.

"*Coming to you live from Co. Kerry, Éire News brings you in-depth analysis into the Rossbladderburst massacre, where, so far, eleven bodies have been recovered from a local woman's vegetable garden.*"

Matthew's face suddenly blanched, while to his rear, an unaffected mob merely yawned and scratched their heads. Stationed directly outside the ill-fated cottage, the on-screen reporter's sense of urgency made a grim situation seem all the more potent. "*While the eleven have yet to be formally identified and their exact cause of death to be confirmed; condemnation of this senseless carnage has been widespread. Issuing a statement from a bar in Ibiza, only minutes ago, the Taoiseach is reported to have said that he was 'shocked' by this 'monstrous atrocity'. By and large, Rossbladderburst is a hub for hundreds of students who flock here annually to attend a summer school. Now, Éire News has gained exclusive access to a group of these students, who claim their landlady, and the owner of this property is, in fact, the architect behind this brutal rampage.*"

As the camera panned to our three conquering heroes, the atmosphere in 4C turned electric. The spectacle of their classmates on live television brought whoops and hollers, although from one minority, namely Dave and Ambrose, a stone-cold silence. None, however, were more eager than Ashley, who made it known that she was 'practically engaged' to one of these lucky celebrities.

"Tell me Kieran O'Dowd," the attractive auburn-haired reporter posed, while thrusting the large microphone in his direction, "Were there any significant clues that led you to believe that the suspect wasn't entirely on the level?"

"You mean Peig Sawyer?"

"No names please, we're live!"

"Oh right, eh yeah just one or two," he confirmed with a nervous titter. "Little things at first, we noticed, like bad smells, insect infestations, or my clothes being torched. But from there on in, things really started to get so much worse. Daily raids on our dorm meant that we were soon without food, clothes and medicine. God knows what she did with half of it. I guess she ate it. Then, of course, the real clincher was finding the skull in her vegetable patch, out back!"

"In the light of what's happened today, Owen O'Brien, how do *you* feel having escaped this chamber of horrors with your very lives?"

As Owen came under the spotlight, he nonchalantly pulled a cold sausage from his grease-stained shirt pocket. "Well Rachael, it was touch and go there for a while," he wielded the sausage for emphasis. "I felt every day was going to be our last. I mean like, what *didn't* we have to put up with? Poisoning, starvation, thrashings. I'd swear she even drugged our cocoa, once. In fact, pretty early on we began to suspect that she might have the odd skeleton in the closet, although nothing on a scale quite like this!"

"Are you intimating that you endured physical as well as psychological trauma?"

"Fizzy your what now?"

"Did she *beat* you?" Rachael rephrased.

Pausing only to take a bite from his sausage, Owen offered a lynching testimony. "Hell yes! I've lost track of how many times I was coshed with either a piece of turf or a wooden spoon. Even Rory there came a cropper after a bunk bed collapsed on top of him, one morning!"

The camera sequentially zoomed in for a close-up on Rory's tragic face.

"Rory Waters, what motivation do you think lay behind this campaign of terror? Greed? A lust for power? Demonic possession? Or a lonely woman's cry for help?"

"Mother, if you can hear me. *Please*, I'm ready to go home now!!!" Rory pleaded.

His devastating appeal triggered a momentary lull, though Kieran readily hogged the limelight again. "Never mind that cabbage!" he swung the microphone back in his direction. "The woman was unhinged, I tell you, just pure evil, and I think I speak for everyone, when I say it was the worst week of our entire lives!"

"Still, isn't a week a rather long time before coming forward with something of this magnitude?"

"On day *one*, our plea for help went ignored!" he cried. "For a finish we were practically blue in the face! Teachers are a law unto themselves, you know, and most of the time they just don't want to listen-"

The throng in 4C were universally riveted, but deplorably, became detached again as the screen suddenly went blank. "Sorry, I think this television must be on the blink too," Matthew murmured awkwardly, amid the roars of umbrage.

While most didn't doubt it was because the plug had been wrenched clear from the socket, highlighting the fact seemed to fall on deaf ears. Seemingly in a flap over the damning news bulletin, the principal dithered over his next course of action. "Right, eh-eh, g-get out the old Ludo there and eh, somebody will be along shortly to keep an eye on things-" he said, before making a hasty departure.

♣ ♣ ♣ ♣ ♣

A silver bullet shot out from the school gates, on a collision course for farthest reaches of the village. Fastened securely in the passenger seat, Catherine herself went ballistic upon hearing the latest developments. "*Eleven* you say?!" she squealed incredulously. "Madness! Absolute madness!"

"Never mind *that*!" Matthew urged, while bumping into fifth. "The truth is, if we don't round up those loose cannons right away, we could be riddled in litigation by teatime!"

"Oh yes, yes, I see what you mean," she concurred. "Well thank goodness for Father Buttimer arriving early and Curly Buckley too. I was really surprised by just how eager he was."

But as the Begleys arrived within spitting distance of the stone bridge, their Laguna screeched to a halt. So widespread was the media circus surrounding the cottage, that the road beyond had become a pedestrianised zone. Among the entourage were helicopters, chip vans, ice-cream vendors, doughnut stands and even Madame Cashmere's caravan, with a sign outside offering a one-day special on tarot reading.

"It's anarchy!" Catherine gasped.

"That's it, we can't go any further!" Matthew wrenched the handbrake.

"You'll have to get out and walk so!" she commanded.

Exorcising a frustrated sigh, he unfastened his seatbelt and alighted. Yet, having ventured no further than a few feet, Matthew was sidetracked by the allure of the candy-floss stand. And to the sheer disbelief of his better half, assumed a position in line.

Close at hand, the interviews were in full throttle, with reporter Rachael Dowling delving ever deeper into the summer school's administrative gaffes. "So what you're saying is, they readily furnished students to a dangerously unsuitable candidate?!"

"That's about the gist of it all right," Kieran nodded. "Even after that scandal last year!"

"Scandal? What scandal?"

At that particular moment, an irate and crimson face cropped through the dense cluster of bystanders. "Uhm, perhaps you'd best ask the principal that!" Kieran flinched. "Here he comes now!"

Chewing agitatedly on his candy-floss, the maligned administrator bulldozed his way through the ranks, only to be barraged by questions as he reached the nucleus.

"Excuse me, are you Matthew Piggott, the Academy's principal?"

"It's Begley!" he snapped. "And *no* comment!"

"Mr Begley, Mr Begley! What have you to say to the allegations of sleaze and complicity in aiding and abetting a homicidal maniac?" the reporter probed.

"No comment!!! And sorry to cut you off there, but these lads are urgently needed elsewhere!"

"Please! Mr Begley! Please, just a few questions!" the predatory horde pleaded in desperation.

Collaring Kieran and his fellow collaborators, Matthew ran the gauntlet while covetously shielding his outsized confectionary. But despite ducking microphones, video cameras and blinding flash photography, the hapless headmaster failed to notice investigators in white jumpsuits hauling a stretcher from Peig Sawyer's front gate. Stumbling gracelessly across the breadth of this unwieldy obstacle, both Matthew and the body bag aboard were sent hurtling to the ground. Amid a hypnotic delirium of unrelenting brilliant white flashes and horror-laden gasps, Begley's eyes finally focused on what was the worst obloquy of all. Sprawled out beneath him, were decimated skeletal remains of victim number twelve. Worse still, half of his precious cargo had become enmeshed in the ribcage. Injudiciously salvaging his candy-floss from the mouldering carcass, the principal scrambled furiously towards the car with his three scallywags in tow. Fortunately, the emergence of yet another body from the site, was just newsworthy enough to throw the insatiable jackals off their scent, for that crucial moment.

Once the trio were shunted into the back seat, Matthew climbed behind the wheel again and hammered the accelerator. "This is terrible! Just terrible!" he said ruefully.

"Yes, no school worth their salt will have anything to do with us after *this* cataclysm!" his wife bleated.

"No my candy-floss, I mean! Look! It's half ruined," he nibbled hesitantly.

"Give me that!" she roared. Seizing the sweet snack from her husband's fingers, Catherine lowered her window and dispatched it into the nearest sheep paddock.

"Now keep your eye on the road!" she ordered.

Observing the couple in a more vulnerable light, Kieran began to wonder if he had been a little harsh on the Begleys. After all, they too, were merely pawns in the old woman's warped crusade for supremacy. And Jennifer; she was generous to a fault.

"I'm sure nobody will blame you or the school," he said, by way of reconciliation. "Anyway, *she's* the one who's clocked up a dozen bodies in her back garden."

"Actually, my mother is on our school's board of governors," Rory stated candidly, "And once I explain you did everything in you power, I'm sure she'll put in a good word!"

This worthy revelation raised hopeful eyebrows at the front of the car.

"What do you say we stop off for ice-cream, once we get to Knockyadown?" Catherine cheered, following some careful deliberation.

♣ ♣ ♣ ♣ ♣

As luck would have it, the whereabouts of Rossbladderburst's most reviled resident had been leaked to the press, and outside Knockyadown Garda station, the paparazzi were maintaining a vigil. Bearing the full brunt of their bombardment, an enraged superintendent battled his way to the front door.

"Make certain those blackguards stay outside!" O'Meara barked at the desk sergeant.

"Yes sir!" the officer acknowledged, parading a state of heightened alertness for the benefit of his superior.

Inside, the main atrium was a flurry of activity, with all available personnel engaged in cataloguing evidence, writing reports or answering telephone calls from a panic-ridden public. At its core was D.S. Danny Boyer; his eyes bloodshot from the hours spent trawling through computer files. As the corpulent senior officer converged, he pretentiously parked himself on his chief investigator's workstation.

"Well Danny Boy," he began, with the faintest hint of ridicule. "What's the latest?"

Exiting the file on screen, the detective heaved a defeatist sigh. "The missing persons database has yielded nothing conclusive, although once the medical examiner's report comes in, we should have more to go on."

"I gather you saw the News this morning?"

"Yes, it's right outside the window."

"Listen, I've just had a very nasty telephone call from *upstairs*, who feel there's been far too much exposure on this case already. They want the whole thing nipped in the bud, by calling for a press conference here at noon tomorrow. So in a nutshell, Sergeant, we'll need something concrete by then!"

O'Meara paused briefly, to glance across at the cells. "Any word on a solicitor yet?"

"Yes, some chap called Lawrence Sharkey," Boyer referred to his notes. "He's coming down from Dublin to represent her."

"*Sharkey*?"

"That's right, but unfortunately he can't make it down 'til tomorrow morning."

"*Tomorrow*?!!!"

"Yes, he's due to appear in court today."

"Oh right, more than one iron in the fire?"

"Eh no, he's up for contempt, apparently."

"Great, that's all we need, another troublemaker! I can't see why she couldn't let a local firm handle the case. Buckley and Buckley down in the village have a solid reputation!"

"I mentioned that, but she was violently opposed to the idea," Boyer said, reaching for a nearby tray of paracetemol.

"Fair enough, we'll just have to plough on, the best we can, I suppose."

A minor scuffle in the reception area alerted Leo to the arrival of their star witnesses.

"That's all right O'Shaughnessy, you can let *them* through!" he signalled.

As the party was released, Catherine stormed towards her brother. "Jeepers Jacks, Leo!" she cried. "As if the infamy weren't bad enough, now we're being attacked on all fronts!"

"Sorry about that, but we've had to beef up security since things went a little berserk!"

"Insanity is what it is! How could *all* these journalists have latched onto this story so quickly?"

"I don't know!" he said petulantly. "Oh and lads, it might be best *not* to speak to any more reporters, it could damage the case for the prosecution, you know."

"Cripes!" Owen gasped. "I hadn't considered that."

"Well I did!" Rory scowled.

"They promised us a cash deal," Kieran warranted, "Which we deserve after being messed about in that crap factory!"

"You won't see a penny of that now," Matthew noted sceptically.

"Yeah, thanks to you."

Bringing this little symposium to an end, the superintendent cleared his throat. "Anyway look, this here is Detective Sergeant Danny Boyer," he said, yielding the donkeywork to his subordinate. "He'll take your full written statements and answer any other questions you may have."

The sergeant deferentially exchanged the usual social pleasantries. "Please, sit down," he gestured, "That is if you can find a chair beneath all this clutter!"

"So if you'll excuse me, I'll be in my office making a few calls," O'Meara bowed out.

As they eased into their chairs, Owen beheld an odious spectre from his recent past.

"Hey! That's the guy that diddled me out of a tenner yesterday!"

All eyes focused on an elderly gent with a peaked cap and unsteady gait, being escorted towards the holding cells. "Teddy Holland?" Boyer noted. "Yes, he's a bit of a confidence trickster. Mostly harmless, though a bit too fond of the drink."

"I wouldn't call getting swindled out of hard earned pocket money, harmless!"

As the inebriated charlatan was jostled down the corridor, thoughts of another degenerate sprung to mind. "So what's the story with the old Sea Hag?" Kieran said negligently, while looking around. "Has she 'fessed up yet?"

"Who? Mrs Sawyer?" Boyer flexed his fingers. "The pursuit of justice can be a long and convoluted affair, I'm afraid."

"I hope you see to it that all she gets is bread and water."

"That's way too good," Owen objected. "Half a coconut is loads!"

"Why coconut?" Kieran frowned.

"I hate coconut!"

And just as they were about to settle down to business, a volcano erupted from Leo O'Meara's office. "What in blues blazes are all these receipts doing on my desk, Boyer?!" he spewed. "€49.95 for a Chateau Monsieur Duffy's La Evening Special?! €31.95 for a Chateau Monsieur Duffy's La Full Continental Breakfast?!! Plus €10.09 for one Chateau Monsieur Duffy Cognac?!!!"

Before the sergeant could respond, a young officer breezed through the front door flaunting a lavish silver-plated tea service. Pausing on route to the cells, he extended a small piece of paper to Boyer, who, in turn, diffidently submitted it to his superior. Holding the receipt at arm's length, the glowering superintendent read aloud its small print. "Chateau Monsieur Duffy's Tasty Indulgences €24.95?!! What the devil is *this*?"

Raising the silver dish-cover, the rookie Garda gestured towards a selection of buttered scones, preserves and Danish pastries beneath. "Elevenses, for Mrs Sawyer."

Realising its beneficiary was none other than a convict, Leo, once more, blew his stack. "Damn it!!! This isn't the Hilton we're running here! That woman has laid waste to half the countryside and you're treating her like a film star!"

"My apologies," Boyer deflected. "She's desperately picky and nowhere but Chateau Mon- Monsieur Duffy would cut the mustard."

"I despair!" O'Meara kneaded his eyeballs. "All right I suppose. It'll only be another day or so before she's arraigned and then she'll be out of our hair for good!"

As Leo returned to his office to cool off, the silver tray and its delectable fancies continued its journey.

"Jammy bleedin' cow!" Kieran murmured rancorously.

"Yes, remind me to murder someone, the next time were in town!" Owen concluded.

♣ ♣ ♣ ♣ ♣

Shortly after midday, the Begleys' station-wagon rolled back into the college grounds. While Catherine went to relieve Fr. Tom Buttimer in the exam hall, the others proceeded on towards 4C. But a shock lay in store for Matthew and company as they entered the classroom. Its entire complement, including Curly Buckley, had inexplicably vanished. "It's the Marie Celeste!" Owen quipped.

"Curly Buckley, more like it!!!" Matthew seethed. "I'll have him up for kidnapping!"

Suddenly remembering Curly's 'field trip' proposal the night before, the principal guessed that the reprobate had simply thrown caution to the wind.

"Right!" he backtracked down the corridor. "You three come with me!"

It didn't take long to track down the elusive mogul and his band of sixty renegades. Dotted across the length and breadth of Curly Buckley's bog (every inch a field trip), the students gathered turf for their new master.

Veering off the main road and onto rough terrain, Matthew's silver Laguna skidded to a halt alongside the golden Rolls Royce. Perched from the edge of the driver's seat, Curly seemed entirely at ease as the fuming principal stormed over, while unwilling to take a back seat, Kieran, Owen and Rory followed in hot pursuit. Shaking his head in disbelief, Matthew gestured to a nearby trailer and the drones who were gradually filling it with turf. "What's this? A chain gang?!"

Curly nonchalantly ditched a blade of grass he had been using as dental floss. "There y'are!" he hailed. "You made it back all right, I see!"

"What? Yes, of course we did!" So blasé was Curly, that Matthew began to question his own reasoning. "Now look here," he cried. "The trafficking of child labour is a drastic deviation from the Academy's cultural syllabus!"

"This is *pure* culture!!" Buckley said, bringing to bear a turf sod. "Not some second-hand nonsense flushed out by an idiot box in some stink-filled classroom!! Anyhow, isn't that same energy only going to waste on the dance floor?! At least out here they can get fresh air and sunshine into the bargain. So you tell me, which is worse?!"

As Matthew scanned the landscape, he had to admire the man's ingenuity, at least. Having fallen under Curly's spell, everyone seemed to be working up quite a sweat. Even the girls, with a cigarette in one hand, giddily flung their contribution into the trailer, while the boys, were in competition to see who could carry the most in a single sortie. Curly, meanwhile, lumbered around to the rear of his car and opened the boot. Inside, surprisingly, were several crates of lemonade and two large boxes of cheese and onion crisps. Clearly, this was a man on a mission. Producing an old brass bell from the glove compartment, which Matthew realised had been requisitioned from *his* desk back at the school, the squire shook it with vigour. All of a sudden, a rapturous horde came rampaging up from the field below. Before they knew what hit them, Kieran and Owen found themselves holding the crisps and Matthew, a heavy crate of lemonade.

"Grub for the troops!" Buckley clarified, while ripping open a second crate of beverages.

As the hungry conscripts converged, Curly's newest deputies began handing out these nutritionally suspect snacks. The presence of the principal, however, raised concern among the workforce. "Here, we don't have to go back already?" one worried face enquired.

Observing the smug 'I told you so' glint in Curly Buckley's eye, Matthew sensed his authority being eroded to the point of obliteration. "I hope we're not hanging our heads in a noose here!" he capitulated. "I'm not certain our insurance even covers such outdoor excursions!"

"Insurance?" Curly scoffed. "That's only for the superstitious!"

19. The Con Acre

With cogs of justice slowly turning in their favour, Kieran, Owen and Rory were finally beginning to luxuriate in the lifestyle their peers had long been taking for granted.

"Well lads, was that steak to yer liking?" their new landlady asked, as she gathered their empty plates.

"Absolutely top notch!" Owen licked the tips of his fingers.

"And the vegetable lasagne?"

"Fantastic, I'm sure Mother would love the recipe!" Rory nodded enthusiastically.

"So what's for afters, then?" Ambrose enquired.

"Baked Alaska, is that all right?"

"Ugh, disaster!"

Appalled by such incredible ingratitude, Kieran took on the mantle of administering a dash of 'under the table' retribution.

"Ow!" the malcontent grabbed his shin. "What the hell was that for?!"

"What was what?" the executioner chirped innocently.

Riled by this gatecrasher's persistent meddling, Ambrose sought vengeance of his own, with a witless gag he and Dave Keogh had been plotting just before dinner. Acknowledging a subtle nudge from his fellow conspirator, Dave initiated the proceedings by adapting a distinctly contrived timbre. "Listen guys, we heard that you'd recently fallen on hard times?"

Kieran, however, decided to come clean, especially since their plight had become a matter of public record. "Okay maybe we exaggerated, just a bit," he began.

"No-no-no, that's all right! And just to show there's no hard feelings, Ambrose and I decided to have a whip round, to help you back on your feet."

Kieran was mortified by the concept. "You what?!"

Producing a decrepit polystyrene cup from his pocket, Dave extended it across the table. "Here you are, only try not to spend it all in the one shop."

"Hilarious!" Kieran snorted, as he peered into the cup "Two cents and a button."

"Yes, the button is from me!" Ambrose added superciliously, "You can put it towards a new jacket, or something!"

An ugly tiff was foiled by a timely knock on the front door. "Now who's that, I wonder?" Mags wiped her fingers on a tea-towel as she went to open it.

"Hi, is this by any chance Mr Beckley's residence?" hailed a beguiling female voice from outside.

"*Buckley*, yes it is!" and inclining her face to one side, Mags vociferously summoned her brother. "Curly! It's for you, I think!"

Intrigued by their mystery guest's alluring inflection, those at the table arched their heads towards the door, only to be pleasantly surprised. "Phowar look!" Owen elbowed Rory none-too-subtly in the ribs. "It's Rachael Dowling, that T.V. reporter!"

"Yes, I know," Rory said, taking none-too-kindly to his freshly allocated bruise. "We met her earlier today."

Their visitor's strangely familiar veneer also struck a chord with Mags, though her queries were deferred as Curly emerged from some unknown recess, with a rolled-up newspaper beneath his arm and braces hanging by his sides. The speculator's eyes lit up at the prospect of a household name standing on his very doorstep.

"Hello there!" he beamed with an outstretched arm. "Curly Buckley at your service!"

"Hi, I'm Rachael Dowling?"

"Oho! Sur' we *all* know who you are! Come in-come in!"

"Oh dearie me," she chuckled, with *faux* self-depreciation. "Basically, we received a memo saying you run a guest house here during the summer months? Is that right?"

"That's right! That's right!" the starry-eyed Buckley grinned avidly. "And winter, spring and autumn!"

"So you *do* have rooms?"

"We do, we do!"

"Oh that's smashing! I'll just let the gang know that we're in the right place! Is it all right if we park our van outside here this evening?"

Buoyed with by the word 'gang' Curly excitedly shook his head.

"Yes-yes, work away, work away!"

As she turned to face the exit again, Rachael cast an eye over the recently inaugurated celebrities sitting at the table. "Oh hi guys!" she beamed. "I didn't realise you were shacked up here too! Say, that was a sizzler this morning. You occasionally laid-it on a bit thick, but let's face it, the public really a get kick out of all that doom and gloom!"

"But everything we told you was legit!" Kieran gawped.

"Sure, whatever. Oh and listen before I forget, I meant to square up with you earlier on, only that you vamoosed so quickly!"

Rummaging through her shoulder bag for a moment, she retrieved a long white envelope and extended it to Kieran. "There you go. Treat yourselves to champagne cocktails, compliments of Éire News!"

With that, the news anchor dashed down the driveway to round up her colleagues who were moored beyond the front gate. Above all, it appeared that all misgivings regarding the media were wholly unfounded.

"Well?" Owen eagerly gazed, as his comrade evaluated their windfall.

"Three hundred quid!" Kieran leered.

"Score!"

"So a fifty-fifty split, I reckon?" Kieran suggested.

"What about Rory?"

"What about him? That plebe's only contribution was to bawl for his Mammy in the middle of the interview!"

"And went down a treat," Owen warranted. "Besides, we're all in this together!"

"Yes, we're *all* in this together!" Dave hazarded.

While Kieran had no intention of including this belated sycophant in the loop, he did concede that Rory *was* a deserving candidate and therefore opted for a three-way split. Naturally, this didn't prevent one or two others from feeling gypped.

"Aren't you forgetting someone?" Ambrose whined.

"Am I?" Kieran said artfully, while stuffing the balance into his pocket.

As Mags tended to her elaborate dessert, Curly massaged oil into his folically challenged scalp; rendering himself presentable for the benefit of his imminent guests. Moments later, a large white van rolled up outside and from it emerged Rachel Dowling and a gamut of her colleagues. "Knock-knock?" the reporter grinned, as she cropped her head through the open door.

"Come in! Come in!" the shimmering Buckley gestured once again.

One by one, Rachael ushered her associates through. "Now this here is Grace our director, Mike our cameraman, Úna our boom operator, Nigella our makeup artist and Tristan our lighting engineer. So it's just the six of us, in all, Mr and Mrs Buckley."

"Only six?" Curly whirred.

"Yes, Declan our runner, was rushed to hospital after eating a mouldy burger."

"Right Mags," Curly clasped his hands. "Six more for breakfast tomorrow morning!"

The Baked Alaska almost slipped from his sister's fingers. "Six?!!" she cried. "That's fine. Although I'm not sure how we're fixed for beds, Curly?"

This was the understatement of the century and apparently the one variable he hadn't considered. Still, not one to be discouraged by frivolous obstacles, our intrepid entrepreneur brushed over the cracks, in true Irish fashion.

"Ah sur' we'll manage!" he pledged, with a reassuring wink.

♣ ♣ ♣ ♣ ♣

As the old hay barn door swung open, a silhouette fumbled for the light switch inside.

"Here we are, lads!" Curly Buckley illuminated. "And isn't it grand and cosy too?"

In ascending order of pessimism, Kieran, Owen, Rory, Dave and Ambrose filed into the silo, each carrying a pillow and a blanket.

"Sur' what more do ye need only somewhere to put your head down for the night?"

"Are there any animals in here?" Rory frowned apprehensively.

"No-no-no! Well, not at this time of the year anyway. You might find the odd *rat* knocking about, but sur' if you don't bother him, he won't bother you! Now lads, sleep tight and don't let the bed-bugs bite!" On that encouraging note, their bombastic host retreated to the manor.

"What beds?" Ambrose spitefully kicked around a tuft of hay. "Everything was going just peachy, until you three spongers muscled in on our turf! And now look at us! Reduced to animal shelter!"

While Kieran, Owen and Rory were willing to take a demotion in their stride, they certainly didn't fancy a lecture from this perennial moaner.

"Put a sock in it you whinge bag!" Kieran revolted. "If you saw a fraction of the rubbish we endured, you'd reckon this was The Shelbourne!"

As the reluctant campers straightened out their blankets, they were mildly surprised by a tap on the door. "Come in?" Owen hesitantly declared.

With that, Mags Buckley appeared; kitted in her dressing gown, slippers and hair-rollers. "Hello lads, are ye decent?"

"Uhm, yeah, sure," Owen nodded.

What's more, the unfortunate middle-aged woman came fully equipped with a pillow and an alarm clock, signifying that she too had been relegated to the barn.

"Don't mind me lads," she said, evidently looking around for a fallow patch to bed down for the night. "I won't get in your way. I've to be up at half-two anyway to cook fourteen breakfasts."

"How come you've bumped down to economy?" Kieran probed.

"Hah? Oh, I couldn't bear to have that other poor sick boy disturbed, so I gave up my own room instead for one of the telly crew!"

"What sick boy?"

"Morrissey," Dave Keogh yawned unenthusiastically.

"What? Sick my ass! It's stoned, he is, I'll bet!"

Allowing their hostess to crawl into some nook for a badly needed forty winks, Kieran plumped up his pillow. "Here, that Curly bloke is a bit ruthless, though," he whispered. "I mean, letting that poor woman sleep in the cow shed, for the sake of a few quid?"

"At least he's not afraid to shell out where it really counts," Owen garnered, as he plucked a strand of beef from between his teeth.

"If the investment is deemed to have a worthwhile return!" Rory hypothesised.

"Actually, if anyone deserves to remain indoors, it ought to be *you*, what with all your allergies and hay fever!"

"Thank you," Rory acknowledged. "But my sinuses have cleared considerably."

"Would that be since you were forced to give up half of that medication?"

"As a matter of fact-"

"Anyway, we didn't fare too badly, today," Kieran said, taking stock of his recent cash dividend. "Plus, you have to admit; even this place is a damn sight cleaner than our previous lodgings!"

"Hell yes!" Owen wholeheartedly agreed. "It even smells better!"

♣ ♣ ♣ ♣ ♣

With the proposed press conference only a matter of hours away, tension was mounting at Knockyadown Garda station. Fortunately, with the arrival of Mr Lawrence Sharkey, a man of short stature with impenetrably thick spectacles, came a renewed hope that the old woman might finally answer to her crimes. In the interview room, all relevant parties had assembled; Peig Sawyer and her legal aid occupying one side of the table and Leo O'Meara and Danny Boyer seated at the other. Setting his Dictaphone in record mode, the detective-sergeant verified the correct time.

"Interview commenced at o-nine-hundred hours. Would the suspect please state her name for the record?"

"You don't have to answer that Mrs Sawyer," her counsel advised.

Instantaneously outraged, O'Meara hammered the apparatus into standby. "Look, damn it! We will not get anywhere, unless you give us some level of co-operation!"

But the equally pompous Sharkey was not about to be press ganged. "Superintendent, I strongly urge you to accord my client with every level of professional courtesy. Otherwise, we may be forced to consider taking this case to the European Court of Human Rights!"

"Let me tell you about human rights!" O'Meara seethed. "Our cadaver drawer is brimming with a dozen people whose human rights were pitilessly stripped away. So don't you lecture me on human rights!!!"

"A dozen, now, is it?" Peig shrugged pessimistically. "That's news to me!"

"Oho! It is, I'm sure. Look, Mrs Sawyer, don't you realise the grave trouble you're in? This isn't a minor misdemeanour we're talking about, this is mass murder! So *who* are these people? *Where* did they come from? And *how* do you justify their pitiful state?"

"They were scarcely in their prime when I met them!" she huffed. "As for names, I think one of them might have been called Robert- what-was-it? Wait, no, it's gone again."

As this marked some semblance of a breakthrough, O'Meara grappled for the recorder again. But before the proceedings could resume, a head appeared just inside the door.

"Not now, O'Shaughnessy!" the superintendent bellowed. "We're in the middle of an interview here!"

The desk sergeant, nevertheless, saw fit to intervene. "Sorry sir," he said, holding up a large brown envelope. "But a courier just dropped this off. I think it might be the lab results you were waiting for?!"

With a weary nod from his superior, Boyer took receipt of the package and opened it. But as the detective studied its contents, a succession of mystified facial contortions suggested an alarming irregularity.

"Well? Anything significant?" O'Meara grilled, following an apprehensive pause.

"If I'm reading this correctly sir; the preliminary results on your initial skull, indicate it to be at least one hundred and fifty years old!"

Automatically suspecting an artifice, Leo grabbed the file for himself. "What? Let me see this."

Even so, a fresh perspective didn't alter the facts. "Just how old *are* you, Mrs Sawyer?" he finally asked, looking from Peig to the dossier and back again.

"Hardly that old, for heaven's sake!" she huffed astringently.

"Then surely, Boyer, there's a mistake on the chart?" he dropped the document on the table.

Straight away, something clicked with the detective, and he suddenly became transfixed with the map of Ireland on the opposite wall.

"Hey! Are you gone to sleep or what?" The senior officer snapped.

With a deadpan façade, his junior grabbed his jacket and made for the door.

"Here! Where are you wandering off to in the middle of it all?"

"Out to follow a hunch," Boyer replied. "It may be a wild goose chase but it's still worth checking."

"Well hurry back or *your* goose will be cooked!" the fractious superintendent cautioned.

♣ ♣ ♣ ♣ ♣

At the behest of The Cultural Academy's academic council, namely the Begleys; Kieran, Owen and Rory were urged to remain at the Buckley manor for an indefinite period of 'recuperation'. Despite a thinly veiled pretext to sluice their loose lips from the public gaze, our elated friends found no shortage of amusements on their host's sprawling estate. Additionally, with the News crew gone since dawn and their hostile housemates having left for school, they now had a free hand to explore.

Curly Buckley's collection of vintage automobiles was a marvel to behold. While peering into an old Triumph, however, Kieran was ambushed by a frisky collie who bounded through an open window. "Hey-hey-hey, take it easy now," he chuckled nervously, spurning the dog's amorous advances. "I'm on my last set of clothes, you know!"

"Bad Peggy! Get down!" Curly bid, as he emerged from around the corner. "Get down now!" And with a remorseful whimper, the dog respectfully retreated.

"How do, lads!" his lordship hailed, "Sleep well last night?"

"Pretty good," Owen granted. "Is that your dog?"

"Yes, she's just a pup and still a bit foolish. Well, what do you make of this little lot?" he gestured proudly towards his private museum.

"Fan-tastic!"

"And have ye seen the ponies, yet?"

"Not yet!" Rory chirped optimistically.

The trio were led around the corner, where they encountered James and Jeremiah stealing a quick snooze on the backs of their shovels.

"Hey you two! Get cracking!" the old man bellowed, to which his multitasking offspring immediately resumed mucking out the stables. "My own two lads," Buckley elucidated. "Dead lazy they are, sometimes."

"Oh right," Kieran said, musingly. "We met briefly in the village, the other day."

"I hope you found what you were looking for?" Owen affably addressed the duo.

But Jeremiah's vacuous stare, suggested no recollection of their previous encounter. "Hah?" he grunted, primitively.

"Uh, nothing, nothing at all!" Owen flinched.

"Now lads," Curly beckoned, "Come over and meet Distemper, my prize mare!" As the wooden hatch opened out, a striking beast with pitch black pelt loomed forward.

"She's a beauty all right!" Rory cooed.

"I expect you wouldn't see the likes of this over at Sawyer's place?!!" Buckley swaggered.

"No," Owen said ruefully, "There was only one old nag over there, and she was only well-fit for the glue factory."

As the dog's superior audible range caught wind something adrift in the ether, she raised her ears and embarked on a thunderous proclamation.

"Whisht up Peggy! Or I'll have ye locked up again!" Curly admonished.

The collie's disquiet, however, was explained when a lime coloured Punto roared into the old bawn, narrowly missing the pedestrians before juddering to an undignified halt. Mairéad Waters virtually garrotted herself on her seatbelt as she teetered out from behind the steering wheel. "Oh lads-lads-lads!" she cried. "Thank goodness ye're all in one piece!"

On this occasion, all three were simultaneous recipients of a crushing bear-hug. Though, when the smell of perspiring armpits proved overwhelming, their love fest swiftly disbanded.

"D-did-didn't you get Mrs Begley's message?" Rory stuttered.

"What? Oh no! My mobile was pick-pocketed! In fact, it wasn't until early this morning when I overheard one of the ladies discussing last night's news that I learned of Mrs Sawyer's arrest for murder. Of course, I immediately phoned Mr Begley who assured me that everything was fine. Anyway, after nearly three hours on the road, I finally stopped off for petrol just beyond Knockyadown. And when I spotted a news-stand, I tell you, I nearly dropped dead of a heart attack!"

Hoisting a stack of newspapers from the passenger seat, Rory's mother distributed the morning editions. "As you can see from these, I hardly knew what to believe!"

Indeed, not only were the reports outrageously contradictory, but some were categorically mythical. "She's right!" Owen exclaimed. "Look! According to this tabloid, we've been written off as dead!!! See here! *Slasher Gran Slays Students*! And correct me if I'm wrong, but aren't those our passport photos they've printed?!"

"Where did they get those?!" Kieran gawped, as he and the others crowded together.

"In a ditch somewhere, knowing those muckrakers," Curly surmised.

"If my father sees this, he'll have a conniption!"

"My parents too!" Owen concurred. "Here, we'd better call to let them know we're still alive and kicking! Mr Buckley, would it be all right if we use your telephone?"

"Work away lads. It's in the parlour; the first door to your left in the hall. Only don't stay on too long."

As the pair hurried off to allay their loved ones' fears, Mrs Waters once more contemplated the array of lurid banners. "I can't understand how they can be allowed to print such tripe!"

"Well there's nothing about us in *this* paper, at least," Rory pored over a copy of the 'The Bladder Bugle'.

Curly Buckley rapidly poured scorn over the complimentary newsletter, which unaccountably had been included in the pile. "Ara pay no heed to that auld trash!" he belittled. "That's another one of Father Buttimer's holier-than-thou vanity projects!"

- THE KERRYLAD -

INSIDE EVERY COPY
Free bag of potatoes
(may contain stones)

COMPETITON
Win your own luxury dream home
(built from straw)

Price €4.10 (inc Vat)

Tuesday June 14

Our Kingdom's Shame

Elderly woman's brutal rampage claims twelve

Alfred Seimers and C. Niall DeMenzies

The Gaeltacht village of Rossbladderburst came under tight scrutiny yesterday, following the discovery of twelve bodies in a pensioner's garden. So far, a cloud suspicion hangs over a 71-year-old woman (Peig Sawyer) who is currently being detained at Knockyadown Garda station. While Gardai maintain that Mrs. Sawyer is merely 'assisting them with their enquiries,' neighbours have been doubly quick to allude to the pensioner's guilt, saying that she was 'a horrible woman; just horrible' and that 'they should impose the death penalty, instead of squandering tax-payer's money on trials and the like.' Some have expressed a fervent desire to see a revival of public flogging and have volunteered their services, free of charge. Curiously, one or two others have actually volunteered to be flogged themselves.

Mrs. Sawyer, apparently, is no stranger to brushes with the law and in 1976 virtually annihilated the local eco-system with a major toxic spill in a nearby reservoir. For her crimes, the 84-year-old reportedly received a suspended sentence and 30 minutes community service.

Incredibly, for the past two decades, Mrs. Sawyer (68) has been a beneficiary of students attending a local summer school in the area.

Assault on Precinct Knockyadown: The ugly scene outside the Garda station, yesterday, where the suspect is currently being held.

Outcry over Ireland's new murder capital

Pamela Butcher and Audrey Topsy

Once famous for its charming wicker baskets, Rossbladderburst is a name that has become synonymous with untold atrocities. A press release issued from Aras An Uachtaran yesterday, quoted the President (who is currently on a goodwill tour of Las Vegas) as being 'deeply saddened' by this 'very bad news'. A spokesperson for the Department of Education claimed that 'while there was 'no justification for these heinous crimes; Coláiste Nathair - which boasts 8 million students annually - could not be held accountable for the actions of one depraved individual.'

The Cross-Examiner

Tuesday June 14

Price €2.90

SLEEPY VILLAGE ROCKED BY PENSIONER'S KILLING SPREE

Above: currently under the spotlight - Coláiste Nathair Naofa - where the students were sitting their state exams. Left: - tragic victims, from top to bottom - Kieran McDowell (16) Owen O' Brien (15) and Roy Walters (12).

SLASHER GRAN SLAYS STUDENTS

Inside: The full story on the Rossbladderburst massacre, plus your full TV listings.

The Daily Stun

25

Tuesday June 14

INSIDE EVERY COPY

FREE DVD

ROSSBLADDERBURST'S 'RESIDENT EVIL'...

'REAPER BY THE DOZEN'

12 bodies unearthed in pensioner's garden

By Gerry Atrick

The Village of Rossbladder-burst in Co. Kerry... Once renowned for its breathtaking scenery but now - Ireland's worst serial killer....

Gardai investigating the discovery of 12 bodies in a pensioner's garden have officially launched a murder inquiry. So far, they have confirmed that a 98-year-old has been remanded in custody. Around twenty-five officers are currently working on the case which is being led by Superintendent Leo O' Meara. The suspect - local woman Peig Sawyer - has been described by neighbours as 'a dried up old husk' and as 'guilty as hell'.

Continued on page 4.

The full story pages: 4 - 21 **Plus: reams of hearsay and conjecture**

FREE

St. Millipede's Parish Newsletter - Vol. 6: June Edition

The Bladder Bugle

Missing Kitten

Lost and feared catnapped:
Fluffy white kitten - 'Tiddles'.
Disappeared on Tuesday afternoon.

Contact: Candy on 555-039-2032

For Sale

Beautiful and rare Abyssinian dwarf house cat.
€200 or nearest offer.

Contact: T. Hayes 555-039-2876

Telephone kiosk plans scrapped as Rossbladderburst fails to go nuclear.

Plans to install a much needed public telephone box in Rossbladderburst collapsed at the eleventh hour last month, after the local authority discovered an untenable deviation in the government drafted contract.

A clause in the agreement stipulated that the area would be automatically designated as a location for a nuclear power station on receipt of the kiosk. The proposed power plant would have imported doubly spent fuel rods from the United Kingdom for the purpose of re-re-processing. The site earmarked for the project was Bladder Beach - only 12 kilometres from the village - considered to be ideal for its proximity to the Atlantic Ocean.

Bladder Beach: The proposed site for the spent fuel re-re-processing plant

The Minister for Unsustainable Development, Douglas Lucan (36) who spearheaded negotiations was clearly disappointed by the u-turn. - 'I never thought they'd read the small print', he claimed. 'Fools! They're all fools! Anyone who would turn down an offer to bolster employment in their local community, truly needs their head checked'. Meanwhile, local councillor Maura O' Driscoll (40) said that she 'regretted any inconvenience caused', and wished Mr. Lucan 'the best of luck in tempting another village with of such a beneficial endeavour'.

At the prospect of obtaining a kiosk without the clause, a string of expletives hinted at Mr. Lucan's scepticism.

The village's previous kiosk was razed following a major earthquake in 1982.

Above: 'Dougie' Lucan - T.D. - Minister for Brown Envelopes & Unsustainable Development

Scuppered: No phoneboxes

Annual flower show coming soon to Rossbladderburst

Faith and begorah! It seems that summer is upon us once more and Rossbladderburst's annual flower is now only mere weeks away!

Despite previous attendance being hampered by locust plagues and indifference, this year's event promises to be a blooming extravaganza. All proceeds are in aid of the local butterfly sanctuary. We can only pray that last year's beneficiaries: (the starving orphaned monkeys of Maluku Selatan) have now gone to a better place. Sadly, the €5 raised; scarcely covered the cost to send one banana via surface mail. As usual, entries cost only €5 and a prestigious ribbon will be awarded to the best in show. Tea and sandwiches will be provided in St. Millipede's hall - courtesy of Candy O' Shea and Mags Buckley. Regrettably, a token admittance fee has been introduced - primarily to recoup the cost of some 1500 corned-beef sandwiches thrown to the seagulls, last year. Following a stern warning from the Garda Siochána; marijuana plants are no longer considered eligible for competition.

In view of last year's record turnout - this year, we aim to attract spectators and hopefully exhibitors.

Having caught her wind again, Mrs Waters finally granted her son early parole. "Well Honey-Bun, if you pack your bags, we'll be on our way. No doubt you're dying to hit the road?!"

Twenty four-hours ago Rory would have jumped at the chance. Now strangely enough, the habitually glum teenager had mellowed considerably. "Well, I *was* looking forward to going home," he sighed, while looking forlornly at his new-found toys.

"Oh, I'm afraid we won't be going *there,* straight away, either," his mother unexpectedly divulged. "As it happens, your Auntie Bridie in Drogheda is suffering from an acute bowel abscess and I promised we'd look after *her* for a few days."

A look of unadulterated revulsion suddenly gripped the teenager, whilst to his rear, Curly Buckley too was making a strategic withdrawal.

♣ ♣ ♣ ♣ ♣

With a press conference brewing in Knockyadown, the feeding frenzy surrounding Peig Sawyer's cottage was weaned down to a mere suckle, with a streamlined Garda presence now monitoring the site. The excavation too was complete and all heavy machinery had been hauled away. This lull afforded D.S. Danny Boyer an opportunity to explore the property unencumbered. Proving his theory, on the other hand, wasn't going to be easy, as the invasion had made a pig's ear of her garden. Indoors, chaos also reigned; though the detective didn't realise that such disarray and squalor were the norm. Fearing the scene had been compromised, Boyer prepared to renounce his quest, until one peculiar glitch caught his eye. It was the white marble table top; which mysteriously covered just one side of the table. Enthralled by this detail, he wandered over and gently slid his fingers across its smooth surface. Ascertaining the slab was simply resting on the wooden frame below, Boyer summoned the assistance of the Garda on sentry duty by the front door.

"Can you help me lift this, please?" he asked.

Venting some grumble about health and safety, the officer assented and both men carefully hoisted the marble. On the flipside, was a mind-blowing deposition that would throw their entire investigation skew-whiff. Yet, the discovery dredged up other revolting questions, such as *why* their crack team of investigators had overlooked such a blatant clue; or *how* anyone could have the nerve to craft a table top from a headstone? Boyer's index finger traced the embossed lettering, *In loving memory: Robert Nugent, 1792-1865*, and following a moment of quiet contemplation, once more addressed the sentry, "Now, whereabouts can I get a hold of an ordinance survey map?"

♣ ♣ ♣ ♣ ♣

Despite a deficit in social graces, Curly Buckley's parlour was yet another testament to his oblique sense of sophistication. Immaculately maintained, his inner sanctum was replete with mahogany furniture and countless charming antiquities; comprising of family heirlooms and doubtless; trophies of many a Plunder Party. More intriguing, was his curiosity cabinet, a haven for what seemed to be, and quite hilariously Owen thought, awards for tractor driving and ploughing; the likes of which, he never knew existed. Deviating from the display of laughable accolades, Owen returned to the leather top bureau, where his friend was wrapping up on the telephone; while distractedly doodling in an open copy of the Golden Pages, where numerous news-outlets had been circled and ticked off.

"Yes, right, okay, yeah-yeah, take care, bye-bye-"

"Well?" Owen enquired as Kieran replaced the receiver.

"My auld fellah hadn't even *seen* the News and knew squat about what happened!"

"Too mean to buy a newspaper?"

"What?!"

"Nothing, at least it's one better than my Mum saying that she *had* heard something, but thought that *we* were in a different Gaeltacht."

"Yeah, same difference it would have made, had we ended up on the side of a milk carton," Kieran groused, as he pocketed a fistful of Imperial Mints from a jar on the bureau.

♣ ♣ ♣ ♣ ♣

Following a punishing nine hour shift, in which she scrubbed the house, cooked for an army, milked the cows and delivered two calves, Mags Buckley was on the threshold of pulmonary failure. As she collapsed into the settee, her brother stepped inside the front door. "Oho! It's the life of Reilly for some!" he declared in his usual self-aggrandising way.

"But I've only just sat down!" she gasped.

"All right yera! No need to eat the face off me!" he backpedalled. "Well, any more developments?"

"They're about to make an announcement any minute now," she said, reaching for the remote.

Delighted at the prospect, Curly made for the liquor cabinet. "This calls for a drink!"

"Ah this is appalling!" his sister demurred. "No grounds for a celebration, at all!"

"You won't join me for a brandy, so?"

"Eh? Just a wee one so, for medicinal purposes."

As Curly poured two unequal measures, Kieran and Owen shuffled through from the hall. "All sorted, lads?" he briefly saluted.

"Yes, thanks, Mr Buckley," Owen sighed.

"Grand so, ye wouldn't like a brandy?"

"I'd love one!" Kieran grinned greedily.

Mags baulked at such a monstrous suggestion. "Oh Curly, they can't be old enough?!"

"Hah? What age are ye lads?" he posed with a gauging squint.

"Twenty-one!" "Sixteen!" Kieran and Owen responded respectively.

"*Sixteen*?!!" Curly scoffed. "Sur' my lads were only six when they had their first snifter!"

Struck by an epiphany, the pair instead plumped for something less intoxicating. "Actually, some lemonade will do me fine," Kieran opted.

"Or an ice cube!" Owen nodded.

As the victory beverages were dispensed, Rory Waters returned to the fold, minus his entourage.

"Where's your Ma, Rory? Is she still outside?" Kieran queried.

"Oh! Is your mother here?" Mags gleaned. "Maybe she'd like to come in for a bite?"

"Eh, well, no, she's gone, actually."

The other housemates looked on in disbelief. "*Home*?" Owen gasped.

"Yes, well, sort of-"

"Good man yourself!" Kieran commended, with a jovial slap on the back. "You're one of the gang now. In for the long haul, like the rest of us!!"

Rory's transmutation, however, was anything but sweeping and he shrugged uncomfortably at the unsolicited attention. Close at hand, events were about to reach a pinnacle as the large screen cut to live coverage of Knockyadown Garda station.

"Whisht up lads!" Curly settled into the settee, with his drink in one hand and a large black cigar in the other. "They're making that announcement now, I think."

"God save us, not more bodies, I hope!" his sister lamented.

"Did they find *more*?" Kieran enquired.

"No, still only the twelve, so far."

"Yes, *so far*-"

♣ ♣ ♣ ♣ ♣

How did it all go pear-shaped? Superintendent Leo O'Meara wondered. This was meant to be *his* fifteen minutes of fame; *his* opportunity to make a mark in the annals of history. But all he could brag was one shifty suspect, a myriad of unanswered questions and a kibbutz of corpses. Stealing one last glimpse through the Venetian blinds, he braced himself for the inevitable onslaught. Outside, the vultures were circling. There was still no sign of his detective and since the noon deadline had now elapsed, further procrastination seemed ill-advised. He would have to bluff his way through the conference, it seemed.

Yet, as Leo plodded from the exit to the makeshift podium beyond, he was fortuitously intercepted by his right-hand man. But relief turned to horror, as the sergeant swiftly relayed his findings. Initially, it all seemed too fanciful, until Boyer's inconceivable theory was substantiated by an ordinance survey map. A lighter shade than death itself, the superintendent tottered towards the nest of microphones that eagerly awaited him. "Ladies and gentlemen, thank you all for coming here, this afternoon," he began rather humbly. "It appears that due to eh, uhm, a slight clerical error, it has belatedly come to light that a tract of land bordering Mrs Peig Sawyer's property has been provisionally *re-zoned*. In effect, those bodies exhumed from her garden were lawfully interred in the adjacent graveyard many years ago. Owing perhaps, to the shifting of tectonic plates in the ground below, those boundaries have apparently gone astray over time-"

Murmurs of incredulity and bewilderment arose from the assembly. Few believed his 'tectonic plates' hypothesis, while many were simply angered at being duped by the mother of all hoaxes.

"It is now evident that any assessment of foul play here is entirely erroneous. Our suspect, of course, will be released forthwith and all charges against her dropped."

That was it. The story was dead. In next to no time, O'Meara's lecture was submerged by the sound of slamming van doors and screeching tyres.

"I would like to take this opportunity to thank my team for their efforts," he rattled on with escalating conceit. "As you can imagine we worked flat out to bring us this wonderful and encouraging result. No doubt you'll all rest easier in your beds tonight, with the knowledge that we no longer have a sociopath in our midst-"

The tardy attempts at self-preservation were to no avail, as the television crews had by now de-rigged and dispersed. Indeed, the final straw came when a lone tumbleweed rolled by, undoubtedly having blown over the road from Domingo Murphy's garage. Trailing off into an incoherent burble, O'Meara finally descended from his soapbox, just as D.S. Boyer was slinking off in the opposite direction with his waders and fishing rod.

♣ ♣ ♣ ♣ ♣

Curly Buckley was stunned into arctic silence. With an unlit cigar protruding from his bottom lip and half a brandy nestled in his palm, the old man stared blankly at the television set, long after it had been switched off.

"So what does this mean?" Kieran scratched his head in befuddlement. "Is she guilty or not?"

"Guilty as sin!" Owen decreed. "But not of murder, I'm sorry to say. She was shifting those boundaries for years, I suspect, expanding her empire by terra-forming the land; inches at the time; under cover of darkness, no less. *That's* why we discovered the skull. We were digging in the wrong place because *she* had pushed the stone wall back, overnight!"

Rory, meanwhile, remained quietly contemplative. With the pending discharge of that perilous reptile, his mother's dismissal must have seemed a shade premature. As Mags Buckley tipped her glass back, the last drop of brandy tickled her tongue.

"I'm glad it all worked out for the best," she said, rising from the settee. "Peig Sawyer may have her quirks, but I couldn't imagine her doing away with all those people!"

"I could," Kieran murmured acerbically, "And plenty more, besides."

♣ ♣ ♣ ♣ ♣

After a crushing defeat, Curly Buckley ventured off in search of a good elixir to nurse his wounds, while our three friends found solace in an idyllic pasture, complete with grazing horses. Propped against a gate, with nothing more taxing than a gentle breeze to whet their appetites for dinner, the good times now seemed assured. But there were winds of change on the horizon; an ill-wind, unfortunately, as a visit from two emissaries would soon bear out.

"Good evening, lads!" vented a voice from behind.

Jolted from their pastoral therapy, the trio turned to face their guests.

"Just checking to see how you're all holding up after today's events?" Catherine Begley said with a tepid smile.

"Yeah, grand, thanks," Kieran nodded charily.

"So I expect ye'll be fit enough to return to the master classes tomorrow morning?"

"Sh-sure, whatever!" Owen shrugged.

"Oh good!" she acknowledged, before turning at her husband with a discernible expression of unease.

"Ehm, yes. We were also wondering about something, else," Matthew said, taking up the slack, "Bearing in mind today's findings, we were thinking, wouldn't it be a lovely gesture if you were all to return to Mrs Sawyer this evening to see out the end of your stay?"

Despite smelling a rat in the pipeline, this beastly proposition was predictably met with sheer outrage. "What do you think we are?" Kieran roared. "Cannon fodder? Why the *hell* would we return to the firing line? So that she can reload and finish the job, completely?"

"Look, all we're asking here is a show of solidarity, if you will, on behalf of yourselves and the school," Matthew sustained.

"Ah yes, you're out to save your own hides! You're afraid she'll sue!"

"No! Don't be ridiculous! Although, need I remind you; you did have a hand in implicating an innocent woman on a very serious charge!"

Employing scare tactics was a cheap shot, but effective, judging by Kieran's anaesthetised silence.

"Have you lost sight that she pillaged her way through our belongings, before leaving us to practically starve to death?" Owen tackled with unmistakeable dread.

"We are aware of Mrs Sawyer's, how should we say, occasional lapses? Which is why we're prepared to make it worth your while!"

"What? How?"

Breezily plucking a cheque book from his pocket, Matthew flaunted it before their eyes. "On completion of your assignment, you have my solemn oath that you will receive a cheque payable to you, personally, refunding the full amount you paid for this course, which is most generous, I'm sure you'll agree?"

"Find some other flunkies for your suicide mission!" Kieran brusquely dismissed.

Owen, on the other hand, was a little less hasty. "Shh, let's hear them out first."

"As added incentive," Catherine proceeded, "And in light of Mrs Sawyer's shortcomings in the catering department, we've smoothed it over with Mags Buckley, who, incidentally, spoke very highly of you, for you to return here for your lunch, every day."

"Whoa, wait a minute," Owen gestured, "If we finish out the remaining week-and-a-half at boot camp, we're guaranteed three square meals a day?"

"Eh no, just *one*," Matthew amended.

"*Three* square meals a day?!!!" Owen reiterated.

Matthew grasped that he was being hustled. "Oh right, well how does *two* grab you, so?" he haggled.

"Matty!" his wife remonstrated. "Mags Buckley never agreed to this?"

"Don't worry we'll square it up later."

With the lure growing consistently juicier, Owen now appeared to be giving their proposal serious consideration. "Plus, I definitely get my three thousand Euro back?"

"Absolutely," the principal nodded, referring back to his old ring binder again. "Of course we may need to juggle the books a bit, but sur' that's nothing new."

Kieran, however, remained steadfast in his decision. "No deal! Just keep the money!"

"Oh hang on," Matthew reviewed his files. "The refund is applicable to *all* except *you*, Kieran, I'm afraid, whose scholarship is firmly ensconced by the Department of Education."

This whopping disclosure, not only undermined Kieran's argument, but at once rendered him enormously unpopular with his two housemates. And while Rory merely frowned contemptuously, Owen was little more verbose in articulating his disgust. "What?!!!" he roared. "Oh that's rich. That's just priceless! After all that endless bitching about how much this trip cost, when all along you were just coasting along on a freebie holiday!"

"Yes all right, let's not make an issue of this, right now," Kieran squabbled.

"You hypocrite! You fraud!! You scab!!!"

"All right, that's enough, now please just shuddup!"

"Don't worry lads, I'm sure ye'll be fine," Matthew said, taking their commitment for granted. "And anyway, twelve murders? Sur' I knew that sounded a bit flaky right from the get-go!"

"Pure codswallop!" Catherine corroborated, "And despite her eccentricities, I've always maintained that Mrs Sawyer isn't a bad old salt really."

"You go and live with her, so!" Kieran proposed in vain.

♣ ♣ ♣ ♣ ♣

Kieran, Owen and Rory were cajoled, bribed and ultimately conscripted into what was branded, by their teachers, as a 'simple public relations exercise'. Ironically, upon delivery of its cargo at the cottage that evening, the silver Laguna made itself scarce again with alarming alacrity. Outside the stone wall, the ensemble lined up to face a force of darkness they had failed to vanquish. Cruelly seized from a life of opulence and once more condemned to the bowels of hell, although remembering Auntie Bridie's bowels determined for Rory that it was two sides of the same coin.

As all three summoned the courage to forge ahead, the green door unexpectedly swung wide open, while a synchronous crack of thunder proclaimed Peig Sawyer's re-ascension to the throne. There it was, a harbinger of doom, tentacles outstretched and ready to ensnare. "Hello lads," she grinned. "Isn't it nice to be back again?"

None were remotely fooled by this smokescreen, as always a warm salutation was merely a precursor to disaster. Their immediate instinct was to take flight, but alas, their fate was sealed when a precipitous downpour forced them to take shelter inside. As O'Dowd and company entered the kitchen, they were immediately overwhelmed by an aura of evil; induced, most likely, by the festering mound of rhubarb leaves stacked behind the door. Of small consolation were two uniformed members of the *Garda Síochána* who had remained to tie up loose ends, but they too were on the threshold of departure.

"Hey you!" she snapped, as the pair lugged a heavy slab towards the exit. "Where are ye going with my table top?"

"Back to the graveyard, where it belongs, Mrs Sawyer," one of them replied.

Kieran grew queasy as he spotted the flipside. "Oh God!" he exclaimed. "I ate my breakfast from that thing every morning!"

Hence, with the iniquitous balance of power restored in the universe, Kieran, Owen and Rory prayed that their extraordinary sacrifice, wouldn't be the ultimate sacrifice.

20. Exodus

Although news of the dowager's amnesty failed to dominate the national headlines, tongues wagged feverishly in local quarters. Indeed, the stomach-churning revelation that their dearly departed helped fertilise her crops, saw a massive surge in laxatives sales.

In spite of her bald-faced felony, no further legal measures were taken against Peig Sawyer; a mitigating factor being the shared culpability in desecrating a dozen graves. Besides, in a town where land-grabbing was hardly a crime and stealing from the dead, practically mandatory, collective amnesia was the order of the day. Nevertheless, as justice had to be 'seen to be done', the bodies and boundaries surrounding her property were eventually restored. Ensuring Peig's compliance and in reparation for damages, Leo O'Meara purchased, at full market value, the land she had recently (mis)appropriated from Evelyn Schalplatten. This was a strategic purchase, however, as O'Meara already had it on good authority that the site was about to be re-zoned as commercial property. Rossbladderburst, evidently, was in dire need of another public house, and Leo, a new retirement plan.

Furthermore, a campaign spearheaded by the wily Mr Sharkey, saw several newspapers make substantial out of court settlements with his 'unjustly maligned' client.

While denied the opportunity to dance on the grave of his archenemy, Curly Buckley didn't walk away empty handed. Having proved his mettle with the mutual appreciation society, his student quota for the next term was not only guaranteed, but doubled. As to *who* was responsible for the anonymous tip-off that sparked off the media frenzy to begin with, remained a mystery.

In due course, some semblance of normality returned to the Academy. As promised, hush money for the traumatised victims was wrung from the coffers and the accounts were duly massaged; thwarting hopes of new computers, for another year. The dearth of training didn't go unobserved either and accordingly, three weeks of master classes were condensed into one, leaving the hapless students truly frazzled, by the end of it all. But it wasn't all hard work and once the dust settled, the *céilí* too was re-instated; so at times, it was positively backbreaking. Live music replaced canned music, while opposition from the 'intelligentsia' was eliminated, following their expulsion. Hacked off at the daily raids on their cellar, the O'Shea's installed Closed Circuit Television, capturing incriminating footage of Daimo, Higgo and Locko pilfering hard liquor and cider, within minutes of its installation. Three stomach pumps later, the evictees were on the next bus home.

Apart from their initial stumbling block, no major catastrophe befell Kieran, Owen and Rory in the days that followed. On the contrary, their circumstances evolved from execrable to adequate. At some point in time, Peig caught wind of their dealings with the Buckleys and not to be outstripped; upped the ante by slipping luxuries such as bread, milk and even sugar into her bill-of-fare. Obviously, not in the same league as Mags Buckley, at least her ladyship's distinctive brand of 'hospitality' never quite plunged to its previous murky depths. Above all, there was no shortage of hot air, with Curly and Peig locked in a perpetual struggle to emerge as a moral champion. Both fished relentlessly for salacious gossip on the other, in the hope of sustaining their outsized egos; a cheap commodity, our friends were happy to provide.

On to the subject of her incarceration, Peig remained strangely composed. If she did have an inkling concerning her wards' accountability in the matter, she didn't let on; or more plausibly; didn't care, given the tidy bundle she had made in the process. Or perhaps she was saving her breath for an exclusive 'tell all' interview which appeared, to everyone's dismay, in the *Kerrylad*, the following Sunday.

On their final morning in the Sawyer firmament, the trio were making a token appearance at the breakfast table when their landlady barged through the front door with a tin of black bitumen and a paint brush. Setting the items aside, she wiped her fingers on her apron before focusing on her outbound guests.

"Well lads, I expect ye'll be sorry to be leaving us?" she enquired.

"Gutted," Owen indifferently stirred his mashed potato.

"Still, ye'll come back and see us again, no doubt?"

"Oh sure," Kieran confirmed, "I might go the whole hog and buy a season ticket."

Overlooking the sarcasm oozing from every orifice, the old woman pulled up a chair and sat down beside them. Hurling her flaccid arms across the table, a wistful gaze sheathed her wizened face. "It's the end of an era, I suppose," she said mournfully, "I doubt the Academy will be sending many more students my way, from now on."

Mistrustful of the apparent self-pity, Kieran nonetheless posed the obvious question. "You're retiring?"

"Goodness no! That's only for *old* people. No, not at all. Only that my name will be mud, if I stick with that crowd any longer, and contrary to what some would have you believe, I'm not a monster!"

Oh the irony, he mused, that such a declaration invariably came from those who were precisely that.

Bounding from the table again, Peig rattled excitedly towards the window. "As from today," she said, raising the net curtain, "I'm going freelance!"

Curious as to what on earth she was flapping her jaws about now, the trio wandered over for a look. Outside, fresh black bitumen trickled down a crudely fashioned placard, onto the stone wall beneath. The message was loud and clear; effective from immediately, Peig Sawyer had joined the 'B&B' brigade.

"Oh I see, the approval came through from *Bord Fáilte*?" Owen hazarded.

"Hah?" she grunted.

"Eh, nothing, c-congratulations, that's all." And glancing at his watch, Owen signalled his intent to depart. "We'd better be heading off, I suppose. Our bus is leaving in an hour."

Alarmingly, the old woman scuttled around to the front door, obstructing their exit.

"Oh but listen, I can't have ye going back to Dublin, empty handed?" she declared. "Now, ye stay there a minute, while I get ye something nice."

Unsure of where this chilling aberration was headed, the trio made no sudden moves; having ventured *this* far, there was no sense in risking any last minute bloodbath. She didn't seem to have a game plan per se, but after a chewing it over for a moment, plucked a threadbare garment from the line above the hearth.

"Here," she placed the improvised gift in Kieran's arms. "*You* took a fancy to *this*, unless I'm mistaken?"

Bamboozled by what initially appeared to be a rag pile, a brief examination revealed it to be something far more contentious. It was the legendary robe, albeit now sky-blue opposed to navy-blue, with more holes than ever and flaking Tip-Ex encrusted on the lapel. Like everything else, three weeks in her custody did nothing to improve its lustre, a notion, perhaps, that hadn't escaped Peig. Even so, Kieran wisely said nothing.

Next she looked to Rory and following another spur-of-the-moment decision, grabbed half a dozen sagging strips of rhubarb from the sideboard.

"Give these to your mother! Tell her she can make a nice crumble out of them."

A thunderstruck Rory hesitantly took receipt of the produce which, judging by its sorry state, had been reclaimed from the fallout zone in her back garden.

Finally she came to Owen. "Oh! I know what *you'd* like!" she shuffled breathlessly towards their dormitory. "One second now and I'll get it-"

As Peig rummaged about in the room below, the trio paused in anticipation of what conceivable horror was going to emerge. None, however, were prepared for the desiccated and decapitated remains of 'Old Healy' the donkey.

"You've had your eye on this, right from the very beginning," she said, brushing away the decades of dust from between its ears.

"Ah no-no-no!" he baulked. "That's far too good! Didn't your husband make that? Surely it must be of sentimental value?!"

Peig, of course, didn't know the meaning of the word and simply dropped the unwieldy object into his arms. "Take it away! Himself was fond of it, but I couldn't stand the sight of the damn thing!"

"Oh right, eh, th-thanks very much, y-you're too kind!"

"And don't forget now, the next time you're coming down, be sure to bring more of your father's quilted paper," she stipulated.

It struck Kieran that her belated fawning was no more than a promotional campaign to bolster her fledgling enterprise. Somehow, these few pathetic keepsakes proposed to erase all misdeeds of the past. Relatively speaking, Owen had hit pay dirt, considering the assets he in particular might endow on future visits. But since her capacity for 'selective' memory was entirely unique, the likelihood of repeat business was infinitesimal. Moreover, with liberty virtually within their grasp, none were about to contradict her ludicrous pipe-dream.

As Peig Sawyer opened the front door, the sheer splendour of freedom finally embraced her brood. Then, surprisingly, came the icing on the cake.

"There ye are," she placed a twenty cent piece in each of their palms. "Buy yerselves a bar of chocolate, now, for the road."

Despite the temptation to wrangle over her derisory bequest, the trio upheld a façade of diplomacy to the bitter end. "Right, well, thanks a lot Mrs Sawyer and eh, take care now!" Owen declared.

"Yeah and thanks for sparing our *lives*," Kieran muttered beneath his breath, as he led the way down her garden path one last time.

"Yera, ye were *no* bother to look after, anyway!" she exclaimed, in a statement wholly contrary to earlier indications. "Come down and see us again soon and bring the whole family, next time, why not?!"

"Why not indeed, so you can fleece them too," Kieran added, as he closed the gate behind them.

Their congenial smiles and waves ended prematurely when a burgundy B.M.W. convertible arrived on the scene and halted alongside. Behind the wheel was a young man with a ponytail and a goatee; to his left, a young woman with an otherworldly collection of facial accoutrements.

"Excuse me?" the driver said, alighting from the vehicle. "Would this be the *Sawyer* guest house, do you know?"

"Uhm, yes, I suppose it *is*," Kieran speculated. "But you'd be crazy to go in there!"

Kieran's apparent insolence provoked an immediate distrust of the students. Worse still, when the donkey's head beneath Owen's arm was spotted, their credibility stakes plummeted even further.

"And *why* not?" he frowned.

Mindful that Peig was still standing in the doorway, Kieran discreetly held the stranger aside. "I haven't time to go into details," he whispered. "But basically she'll take you to the cleaners, mister. As for the food, trust me, it's pure muck!"

But the sceptical newcomer was already sliding away. "Okay, well thanks for the tip but I think we'll take our chances. Besides, this place featured on a telly documentary recently, and it's unlikely to be mentioned, unless it was pretty darn good!"

"Or damn awful!" Owen amended. "That was definitely a news bulletin you saw!"

"Look, all we want is a nice quiet holiday!" he asserted. "Last year we went to Donegal, which was just diabolical. So nothing, I repeat *nothing*, can be as bad as that!"

"It's your funeral mister," Kieran sighed, making a reluctant withdrawal. "Although don't say we didn't warn you."

As expected, Peig Sawyer's curiosity compelled her to the fore. "What's wrong?" she enquired. "Are they looking for directions or something?"

"Eh no we're the Finches actually!" the young man proclaimed. "I'm Justin and this is my wife, Guinevere-"

Duly noted was the bloodcurdling smile that shaped the old woman's chapped lips.

"Ah yes, of course! The Finches!" she beamed. "I've been expecting ye! Yes-yes-yes, come this way, come this way!"

"Come on Guinevere," Justin said, heaving two mismatched suitcases from the boot. "We're in the right place!"

As to *how* she had so expeditiously finagled new guests was anyone's guess, but for Kieran, Owen and Rory it was like watching lambs being led to the slaughter. In view of 'Guinevere's' penchant for facial armour, Kieran could only surmise that their successors were a pair of masochists. With this, the exiles walked away from the old cottage and never looked back, for fear of being turned into pillars of salt.

♣ ♣ ♣ ♣ ♣

A haze of activity swathed *Coláiste Nathair.* All and sundry had emerged for the big send off; all except Peig, whose priorities were rooted elsewhere. Outside the school gates, two glistening carriages awaited to take the students on their homeward bound expedition.

The hapless driver of St. Grizelda's coach, who in all probability faced a grisly afternoon in a gaseous nebula, was on hand to facilitate the storage of luggage. Awaiting the next batch to filter through, he casually drifted over to his opposite number. "Well Tony, a lovely morning for it, isn't it?" he hailed.

"Ah yes, Christy, not too bad at all."

"Here I don't suppose you'd fancy swapping places and driving this *other* lot up instead?"

Noting the cluster of girls who were puffing away by the railings, *Scoil Gailseach's* driver judiciously declined. "Ah no-no, you're all right, there!"

"No, I thought not. Three days, would you believe, I spent hooked up to a nebuliser after our last trip! They just don't pay us enough to suffer these little scuts!"

But the nearby spectacle of Domingo Murphy bidding a tearful adieu to his party of five, softened Tony's heart. "Ah sur' isn't it all a bit of an adventure for them anyway?" he warranted.

"Huh, but do they actually learn anything at the end of the day?"

"You can always ask one of them there?!"

Departing from the emotional Domingo who was still waving his handkerchief, Ashley turned to make eye contact with her driver.

"Say something for us, in Gaelic!" Christy said, relieving her of her suitcase.

Ashley was only delighted to boast her new-acquired linguistic skills.

"Tuve un buen momento, pero estoy ansiosa de volver a casa!" she replied lithely.

Her fluency enormously impressed both bus drivers.

"Did you hear that?!!" Tony gasped.

"Yes, I have to admit, that's not bad at all!" Christy acknowledged.

"I think I'll send my own kids here next summer!"

"A sound investment!"

Later than most, Kieran, Owen and Rory arrived on the scene. They, naturally, had been relieved of their luggage far in advance; although compensating for that, was the profound emotional baggage they were bringing home. Rory's rhubarb had also taken a plunge into the river Sualach on the way over; after Kieran highlighting its probable unsuitability for vegetarians. Owen, nonetheless, hurled Old Healy into the undercarriage, before being accosted by the belle of St. Grizelda's.

"¡Hola!" she exclaimed.

"Oh hi Ashley!" Owen smiled, apparently having learned to take these surprise attacks in his stride.

"Here's my number," she placed a post-it in his hand. "And don't you forget to call me, now!"

"Don't worry, I'll give you a shout when I get back this evening."

And with a parting peck on the cheek, Ashley skipped with elephantine grace back to her own bus.

"That'll be going straight into the dustbin, no doubt?" Kieran jibed.

"No-no! We've arranged to meet up next week," Owen said, pocketing the post-it.

"What? I thought you said she had a face like a bag of chips?"

"No I didn't! Anyhow, her father has the complete *Murder She Wrote* on DVD, so if my luck holds, I might just catch up on those episodes I missed."

"Oh, I see!"

"And did I mention she's given up smoking?"

"Yes, five times. That piece of lung she coughed up during Thursday's *céilí* was the clincher?"

"Yeah, having the last rites was a real wake-up call, she said."

Just as Kieran was thinking that wonders would never cease, Sharon arrived and placed *another* post-it in *Rory's* hand, before scampering back to her sniggering enclave. As to whether it was bona fide or not, Rory kept schtum, but a wry smile hinted that Mrs Waters might have a rival for his affections.

The echo of a familiar and rather irksome car horn suggested that a certain Rolls Royce had entered the arena. Although the big man himself didn't materialise, Dave Keogh surfaced with his holdall in one hand and a large watermelon in the other.

"That's an impressive packed lunch you've got there!" Kieran observed.

"It isn't for *me*," Dave said, looking around.

Before the opportunity arose to clarify, a heavy-set teenager accidentally backed into Kieran.

"Oh sorry O'Dowd, I didn't see you there, my fault entirely."

"Who's that?" Kieran enquired, as the stranger climbed aboard their bus.

"Morrissey!" Dave revealed.

"*Dave* Morrissey?!"

"The one and only! I barely recognised him myself, but you'd be surprised what three weeks in bed, good grub and a break from glue sniffing can do."

As the crowd began to thin out, pangs of disappointment suddenly gripped Kieran. His sole guiding light in this squalid outpost had apparently failed to turn up for a final reunion. Her absence was all the more crushing since their friendship had blossomed into something very special, during the past week, or so he thought.

With almost everyone now on board, Miss Colic finally crawled out of the woodwork. Observing Kieran sauntering aimlessly about with a red rose in his hand, she was bound to be curious. "Are you waiting for someone, Mr O'Dowd?" she enquired.

As he turned to face his teacher, a wave of relief swept across his face.

"Ah, *mon amour*!" he waved theatrically.

Logically assuming his advances were directed at *her*, Miss Colic turned crimson.

"What?!! *No*! You mustn't, not *here*!" she pleaded.

But Kieran walked straight past the babbling spinster and into the arms of Jennifer, who approached from directly behind.

"Phew! For a minute there, I thought I'd been left in the lurch!" he grinned.

"Perish the thought!" Jennifer smiled. "No, I actually bumped into Mrs O'Shea; the biggest gas-bag in the north Atlantic. Although after the usual third-degree, she offered me a temp job in her tavern, believe it or not!"

"Will you take it?"

"Mmm? I'll need *some* distraction until the results come out in August. After that, who knows? I might even end up studying in your neck of the woods, if my luck holds."

"That would be brilliant! And don't worry, I'm sure you'll do fine! Oh! And eh, this is for you," he handed her the rose.

"Oh it's gorgeous! Thank you! But listen, in the meantime you'll come down and see us again, won't you?"

"Oho-ho-ho, I don't know about that!" he chuckled derisively. "This place makes Cabot Cove look like a holiday camp!"

"Yes, all right, just because you got off on the wrong footing, and okay, maybe ended on the wrong footing; it doesn't mean Rossbladderburst is without its rewards!"

"Name *one*," Kieran said, throwing down the gauntlet.

Jennifer sealed her testimony by bequeathing a long and passionate kiss. In the midst of their embrace, boisterous chants of encouragement erupted from *Scoil Gailseach's* coach, which alarmingly began rocking from side to side.

Miss Colic was agape. Although crestfallen to discover that her betrothed only had eyes for another; she mostly felt very foolish for having spent the past fortnight in a drunken stupor. Kieran, of course, revelled in the moment and when it was all over, gormlessly scratched the back of his head in an attempt to gather his thoughts. "Yes, ehm, yes, m-may-maybe," he said wistfully. "Maybe a long weekend before I go back to school, mightn't hurt. I hear there's a new bed and breakfast just after opening up."

Edging slowly up the steps, he blew several parting kisses to his beloved, while a twitchy and shamefaced Miss Colic followed on behind.

"Is that everybody now?" she croaked, once they were both aboard.

"Just about, I reckon," Dave Keogh acknowledged. "Listen eh, we got you a little something just to show our appreciation for all your hard work!"

When presented with the large watermelon, Miss Colic's despair seemed to fade away. "Oh! Oh, thank you very much! That's lovely and a very sensible gift too!"

"Yeah well, you know, we all thought you seemed a bit eh, melon-*colic* lately."

When raucous laughter suddenly filled the air, the liaison teacher realised she'd been suckered again.

"All right, enough of your lip, Mr O'Dowd, I mean Mr *Keogh*! Sit down now!"

Once the doors hissed shut, Jennifer relocated to the footpath where Fr. Tom Buttimer and her parents were standing. Matthew and Catherine appeared principally concerned with the shameless exhibition they had just been privy to, and were looking to their daughter in anticipation.

"What?" Jennifer defensively folded her arms. "Just looking after the clientele," she elucidated, speaking in terms she hoped they would understand.

"Aaaahh!" The couple hummed favourably, sensing that their life's work hadn't been in vain.

"So that's it so, anyway so," Fr. Tom hummed nonsensically, clasping his hands.

"Yes, indeed!" Matthew concurred. "All in all, I have to say it went pretty *well* this year. Plus, four more coaches arriving, this time tomorrow!"

"Four?!!!" the cleric gasped.

"That's right!" Catherine confirmed. "It just goes to show, doesn't it, there's nothing such as bad publicity!"

The ease at which the pair could whitewash recent history frustrated the priest.

"What's niggling *me* is that we still haven't located Mrs Schalplatten!" he frowned. "I genuinely feel we lack proper closure there!"

"Rest assured, Mrs Schalplatten is in a better place, now," Catherine warranted. "And the sooner you realise she isn't going to just roll back into town, the better. Isn't that right Matthew?"

"What? Oh yes, definitely!" her husband dutifully concurred.

Fr. Tom Buttimer sighed resignedly as he watched the two buses pull away. It was then, extraordinarily, that that he noticed an eerie looking article parked on the other side of the road. A battered box, emblazoned with dozens of stickers, heralding worldwide destinations including Bangkok, Moscow, Sydney and Toronto, upon a decrepit trolley, on the brink of collapse. Approaching the casket, his suspicions were confirmed as he wiped away a thick layer of grime from the brass nameplate. Saints be praised, Mrs Schalplatten had returned. A jubilant Fr. Tom Buttimer wanted to proclaim this miracle to one and all, but in looking up, he realised all had gone home.

♣ ♣ ♣ ♣ ♣

"So what is it ye do for a living?" Peig probed as she poured the tea for her new lodgers.

Justin Finch stared disdainfully at the battered spaghetti tin purporting to be his mug.

"I'm an artist, and Guinevere is an interior designer," he scowled.

"But come here to me," she whispered, while hovering a little too close for comfort. "What happened to that poor girl's face? Was she in an accident?"

The perplexed gentleman looked to his wife, who was stirring her tea, opposite.

"Hah? Oh! Those are just facial piercings Mrs Sawyer; quite harmless, I assure you."

"You mean she chooses to go around with a face like a breakers' yard?"

Suddenly growing impatient, Justin arose from the table. "Uhm yeah, eh, perhaps you might show us to our room now, Mrs Sawyer?"

"Oh yes of course, ye'll want to get settled in, won't ye?" Peig scurried over towards the dormitory. "And yer in luck too, as it happens, our honeymoon suite was vacated only this morning!"

"Ooh wonderful!" Justin chirped, picking up a suitcase as he followed her.

But his optimism quickly waned as she opened the door. From eye gouging bedsprings and jagged bedposts, to its heady aroma and buzzing insects circling a half-eaten corned-beef sandwich, Peig Sawyer's honeymoon suite offended all his senses in a single blow.

"Did you pack the Trench Mouth tablets, Guinevere?" Justin finally gulped.

His gum-chewing wife appeared less fazed by this veritable battlefield. "I quite dig the grunge theme, actually, Justin?"

"Yes, I'm afraid the last mob tended to be a bit unruly at times," Peig said musingly. "So it's standard policy now, to ask for a twenty Euro deposit, in case of breakages."

"What's to break?" Justin squabbled.

"There's still two perfectly good beds over there!" she snapped.

"Oh right, well eh, here you are then," he appeased her with a banknote drawn from his wallet.

"Each!" the old woman expounded, with her hand open for more.

Rolling his eyes in disbelief, Justin coughed up the balance.

"Now folks, if there's anything at all I can do, ye're at my disposal," Peig smiled, while stuffing the cash into her apron pocket.

"Eh? Oh eh no, you've been to a great deal of trouble as it is," her new tenant gleaned, as he looked around. "Eh, Guinevere, have you got the other suitcase there?"

"No, I thought you had it?"

"Yes, but didn't I give it to you?"

"No."

"Ara, I think ye might have come in with only the one case?" Peig suggested.

"Did I? But I could have sworn- Oh never mind, I'll just fetch it from the car."

The keys were no sooner out of his suede jacket pocket, when the old woman sunk her talons into his hand. "Sur' let me do that! Ye're guests here now, after all," she magnanimously offered.

"Ah no-no, you're all right," he recoiled.

"No-no-*no*! Ye take it easy there now and relax. Sur' ye must be exhausted after ye're long journey?"

Bearing in mind the fact that she already had the squeeze on him, the novice relinquished the keys. "Okay well, mind the paint-work please, Mrs Sawyer, she's only two days out of the showroom."

"Not to worry, I'll take good care of it!" she winked, before gently closing the door.

Once the old bat was out of earshot, the couple felt at liberty to drop the charade. "God almighty, I don't think we'll stay the course in this hole!" he flailed his arms in antipathy.

"Well Justy darling, you did say you were looking for a challenging new environment to stir your creative juices?"

"Challenging maybe, but not hazardous!"

On edge concerning his curvaceous new mistress, Justin wandered over to the window for a routine check up.

"What the devil is she doing *now*?" he said, winching the net curtain.

Peering out alongside her husband, Guinevere seemed equally baffled. Outside, their esoteric hostess was apparently searching for their luggage while seated behind the steering wheel of their B.M.W.

"Doesn't she realise that normal people store luggage in the boot?" he barked.

"All right, calm down," she urged. "I'll go out and talk to her."

But as Guinevere made for the exit, she hit a snag. "I think this door is locked!" she said, vigorously shaking the handle

"Maybe it's stuck," Justin proposed. "Hang on, I'll open the window-"

His attempt to raise the lower sash, also met with frustration and it didn't take long to discover why. "What is this?!" he roared. "Look! The window is nailed down!"

What happened next clearly breached the realm of casual curiosity. To their sheer horror, the engine was ignited and the car began to judder slowly along. As the old woman rapidly found her feet, her two prisoners pounded ferociously on the Perspex window. In one fell swoop, Peig Sawyer and their cherished wheels vanished in a cloud of dust.

About the Author

A.J. Ó Coileáin's passion for storytelling began many years ago when the author was at school. A roving mind led to the creation of many fanciful characters, often brought to life in comic-strip format. While to the amusement of some, such cartoons occasionally scandalised his honourable teachers. Having received his education in Ireland and the U.K, majoring in Media and Communications, A.J.'s storytelling mission expanded into the collaborative process of film production. His interests are many, not least watching the ducks toddle by on a lazy summer afternoon.